A Hard Darkness

A Hard Darkness

Ray Turner

The characters, businesses, locations, and events portrayed in this book are fictitious. Any similarity to real persons, living or dead, is coincidental and not intended by the author. The city of Eola described in this text is entirely imaginary and should not be confused with real communities of same name.

ISBN: 979-8-9911917-0-8

Cover Illustration by Savannah Forrester. Design by Matthew Creviston.

Dedication

For Lenore: my love, inspiration, and support for all these years.

Table of Contents

CHAPTER ONE

A private eye is widely believed to live a glamorous, dangerous life on the edge. Like so much else, it makes you wonder how popular wisdom got the name.

It was after 1 a.m. on a lonesome October night. I was sitting on the edge of my bathtub in underwear and rubber gloves, pawing through a bag of stolen garbage. I had a glass of Wallams Red Top whiskey and a fresh pack of cigarettes ready on the rim of the sink but couldn't touch either of them. The biggest danger I faced was wanting to rub my eyes.

Most PIs agree, you learn more about a person from what he throws away than by strapping him into a polygraph machine. At the Transcontinental Agency where I used to work, the garbology guru explained it this way: "A lie detector only tells you what the subject believes about himself. His trash shows you who he really is."

So, handful by handful, I sorted my client's trash into three piles on a disposable tablecloth lining the tub.

The food pile was the worst: fat-slimy chicken bones; hard, sweaty lunchmeat the color and consistency of fruit leather; vegetables in a cream sauce gone furry with refrigerator mold... And all of it sodden with old coffee grounds--my toes could already feel the grit on the bathroom floor.

The beverage containers were somewhat better. Preston Curtiz mostly drank store brands of juice and diet soda, though I also found an imported beer can and the cork from a bottle of red wine.

The most revealing trash is usually paper, but in this case, Curtiz shredded most of his to confetti. None of his bank statements, bills, canceled checks, purchase receipts, or drafts of works in progress were left intact. Even his junk mail went through the shredder. Curtiz was either preparing for a victory parade or he was as paranoid as a Supreme Court nominee facing a hostile Congress.

I did find an empty box from a "healthy" cereal with a coupon cut out. The trash bag also contained the packaging for a blow-dryer, two empty boxes of Sobranie party-colored cigarettes, a fistful of wrappers for granola bars, and the top tab from a box of Zeus condoms ("For the feel that makes you a god!"). Mercifully, there were no used condoms present.

Unfortunately, I did not learn much about my client that was new. He was particular about his appearance and careful about what he ate, but not obsessively so. He didn't seem to have a drug or alcohol problem. He liked expensive cigarettes but in other areas was surprisingly frugal.

Where sex was concerned, the condoms tab indicated that Curtiz was not interested in celibacy, fatherhood, or debilitating disease; but it showed nothing about his sexual orientation. The absence of any used condoms possibly implied that his sex life was not very active.

I wrapped up his trash in the plastic tablecloth and put the bundle into a fresh garbage bag. I sprayed down the walls of the bathtub to remove any stray refuse.

I washed my hands and took my whiskey and cigarettes out to the living room, where I sank into the couch, exhausted. The sounds of its springs echoed hollowly through the apartment.

The cardboard boxes that had been scattered around the room were gone now—Mara must have collected them while I was out. Most of our videotape library remained stacked up neatly beside the TV table. It was the last stage of her leaving, the final proof of a marriage gone sour and defunct. The apartment already felt empty and depressing without her.

I took a long slug of whiskey and lit a Camel; orange flares twisted and crawled along its edge like glowing snakes. I drew deeply on it but my throat was so coated from its comrades that I barely felt the smoke.

It had been a long, wasted day. I'd spent most of it in my car outside Curtiz's house just waiting.

Since Curtiz never came back, I ended up watching his secretary instead through his office window. My miniature binoculars had showed her to be a slim twenty-something blonde with a shoulder length pigtail and a pleasant oval face that looked bland from lack of make-up. She spent a lot of time staring into a computer monitor that cast a green glow over her pale complexion. She occasionally buckled down to some furious bouts of typing, but these never lasted long. She smoked almost as much as I did, and once or twice I caught her picking her nose. That was nothing to me, of course--people who pee in glass jars can't be real sticklers for etiquette.

The one break in the day's routine had come in mid-morning when two stone-faced men in suits and long camel coats arrived in a black BMW. The secretary let them into the office and tried to talk very animatedly with them. I couldn't see the men from the street, but the woman's gestures made it clear that the interview went badly. Finally she shook her head and handed them some papers. The men let themselves out and drove away, but I managed to get their license number first.

It wasn't much of a highlight.

I kept watch the rest of the day, relocating my car to various removes along the street. At 5:30 Curtiz's secretary brought out a bag of trash from the house and lugged it down to the curb in a metal trashcan. Then she left in a red Volkswagen Beetle.

I continued to wait for Curtiz until nearly midnight. Then, finally giving up, I retrieved the trash bag from his garbage can and brought it back to my apartment, hoping it would shed some light on the secret he was so desperate to hide.

Instead I found nothing. After three days on the job I was no closer to finding out who was blackmailing my client or why.

CHAPTER TWO

I first met Preston Curtiz three nights earlier at My Cat Jeoffry's, a divey night-spot on the northeast side that catered exclusively to an upscale crowd. As Eola's most celebrated author, Curtiz was in his element among the smart-set lawyers, politicians, and local celebrities who hung out there. I conspicuously was not.

The maitre d' led me across the dimly-lit dining room through a maze of crowded tables and sprawling patrons. Thick cigarette smoke filled the air and parted in waves where we walked. My feet felt like bricks and my legs wobbled a bit, but I doubted it would show in the general gloom. It turned out I was wrong.

"Mr. Tobin, you're late," the writer said when I reached his booth. "And you're drunk!"

I sat down and shrugged; there was no point denying either charge.

"I only got your message twenty minutes ago. It was too late to reschedule so I had to come as I am."

"Hmmm," he hmmmed.

Curtiz's square face was taut and unnaturally dark, the tan of a man obsessed. He appeared to be in his late forties or early fifties, had short dark hair greying at the temples, and wore a conservative charcoal suit with a microscopic pinstripe. His dust-brown eyes were like an old man's, intense and dissipated, gripping and repellent all at the same time. From his book jacket photos, I had always pictured him younger and with a lot more swagger.

So this was Eola's literary lion whose works were the toast of two continents. A particular favorite of the French, I believed. The burled walnut grain on the high-backed bench surrounded Curtiz like a smoky aura.

I suppressed an urge to belch.

A tuxedoed waiter came to our table: "What would you gentlemen like to drink?"

"I'll have a white Russian," I said. "With extra cream."

Curtiz never took his eyes off me. "Just two coffees. Black."

"Very good, sir." The waiter grinned and left.

I cleared my throat. "Did you ask me here for a temperance lecture or was there something else?"

Curtiz folded his hands on the table and leaned back.

"I'm sorry, Mr. Tobin, but I can already see that this is not going to work. I am in a position that will require very delicate handling. More delicate, I'm afraid, than you are likely to provide." His tight-lipped face and dismissive tone made it clear our interview was over. My one big chance to work for a wealthy client and I'd blown it to hell before it even began.

"Believe it or not, my work often involves some delicacy, Mr. Curtiz. It may not come easily, and it usually leaves me drained for a week, but I do manage when I have to." I slid out from the table and stood up. "There are certainly a lot of other private investigators in the phone book. Perhaps you'd be happier with one of them. But if it's a diplomat you want, you should call the UN. Good night."

I turned to walk away, but Curtiz's voice stopped me.

"No, wait!" he said, louder than the distance warranted.

Several restaurant patrons turned, and Curtiz immediately shrank back into the deep booth. I could only see his hand and suit sleeve beckoning me to return.

Sensing a change of heart, I went back and resumed my seat. I'd have taken this job even if it meant shadowing his poodle with a poop-scoop.

"Maybe I was wrong," Curtiz said, leaning forward across the table. "You're younger than I expected, but you may be just the ringer I'm looking for."

"I've done this for five years now," I said. "Two of them on my own." I tapped out a Camel and lit it. "Now, then, what is it you want me to do?"

"First, you have to understand, your work for me must be kept strictly confidential. I cannot afford scandal or controversy in my life--not now, not ever. I have too much to lose and there are too many jackals waiting. Is that clear?"

I nodded. "What you tell me is safe. Wild mushrooms couldn't drag it from me."

Curtiz paused as he came to a decision. "All right then. I need you to find someone."

I brought out a small notebook and pen to jot down the details.

"That sounds straightforward enough. I just need the person's name and description, a picture if you have one. Also some background: their last known address, why you want them found, whether they know you're looking. That sort of thing."

"I thought you understood. My situation is delicate, dangerous even. If I tell you all that, it will be obvious who sent you. You'll be traced back to me immediately. That is out of the question."

"Then what can you tell me?"

Curtiz remained silent, merely shaking his head.

"You're kidding, right? How am I supposed to find someone if I don't know who I'm looking for?"

"That is your problem." Curtiz's brown eyes were cold and

implacable like dirty glaciers. "I've told you all I can. If you are not willing to take this on, then, as you said, there are a lot of others in the phone book..."

"You must give me something more to go on. Anything..."

"Just this."

Curtiz pushed a tight stack of twenty-dollar bills across the table, enough to paper my apartment. I counted them in my lap and came up with something like forty. Jackson was fast becoming my favorite president.

While I counted, Curtiz laid out the ground rules:

"That should cover your fees and expenses for the first week. My secretary will call to check on your progress and to arrange future payments. If that should not be enough, you can speak with her and reasonable adjustments will be made. You are not to contact me directly under any circumstances. Now, what is your answer?"

It should have been a "gimme." My ailing bank account was strung-out in the throes of heavy withdrawal and desperate for its next fix. Still, my instincts told me to walk away. Curtiz's paranoia about his reputation seemed almost an obsession.

A single word clicked in my mind--blackmail. It was the only explanation that made sense. Curtiz certainly made a tempting target. He was rich, internationally known, and so afraid of scandal that he would never go to the police for help. Maybe he thought having a private eye poke around would be enough to frighten off his blackmailer. If so, Curtiz was being straight with me on one point at least--the situation could be very dangerous.

I stubbed out my Camel and shifted on the hard wooden bench while I tried to make up my mind.

A low murmur from nearby tables filtered into our booth and resolved into shards of conversation. Two businessmen beside us were celebrating their hostile buy-out of a long-time senior partner. The men boasted, laughed, and ordered Manhattans. Their faces glowed with satisfaction and the sheen on their sharkskin suits was a joy to behold. The woman in the booth behind me hiccupped from drinking her champagne too fast. Her low chatter with the man beside her was filled with the thrill of fresh adultery.

I scowled and, almost on impulse, stuffed Curtiz's bills into my sport coat pocket. My thumb riffed the ends, making a pleasant sound like cards being shuffled. I scrawled out a receipt and handed it to Curtiz.

"Then I guess I'm your man," I said.

* * *

I left My Cat Jeoffry's a few quarts low on self respect but eight hundred bucks to the good. A cold drizzle was coming down and the overcast sky glowed dull orange from the city below. I bought a bottle of Stolichnaya vodka at a packaged goods store and set off for the long trudge to my car. Water droplets rolled down my hair and neck like crawling insects, but the vodka warmed my blood vessels and numbed my nerves. It was almost like the first flush of love. Almost.

The street lamps were out on Algonquin Row and the large houses that lined it were dark. I turned into the block and did an unsteady tightwire walk along the curb, taking care not to jostle the Jaguars, Mercedes, and Porsches that were parked there. My old Chevy looked like a poor relation at a society ball.

I tipped the bottle up for another drink. Rain splashed against the paper bag with a loud, random patter. I heard nothing else. It was just another night on a binge and they were getting to be routine.

Whoever came up behind me was good. Or at least quiet. The first sign of trouble was a sharp "thwack" and the back of my head exploded. The vodka bottle fell from my hand and shattered on the street. Even as my knees buckled, I looked up stupidly to see if I'd bumped my head on a low tree branch. Instead, I saw a leather-lined sap as it came down hard on my forehead...

* * *

When I came to, I was in my car but had no recollection of getting there. My head throbbed like a rotten tooth, both from the hangover and the sapping. It was a classic case of cerebral claustrophobia--my brain wanted to be let out to breathe.

When my head cleared a little, I grabbed at my pockets for Curtiz's money but found them empty. It wasn't on the floor or under the car seats either.

I'd been mugged plain and simple. Rolled like a drunk in the street. I pounded my fists on the steering wheel, setting off the horn. "Stupid, stupid, stupid, stupid!" I'd lost a wife and a big retainer in a single week. And people hired me to find things?

CHAPTER THREE

After three days the swelling above my right eye and the thick bruise on the back of my head were nearly gone. But that was almost all the progress I had made. If I did not find something soon, Curtiz would not rehire me for a second week and all my work would be for nothing. Literally.

Despite my late night with Curtiz's trash, I got up early the next morning and resumed watch at his house before sunup. He lived in an elegant stone townhouse on Tamur Lane, a few blocks away from My Cat Jeoffry's. Although detached, the narrow three story structure was set so close to its neighbors that it might as well not have been. The house had a wide, window-filled turret facing the street and a dark archway over the front door. There were no lights on inside and all the blinds were closed. Curtiz's garbage can was the only one by the street.

A scrubby little park with swing sets, slides, and jungle gyms sat across from the row of houses. The park equipment loomed like scaffolds in the grey morning mist.

I took a sip of scalding coffee to keep awake. I had brought all the essentials for a successful stakeout: a blueberry bagel, a thermos of donut shop coffee, two fresh packs of cigarettes, a mixed pill bottle of aspirin and caffeine tablets, and most important, an empty orange juice bottle with a screw-tight lid. I also had a copy of Curtiz's most famous novel, My Brother's

Keeper, for when things got slow.

As the sun rose, it drove off the fog and cast narrow bars of light between the houses. These gradually retreated across the road like a tide washing back from the beach.

Curtiz's car, a white Buick, was not parked on the street, so I took a walk around the block to look for it. The brisk morning air and exercise revived me somewhat but was no help in finding his car. I returned to my Impala and settled back with a cigarette to wait some more. He has to come home eventually, I told myself. But, of course, that's just what I had said the day before...

To have any chance of identifying Curtiz's blackmailer, I needed a lot more information than I had gathered so far. My plan of attack was first to find out why the writer was being blackmailed and from there to work out who might know about it. This meant approaching Curtiz's life like a blackmailer would, keeping a sharp eye out for any salable dirt.

I had done a similar muckraking investigation once before on behalf of a scurrilous politician who wanted to smear his opponent. In that case I'd been successful but I still didn't feel good about it. The opponent turned out to be an alright guy despite some flaws, and when the election came I even voted for him. But no one else did. No life can bear too close scrutiny. If you look hard enough for something, you're going to find it.

But three day's looking had still not uncovered anything derogatory about Curtiz. There were no run-ins with the law, no messy court cases, no kiss-and-tell biographies. Even the most aggressive scandal rags were unable to dredge up any juicy gossip about him.

And Curtiz's credit rating was flawless. Although the royalties income from his books appeared to be waning, he still held a plum position at the University of Eola. He had bought his house on Tamur Lane outright and also owned a condominium apartment in the city's Shakytown neighborhood. Both properties were actually registered under his father's name (as "Delaney Curtiz Inc.") but Preston Curtiz was paying all the taxes and had certified that the Tamur Lane house would be his primary residence. According to my research, Delaney Curtiz worked for a religious book publisher in New York.

As the morning dragged on, the neighborhood remained surprisingly quiet. Even the children who came out to play in the park seemed remarkably subdued. At least at first...

A wild whoop rose up behind me. I turned around and saw that one of the boys was hanging upside-down from a swing set with the chain wrapped around his ankles. The other children were pushing him as high as they could, trying to make him loop over the cross bar. Soon they were all jumping up and down, clamoring to be next in this great game.

A sleepy-looking mother leaned out a window across from me and hollered, "Now, kids, you stop that! Right now! Get inside and watch cartoons!" The children reluctantly began to drift back toward their houses.

It must have been Saturday already. That's why the kids were not in school, why no one was going to work. Everyone was spending the morning at home with their families, relaxing. Everyone except me.

Mara and I had always used Saturdays to regroup after the pressures of the week. We slept in, made breakfast, drank coffee together, or went through any of the other little rituals that were the happiest part of our marriage. It was the day we'd been best together and could actually believe we were in love. The day I dreaded more than any other now that I was alone.

"It was cute for a while," Mara had told me. "Like living on the set of an old forties movie. But I'm tired of it now. I'm so tired of slumming."

"That's all this has been?"

"Yes," she said earnestly. "Yes."

We both knew she was lying. But I also knew she would eventually come to believe it. My place was assured in her history, and only there.

"We're just not going anywhere." Her voice had been desperate, trying to make me understand. What I understood was an accusation that I wasn't going anywhere.

Without looking at me, Mara had solemnly removed her wedding ring and laid it on our dining room table. There was nothing else to say.

The memory of that moment arced through my being like a spark between the poles of past and present. A chasm opened in my gut, and I began to fall into it...

"At least you have something to do."

A dark voice, full of confidence and purpose, percolated up from some remote corner of my mind. I latched onto the strength it contained, afraid to let it go. The voice seemed independent of me, but its power became my own and kept my panic-depression in check. Slowly, the black spell of vertigo subsided.

I glanced back at Curtiz's house and took a bite from my hard, dry bagel. It was not much, but I did have something to do.

CHAPTER FOUR

The morning grew unseasonably warm and humid and eventually wore into afternoon. With nothing else to do, I made real progress in Curtiz's novel.

My Brother's Keeper told the story of a family conflict that arose between a strict fundamentalist father and his two sons. A stubborn man of harsh judgement, the father turned his first son's teenage rebellion into a battle of wills that lasted their whole lives. The son eventually became a pornography tycoon who made a fortune out of flouting his father's most deeply-held values. The son was never truly satisfied in his dissipated life-style, however, and his health quickly degenerated from constant drug use and alcohol.

My Brother's Keeper was written from the point of view of the younger son, who tried desperately to rehabilitate his brother and make peace between him and their father. This younger son was the book's only sympathetic character, perhaps by virtue of his first-person narration.

Curtiz's writing was powerful enough but it had a strident edge that sometimes made it seem more like a raging debate rather than a novel. Still, I had to admire his skill in putting it together when he was only twenty-four. It was Curtiz's first novel and also his most popular. The dust jacket described it as "the most personal book Curtiz ever wrote." The dedication ran: "To my father, Delaney. Just because..."

The author still hadn't returned by four o'clock. After sitting in the car for ten hours with only negligible breaks, I felt as stiff as a relic from the mummy's tomb. I got out to stretch my legs and took the opportunity to interview some of Curtiz's neighbors.

I had already spoken to several of his colleagues at the University of Eola three days earlier, but none of them seemed to know him well or considered him a friend. His fellow professors found him "reserved and stand-offish," even "cold." They seemed to relish my vague hints that Curtiz could be party to some secret scandal, but everyone agreed it was absurd.

His neighbors didn't have much to add. Preston Curtiz was "a very private person," they said. He didn't socialize much. As one old woman put it, "Some people don't like people. And there's no reason they should." She threw me an accusing look as though I were somehow to blame. It's one of my most endearing qualities--I bring out the misanthrope in people.

I did learn that Curtiz often traveled to California and that seven or eight months ago someone had tried to break into his house during one of his trips. But that was it.

I returned to my car and settled in to wait.

* * *

The only person I met so far who had any strong opinions about Curtiz was a creative writing student I had talked to outside of Curtiz's university office on Thursday.

I had been waiting for Curtiz's office hours to end so I could follow him home. I sat on a bench in the English Department hallway, dressed in my high school letter jacket (with the year patches torn off) with a baseball cap turned low over my face. To pass the time, I read from Melville's "Sermon to the Sharks" in Moby Dick.

A boy of sixteen or seventeen came over to me from the

bench opposite Curtiz's door, wearing black jeans, a sports jacket and tie, and carrying an expensive leather briefcase under his arm. The boy's long bangs were constantly falling in front of his eyes so that he had to brush them back in order to see. His expression was a self-satisfied smirk that made it hard to resist slapping it off him.

"I read that," he said to me. "They should've called it 101 Uses for a Dead Whale. Listen, do you have the time?"

"Yeah. It's 4:10."

"Shit. That's what I thought. She always runs long."

"Who does?"

"The girl in there. My appointment is at four, but they never finish by then. And it's not like they have much to talk about--all she writes is stupid death poetry. No one's going to buy that crap."

"You're a writer too?"

"I will be. Once I'm published and paid, which shouldn't be too long now. I'm almost finished with my first novel."

"It must be great for you to work with Preston Curtiz."

The boy waved his hand derisively at Curtiz's door.

"That has-been!? He should be paying me! All I get from that bastard is a name to drop in query letters..."

At that moment, the door opened and the young novelist's nemesis came out. It was easy to forget the boy in her presence. She was taller than he was and possessed a languid poise that made her seem many years beyond him, although she was only in her late teens. Her vaguely feline face was pale and translucent with high cheekbones like an Egyptian funerary mask. Dark pits of eye shadow gave her eyes a sunken look, but they blazed out with a brilliant violet hue, decadent and exotic. Her short hair was greased and teased into sharp, black needles. Despite her extravagant style, however, she possessed a stunning beauty, one almost worthy of worship. She was a punk icon, a

Goth goddess, Our Lady of Immaculate Spikes.

The girl waved back into the office and started down the hallway, turning to smile briefly at the boy and me. Her blood-red lips looked like a bayonet wound to a fresh corpse, but her fleeting smile lit up the world. She pulled a bus pass from her bag and walked away. The boy and I just stared after her.

When she was gone, the boy pushed his hair back over his forehead and muttered "bitch" to the space where she had been. He took his case and went into Curtiz's office.

I opened Moby Dick again and tried to read but couldn't stop thinking about the girl. Somehow her dark, baggy clothes managed to convey more about her figure than a tight lycra body-suit. Despite her youth, she had a profoundly sensual air, a kind of reckless assurance that came across almost as a challenge. The overall effect in one so young had been both disturbing and irresistible…

* * *

I shook myself out of my torpor and glanced back at Curtiz's house.

Thursday afternoon had been the last time I saw Curtiz. When I followed him away from the university, I had to run a red light to keep up and got pulled over by a cop. Needless to say I lost him. Since then it was as if Curtiz had disappeared completely.

More hours passed. The sun went down but the air remained heavy, warm, and still. My back and arms left damp spots on the vinyl upholstery like slug trails under the moon. Patience is a virtue that can be taught--even to private eyes. You learn it in your office filling out crossword puzzles without looking at the clues. You learn it in motel parking lots pulling betrayal detail. You learn it in police interrogation rooms trying to make your genuine ignorance sound convincing. You learn it, but you never learn to like it. Even virtues have their limits.

By eleven-thirty I was ready to call it a night. I started driving back towards my apartment, but as I crossed Haversham Bridge going into downtown, the rush of the highway air and the radio playing Elvis Costello revived my spirits. The grand vista of Eola at night took my breath away; the way its glittering glass towers thrust defiantly at the black sky. The city had a seething beauty, a man-made grandeur wrought from sweat and intellect. No natural scenery could compete with it. In the face of such electric majesty, my own problems paled to insignificance. It was a noble city, it was my city.

Instead of heading home, I took the North Shore Road exit and barreled southwest along the river, with a smoke on my lips and a song in my heart, "Watching the Detectives." Past the stadium, past several industrial plants, past the foundering foundry. Until I recrossed the river into Shakytown.

CHAPTER FIVE

Shakytown isn't listed on any map and there are no signs that say when you get there. Located at a strategic fork in the Eola river, Shakytown was where port and factory workers used to live in housing that supposedly shook every time a truck or train went by. Most of the industry is gone now, and the port is so heavily subsidized that even the Longshoremen have abandoned it. The only train left is a small commuter line that runs up from the south suburbs.

The old company houses remain, however, home now to Eola's latest immigrants. Vietnamese, Chinese, African, Hispanic, Indian, East European, and Russian communities have all settled there in a mishmash of ethnic neighborhoods and low-income enclaves.

According to his tax sheets, Curtiz had a condominium apartment on Flyte Street, a meandering one-way road that ran parallel to the river on the northern edge of Shakytown. Crumbling apartment buildings and run-down shops pressed in on the narrow street from both sides like vegetation over a rain forest stream, all of it shot through with the dank smell of the river and creeping urban-jungle rot.

At that time of night, the street was completely parked up so I had to circle the block and leave my car a considerable distance away beside a derelict warehouse. I wasn't too worried about anyone taking my Impala, but I doubted that Curtiz's white

Buick would have lasted there for more than forty minutes.

The condo building was a four-story brick structure on the right side of Flyte Street with a litter-strewn alley beside it. A half dozen garbage cans that looked like they hadn't been emptied in weeks, stood against its wall facing the alley. The apartment buildings across the street were similar to Curtiz's but not nearly as well maintained. A sheltered bus stop in front of one of them offered a good view of his entrance if I ever needed it.

Inside Curtiz's foyer, a video camera was trained on the entrance to record anyone who came in. The inner security door--a thick glass panel laced with wire mesh--was locked. Looking over the bank of electronic doorbells, I found the name slot beside Curtiz's apartment empty. I pressed his bell button several times but there was no response. I doubted any of the other residents would let me in either.

Judging from its number, Curtiz's condo must have been on the second floor. I guessed it was somewhere at the rear of the building.

I went outside and walked down the alley to a small paved area in back. Light from a streetlamp across Flyte Street penetrated only half-way into the alley, leaving the cement lot behind the building completely dark. Beyond this lot was a fenced-in field, full of rubbish and broken furniture. At the center of the field, a group of brooding figures stood drinking around a metal-drum bonfire, looking no more substantial than shades.

The balconies on the back of Curtiz's building were all connected by wooden stairs to serve as a fire escape. Lights were off in all the second story windows except one, and the curtains in that window were drawn. I started up the fire escape, confident no one would notice me in the darkness.

As soon as I put my weight on the bottom step, a spotlight

flashed on above me and flooded the stairs with light. A large black dog that had been asleep on a third floor balcony started barking furiously and raced down the stairs, dragging a metal chain. I leapt off the fire escape and sprinted out of the alley. There was a yelp and tumble behind me as the dog reached the end of its tether on the stairs. I walked the rest of the way to my car.

By all appearances, my Shakytown excursion was another washout. The apartment building didn't look like anyplace Curtiz would live or even stay. Most likely he rented it out, probably through a rental agent. Given his penchant for privacy, Curtiz's tenants might not even know who their landlord was.

I had done enough empty real estate watching for one day; it was time to go home.

But I didn't. Tired as I was, and still convinced I would be wasting my time, I stayed. Something, instinct or plain stubbornness, told me this was where I needed to be. I sat slumped against my car door and kept my eye on the distant entrance to Curtiz's building until eventually I was caught up by another inner necessity. I fell asleep.

* * *

Gunshots awakened me--five or six fired in quick succession. Their loud echoes rolled away down the street. Glass from a warehouse window crashed to the ground beside me and its shards pelted my car. I hunched over, listening for the next round but heard only the fading echoes of the earlier shots and a staccato heartbeat pounding in my ears. I peered out cautiously.

Nobody.

The strained silence that followed was finally broken by a lone dog's barking. Then, windows were slammed shut up and down the block. Gradually, the night rumble of truck traffic and distant sirens returned.

The street was empty except for parked cars. Lights were on in a couple houses but no one came to their windows to see what had happened. Nothing looked out of the ordinary, but there were ominous patches of darkness that the street lamps couldn't touch. A gunman could have lurked in any one of them.

My own gun was locked away securely in my office safe. I started up my Impala and took off down the street, my rear tires spitting glass and gravel.

After two blocks, I burst into an intersection where some idiot had dropped a large wooden crate in the middle of the crosswalk. When I swerved to avoid it, I lost control and my car fishtailed rear-end first against the left curb. The impact threw my chin into the steering wheel. It hurt like hell, but at least I didn't lose any teeth.

I looked back and noticed a large creamy smear on the street around the crate, like an industrial-sized mayonnaise spill. It was an update to the old mugger's trap of creating an oil slick on the road and robbing the drivers who skid out of control. Mayonnaise worked just as well as motor oil and was safer for the environment. It was small comfort to know I was about to be stuck up by an Earth Firster.

But no one jumped out or came running to my car. The only other person in sight was stretched out on the road behind me. He wasn't moving.

I got out of the car and went over to him. His body lay spread-eagled on its back, a crowbar clutched in his left hand. I didn't bother to check for a pulse. The ragged hole in his forehead--as big as a toddler's fist--made it clear he was dead. Blood had pooled in the wound and a slow trickle oozed down his brow into his hair. I was actually grateful for the blood; the brain mangle that lay behind it was not something I wanted to see. The man had been shot in the chest as well.

This was where the shots had been fired. Their echoes had

been loud enough to rattle the broken window at the warehouse and to shake glass loose from its frame. That meant I hadn't been a target after all, which was certainly a relief. But not one I could dwell on. I had more pressing issues to attend to--the second body, for instance.

This one was pinned between my rear tire and the curb. The man had been lying in the gutter when my car slid into him. My tire had caught him in the stomach, doubling him over like someone about to puke. A faint flutter in his chest showed that he was still alive.

I quickly moved the car off him and set my hazard lights flashing. When I went back to pick the man up, I noticed three ejected cartridge cases on the street. The mugger's gun, a snub-nosed revolver, was in the gutter beside him, so the casings were not his.

I laid the man out flat on the sidewalk. His shirt was so blood-soaked that its original color would be impossible to guess. He had also been shot, but his wounds were cleaner, without the tearing I'd seen on his accomplice. Under the best circumstances his young face would have been pale and colorless, but now his skin had the white pallor of a snake's belly. He seemed to be in no pain; the circuit breakers of his nervous system were already switched off. His staring eyes were focused on nothing and he moved his mouth forming words only he could hear. Periodically he took long wheezing breaths as though breathing were already becoming an afterthought for him, a nagging, irrelevant memory. Tiny air bubbles formed like flat red champagne around the bullet holes in his leaking lungs.

A faint siren sound was getting louder.

"Just hold on," I told him. "They're coming. You're going to be all right."

He seemed to understand. His lips and throat made awkward gurgling noises as he tried to croak out a response.

What came out, however, was an enormous gusher of blood that spilled across his chest and splattered over the pavement. It spoke eloquently to my lie--he was not going to be all right. His breathing stopped and his pulse disappeared. He was gone.

I lit a cigarette and got back into my car to wait for the authorities. I would have some serious explaining to do about those tire treads left on the dead man's chest.

Yo Ho Ho, and a bottle of rum.

CHAPTER SIX

A blue and white squad car came screaming into the intersection and went out of control at the crate. The driver almost managed to pull out of it, but after a three-quarters spin, the car slammed (WHUMP!) into the opposite curb and rocked back and forth on its shocks. The siren died away, but the blue light on its roof continued to turn.

The woman officer who was driving pounded her dark fists on the steering wheel and swore up a blue streak. The profanity that streamed from her window was soon eclipsed by an even fouler torrent directed at her partner for being too slow getting out of the car.

"Get out and check on those two! I mean NOW!" she yelled. At least in essence. She had a natural flair for obscenity that would have made a sailor blush and an NEA official stand up and cheer.

As her partner stood shakily out of the car, the driver began to talk into the car radio. Her voice was now too low for me to hear, but her dark face looked cool, dispassionate, and controlled.

Her partner was a tall white man. He came across the street and examined the two bodies cautiously. He kept his head turned in my direction even as he checked them for a pulse.

Satisfied that both men were dead, he came over to the driver's side of my car. He didn't have his gun drawn but looked like he wanted to. As he approached, I put both hands on top of the steering wheel.

"Sir, get out of the car slowly... Good, now turn around. Put your elbows on the roof and spread your legs."

I did as he asked and resisted the urge to crack wise.

The cop frisked me painstakingly but not very well. If I had a Derringer in my sock, he would have missed it.

When he finished, he said, "Stay here. Outside the vehicle."

He went back to the patrol car to get fresh instructions from the other officer. She was done with the radio and was now standing behind the police car's open trunk. She pointed to several items inside and indicated what her charge was to do with them. He nodded earnestly at everything she said. He collected a number of road flares and a roll of yellow police tape and proceeded to mark the mayonnaise slick with the flares.

Meanwhile, his partner went to the corpse in the street and examined it with a camp-style flashlight. When she was done, she came towards the second body, shining her light along the curb en route. At one point, she stooped down for a closer look at something.

She frowned when she reached the second body and bent over to do her own examination. Something was wrong. Maybe it was the way it was placed. She looked up at me briefly.

"Nice morning," I said.

She didn't respond, but her scowl showed that she disagreed. I lit another cigarette and left her to her postmortem.

When her partner finished with the mayonnaise slick, he proceeded to mark off the crime scene with yellow plastic ribbon. He strung the tape around the fire hydrant and street lamp on the other side of the street and brought it around a trash can and the bus stop shelter on the near side. In addition to the two bodies, the patrol car and my Impala were trapped inside the resulting trapezoid. When he was done with that, he returned to the squad car for a camera.

The senior officer shone her light on the curb by my car. She knelt down to sniff the revolver that was lying there.

"He didn't get to fire it," I told her. A cheap gun like that would have sprayed burnt powder all over his shooting hand and there wasn't any.

She stood up and came over to me, shining the light in my face for intimidation.

"Yeah, the gun's clean," she said, but her tone and expression showed she had doubts about me. "Do you have any ID?"

I reached slowly into my back pocket, took out my wallet and gave her my driver's license.

"Nash Tobin?"

I nodded.

"Mr. Tobin, do you know what happened here tonight?"

"I have a fair idea. But I wasn't an eyewitness if that's what you mean."

"Leave out the speculation for now. Just tell me what you saw." She glanced back at the body I had moved, and added, "And what you did."

I briefly described everything from when I'd heard the shots. The officer listened attentively without interrupting, not even for clarification. She only began to ask questions after I finished.

"So, what exactly were you doing out here at 2:00 in the morning?"

"Sleeping," I admitted. "On the job I'm afraid."

"What job?"

I handed her one of my business cards. A look of scorn came over her long face when she read "Private Investigator."

"And you're going to tell me you're here on confidential business?"

It went without saying, so I just nodded.

"All right--seeing as you're a pro and all--what do you think happened here?"

"As I see it, these two men made the mayonnaise slick and set the crate in the road. They planned to mug any drivers who slid out of control."

"That's obvious."

"But one of the cars they trapped was more than they bargained for. Someone in the car was armed, probably more than one person. When the muggers came at the car, they were both shot. Probably the gunmen in the car were professionals, or at least criminals of some type."

"What makes you think so?"

"I only heard five or six shots. From the wounds on the bodies, all those shots must have hit the muggers, and all in the head and chest. That's amazing shooting under the circumstances. And whoever was in the car didn't wait around after shooting these guys. They were already gone when I got here less than 5 minutes later."

The officer nodded. "Makes sense. I agree there were two shooters. From the damage to that one," she pointed to the body in the street, "Looks like dumdums were used. But on this one, the wounds are clean. Probably the 9mm automatic that left its cartridges on the ground."

Her young partner, who had been taking Polaroid pictures of the bodies, came up to us.

"Okay, boss. I got the stiffs, the gun and the brass. Anything else we need?"

"Yeah, one more thing. Mr. Tobin, you too. What do you make of this?"

She led us to a spot halfway between the two bodies and pointed at something in the gutter. It was what she had stopped to look at earlier. Apart from scratches on the high curb, I saw nothing.

The junior officer bent forward, shining his light carefully on the curb and the ground around it. The strain of his concentration was almost painful to watch.

"Tire marks," he said finally, straightening up. "Smudges from grey-wall tires on the curb."

"Not bad, Boze," the woman said with a clipped smile. "Also a scrape of red chrome on the top edge from the hub cap. But what about the gutter itself?"

Her partner leaned forward again. His lips grew tighter and tighter with frustration as he scanned the gutter. I couldn't blame him; I was as baffled as he was.

The woman took her flashlight and set it down sideways on the street by the curb. The horizontal beam of light picked up a pattern of clear, shiny lines on the cement gutter.

"A tire print!" Boze said excitedly.

"In mayonnaise," I added, leaning over for a closer look. "The shooters' car hit here." How she'd ever noticed it was beyond me.

The policewoman flashed a self-satisfied smile. She was good. We all knew it.

While she and Boze were occupied with trying to photograph the tire marks and print, an ambulance arrived. The two paramedics went directly to the police to find out whether they had wounded people to help or corpses to transport. After doing their own check on the bodies, the paramedics went back to the ambulance and sat in the cab listening to rap music.

A few sleepy people had come out on the street to watch the proceedings. A few more settled for window seats, watching from their apartments above the street-level stores. The spectators were quiet and interested.

A second police car arrived, soon followed by an unmarked grey sedan.

The officers from the second squad car conferred quickly with the woman officer and Boze. The newcomers went to ensure that none of the civilians intruded on the crime scene. No one seemed all that eager to do so, anyway.

The woman officer escorted me back to my car. The plainclothes detective from the grey sedan ducked under the yellow tape and came to meet us. His beard shadow was heavy and the dark circles under his eyes seemed to engulf his face. His shirt was only half tucked in but his tie was immaculate.

"Officer Nance," he began.

"Yes, sir." The policewoman stood up straight.

"Who is this?" He jerked his thumb in my direction.

"He's sort of a witness."

"You get his statement?"

"Yes, sir."

"Name and address?"

"Of course, sir."

"Then get rid of him."

She stared at the man for a second. Her eyes said all that her mouth held back.

The plainclothesman didn't notice. He was already on the ground frisking a corpse for its wallet. He emptied the dead man's pockets onto the pavement and put all the contents in a single pile. He examined each item, holding each one in his fingers, leaving his own prints on everything he touched. A penknife fell from the policeman's pocket but he didn't recognize it and added it to the pile of the dead man's personal effects. His procedures were enough to make a prosecutor weep and a defense attorney rub his hands in anticipation of "legal technicalities."

Officer Nance hurried after him.

"Sir, Ident should be here any time now. Why don't you leave that for them?"

The detective stopped for a moment.

"Nance, you're bucking for detective." He made it a

statement, not a question. "Let me tell you, you don't get there by telling your superiors how to do their jobs. Am I clear on this?"

"Perfectly, sir."

"Good."

Officer Nance came back to me, her lips clenched.

"I hate working for... jerks," she said, though not nearly so delicately. "You got that problem?"

I nodded. Being self-employed, you could say I was my own jerk.

She went on, "Everybody does, I guess. Goes with the territory. The thing is, with this clown the case is already closed. Unless ballistics turns up something solid, he's not going to follow this up at all. 'A couple scumbags popped off in the street. Saved us the trouble.'" She paused for a moment and gave me a hesitant smile. "Don't know why I'm telling you this."

I didn't either. Telling me their problems was just something people did.

"Goodbye, Mr. Tobin." She went back to watch over the detective's plundering, taking whatever notes she could.

The clown soon finished looting the gunshot victims. He gestured to the paramedics, who collected the bodies on stretchers and stashed them in the ambulance. The paramedics drove away to wherever corpses are kept at 3:00 in the morning.

Wherever that was sounded like home to me, but the paramedics were gone before I could ask for a lift. Instead, Officer Nance lifted the yellow tape for me and my car to leave.

I returned to my apartment to find the mail box stuffed with junk mail and a long string of messages on the phone answering machine, which I ignored. I went straight into the bedroom and without bothering to put on sheets, collapsed on the bare mattress.

Tired as I was, though, I didn't fall asleep quickly or easily.

When I closed my eyes, I kept seeing tiny air bubbles leaking slowly from a dying man's lungs.

CHAPTER SEVEN

I slept well into Sunday afternoon and watched football on TV for the remainder. It was a rainy, drizzly day in Eola, and the players' uniforms were so caked with mud by the end that it was hard to tell the two sides apart--at least our quarterback seemed to think so. I spent the evening drinking beer and leaving ring patterns on my coffee table in the shape of Olympic emblems. I played several games of chess on the electronic chess set and lost them all.

The phone rang at nine p.m. but I let the machine take it.

"Nash, it's Mara. Listen, if you're there, there's no need to pick up. I don't have anything new to say, just thought I should leave my number in case anyone has to get hold of me. For the time being, I'll be at [555]-6432. I'll try to let people know so they don't bother you." There was a long pause, then, "Nash, please don't come looking for me. It won't make any difference. I just want for us both to be—…" The machine beeped and cut her off. She didn't call back.

I quickly scanned the earlier phone messages and deleted them all. They were mostly Mara's friends asking how to reach her. Finally I got to Mara's message and played it over, copying down her new telephone number.

I should have known better but couldn't help myself. I picked up our contacts notebook and quickly glanced through it for the entries I had not put in there. Mara's new number was listed for

Andrew Carter, a colleague at the clinic where she worked. I remembered meeting him at an office party, a tall, doctorish-looking man, with a good sense of humor and an infectious laugh. He was probably even a nice guy. But I had despised him instantly. Carter had looked right for Mara in a way that I never did--and now never would.

There's something wrong with a world where you can spot a good mate for the person you love but can't for yourself.

I picked up my keys and left for my office where the liquor cabinet was better stocked.

* * *

That night I dreamed of Mara and Preston Curtiz together. She was dressed like a dog with pointed ears and a long snout. Her long tongue licked at Curtiz's face but he seemed not to notice. She ran around him barking, trying to get his attention, but Curtiz just stared at me. His cold eyes never blinked. Mara's activity increased to a fever pitch until she collapsed panting to the floor. She crawled back to me and I knew we would never part again. Contentment flooded my being at the thought.

"Nash, my love," Mara said, "If I were a jackal, where would I hide?"

* * *

When I finally woke up, my office was flooded with late morning sunlight and I was sprawled across the floor. The room reeked of mezcal and cigarettes and my breath did too. I stretched out luxuriously and scratched everything that needed scratching, oblivious to the woman in front of my window.

"Oh!" she said in a startled voice. "I mean, excuse me!"

I stopped scratching.

She stood silhouetted against the incoming light, her hand holding the venetian blind cord. Her brown suit was either tailor-made or a very happy accident off the rack. It melted around her slender figure like a fudgsicle on a summer night. In hot weather the woolen material would feel just as sticky. Sunlight blazed in a nimbus off her blond hair while her face remained in shadow.

"Morning, angel," I said.

She snorted and brought her hand to her mouth. But when she dropped the cord, the metal blinds came crashing down to the sill. The room went dark again and my eyes were grateful.

"I hate those things," she muttered. She pulled the blinds back up until they stayed. "Mind if I open the window? It's stuffy in here."

"Go ahead." I pushed myself up onto the couch. My head was beginning to clear, and in a moment, I would have thought to ask what she was doing there.

"Your door was open, so I came in to wait. I didn't mean to wake you." She came back from the window and sat down in a folding chair in front of my desk. She crossed her legs, pulling the skirt over her knees.

"I hope you weren't waiting long," I said.

"Not at all. Honestly, if I'd known you were there..." Either she stopped or I missed what she said when I recognized her. She wore little makeup but her pretty oval face didn't need it. She had round cheeks and a narrow chin. Her expression was a pleasing blend of confidence and vulnerability. My binoculars hadn't done her justice.

"...I'm Vera Marshall, Preston Curtiz's personal assistant. I understand you have a contract for me." She took a plain white envelope out of her purse and laid it on my desk. "And I have your fee for the second week, starting tomorrow."

I crossed from the couch and sat down behind my desk. I pinched the envelope: it felt just the thickness of forty bills.

"So he wants me to go on with this."

"Definitely. He has every confidence in you."

"Uh-huh." I pulled Curtiz's contract from my drawer and looked it over. "This is almost done. I just need his phone number for my records. He forgot last Tuesday."

Ms. Marshall's hands fidgeted.

"I'm not sure I can..."

"Even his office phone would be fine. But something's come up and I need to talk with him. It's important."

"Mr. Curtiz is in California right now. He has been for several days. But I can certainly pass along any message you have. And I will ask about giving you his number..."

Her hopeful smile won me over. From my interview with Curtiz, I doubted he would change his mind, but I didn't feel like grilling Ms. Marshall about it.

"All right," I said handing the contract to her. "Excuse me a moment..."

I stood up and went into the bathroom. As I stood before the toilet, I began to cough, hacking up hard bits of brown phlegm flecked with blood and spitting them into the water. My ribs ached by the time my fit subsided. I washed my hands and rinsed my face.

Ms. Marshall was still reading the contract when I returned. I put a cigarette in my mouth and moved the ashtray between us.

"Feel free to smoke," I said, rummaging through my desk drawer for a matchbook.

"I don't think I should encourage you."

"That's all right, I don't need encouragement."

She reached up with a gold lighter to light my cigarette and for a long moment our eyes met. Hers were a beautiful chameleon shade, blue mixed with green and grey. They would change color depending on what she wore and the light. Behind a cautious veneer, her eyes were warm. It was a look I approved of.

She glanced down and lit a cigarette of her own. When she

looked up, our eyes met again and held each other with the same magnetic power.

"Is there something I can do for you, Mr. Tobin?"

Nothing. Not a thing. Except maybe to ask if I know how to whistle. My lips were pursed if she only gave the word.

"Better watch your ash," she said. "It's about to fall."

Even as she spoke, it did. I swept it off the desk, leaving a grey smudged arc. A smile burst across Vera's face and her eyes sparkled.

"Thanks for the warning," I said. "Can you call races at the finish line too?"

"Well, I can, but only because I'm never wrong."

"Ah, inerrant and modest."

Vera began to say something, but stopped. She looked away and took a long drag on her skinny cigarette. When she turned back, her spontaneity was gone, replaced by a polite, smiling mask.

"Mr. Curtiz also asked me to pick up your progress report. Do you have it?"

The shift from Bacall back to business nettled me.

"Almost finished."

I put out my cigarette and took a blank sheet of paper from my desk. I wrote my name and the date at the top of it and the title "Progress to Date."

"Okay, it's done," I said, handing the sheet to her.

"There's nothing here..."

"Exactly. I've made no progress. I am not likely to until your Mr. Curtiz tells me who he wants to find."

She looked at me but this time our eyes didn't meet.

"I don't know anything about it. But I do know that this is not acceptable." She mashed her half-finished cigarette into the ashtray and stood up. "I suggest you report whatever it is that you do. Progress or not, it's what you're paid for."

She turned away and started toward the door.

Suddenly it seemed very important that I stop her. It was as if an elevator door out of hell were about to squeeze shut.

"Ms. Marshall... Vera! Just remember, first impressions aren't everything."

She looked back from the doorway; her mouth relented, but only a little.

"And you remember, sometimes they are."

With a shake of her ponytail, she was gone.

After she left, I thought about how the sun had caressed her figure in the window, and how her eyes sparkled when she laughed. I suddenly pictured her together with Curtiz in a stormy and sleazy relationship. I couldn't imagine Curtiz in any other kind. That I jumped to this conclusion so quickly and based on no evidence showed how strongly I wanted it not to be true.

For a moment, Vera Marshall and I had clicked, that was all. I shouldn't make anything more of it. But I did. Something about her had appealed to me in that moment and reminded me of hope. It recalled a world of possibility and promise that I thought was lost. Besides, I've always had a soft spot for beautiful women who pay me in cash. Maybe I'm in the wrong line of work.

I counted out $800 on my desk and replaced the bills in the envelope. I put the money into the inner pocket of my jacket and went outside to take it to the bank.

The morning was bright and brisk. Rush hour traffic was tapering off, but the sidewalks were still crowded with people on their way to work. As I passed a store window, I thought I glimpsed the reflection of a man watching me from the other side of the street. I turned quickly, but didn't spot him again. I quickened my step and reached the bank with a feeling of relief. It was such a comfort to know my money was federally insured up to one hundred thousand dollars.

I returned to my office and remembered that I had not yet run a license check for the black sedan that had come to Curtiz's house on Friday. Something about those two men still made me think they were connected to what Curtiz hired me for. I filled out the request form and kicked in the extra fee for "express" treatment. Vera Marshall was listed in the phone book so I didn't bother with her Volkswagen's plate.

With Curtiz away in California, there was no point in my staking out his house or condo again. It struck me now that when I had followed him from the university on Thursday, he had taken a route leading towards the airport. If I hadn't been pulled over, I might have known back then that he was leaving the city and saved myself a lot of time and frustration. Still, at $800 week one has to do something. The question was, what now?

I spent the afternoon working on Curtiz's progress report. I hoped it would give me some new ideas or perhaps point me in a direction I'd missed. Instead, it just confirmed that I was going nowhere.

I went across the street for supper at the Woolworth's lunch counter and skimmed the Eola Evening Graphic while the waitress grilled me a hamburger.

The national news was nothing to brag about. It was the same at the local level but on a smaller scale. A brief paragraph in the city section reported the shooting deaths of two hoodlums in Shakytown and gave the victims' names. The police had no suspects in the killings.

All in all, the Evening Graphic contained nothing to interest a struggling private eye with time on his hands and an absentee client.

Except one thing I missed on the first pass.

It was just a photograph in the newspaper. A simple death with a bizarre twist that put it on the front page rather than in the obituary section. In the grey half-light of dawn, a young woman's body dangled from the top of a conveyor belt over a huge mound of gravel. Her arm had caught on the conveyor's crossbar like the stem of an autumn leaf reluctant to fall. In the photograph gravel yard workers and police stood at the base of the mound, staring up at the grisly silhouette. An arresting picture to be sure, and one guaranteed to boost circulation. But the smaller picture beside it was what caught my eye.

This one was a standard high school yearbook portrait with the girl's face posed expectantly, as if looking out at the prospects of her beckoning life. But the girl's smile looked ironic in the grainy reproduction. Dark lipstick looked like crayon scrawl on her pale face and grey blush made her cheeks look hollow. The black spikes of her hair left craggy shadows on the photographer's backdrop.

The yearbook photo was placed on the page so that the girl's gaze was focused on the hanging corpse at the gravel yard.

It was the same girl, and I recognized her. She was the punk poet from Curtiz's university office.

CHAPTER EIGHT

The newspaper story ran:

> Death comes in many forms these days, and for a local teenager it came as an unconventional exit to an unconventional life. The body of eighteen-year-old Rudi Alsmith was found early Monday morning hanging from a conveyor belt at Weibrecht Gravel Yard south of the city. Workers at the yard failed to notice the woman's body when they turned the machine on, and the corpse was carried to the top of the conveyor where its arm caught on a cross bar. The body was pelted with gravel for nearly a minute before it was spotted.
>
> "It was horrible," foreman Mike Lamond commented. "I was the first to see her, and it took me a while to figure out what was

happening."

The two employees who were working the conveyor belt requested that their names not be released.

"They've gone home for the day," Lamond said, "and I don't blame them. They were pretty shook up."

Burton County police had no official statement except to note that the University of Eola freshman was dead before the first gravel yard employees arrived at 7:00 a.m.

But unofficially a police source told this reporter, "You don't have to look too far for the cause of this tragedy. It's drugs. Her eyes were the size of bowling balls when we found her. It was like looking into empty sockets. I just wish kids knew what they were getting into when they mess with that [stuff]."

Police don't know yet whether Ms. Alsmith crawled onto the conveyor belt herself or was placed there by some other person.

While attending Worthington High School, Ms. Alsmith was a strong academic student with an interest in creative writing and poetry. She was a member of the

National Honor Society during her junior and senior years, and last February was a finalist in the America Sings poetry contest. Ms. Alsmith started classes at the University of Eola a month ago, commuting from her parents' home in Hanover.

"She was very popular," neighbor Judith Sachett of Hanover said. "We'll all miss her. You can't judge by appearances; Rudi was a sweet, sweet girl."

Ms. Alsmith's parents were not available for comment. Funeral services have not been arranged pending further police investigation.

Further police investigation sounded suspiciously like coroner cut-and-paste.

I set the paper down on the counter and stared at the picture of Curtiz's dead student. A beautiful girl, no question. And such a waste.

But it wasn't the tragedy that struck me. Professionally speaking, Rudi Alsmith's death came far too close to my client to be ignored. Detectives don't like to accept coincidence easily and never concede it without a fight. Our livelihood depends on making sense out of chaos, of fitting disparate pieces into a logical whole, of finding meaning behind events that outwardly seem unrelated. Of course it is also true that coincidence happens every day and there is precious little meaning to go around. So much the worse for us detectives.

More importantly, while Curtiz was away in California, the girl's death gave me a new angle to work, a new direction. It may only have been a tangent, but even a tangent is better than nothing.

* * *

The next morning I stopped by my office to pick up my gun and had breakfast and coffee at Woolworth's. I found the address for Weibrecht Gravel Yard in the yellow pages and even located it approximately on the phone book map.

I drove east through town and turned south onto the North-South Highway. After crossing the river, I soon passed out of Eola's city limits and eventually reached the access road to the gravel yard. The narrow road ran directly off the highway, leading down a steep embankment and circling around behind the yard to a small parking area.

The yard was dominated by huge gravel mounds, some nearly thirty feet tall, that stretched out like a mountain range. Only the bulldozer tracks that led up their sides and the conveyor belts that peeked out above them gave their true sense of scale.

The office was in a long white trailer at the back of the site and there were grey utility sheds scattered around the yard's outskirts. Yellow power shovels, bulldozers, and other heavy equipment were parked beside the office trailer. Behind these, a corrugated metal silo on a cement base towered above everything else. A funnel-shaped chute jutted out from the silo over a rusty string of railcars.

There were two main conveyor belts on the lot and several smaller ones. All but the smallest were wedge-shaped and built on metal frameworks. A torrent of gravel was spewing off one of the large belts onto the tallest mound.

I climbed over the low barrier of stacked railway ties that surrounded the parking lot and headed towards the belt that was running. Coming around one of the smaller mounds, I found two workmen loading gravel into a hopper that fed the main belt. The older man, in his late forties or early fifties, sat in the cab of a yellow power shovel, while his younger partner stood in front, pushing the gravel out of the scoop with a hand shovel. The younger man's flannel shirtsleeves were rolled up and the veins in his thickly muscled arms popped up like vines on a tree trunk.

I moved closer and shouted above the noise of the equipment, "Hey, can I talk to you guys about that girl they found yesterday?"

The shovel driver shook his head. His dark weathered face was unshaven and looked like poorly cured leather.

The other man's face was tanned equally dark, but the sun hadn't yet taken its toll on his smooth skin. His stringy brown hair spilled out from under a baseball cap. He set down his shovel and wiped the sides of his face with his shirt.

"Sure," he said. "Time for a smoke break anyway." He pulled a package of Camels from his shirt pocket and gestured for me to follow him. We moved away from the hopper and went behind a medium sized gravel pile to escape the loud clanking of the conveyor.

When we both had cigarettes going, he asked, "You from a newspaper?"

I made a noncommittal grunt that could only be taken as a yes, and asked, "So what happened yesterday?"

He broke into a broad grin.

"It was something, I tell ya'. Cops were sniffing around, some of your buddies were out here asking questions. The boss was having fits. Easiest shift I ever had!"

"What about the girl? Any idea what she was doing here?"

The man shook his head. "I don't think anyone knows. I sure don't."

"You ever see her before?"

The man's smile quickly died on his face.

"No. I only saw her when they brought her down... That was enough. The gravel messed her up, man." He looked up at the sky and puffed his cigarette. The clouds were getting darker, heavier.

"Bloody?"

He brought his look down again.

"Yeah, you could say that. Only more purple than red, like wine almost. When the police left, I had to hose off the pile."

I glanced back at the gravel which continued to pour off the conveyor. The damage it would do to a human body would be like spraying a fly with a sand-blasting machine.

"Do you have any security here at night or on weekends?" I asked. "A night-watchman maybe, or anyone else who might have seen something?"

"No way. I mean, look around. What's to steal? It's just gravel. Lots and lots of little rocks."

"Do kids hang out here then? Maybe they use it as a make-out spot. Or a place to party."

"Nah, nothing like that. If they did, we'd find traces of it. The location is too close to the highway. There's cars going by here all the time. It'd be too easy to get caught."

He was right. The highway curved above the gravel yard and headlights from traffic would sweep over the lot as effectively as any searchlight. But on the other hand, the gravel mounds and heavy equipment offered plenty of places to hide.

"So why didn't they see the body on the conveyor belt when they turned it on?"

"I wasn't working that machine yesterday," he said almost defensively. "But Charlie was." He jerked his thumb back towards the power shovel operator. "It was still mostly dark out, and she was pretty high up the belt. And, Jesus, who'd think to look for something like that?"

"How far up was she?"

The man moved out from the shelter of the mound and I followed. He pointed to a spot two-thirds up on an idle conveyor, about 25 feet off the ground.

"Charlie said she must have been at least that high. Otherwise, he swears he'd've seen her."

"I see. Why doesn't Charlie want to talk to me?"

"Beats me. He's a stubborn old fart. He didn't talk to anybody yesterday either, so it ain't personal." After a short pause, the young man added, "It was sort of funny. The old guy was nearly in tears when he saw her hanging up there. Maybe it's cause he's got a daughter..." He shook his head again. Funny was clearly not the right word, but I knew what he meant.

"What about the police? Did they find anything?"

"You mean like a clue? You'd have to ask them. It looked to me like they got squat."

I dropped my cigarette to the ground and crushed it with my foot.

"Well, thank you, Mr. ..."

"Morgan," he said. "Russell Morgan. You can say I'm an assistant crew chief here."

That was good on a crew of two.

"Thank you. You've been very helpful." I started towards the idle conveyor Morgan had pointed to.

"Hey, how come you didn't take notes?" he asked. "And which paper will this be in anyway?"

"I've got a phonographic memory. I'll remember every word you told me. Just check the Graphic this week." A friend of mine worked at the Eola Graphic and I did what I could to boost his circulation.

Looking very pleased with himself, Morgan turned around and went back to work. He tried some banter with Charlie but the older man merely shook his head. They seemed to be the only two working today.

The conveyor belt the girl had been found on was over three feet wide and seventy or eighty feet long. Standing at its base, I was reminded of the first, tallest hill of a roller coaster--with the big drop to follow. The belt itself ran on rollers along a slender metal lattice, mounted on a sturdy frame of steel I-beams. At the top of the conveyor, there was a small motor with orange shielding on a crossbar. At the bottom, a small hopper and short flat belt were set up to feed onto the large one.

Staring up the belt, several things bothered me. First, I couldn't see what would possess Rudi Alsmith to climb up all that way, no matter how wasted she was. Nor could I understand how the workers missed seeing her there. With any light at all, she should have been perfectly obvious.

Unless the body had been covered with gravel... But that didn't make sense either. Why would someone go to the trouble of hiding the body on a conveyor belt when there were so many better places on the lot to dispose of it? In one of the railcars, for instance, or buried in one of the outlying gravel piles. It might have been weeks before Rudi Alsmith was discovered.

As I walked alongside the conveyor belt, the gravel mound at its end loomed ahead like an ancient pyramid or earthwork where a forgotten people once performed human sacrifices. I almost thought I could see traces of the girl's blood despite the best efforts of Russel Morgan and his hose. A large bank of clouds rolled across the sun and cast a moving shadow that enveloped the yard. I shivered involuntarily. From atop its perch on the metal silo, a large black bird cawed out several times.

"Hello there!"

A man came towards me from the white trailer, waving. His loud voice had the forced friendliness of a salesman. He wore a tan suit and a red tie with the knot pulled down from his open shirt collar. When he was close enough, he reached out to shake my hand and clapped me on the back like a high-school football coach.

"Howdy! I'm Mike Lamond, the manager here," he said, steering me toward the trailer door.

"What a coincidence, I'm Mike too," I said, "Mike D'Angostino. Yes, I did want to talk to you."

"Great! I'm always happy to get a new customer. Whatever you need, Mike, we can get it. Any grade, any amount."

He led me up a pair of cinderblock steps into the gravel yard office. The room was narrow, taking up only half the width of the trailer. There were windows in the outer wall, but they were covered by sheer white curtains. The walls were paneled with cheap wood veneer. The inner wall was hung with framed photographs and business certificates, most of them slightly crooked. One picture showed a little league team. Another commemorated the ground breaking ceremony for the gravel yard with several fat middle-aged men wielding shovels.

We settled into comfortable chairs on either side of Lamond's large desk.

"Like some coffee?" he asked, pointing to a drip coffee maker by his desk.

"Sure, so long as it's not decaf."

"Never touch the stuff."

He poured some coffee into a styrofoam cup and handed it to me. It tasted rancid and burnt.

"It's good, thanks."

Lamond sank back into his chair and folded his hands over his belly.

"So, Mike, what can we do for you? I think you'll find our prices are lower than anyone's in the area. And if you do find a better deal, we guarantee we can beat it. It all depends on what you want."

"Actually I'm not really looking for gravel right now. What I want is information."

A pained look stole across Lamond's wide face. "What are you, a reporter? You here about that girl?"

I nodded.

"A terrible thing," he said, "But I don't see how I can help."

"Do you know who she was?"

"Only from the paper. Nobody here ever saw her before."

"How did she get here?"

"She didn't leave a car so she must have walked."

I let that pass. The gravel yard was miles from anywhere.

"And you don't know what she was doing here?"

"How could I? She was a junkie, for God's sake. Who knows what was going on in her head? I can't see why everyone's making such a big deal out of this..." Lamond's blood pressure was rising and his broad face and balding head were becoming tinged with red.

"Well, I hate to say it, but making a big deal out of nothing is my job. And people are interested. What I'm looking for is something new, something exclusive. Is there anything you didn't tell the other papers? Did the police find something they're not letting on?" I pulled my wallet out and set it in my lap. Private eye rule number 21.C, 'When all else fails, offer money.' The venality check.

"Look, I'd like to help you, but there is nothing." There was an oily smirk on his face, but his color continued to rise.

I was running out of questions. I glanced around the room for inspiration. Perhaps I should ask about his interior designer. The photograph of the ground breaking ceremony caught my eye. One of the men holding a shovel was Lamond, looking younger and with more hair. Another man next to him had an arm on Lamond's shoulder. Both men had the confident look of men-of-the-world, but the second man was much older. His hair was white, he had an aquiline nose and stood partially stooped over. The photo was inspiration enough: Lamond's partner was

Winston Graham, Eola millionaire, businessman, mobster.

I looked quickly back to Lamond. He'd been watching me and his face was on the green side of beet red.

I pointed to the picture of the little league team which was beside the one I'd actually been studying.

"You sponsor little league," I said. "How do they do?

Lamond let out a long breath.

"They usually lose but what matters is how they play the game."

I nodded sagely.

"So true. Well, I guess that's it for me then." I put my wallet back in my pocket and stood up. "Appreciate your time, Mike." I reached across the desk and shook Lamond's hand. His palm was unpleasantly plump and damp.

"No problem. Sorry I couldn't help. But if you ever need gravel, you know who to see..." Lamond stood up as I went to the door.

I waited until I was outside to wipe my hand on my pant leg.

Charlie, the older, taciturn worker, was standing in the parking lot near my car, smoking a cigarette. I nodded to him as I passed.

"You're no reporter," he said in a low drawl. "And you're awful short for a cop." As he spoke, he kicked his feet together the way people do in winter, even though the day was not cold. "I have nothing at all to say to you."

Charlie dropped his lit cigarette into a small clump of grass by his feet and headed back to work. As he walked away, he turned his head several times to watch me.

His manner was very odd. Even while he claimed to have nothing to say, he seemed to be trying to tell me something. And the cigarette he'd tossed away wasn't even half finished. Its smoke rose up from the small patch of grass like a signal flare.

I bent down and poked carefully through the grass until I

found what was there--a small crystal unicorn from a necklace or bracelet. The charm was coated with a dusty film that had become caked on during a rain storm and a thin blade of grass was stuck to it. As I picked it up, some of the gravel dust rubbed off on my thumb and index finger.

The unicorn's horn and one of its legs had broken off and the ring on its back where the chain would go was also broken. The sticker on the unicorn's belly read: "The Crystal Cave--Hanover."

I put the charm in my pocket and stood up. I looked around for Charlie to thank him for the tip, but he was already gone. Obviously he believed the charm had something to do with the dead girl but he didn't want to become involved. By pointing out the charm to me, he could take it off his conscience. It was mine to run with now.

If the unicorn was Rudi Alsmith's, the implications of finding it in the parking lot were major. It meant she probably came to the gravel yard by car, and since there was no vehicle in the lot when she was found, someone else must have come with her. Someone who left her here.

It was of course possible that the charm was not hers--anyone could have dropped it in the parking lot. But the coincidence of Rudi Alsmith and the unicorn both coming from Hanover was too strong to pass up.

CHAPTER NINE

In a word, Old Hanover is quaint. Nestled in a valley on a southern tributary of the Eola river, the historic village's narrow winding lanes and stone buildings hark back to a time when horses were the only form of rapid transit and power was generated by paddle-wheel. The county seat for Burton County, Hanover started out as one of Eola's competitors and ended up one of its suburbs. Modern Hanover sprawls west out of the valley, a nondescript community of strip malls, car dealerships, commuter highways, and cookie-cutter subdivisions.

But the Old Hanover section has maintained its antique charm, along with its original buildings. The local ordinances are the strictest of any in the state: they require that TV antennas be "discreetly" hidden on the roofs and that all electrical and telephone lines be run through underground cable. All the signs for the boutiques and "shoppes" that line the streets must be hand-painted; their Gothic lettering may just be local convention.

The Crystal Cave was in a dark stone building on Main Street. I brushed my hand lightly against the building's wall and a gritty dust fell to the sidewalk like sand. The leaded glass panes in the storefront's windows were small and smoky. The door was made of oak and studded with black iron fittings. The round transom above the door made it look like the entrance to a real cave.

Inside, the store was dimly lit and snug enough to make a bear grumble. The whole floor was covered with glass shelves and cases filled with crystal bric-a-brac of every shape, color and size. The shelves had built-in halogen lamps so the dolphins, eggs, fairies, etc. all seemed to glow with an inner light.

A bookshelf of "Quest Literature" lined one wall, with titles ranging from the esoteric (like Touching the Goddess, Vol. I--Getting to First Base and The Wicca Man) to the more practical (Channeling in the Television Age and How to Make Your Man Love You Whether He Wants To or Not.)

Two customers, a mother and daughter, were standing at the back by the cash register counter, meditating. The woman had her hand resting lightly on the girl's shoulder. The mother's tight key-lime dress showed off a well-worked figure. The girl was plumper than her mother and looked about fifteen. She wore black stone-washed jeans and a pink tank top with a blue windbreaker tied around her waist. Her eyes were closed tight with concentration.

The girl's hands lay flat on the counter, palms up, with a crystal figurine resting on each one. When I reached the register, I saw that she held a coyote and an eagle.

The elderly saleswoman behind the counter kept a respectful distance from the pair. Her deep wrinkles looked like hatchet marks on a chopping block.

"Excuse me," I said in a low voice, "I wonder if you can help me."

The clerk anxiously brought a finger up to her lips.

The mother did too, adding,"Shhh!" for emphasis. Then she resumed communing.

It hurt, but I lowered my voice even more.

"Sorry," I whispered, leaning towards the saleswoman. "But I have a quick question. I'm trying to find the person who bought this..." I took out the three-legged unicorn and set it on the counter. It fell on its side making a light clink on the glass counterpane.

"For Christ's sake, can't you wait?" the mother snapped. "She's choosing her totem!"

"Then maybe she should pick a jackass, since it seems to run in the family."

The mother's jaw dropped. The girl's eyes snapped open and she stammered, "Mo-mommy!?"

The saleswoman jumped in hastily: "I'm very sorry, please continue. I'll take care of this." She picked up the unicorn and started towards a door marked "Employees Only" at the back of the store. "Sir, this way, please."

I followed her back into the stock room and closed the door behind me.

"Thank you for ..." I began, but the saleswoman whirled round.

"What kind of asshole are you?"

"I'm not... I mean, I'm a private detective." A fine distinction, admittedly, but to me an important one.

"You had no right to treat them that way."

"You're right. I'm sorry, it slipped out. But what I'm working on is very imp-..."

She interrupted again:

"And what they're doing is important to them."

The woman's grey hair and prune face reminded me of my third grade teacher, or maybe it was her look of disapproval.

"Like I said, I am sorry. I've always been bad with totems and taboos. It's not something I'm proud of."

"Why don't I believe you?" she said, bringing the charm up to her face and examining it closely. "Well, it's definitely one of ours. But I don't know what else I can tell you."

"How about who bought it?"

"I'm afraid not. This is one of our most popular items..." She reached up to a storage shelf and pulled down a cardboard box labeled "Unicorn. 200 count. Product of Korea." She took out an item wrapped in brown tissue paper and handed it to me. I opened the paper and found a crystal unicorn just like the one from the parking lot, only intact. The facets on the clean figure sparkled like diamond.

"They're nice pieces," she went on. "Not too expensive. We sell dozens each year."

I brought the newspaper picture of Rudi Alsmith out of my pocket and showed it to the woman.

"Have you ever seen this girl?"

The saleswoman looked at Rudi's picture carefully. Finally she nodded.

"I think she was here a month or two ago, with her father. He did buy her one of these." She paused. "At least I thought it was her father. I hope so anyway."

"Why?"

She hesitated before answering.

"Well, they seemed close, that's all. Even though he was much, much older. His hair was all white." The saleswoman stopped and frowned.

"Anything else?" I prodded.

"No, probably nothing."

But from the look on her face, I had an idea what the nothing was.

"You thought they were close--how close?"

"Well, very close, but maybe not like relatives. I got the impression they were romantic together. Don't ask me why. They certainly didn't do anything I could put my finger on. But something about them just didn't seem right."

"Are there any store records that might show who the man was? Did he pay by credit card? If he wrote a check, did you keep his address for mailings?"

The woman frowned. "No, we don't keep records like that. Besides, he may have bought it with cash--a lot of people do. I only remember the girl because she has a face you don't forget. Like a model. I hope she's okay."

"Why wouldn't she be?"

"I don't know. The way you asked about her made me think she might be in trouble."

"Not anymore," I assured her. "Did you notice anything else about the man she was with? Apart from his being too old for her?"

The saleswoman lowered her eyes briefly and then looked me in the face.

"Only that I didn't like him. He was so ... cold. Just rubbed me the wrong way."

That was all the saleswoman could remember. I thanked her and took the broken unicorn back out into the store.

The crystal eagle was standing on the counter by the register, but the mother and daughter were both gone. So was the coyote figure. The girl had chosen well after all; scavengers know their own.

Since I was responsible for her loss, I paid the saleswoman for the stolen coyote before I left. It was a small price to pay for the elation I felt stepping out into the mid-afternoon sun. For the first time in months I felt focused. My work for Preston Curtiz actually seemed to be going somewhere. Someone had taken Curtiz's young protegee Rudi Alsmith to the gravel yard and left her there, either dead or dying. Since her body was left out in the open, her death may have been a message, perhaps to Curtiz himself. A brutal signal that he could run to California, or Timbuktu, but his problems at home were not going to go away.

* * *

Rudi Alsmith's parents lived outside Hanover in a brand new

subdivision called something-or-other Estates. The houses were grand and expensive, designed to look like English cottages on steroids. The rustic architecture looked out of place on the large, flat lawns where the only trees were tiny saplings.

The Alsmiths lived on George III Way in a two-story brick home with Tudor-style beams and a large bay window. Their house looked modestly elegant compared to some of the more grotesque structures on the block. A bright red Mazda RX-7 was parked at the top of their long driveway. I left my car on the street and wandered up the stone walk to the front door. I pushed the doorbell and waited.

Before long, a tall, middle-aged man with a ferret face and thin blondish hair came to the door. He was wearing a silk tie and the vest from a three-piece suit without the jacket. I could smell his aftershave through the screen.

"Yah," his voice was low and serious with a thickly Scandinavian accent.

"Mr. Alsmith? I ..."

"No, I'm sorry, he is not available."

"Can I speak with Mrs. Alsmith then?"

"This is a bad time for them both. You must come back another time." The man began to close the door.

"No, look, I'm here about their daughter. It will only take a minute."

The man looked back uncertainly into the gloom of the house.

I took out their daughter's unicorn and held it up to the screen.

"If you show them this, I'm sure they'll want to see me..."

"Okay, but you wait here."

The man opened the screen door and took the figure. He went back into the house, closing both doors after him.

Five minutes later he came back, opened the door briefly,

and threw the crystal charm far out into the yard.

"Mister," he said, "I don't know who you are or what you want, but it must stop. If you don't leave, I will call the police. You understand?"

"No. Did you even show it to them?"

The man raised his voice: "Leave these people alone!" He slammed the door in my face.

I stood at the doorstep, wondering if I should try again. I didn't really think the Alsmiths would press trespassing charges at a time like this, but I also doubted harassing them further would do any good.

I went out into the yard and searched for the unicorn in the waning daylight.

It made no sense. Why did they refuse to see me? I would have thought they'd at least want to know how I got their daughter's unicorn. But they hadn't even kept it. Didn't they recognize it?

I found the crystal just before it became too dark to keep looking. I got in my car and drove slowly along the street, reading the names listed on the mailboxes. When I reached the end, I turned around went back along the other side.

A mailbox for "Sachett," the woman interviewed in the paper, was across the street from the Alsmiths and two houses down. She lived in a one-and-a-half story stone house with squat walls and a steep-sloped roof. I parked in the driveway and went up towards the front door.

On the way, I passed a huge picture window I thought would have been for the living room, but the room inside was surprisingly small. There was a potter's wheel on a desk, two easels with half-finished paintings, and an old-fashioned sewing machine stuck away in a corner.

The bronze knocker on the front door had the shape of a lion's face, and when Mrs. Sachett finally answered, she looked equally ferocious. Her white hair was contained in black netting and her wrinkled complexion was as coarse as sandstone. Garish lipstick, rouge, and smeared mascara made her look like a castoff from Jack the Ripper's Whitechapel.

"Judith Sachett?" I asked, making a show of looking in my notebook.

"That's right." She spoke with a weary croak. Her breath reeked of cigarette smoke.

"Hi, I work for the Eola Gazette," I began. She'd already been interviewed by the Graphic and I didn't want her to leave anything out that she might have discussed earlier. "... If it's all right, I'd like to ask you a few questions about your neighbor, Rudi Alsmith."

"I already talked to someone from your paper," she said. "A John somebody. What happened to him?"

"He was reassigned to a different story. I'm taking over for him. Can I come in?"

"I guess so. You have any ID?"

I did, of course. Several. But my only press card was for the Graphic.

"I'll be straight with you," I said. "I'm not really a reporter, I'm a private investigator. My name is Nash Tobin." I held one of my regular business cards up to the door.

She took the card and scrutinized it carefully with her left eye; her right eye looked glazed like a carp's.

"Come in, then," she said simply.

That was me all over; master of lies, trickery and deceit when honesty is the best policy.

Mrs. Sachett led me through a small foyer into the living room. The room was decorated with bright noisy paintings all done by the same hand, presumably Mrs. Sachett herself. Years of accumulated smoke had turned the white plaster walls a dingy gray. Homemade ceramic ashtrays, crammed full of cigarette butts, were scattered all over the room with smoke rising from several of them at once. An old black and white photograph of a soldier stood on the stone mantlepiece over the fireplace. A television set was on in a corner, tuned to a local news program. Mrs. Sachett directed me to sit on the couch while she settled back into an easy chair. She muted the TV with a remote control.

"What do you want to know about Rudi?"

"Everything," I said. "At least anything that might explain why she died."

"If I knew anything like that, I would have told the police. How can anyone explain it? It's such a waste!" Her tired voice was full of despair and disbelief. "She was so young and had such a bright future..."

"What was Rudi like?" I asked.

"I knew her quite well, better than she knew herself in a lot of ways. She talked with me about things she'd never discuss with her parents. She was a beautiful, creative, and loving girl. But confused. The teenage years are so difficult. The terrible things in life can seem so overwhelming. Now Rudi will never know that it gets better." Mrs. Sachett blinked to keep tears from forming.

"What terrible things?"

"Love, sex, despair... Not necessarily in that order." She tried to smile, but combined with her blinking, the effect was almost comical. She realized it herself. "Why do people always look ridiculous when they're unhappy?" she asked.

She took a Kleenex from a box on the coffee table and daubed her eyes. It smeared her mascara even more. In spite of her fearsome appearance, I sensed an openness about her that would be easy to confide in.

I waited while she composed herself and then prompted, "What about drugs?"

Mrs. Sachett was silent a moment and then admitted, "Yes,

she used drugs. Sometimes. Not often. I know she wasn't addicted."

"How do you know?"

"She told me."

"You talked with her about it?"

"Some. I wasn't really comfortable with it though, and Rudi knew that."

"Did she say what she used? Marijuana, cocaine, heroin, pills maybe, something else?"

"The first two, at least. I don't know about anything else. But she said she only used them to 'free her mind' for her writing. She was a very promising poet."

"I'm sure she was," I said with more sympathy than conviction.

It's almost inevitable. Whenever someone dies young, they are invariably said to be on the brink of some great accomplishment in one field or another. I once read about a frustrated young California playwright who killed himself as a publicity stunt. The critics who read his work afterwards admitted it was unproducible, but they were unanimous in declaring that he "showed real promise." I just had to laugh like hell.

"Here, I'll show you." Mrs. Sachett stood up and walked slowly into the dining room. From the couch, I watched her rummage through the top drawer of a bureau, looking for something. She pulled out a sheet of paper and picked up a small photograph in a plexiglass frame from on top. She brought them back and placed the paper and picture on the coffee table in front of me, then returned to her chair.

"The picture is nothing. What I've told you is nothing. But that... is Rudi."

The sheet of paper was an expensive typing bond. The untitled poem was written out with a felt-tip calligraphy pen.

There were still traces of ruled lines in pencil that had been erased after the ink was dry.

The eyes that have seen too much
Stare into me
I know what they want
Like cold steel razors
They strip me bare
Leaving clothes intact
They cut flesh and bone
And pause, leering before my empty soul
I give my self up to the blades
To their gleaming flashing frenzy
My silence is
The final
Surrender

It wasn't what I expected. The boy in front of Curtiz's office had called it "stupid death poetry," but what Rudi saw was bleaker than that. Through her eyes, life itself seemed an abomination. I looked up briefly at Mrs. Sachett and nodded. I had seen what she wanted me to see.

"It's hard to believe it's the same girl in the picture," she said.

The photograph showed Rudi sitting in the school cafeteria with two friends, a boy and a girl. Unlike the yearbook photo in the newspaper, there was no mocking laughter; Rudi seemed genuinely happy here. Her face was made-up the same way I'd seen her, pale powder with cheeks greyed to make her look gaunt, violet eye shadow and heavy black liner and mascara. But her smile belonged to a silly school girl, goofing off with her friends.

The boy sitting beside Rudi was wearing a tuxedo T-shirt and a tie around his neck. Rudi pulled the tie up over his head, and he mimicked being hanged; his blond hair was in disarray, his eyes rolled upward, his head slouched to one side, and his tongue stuck out the side of his mouth. But through all this, he continued to smile for the picture.

The other girl sat a little back from the table with her arms crossed. Her bowl-style haircut emphasized the pudginess in her features. She had a weak, diffident smile, as if she didn't find the gruesome pantomime amusing but didn't want anyone to know. Or maybe she just didn't like having her picture taken next to Rudi. Beside her more fascinating friend, she just seemed to fade into the background.

"Who's the boy in the picture? A boyfriend?"

"That's Jim. One of them, yes."

"She had others?"

Mrs. Sachett laughed. "Does Peking have Chinamen? Yes, she had many boyfriends."

"Would you call her a flirt?"

"In my day she would have been called something worse. But today's standards are different, I guess." Mrs. Sachett paused. "Frankly speaking, Rudi liked men, lots of them. She had boyfriends her own age but she preferred older, more mature men. They made fewer demands on her. Besides, they could afford motel rooms."

"These men, were they the ones who supplied her with drugs?"

"Almost certainly," Mrs. Sachett said. "Rudi didn't have money of her own. Her parents tried to keep her on a tight leash."

Not tight enough, it sounded like. Today's standards weren't all that different from when Mrs. Sachett was a girl. Only the form of currency had changed. A beautiful young girl with no money and an expensive appetite for drugs and sex, Rudi Alsmith sounded like a walking prescription for disaster. But she had also been much more than that. The keen intelligence I'd seen in her eyes at Curtiz's office had been unmistakable. And she wasn't walking anymore.

"What about her other boyfriends? What were their names?"

"Well, she went with Jim for a while. Before him there was a Roger. She called him her big hulking thug. There was also someone named Win, but that might have been short for Winter. There were others, but those are the ones I recall."

"Do you know any of their last names?"

Mrs. Sachett shook her head.

"Sorry, I don't think Rudi ever mentioned them."

“What about the girl in the picture? Do you know her name?”

“No, I’m afraid not.”

I frowned as I looked down at the picture. The carefree moment seemed so disconnected from the rest of Rudi’s life.

"Did Rudi's parents know all this was going on? The drugs, the men, and so on?"

Mrs. Sachett's eyes briefly roamed over the ashtrays in the room. Before answering, she lit a fresh cigarette, leaving the others to burn themselves out.

"They probably suspected some of it. They tried to control her as best they could. Her father especially. He refused to let her have a car of her own. He insisted she live at home when she started college. But really there wasn't anything they could do. Rudi was who she was and no one else could change that. If she had lived long enough, she would have outgrown her problems. Most of us do."

Mrs. Sachett paused for a moment and glanced up at the soldier's portrait on her mantlepiece.

"She wasn't really wild, you know," Mrs. Sachett went on. "Not for wildness' sake. The drugs, the sex, even her writing were Rudi's ways of blotting out life, of making time pass without having to think or feel. She was very hurt inside, desperate for something she never found. I think somewhere deep down, Rudi wanted to die. I know she didn't want to live. It's so sad. If only she'd had more time..." Tears formed in Mrs. Sachett's eyes and nothing she did would stop them from flowing.

"You think she may have killed herself?"

Mrs. Sachett sobbed.

"I don't know," she cried, "I don't know."

I took the crystal unicorn from my pocket and set it down on the coffee table.

"Have you ever seen this before?" I asked.

Mrs. Sachett rubbed her eyes with her sleeve.

"It looks like one she wore on her necklace. She called it her secret charm." Mrs. Sachett reached across and picked up the crystal figure. She grasped it tightly as though it were a talisman that could somehow bring Rudi back. "Her boyfriend Win gave this to her. She said it was the only thing she'd ever seen hornier than she was."

With symbolism like that it's no wonder her parents didn't know about it. It also confirmed the Crystal Cave saleswoman's suspicion that Rudi and the older man who bought the charm had been lovers.

Mrs. Sachett looked up at me. Her tears and mascara left black tracks down her cheeks.

"Mr. Tobin, I have to know. Did Rudi do this to herself?"

"I don't know yet," I said. "But I can say she wasn't alone when she died..."

"I hope you get the bastard who was there..."

Mrs. Sachett's painted lips pursed tightly and her eyes blazed with reflected light. The pain and impotent anger in her face taught me something I hadn't realized before. The tragedy here wasn't Rudi's. It belonged to the people she left behind. This lonely old woman had lost a young friend, confidante, and fellow artist--even a surrogate grand-daughter. And despite all their efforts to keep their daughter safe, Rudi's parents had lost their child forever. The conflict sparked by Rudi's rebellion against their rules would now never be reconciled. And who could tell? American poetry may have lost the defining voice of a generation.

Mrs. Sachett's unanswered plea hung over us like a hovering spirit.

"I'll find him," I said finally. "I promise."

Mrs. Sachett brought her hands up to her eyes and began to sob again. There was something achingly sad about the old woman's pain. To have lived so long, only to be left vulnerable and alone with no one to turn to for comfort. I stood up and went behind her chair. I put my hand on her back offering what consolation I could.

From behind her, I watched the mute images on the television screen. It showed the silent antics of a noisy crowd of protesters on the plaza at city hall. The protesters wore feather head-dresses and war paint. From the printed signs they carried, I gathered that their beef had to do with the way Eola's mayor treated school teachers and Native Americans. It was a strange coalition certainly, but I knew better than to speculate on political motives or bedfellows.

I closed my eyes to the silent cacophony and felt once more the gentle pulse of Mrs. Sachett's weeping.

CHAPTER TEN

Mrs. Sachett let me take the photograph with me when I left. It was chilly and still as I trudged out to my car in the driveway. Wispy, moon-limned clouds crept across the sky in front of stars that were too tired to twinkle. In the frosty air Mrs. Sachett's house looked even more weighed down and dejected than when I'd arrived. In a brighter mood I might have looked forward to the upcoming change of seasons. Instead, I felt bleak and hollow. For several minutes I sat on the dark driveway, coaxing my car's hesitant engine along and clouding the cold windshield with my breath.

Despite my mood it had been a productive day. I now knew that the unicorn charm from the gravel yard was given to Rudi Alsmith by someone named Win or Winter, a man old enough to be mistaken for her father. I didn't know whether her attachment to him was based on love or a craving for drugs, but I suspected the worse. The same held true for Jim and Roger and any of the others whose names Mrs. Sachett had forgotten or never knew.

Perhaps for Rudi Alsmith the distinction between love and craving did not even exist. If she was an addict (despite what Mrs. Sachett believed), then her need for chemical stimulation would have filtered into every aspect of her life, including how she experienced love. She may have been attracted to any man who could feed her addictions.

It was a depressing thought: a teenage girl, locked into a

world where love and sex were commodities and where drugs offered the only escape. Such a world left little room for hope. It made me realize how much I wanted a drink.

I backed out of the driveway and started down George III Way towards the exit. My headlights cut a swath across the show-case neighborhood. It wasn't supposed to be like this. Not here, not among these premier homes with manicured lawns and royal street names. When I first arrived, the subdivision had reminded me of a secluded island amidst the dry scrub of empty fields, a sheltered place where wealth and security kept an ocean of problems from washing up on its shores. What happened to Rudi Alsmith showed that prosperity was no bulwark, that no amount of landscaping or architecture could hold that sea at bay. The deluge began when the first resident moved in. As I pulled out of the development onto the highway, I glanced at the lighted marble sign by the entrance. The name of the development was Avalon Estates.

* * *

The landscape seemed deserted as I drove east along the narrow rural highway. It was punctuated by occasional clusters of dilapidated houses, weather-beaten feed/grocery stores, and vacant gas stations. The only traffic signals were flashing yellow caution lights.

At the edge of one of these small settlements, I waited at a railroad crossing for a freight train to pass. Each car made heavy rhythmic "chuck-chuck" sounds as the wheels rolled over loose cross-ties. The long parade of maroon cars seemed endless.

A grey Jeep Cherokee, bristling with antennas, pulled up behind me and its headlights blazed through my rear window. It looked familiar somehow, as if I'd seen it somewhere before without really noticing. The Jeep had been following behind me for at least the last ten minutes, and even though my speed had not been particularly consistent, its driver had maintained a constant distance between us. I looked back to see who it was but could not see into the dark-tinted windshield.

Still cautious after my Saturday night trip to Shakytown, I took my gun from the glovebox and laid it on the seat beside me.

Finally the train's caboose went by. Before the railroad crossing lights even stopped flashing, I pulled across the tracks and started down the highway. The Cherokee accelerated more slowly, betraying no overt sign of trying to catch up. But it never really fell behind either.

I turned left at the first intersection and followed a small country road that led away from town. The Cherokee took the same turn behind me.

I swerved again onto an even narrower road, winding through the dark countryside. This one was lined with hedges that made it hard to anticipate the twists and turns as they came. I could no longer see the Jeep, but every once in a while its headlights lit the tops of the hedges behind me.

It's a coincidence, I repeated to myself. It's just a farmer on his way home. Certainly nothing to get paranoid about. Eventually he would turn off on one of the small unnamed roads and I'd never see him again. I'd go home, open a beer, and chuckle a few times over it. Eventually I would forget the incident completely.

But the Jeep didn't turn off.

So I did. The next route I chose led into the heart of empty farm country. Beyond the hedges were fields and fields of chopped corn-stalks, shining like bones under the pale moon. No farmhouses were visible, no lights of any kind.

I spotted the Cherokee once more as it passed over a rise in the road behind me. It was closer now. My hope that the driver was just a local was getting slimmer with each mile. There was no civilization out here, no place to come home to. Instead, we were driving deeper into darkness and isolation.

I pushed the accelerator pedal down and my Impala's engine roared to life. Its eight cylinders pulsed with the hum of vintage American manufacturing. The beast roused itself like a dinosaur from the modern swamp of PCV valves, MPG standards and unleaded gasoline. Exhaust belched from its tailpipe, and the speedometer reached seventy before I knew it. The Impala's huge snout covered the road as we tore around corners, filled with the animal exhilaration of reckless speed. Coming around one blind curve, I almost ran head-on into a Volkswagen Bug. Its driver swerved off the road and pumped his puny horn. The doppler shift on the horn made it sound like a dog's squeak toy as I went by, but I didn't slow down.

The Jeep was still trailing me but it had fallen farther back. After rounding another sharp turn, I hit my brakes hard and pulled onto a patch of gravel at the side of the road.

The gravel was part of a tractor entrance through a low stone wall into an empty field. I turned off my headlights and got out of the car, taking my gun with me. I went through the gap in the fence and ran ten yards back along the wall in the direction of the curve. My feet sank into the soft dirt at every step and the earth clung to my shoes.

I crouched low behind the wall, waiting for the Jeep to come around the corner. If it stopped, I would be well out of its headlights. I still half-believed it would drive right by. The idea that someone was following me made no sense. Why would someone be after me? What could they possibly want?

And what was Rudi Alsmith's body doing at a gravel yard owned by the gangster Winston Graham? Could he be the mysterious older lover "Win" who bought her the unicorn?

What was I getting involved with? The meager threads I'd pulled together on this case all seemed to unravel in various directions, the most ominous of which was Graham himself.

There was so much I didn't know... And in my line of work, what you don't know can hurt you.

All I knew was, I was armed and hidden behind a crumbling stone wall, out of harm's way if harm was approaching. I told myself I was ready for anything.

Except for nothing. The Cherokee had been two minutes behind me at most. But my wait stretched out to ten. My knees were getting stiff from their long crouch, so I sat down flat in the dirt and stretched my legs out in front of me.

And still the Jeep didn't come.

It should have been a relief, but it wasn't. There had been no intersections on the road for the last few miles. There was nowhere for the Jeep to get off. That meant the driver had stopped. He was waiting for me, just as I was waiting for him.

I stood up and started walking back along the inside of the low wall towards whomever it was. The hedges provided cover for me but they were not so thick that I would miss the Cherokee if I came to it. I trudged on for several minutes but there was no sign of the other vehicle.

Maybe I was wrong. Maybe I had missed an intersection along the road, or a hidden driveway, as I went speeding by. My eyes had been so focused on the road that it certainly seemed possible...

I heard the Cherokee before I saw it. Its engine was in slow idle and its headlights were off. I crept silently behind the bushes until I was past the car. Through a thin gap in the hedge I could see it parked on the shoulder with its passenger side tires partway down a shallow ditch. The driver inside held a car phone to his head with his right hand and the lighted numerals cast a faint green light on his cheek. His left hand held a cigarette which he periodically brought up to his mouth.

I pushed myself into a large break in the hedge and held still, watching and waiting. I was in no hurry now. The driver did not look particularly attentive, but if I left my hiding place there was still a good chance he would see me in his side mirror.

The driver hung up the phone and stubbed out his cigarette in the car ashtray. He shook out another from a pack he took from his pocket. As he concentrated on lighting his second cigarette, I made my move.

I pushed through the bush and ducked behind the car. I had no way of knowing if he had seen me but at least I didn't hear his door opening. I came out around the driver's side and moved at a crouch toward the front of the car, keeping below the view of his mirror. Faint strains of country music emanated from inside.

When I reached the driver's door, I took a deep breath and stood up quickly, my body shaking from adrenaline overload. I rapped the window with my gun. The driver's wide white face jerked around at the sound. His startled eyes, half-open mouth, and bald pate made him look like a frightened fish.

"Get out," I said loudly.

The man hesitated, glancing at the glove compartment to his right.

"Don't even think about it!" I said, pounding firmly on the glass. It was enough to get his attention away from whatever was in the glovebox.

As he looked back at me his expression softened to one of recognition. His body slackened. He held his right hand in the air and with his other hand pushed a button on the door to roll down the window.

A cold smile played across his pale lips.

"Well, boy, ya got me," he said with a Texas drawl. His voice was slow and relaxed, friendly to the point of being insipid. "Yup, fair and square. I should have known you were up to something." As his grin grew wider, the ends of his mouth stretched back towards his neck, like a snake greeting dinner.

"I said, get out."

He slowly pushed the door open and climbed out. He was a big man, taller than me by half a foot and wider by the same margin. He wore a beige suit of sorts, rumpled and comfortable looking, but no tie.

"Turn around and put your hands on the roof," I said.

He turned to face the car and did as he was told. I patted him down carefully. In spite of his flabby appearance, the driver was heavily muscled. He must have worked out every day and it wasn't because he was particular about his looks.

"Careful back there," he said, turning his head. "I'm a trifle ticklish."

I put my gun against his thick neck.

"No, you be careful. Otherwise my trigger finger's liable to get a little ticklish."

"Come on. You're not going to shoot me."

"Maybe not. But if I did, I'd get away with it. So for now, I make the rules and you follow them. Got it?"

His only answer was a grunt.

When I was satisfied that he didn't have a gun, I lifted his wallet from a back pocket. I flipped the billfold open but it was too dark for me to read any of the IDs inside.

"All right," I told him, "Stand away from the car." I gestured with the gun for him to move back.

"What? In the middle of the road?"

"If a car comes you can move."

He stepped back to the center line.

"Son, this is all unnecessary. I'll tell ya who I am."

"I'm certain of that."

I opened the door to his car and examined his wallet under the dome light. His driver's license identified him as Lance Talbot, born in 1950, and two credit cards confirmed the name. But he also had driver's licenses under the names Wallace MacShane and Douglas Murphy and credit cards for those names as well. He kept business cards for each identity in separate slots of his wallet. The cards all bore the company name "Axiom Security" with an Eola office address and phone number. The cards were nearly identical except that Talbot was listed as the "chief investigator" and MacShane and Murphy had no job titles.

The wallet's money pocket had only forty dollars inside, but hidden away behind the lining were ten fifty-dollar bills. Talbot had no personal items in his wallet, no pictures of family, no library or video store cards, not even any jotted notes or reminders. It was all strictly business.

I pocketed one of his cards and tossed the wallet back to Talbot. He caught it with his left hand.

"So which is it? Talbot?" I asked.

"Yes."

"That's quite a collection."

"Extra identities never hurt, I'm sure you know. Especially since I pay myself under three names. We all pay taxes, but not much!" He smiled a good-ole-boy grin and started coming back to the car.

"I didn't say you could move." I gestured with the gun for him to move back.

I ducked back into the car. It was equipped with enough electronic gadgetry to fly an F-15; the only thing missing was an altimeter. In addition to the phone, there was an expensive scanner that I recognized from trade publications; it could pick up conversations from both cordless home phones and mobile cellular ones.

Mounted on Talbot's dashboard was a small round screen marked with concentric circles and intersecting straight lines, like a radar display. I flicked on the switch for the screen and a stationary green blip appeared on its face. My Impala was apparently host to a radio-transmitter parasite. A collection of large-scale maps of the Eola area lay out on the passenger's seat.

I glanced briefly back at Talbot to make sure he was staying put. He continued with his meaningless smile as he watched me but didn't move.

A miniature voice-activated tape recorder was lying on his passenger seat. I opened it up and found the microcassette inside labeled "Tobin--October 17." I rummaged quickly through his glove compartment and found a box of blank tapes and several fresh packages of menthol cigarettes. Talbot also had a .357 Magnum Colt revolver attached to a holder on the roof of his glovebox. All the chambers were loaded. I put his gun back in place, but put the tape with my name on it into my pocket.

As I was getting out of the car, my head bumped a protrusion above the door. I reached in and found a leather-lined sap mounted there.

Immediately, the back of my head began to tingle. I put my gun away and shifted the sap to my right hand. Only then did I motion for Talbot to come back.

"Okay," I said. "Now we talk."

"High time, too." From the jovial tone in Talbot's voice, it was obvious he missed the edge in mine.

As he approached I gave a fast swing with the sap and landed the blow on his arm. I hadn't thought to do it, but the memory of having it used on me made me want to lash out. Talbot yelped and grabbed at his bruised limb. My anger was building and it felt good to strike him. I wanted to do it again.

"Not here. Around the other side," I said, pointing.

Fear was beginning to show on his fat face now. He looked up and down the road, hoping perhaps someone would drive by and save him from his predicament. But he needn't have bothered--the world was deserted except for us two.

I ended his hesitation by slamming the club on the hood of his car.

"Now!"

I followed him around and gestured for him to stand at the bottom of the ditch. His expensive shoes squelched in the brackish mud.

"Why are you following me?" I said.

"You know I can't tell you that. That's strictly between me and my client."

"That's your problem, not mine. You've been watching me for a week now. I want to know who hired you and why."

"Look. I just do what I'm paid to do. The whys don't matter to me. Maybe you've been screwing with someone's wife... You got something on your conscience, kid?"

His face was one big smirk. He knew that I was not even involved with my own wife, let alone someone else's. His comment set me off again and I took a sharp swipe with the sap to the side of his knee. His leg collapsed and he went sprawling forward into the rank mud.

He slowly got back on his feet but stood stooped over, rubbing his leg.

"You know, I really don't like you," he said. "If I did, I still wouldn't tell you anything. I haven't enjoyed this, except maybe for watching you make a fool of yourself. But it has been awfully easy. So easy I got careless." Talbot laughed derisively. "I don't even know what you're doing in this racket. You're a goddamned college boy who never worked your way up. You haven't the skill or the talent or the knack to make up for it. You're a disgrace to an honorable profession. Come to think of it, maybe I should've followed your wife instead. That might have been a whole lot more interesting!" His leer came through even in his voice. He wanted to rile me and was succeeding.

I started towards him.

"Right," I said. "You knocked me senseless when I was drunk and robbed me. You set a nice standard yourself--a consummate professional. A goddamned paragon."

"I don't know from goddamned paragons, but if this is about money, I can pay you back. I've got money right here..."

Talbot reached back to take his wallet out of his pocket. He was still stooped over, but in the darkness I missed a slight shift in the position of his feet. One foot was now planted firmly on the rear wall of the ditch. As he brought his wallet out and extended it towards me, my gaze followed his hand.

Pushing off his back foot, Talbot launched into me. I didn't even have time to swing the sap. He drove me into the side of his car, right onto a passenger side mirror. The aluminum bars that held the mirror broke and stabbed into my back. The pain was like an underground bomb test, the shock wave moved through my whole body. Before I had a chance to recover, Talbot grabbed my arms and threw me against the car again, once, twice, three times. After that I was beyond counting. With each blow my strength drained out until I was left as limp as a rag doll.

Talbot let me go and I slid down the side of his car. Talbot reached down and lifted me up by my armpits. He carried me to the center of the ditch and dropped me into the mud. He ground my face down with the heel of his shoe.

"You want to play with big boys, huh? First you gotta learn the rules for hardball. Here's lesson one..." Talbot pulled his foot back and kicked me in the ribs on my left side.

I barely felt it. Aftershocks throbbed throughout my system, drowning out any local hurt. I moaned loudly and pulled up onto my knees. He kicked me again and I cringed, bringing my arms into my sides. I slipped my right hand into my jacket pocket and felt the gun there. I let out another moan and tried to bring the gun out.

But Talbot saw what I was up to. He grabbed my arm and shook the pistol out of my loose grip. He picked up the gun with one hand, and reached into my pocket with the other. He removed the micro-cassette tape and his business card.

"Now who has the gun, eh?" he said, holding the muzzle to my temple. "Whose finger's ticklish now? Just so you know, there is nothing that ties me to you. When I kill you, you can be certain I will get away with it, dead certain. I wanted you to know that for the last minute you have before dying."

He could do it, I knew. The coldness in his voice more than his words showed that taking my life meant nothing to him. Nothing I could say would change his mind. A light squeeze of his finger and my head would be splattered across the ditch, burnt bits of brain and bone that would be food for insects and roadside weeds. Talbot could cover his tracks well enough that no one would ever suspect him. There'd be a perfunctory police investigation but in the end nothing would be done because nothing could be done. My life would end as a momentary blip of crime statistics, the sum of my experience reduced to a one versus a zero on a police computer memory chip.

But for all that, I wasn't afraid.

No, that's not true. I was afraid. But other feelings masked the fear and pushed it aside as irrelevant. I gulped at the depth of my regret: regret that I could not see my parents before this moment came and tell them I was proud of them, proud to be their son; regret that Mara and I had parted so bitterly--as if the good things we'd shared had never existed; regret for so many things I had wanted to do but always put off for the mundane necessities of living.

There was sorrow too. Not for myself, but for what I could never now understand. What made Talbot so cold? What could blind him to the importance of what he was taking away? So much seemed obvious to me, but I could never make him understand. As my life was about to end, my heart went out to Rudi Alsmith and I hoped that the drugs she took had not clouded the clarity of her last moments.

But most of all, I was overcome by awe. Awe of the one true mystery--when everything's over, what's next?

Talbot laughed. He opened the gun's cylinder and emptied the cartridges one by one into the muck. Then he put my revolver into his pocket.

"These things aren't toys for children, you know," he said. "I hope you enjoyed today's lesson in hardball. Let me know if you ever want another. I'll see you."

Talbot got into his Jeep Cherokee and drove away.

After a while, I removed my coat and lay on my back in the ditch, letting the warm mud seep through my shirt. I put the jacket over me like a blanket. I don't know how long I lay there, but at least two cars went by on that little-traveled road and I made no attempt to stop them. Most of the time I kept my eyes closed. When I did look up, the sky was full of stars in patterns within patterns.

The ache in my back and ribs finally subsided enough that I began to feel cold and my whole body began to shake. It was time to move on. I got up and walked slowly back to my car.

Before getting in, I took off my muddy shirt and undershirt and dropped them to the ground. I tried to clean up the mess on my back with a cloth towel, but it wouldn't come clean. It took me a while to figure out why: the muck on my back was blood, not dirt. There was a long gash in the skin where Talbot's broken mirror-mount had stabbed me like a dull blade. Luckily, my jacket had kept the bar from piercing my skin too deeply and let me off with a flesh wound.

Talbot had taught me a humiliating lesson. Like it or not, I was playing with big boys now in a game where I didn't know the object or the rules. But Talbot would learn something too--college boys can be quick studies.

CHAPTER ELEVEN

I pulled into the alley by my office sometime after 1:30 a.m. My back muscles knotted up during the long drive from the rural reaches. I felt even worse than when I started. My wool jacket chafed my goose-flesh skin like sandpaper.

I unlocked the warehouse door and punched the "Up" button for the elevator inside. The sluggish machinery grumbled to life. But when the empty cab arrived, I just stared at it. It was obvious my stab wound required more attention than I could manage on my own.

I turned and followed the long corridor to a ground-floor apartment and rang the doorbell several times. I eventually heard footsteps inside. The door opened a crack, and an old, tired eye peered out.

"What the hell..." My landlord and sometime drinking partner, Alphonse Andeo, stopped when he recognized me. The eye disappeared as he fumbled with the chain, and his voice told someone inside, "No, it's okay, Hil. You go back to bed. I can take care of this..."

The old man pulled the door all the way open and stood before me in rumpled boxer shorts and a yellowed dago-tee. His white hair was ruffled back over his head like eagle feathers and his limbs looked sad and scrawny in the bright living room light. His ankles were lost in a pair of tattered blue corduroy slippers.

He could not have looked more different from the tough, bad guy roles he'd played back in his Hollywood heyday.

"Nash, you look like guano! What's wrong?" Andeo motioned me in and closed the door.

"I got hurt," I said. "It's my back."

"What happened? Take your jacket off, boy. What's that towel for?"

I removed my coat and unwrapped the towel carefully to keep the blood from dripping on his floor.

"I got hurt," I repeated, turning to show him.

"What you got... is a trip to the hospital! You're bleeding a bitch!"

I shook my head.

"I can't afford it." Health insurance was one expense I had let go early.

Andeo's wizened face turned sour. "Well, that's plain dumb!" But his exasperation sputtered out before it really got going. "Never mind. Let's see what I can do."

He led me through his apartment to the bathroom and sat me down on the commode. He took some gauze pads from a box under the sink and pulled a bottle of antiseptic mouthwash from the medicine cabinet. He opened the bottle, held one of the pads over its mouth, and tipped the bottle over, soaking the pad.

"This will probably hurt," he said, gently placing the gauze on my back.

He was right; it did. The alcohol attacked every nerve in the wound and felt like a cigarette lighter going off under my skin.

"Don't you have hot pokers?" I asked.

He tossed the pad into the sink. It splattered red across the white basin. Even soaked in mouthwash the pad still absorbed a lot of blood.

"I don't know. That gash is awful deep. I think you should have it seen to properly."

"No."

Shaking his head, he tipped the bottle into a new pad and pressed it to my back. "How'd this happen? That wife of yours come at you with a potato-peeler?"

I knew there was a retort in there somewhere about Mara stabbing me in the back, but I was too tired to find it.

"Someone threw me into a car mirror."

"You're not a big man," he said, swabbing more deeply at the wound. "You're supposed to make up for it by being smart--smart enough to stay out of situations like that."

The old man was right, of course.

Talbot had gained the upper hand because I let him. It had been mine to lose, and I lost it by not controlling my anger. Talbot read me perfectly; his provocations were deliberate and calculated. And I played right into his hands...

However, Andeo's comment resonated more deeply than a reproof for getting careless. I hadn't just been angry, I'd been afraid as well. Talbot was acting as someone's agent. I had no idea who sent him or why. That realization brought fear--fear of what I was getting involved in, fear of making a mistake, fear that I might be in over my head. Fear, in short, of the unknown.

But I could never know everything. Ignorance is the human condition, and has been, ironically, since our ancestors first filched from the tree of knowledge. If I was uncomfortable with that, I might as well return Curtiz's money, close up shop, and plead for my old job back at the Transcontinental Agency. Then real detectives could gather up the facts while I only needed to bundle them together into nice, tidy reports.

"Make do with what you know," a Transcontinental op once told me. "It's never enough, but it's all you have. That's being smart. If you do that, 95 percent of the time you'll come out okay. And most of that last five percent is out of your hands anyway, so you can't let yourself worry about it."

What I hadn't been was smart.

"There, the bleeding's mostly stopped," Andeo said. He took a roll of plaster tape and stuck about six dry pads over the wound. The long ribbons of tape stretched from my shoulder to my waist and wrapped around my side. "That should hold it."

There were several reddened pads sitting in the sink. The former actor wiped his hands up and down his thin undershirt, leaving bloodstained stripes on his flat belly. His gesture looked completely casual but also cinematic, as if he'd done it a hundred times before. The dipsomaniac doctor who removes a bullet from the desperate gangster; the solitary grave robber, wiping his hands on a Burke and Hare shirt.

"Thank you," I said, standing up. "It feels a lot better."

"No, stay here." He left the bathroom and marched down the narrow hallway, his bandy legs moving like a puppet's. He rapped gently on his bedroom door, whispered "Hilda..." and went in, closing the door after him. A moment later he returned with a grey and black plaid flannel shirt.

"Here, take this," he said. "It's too big for me."

I took the shirt and let him help me put it on.

"Thanks," I said. "For this and for what you said. I'll remember it."

"Never mind what I said. Just go see a doctor." He led me through the living room and handed me my jacket. I shook his hand before I left.

Andeo's door didn't close until I was nearly to the elevator.

CHAPTER TWELVE

I spent the night on my office couch and didn't wake up until 8:30. The sleep seemed to do my back some good--it only hurt now when I moved, breathed, or stayed still.

I washed up in the bathroom and checked the bandage in the mirror. It was holding tight, but the green-black-purple bruises that surrounded it looked like a disturbed child's finger painting. I took a new undershirt from under the sink and gingerly put it on along with Andeo's flannel shirt. My reflection did not look great, but it was definitely better. Guano no more, I had reached the level of rabbit pellets at least: my appearance improved excrementally.

I made coffee and spent the next hour at my desk updating my progress report for Curtiz. I was perfectly up-front about the direction my investigation was taking. There was no guarantee that Curtiz's blackmailer was somehow connected with Rudi Alsmith's death, but it seemed a reasonable area of inquiry. Especially since it was all I had to go on. I gave only a brief account of my run-in with Lance Talbot, merely noting that another private eye had been following me and that an altercation broke out when I confronted him.

I folded the report into a large stamped envelope and addressed it to Curtiz's Tamur Lane house. I would have liked to drop off the report personally in the hope of seeing Vera Marshall again, but if I was still being followed, the less direct contact between Curtiz and myself the better.

I left my office and went out to drop the envelope into a nearby post box. The morning air was cool but pleasant, more like spring than fall. On my return trip, I stopped in the alley where I'd parked and went over my Impala for Talbot's transmitter. I dreaded the idea that I might have to slide under the car on my back to find it.

But I was lucky. The small square box with a coiled antenna was fixed by a magnet to the inside of the rear bumper. I removed the device and stuck it to a semi-truck with Kentucky license plates that had stopped at a traffic light. Talbot probably wouldn't fall for an interstate wild goose chase, but it was worth a try anyway.

With the bug gone, I got into my car and drove south again to Hanover, this time to Rudi Alsmith's high school.

* * *

From a distance, the buildings of Worthington Senior High looked like blobs of brown clay left out to dry in the sun. As I got closer, the complex began to look more like a country-club prison; the buildings had very few windows and doors, but there was an indoor swimming pool and even a planetarium to keep the inmates happy. The school was surrounded by immaculate sports fields and tennis courts. Phys Ed students in shorts and T-shirts were outside knocking golf balls across an empty green.

The students' and visitors' parking lot in front of the school was a sea of gleaming sedans and muscle cars. Even here my car was an embarrassment. I should have parked out back with the teachers.

I went in through the main entrance and found myself in a large, open area with cinderblock walls painted light blue and decorated with student-drawn pictures of fish. "Go Piranhas!" blazed out in large letters above the doors. It wasn't much as slogans go. "Small fry with teeth!" would have been better.

A few students were grouped around tables in the open cafeteria, but the building still seemed strangely empty.

The principal's office was close to the main entrance on the right. A young secretary inside was drinking coffee behind a high reception desk. She looked harried despite having nothing to do. I gave her my card and asked to see her boss. I had the sheepish feeling that I should have handed her a hall pass instead. Without a word, she looked at my card, stood up, and went to a door at the back of the reception office. She knocked and went inside, closing the door behind her. A moment later she came out and gestured for me to go through. I nodded my thanks as I went by but she turned away.

The principal's inner sanctum was plush compared to the reception area, with good carpeting, glossy paint, and large wood bookcases. The room was overrun with potted plants: flowers, shrubs, ferns, creepers, even a small tree or two. No doubt they were intended to brighten the room but instead they had the opposite effect. They were all drooping and dry, their colors subdued with brown and grey. Fluorescent lighting must not have agreed with them.

The principal, Mrs. Wiggins, according to the plaque on her desk, sat behind her desk in a leather and chrome chair. She held my card, scowling. Her conservative nutmeg-colored suit looked big on her, perhaps a full dress-size too big. Her wide face was carefully made-up but still pale. She looked barely forty but there was already a heavy tone of silver in her blond hair. I guessed the lighting didn't agree with her either.

She set my card down on the desk and pushed it towards me. She made no effort to get up or shake my outstretched hand.

"Mr. Tobin," she said, "You have an interesting line of work. Are you here for career day or is this a business call?"

"Business," I said, sitting down opposite her. My chair felt a lot less comfortable than hers looked. "I can't honestly recommend my job to young impressionable minds."

"Too bad," she said. "We've got several here who won't amount to anything better."

I searched her expression to see if I misunderstood, but there was no mistake; the insult was deliberate. She returned my look with open hostility, a harsh pout woven into the wrinkles around her mouth. She was an unhappy woman with an axe to grind on any private eye unfortunate enough to stumble into her lair.

"That's funny," I said. "In my day we had a saying, 'Those who can, do; those who can't, teach. And those who can't teach, administrate.' Do kids still say that, I wonder?"

"Mr. Tobin, I have more important things to do than waste words with you. Just tell me what Roland wants and then please leave."

"Personally, I don't know. But let me think about it. I may come up with something."

"What? More papers? A bout of flu so he can't leave the Caribbean? You tell the bastard flat out, he's not getting the house or anything in it. He should have thought of that before he--"

I cut her off.

"If I meet him, I'll tell him. But I'm not here for Roland."

Mrs. Wiggins stopped and bit her lower lip.

"You're not here about the divorce?"

I shook my head.

"My husband didn't send you?"

"No."

"Then what are you here for?"

"A student of yours. Ex-student actually."

"Oh, I'm sorry! I assumed since you're a private detective... Apparently I was wrong."

"Actually, I don't like doing divorce work. Most of us don't."

But it beats having no work at all.

"It's just... Well, it's a hellish time for me. You can imagine."

"I understand completely."

Mrs. Wiggins took a Kleenex from a decorator box on the desk, blew her nose into it loudly and inspected the results. It was the habit of someone who spent too much time alone in an office. A habit I knew well.

"So then why are you here?" she asked.

"I have some questions about a girl who graduated last year. Rudi Alsmith."

Mrs. Wiggins looked away from me to a small bonsai plant on her desk. She absently ran her finger along one of its branches, brushing off the dry, dying needles.

"Rudi is dead," she said without the slightest twinge of sentiment. "Were you aware of that?"

"Yes I know. I'm trying to find out more about how and why she died. Can you tell me anything about her friends here and what they were like? Did she hang around with the wrong sort of people?"

"Mr. Tobin, Rudi Alsmith was the wrong sort of people."

"How do you mean?"

"While she was here, we had a number of very serious, nasty incidents. I believe Rudi was at the center of many of them. As the instigator if not the actual perpetrator."

"What kind of incidents?"

"During her junior year, someone started a fire in the locker of a girl who called Rudi a name just two days earlier. Of course, we couldn't prove Rudi was involved. She was in class at the time on her best behavior. She was smiling and attentive, which was highly suspicious in itself. Her teacher said Rudi actually seemed smug.

"Rudi also had a brief affair with a young football coach here. Not because she liked him, but because she didn't. She told him so afterwards. Obviously, he was incredibly foolish, but Rudi ruined his career and his marriage, just because she could."

"What about drugs?"

Mrs. Wiggins stiffened.

"We have never had a serious problem with drugs at our school. But they haven't been entirely eliminated either. Rudi and one of her boyfriends may have done some selling on a very small scale. We searched their lockers once on a tip but found nothing."

"Did you ever catch her at anything?"

"Not Rudi. She was too smart for that. Apart from the affair with the coach, she never got into any real trouble. We caught her friends often enough, though. Usually they were involved in some prank that was a lot more clever than they were. They claimed to be acting on their own, but you can bet Rudi was behind it. She was their undisputed leader. She could get them to do anything. One boy is dead simply because he knew Rudi Alsmith. I'm sorry, but I can't work up a lot of sympathy over her."

"What boy was that?" I asked.

"Jim Boughton. No winner exactly, but he did have possibilities. Or would have if he'd applied himself. But he and Rudi started dating their junior year, I think. After that he began to fall apart. His grades slipped from good to hopeless. His attendance became erratic. No doubt, drug use was part of his problem, but chiefly it was Rudi's influence on him."

I took out the photograph Mrs. Sachett had given me. Mrs. Sachett had said the boy in the picture was Rudi's boyfriend Jim. I showed it to Mrs. Wiggins and pointed to the boy.

"Yes, that's Jim Boughton," the principal said.

"How'd he die?"

"Last winter, the first period swimming class found him floating face down in the swimming pool. But he didn't drown.

The night before, when no one was here, he jumped off the diving board with a pistol in his mouth and pulled the trigger as he came down. I had to pay someone to scrub the bottom of the board. The whole pool had a pink tinge to it when they found him. I never knew there was so much blood in one person."

Mrs. Wiggins' face tightened as she remembered and she went silent.

My own thoughts were more selfish. For me, Jim Boughton was a promising lead now come to a dead end.

"Did he leave a note explaining what he did?" I asked finally.

"He did, as a matter of fact. He left a note in his locker that said, 'Rudi, why not?'"

"That's it?"

"That was all."

"Did Rudi know about the note?"

"No. The police thought he was trying to put some kind of guilt trip on her. They talked to her of course, but they never told her about the note."

"The police must have found something. Why did he kill himself?"

Mrs. Wiggins pushed her chair back and retrieved a paperback book from one of the shelves. She opened it to the very beginning and handed me the book.

"It's on the first page so it's easy to find."

The book was The Haunting of Hill House by Shirley Jackson. The first page began...

"No live organism can continue for long to exist sanely under conditions of absolute reality; even larks and katydids are supposed, by some, to dream. Hill House, not sane, stood by itself against its hills, holding darkness within..."

I knew the novel from my own high school days, a creepy ghost story about a woman's descent into madness. It was a disturbing book but not a dangerous one. I could see no connection between it and Jim Boughton's suicide. My confusion must have been obvious.

"They were all a part of a group or clique," the principal explained, "Jim and Rudi and some others. 'The Hill House Preservation Society' they called it. The members took an oath to live 'only under conditions of absolute reality.'"

I still did not see the connection.

"So why did Boughton kill himself?"

"I guess he found reality harder to take than he thought."

"But what does that mean, 'conditions of absolute reality?' What were they looking for?"

"They believed in a sort of blanket disbelief, if that makes any sense. They renounced all preconceptions, all hopes and illusions. They wanted to look at life squarely and coldly, attributing no false significance to anything they saw."

It was a curious creed for high school kids, a kind of nihilistic anti-glee club. Or maybe I was already forgetting what those so-called golden years were really like.

"Were there many people in this clique?"

"No, only five or six. The Preservationists broke up after Jim's death. They received counseling and that was pretty much the end of it."

"Who else was part of that group?" I opened my notebook to a fresh page.

"I'm afraid I can't tell you that. Only the dead have no privacy."

I pointed to the second girl in Mrs. Sachett's photograph.

"What about her? Was she in the group?"

"Sheila was a friend of Rudi's. I can say no more than that."

"I take it then that the other Preservationists are still alive. Except for Rudi..."

Mrs. Wiggin's mouth took a wry turn and her wrinkles briefly disappeared.

"It wasn't a suicide pact, Mr. Tobin, it was a group of kids fixated on an idea. A stupid idea at that. I've got kids here today with much more dangerous fixations. I've no doubt some of them will be institutionalized within three years, correctional and otherwise. Some won't make it through high school at all.

"The point is, ideas matter. They matter more to adolescents because they often have less common sense to temper their idealism. They get caught up in an idea's importance because they feel unimportant themselves. The ideas themselves may change, but the strength of their hold stays constant. At one time it was Objectivism, before that Existentialism. Now we have radical environmentalists, Satanists, even young Republicans. Jim Boughton was crushed by a reality that was too big for him."

"You said Jim's suicide was Rudi's fault. How was she to blame for what he did?"

"Rudi started the Hill House Preservation group. She was its leader and idealogue. She was a very charismatic girl, an expert at manipulating the people around her. The others would do almost anything for her."

"But to get someone to commit suicide..."

Mrs. Wiggins pressed her lips together in a thin bloodless line. Her hands gave a brief upward flutter before coming back down to rest on her desk. Her non-committal gesture was less an "I don't know" than an "I wouldn't rule it out."

"Were you aware of any older lovers Rudi might have had? Older than the football coach even?"

Mrs. Wiggins shook her head. "No, but it wouldn't surprise me if she did."

"Is there anything else you can tell me about Rudi or her friends?"

"I have probably been too frank with you already."

"Well, thank you for your frankness. I appreciate it."

I stood up and made my way to the door. I stopped there and

turned around. "Do you mind if I have a look at your school library?"

"No, go ahead. It's upstairs. Just take the stairway outside the attendance office."

"Thanks again. And if you need an investigator as part of your divorce, give me a call."

She nodded politely but didn't touch my card on the desk.

I left and went up the main stairway to the second floor. The library area was even bigger than the cafeteria downstairs, taking up the whole central hub of the main building. It was furnished with study carrels, tables, and low book-shelves, but even these seemed sparse. The classrooms on this level were presumably behind closed sets of double doors in three of the library's high walls.

A few students were grouped around some of the library tables with open books in front of them. One or two kids were even seated in the carrels. Most of the study hall students, however, lounged in noisy clusters on and around couches scattered through the library. In spite of the noise, some of them were sleeping.

Behind a desk at the far end of the room, the librarian, a tall black man with a huge mustache, stopped what he was doing and watched me, almost suspiciously, as I approached.

"Yes, sir. What can I do for you?" he said.

"Hi. Do you keep copies of the high school yearbook?"

"Yes, of course."

"Fine. Then I'd like to see the ones from last year and the year before. Mrs. Wiggins said it was okay."

The librarian went back into a small office and came back with the two books. I thanked him and took them with me to an empty carrel.

My main purpose was to find out the last name of Rudi's friend Sheila. But I also hoped there might be a picture that identified other members of the Hill House Preservation Society. I started with The Horizon, the yearbook from Rudi and Jim's junior year. It was slow going, about as exciting as the slide show of a great-aunt's vacation to Arkansas. High school yearbooks are generally insipid and this was no exception. As I pored over its pages, my mind wandered and my eyes glazed.

Rudi and Jim were not very active in the school. The only picture of Jim, apart from his class picture, was as a member of the swimming team. Rudi was pictured as a National Merit Scholar and listed as a member of the school literary club. I didn't find any of their classmates named Sheila.

The next year's yearbook was Vistas on the Future. The only picture of Rudi was her senior class photo, the same one the newspaper had run. She was still listed as being in the literary club, and there was a brief mention of her studying with Preston Curtiz, but there was no picture of her at any of the club events.

Jim apparently dropped out of the swimming team that year. He only appeared once in the book, on a special In Memoriam page. His face had gone through an unmistakable change since Mrs. Sachett's photograph. In the earlier picture, his full, smiling face had been cheerful, vigorous and full of personality. By his senior year, he had put on weight; his face became fleshy and sullen with dark bags under his eyes that even the photo-refinisher's art couldn't hide. What people call the "sparkle" had disappeared from his eyes; they were as dead and unfocused as the frozen inventory at an eye bank. Something had died in Jim Boughton long before he pulled the trigger on his final dive.

Once again none of the students in Rudi and Jim's class were named Sheila. I turned to the index at the back of the yearbook and painstakingly went over the seeming thousands of names listed there. Still no Sheila.

I closed Vistas and returned to The Horizon. I had to go through the index twice, but finally found a listing for "Lee,

Sheila p. 215." Sheila Lee was a year ahead of Rudi and Jim and had graduated their junior year. The single citation for Sheila turned out to be for her senior portrait. She belonged to no clubs or teams and her favorite phrase was "What was the question again?" She had a pudgy face, pleasant enough but with a nervous, uncertain smile. Her bowl-cut hair was parted in the middle and her long bangs appeared to be on the verge of falling forward over her face. I got the impression, if they ever did she would disappear altogether. She had the look of a hanger-on, a person no one paid attention to.

I closed the yearbooks and returned them to the librarian. There had been no mention of the Hill House Preservation Society in either of them, no hint of the strange undercurrent that had passed through the school. The yearbooks maintained the image of happy, untroubled students in the prime of their lives, and nothing in their pages was permitted to break that cheerful illusion. Whatever didn't fit the mold of this ideal was left out, blinked at, and denied. Even the students themselves would gradually forget the reality and come to believe the big lie, captured for all time like a fly in rose-tinted amber.

On my way out of the library I ducked into the fiction stacks and carefully looked through the J-section shelves. There were no Shirley Jackson books at all. And people complain our educational system isn't responsive.

CHAPTER THIRTEEN

With Jim Boughton out of the picture, Rudi's friend Sheila Lee became my only lead. She was the one person I knew who might tell me what Rudi had been involved with. Or with whom.

I returned to my office and began my search in the Greater Eola white-pages. There were no Sheila Lees listed but I did find fifteen entries for "Lee, S." Since none of the addresses were near the Alsmiths in Hanover, I resorted to Sherlock Holmes' old standby, the science of deduction. One after another, I called each S. Lee and if the number didn't belong to a Sheila, I deducted it from my list. Sometimes I wonder if the goal of human progress through the ages has not been simply to reduce legwork for the weary private eye. Today's gumshoe is more likely to have a calloused index finger than fallen arches. Within twenty minutes, I had narrowed the field to five, two in Eola and three in various suburbs. Letting your fingers do the walking will only carry you so far.

It was one o'clock when I hit the streets looking for the two city residents. The first S. Lee turned out to be a souvenir shop owner in Eola's Chinatown; the second was an old coot named Serge who lived in a retirement home east of the river. Neither had ever heard of Sheila or recognized her from her picture.

I drove north out of Eola to Potters Mill to check out the next person on my list.

This address was in a lower-middle class neighborhood within easy crashing distance of the airport. Waist-high bushes surrounded the yard with only a narrow gap for the cracked cement walkway. The small white house had a full-width front porch and forest green shutters. The name "Kellogg" was emblazoned in gold decals on a post beside the porch steps.

A grey wooden staircase crept up the left side of the house to a second floor apartment. The weathered stairs looked like they had been stained with surplus battleship paint shortly after World War II. A plain metal mailbox, its red flag standing jauntily erect, was fastened to the handrail at the bottom of the stairs. Someone had painted "LEE" on the box in an unsteady hand. I took a quick peek at the outgoing mail but there was only a phone bill in a pre-printed envelope and a subscription renewal for a religious magazine. The name for the return addresses had just the initial "S." but for whatever it was worth, the handwriting looked like a woman's.

You develop a sixth sense in this business, or the great ones do anyway. The rest of us act on our hunches as if we could trust them and muddle through as best we can. But as I walked up the creaky stairs to the apartment, I had the strong feeling that I had found Sheila Lee. Maybe it was nothing more than an impression that the mousy, somewhat addled girl from the photo seemed to fit these surroundings.

I knocked loudly at the apartment door several times but there was no response. No one was home.

When I turned to leave, I found a twiggy old woman in a blue-flowered dress standing at the bottom of the stairs. She looked about eighty and held a bright yellow aluminum baseball bat in her hands.

"What's all that racket?" she wanted to know, pointing the bat up at me. Her frail appearance was deceiving. She had a strong voice and handled the bat with a sure touch. I suspected she put in time every week at the local batting cage.

"I'm here to see Sheila," I said, coming down the stairs.

That changed everything. Mrs. Kellogg, the landlady, practically beamed and invited me onto the porch for a cup of tea. We sat down in white wicker chairs and I sipped tea while she told me--and everyone else within a hundred yards--about Sheila. Mrs. Kellogg's voice was loud enough to carry above the roar of landing jets, even when there were none.

According to Mrs. Kellogg, Sheila Lee was a quiet, reliable tenant. She worked at the office of an Eola lawyer--Mrs. Kellogg couldn't remember which one--and always paid her rent on time. She never caused any problems except for maybe some Saturday nights when she played her piano too late. But even then, she played so well that Mrs. Kellogg seldom complained.

Mrs. Kellogg was clearly fond of her young tenant but she thought Sheila was too serious for a woman her age and needed more fun in her life. Her description made Sheila Lee sound like a lonely girl, even a little sad, with no family in the area and very few visitors. But "the biggest shame," as Mrs. Kellogg put it, was that Sheila had no boyfriend. Yet when her landlady tried to introduce her to "some nice young men," Sheila did not seem interested or appreciative. Maybe she was just too busy. Between her work schedule, her commitments at church, and her classes two nights a week at the community college, Sheila had very little time for herself.

All this without my prompting.

"But I think she has tonight free..." Mrs. Kellogg added, with a definite sparkle in her eye. She raised the teapot to refill my cup. I declined.

"And where do you know my Miss Sheila from?" Mrs. Kellogg asked.

I told her I was a friend of a friend and stood up to leave. I was certainly grateful for what she had told me, but the fact is,

Mrs. Kellogg made me uncomfortable. It was almost unseemly how eager she was to volunteer personal information about her tenant to a complete stranger. Working for a lawyer as she did, Ms. Lee needed to give her landlady a good talking to about the constitutional principle of privacy. I would have done it myself, but after leafing through Sheila's private mail, I probably couldn't generate a lot of conviction.

I thanked Mrs. Kellogg for the tea and reassured her that I would return later after Sheila got back from work. From what she told me, that would be sometime between 5:30 and 6:00.

I left Mrs. Kellogg and went back to my car. My back was beginning to throb again so I drove back to my office to take it easy for a couple hours.

* * *

Two important phone messages were waiting for me on the machine when I got back. The first wanted to know if I had ever given serious thought toward purchasing lakeside vacation property. The second informed me that now was the time to buy burial plots and bulk rates were available. The solicitor's voice for both messages sounded so similar that I wondered if I could combine the two offers and get a beachfront mausoleum.

While mulling my real estate options, I downed a handful of aspirin with cold coffee and called the county police headquarters in Hanover.

A woman answered the phone.

"Burton County Police Department. If this is an emergency, you dialed the wrong number. Please hold." Then, limbo.

I stood at my window and looked out into the partly cloudy afternoon sky. I cradled the receiver with my shoulder and raised the sash to let in the cool city air. The traffic noise was comforting in its randomness. I went back to my chair and sat down with a pillow propped behind me.

Eventually, the woman's voice returned.

"Burton County PD. This number is for non-emergencies only. How may I help you?"

"Yes, I'd like to speak with the detective in charge of the Rudi Alsmith case. It's an emergency."

"I'm sorry, sir, but this is not the number for..." She stopped. "I see, sir. Then you want CAPERS section. The number there is ..." and she gave the number. "However, I'll connect you now."

She consigned me to telephone purgatory once more and then a new phone began to ring. A man finally picked it up.

"Hello?" he said, sounding annoyed.

"CAPERS?" I asked.

"Crimes Against Persons section, that's right. What can I do for you?"

"I need to speak with whoever's investigating Rudi Alsmith's death."

"Clark in Homicide, then. Hold on." I heard the man's muffled voice calling for someone as he held his hand loosely over the mouthpiece. At least he didn't put me on hold.

"Dave Clark speaking." A smooth, rich baritone voice resonated over the line. Clark sounded more like a radio announcer than a cop. I felt like the tenth caller waiting to find out what I'd won.

"Detective Clark, you're looking into the Rudi Alsmith case?"

"That's right."

"And treating it as a homicide?"

There was a brief pause.

"Who is calling, please?"

"My name is Nash Tobin. I'm a licensed private investigator in Eola. I've been following the case and would like to discuss some of the details with you."

"Hold a minute," he said, and went away, apparently to

check something. Finally he came back. "Yes, Mr. Tobin, given the circumstances, we are investigating that death as a homicide. And what is your interest in the case?"

A slow shiver of excitement ran through me. Don't believe what you read in books--it is actually very rare that a private investigator gets to work on a murder case, once a decade perhaps, if then. I had been on my own for two years now, and this was my first one. Though scarce as hen's teeth, such cases have the potential of making a private detective's career. The Chandlers and Hammetts of the world have created an unreasonable public expectation that private eyes solve murders. Never mind that the police are infinitely better equipped and manned for such investigations. But for any PI lucky enough to meet that expectation, the payoff in media attention and word of mouth advertising is like hitting the state lottery.

Since my interest in the case was mostly mercenary, I ignored Clark's question and asked one of my own.

"Given what circumstances?"

"Well, if you've followed the case, you're aware of the background: drug use, assault,..."

I interrupted him, "Assault--sexual assault?"

"There was recent sexual activity but that may have been consensual. The victim was no babe in the woods, believe me. No, I mean she was beat up. If you'd seen the deceased on the table, you'd know what I'm talking about. We're keeping the specifics confidential for now, along with other pertinent details."

"Was she killed at the gravel yard or someplace else?

"Why?"

"I found an item she dropped in the parking lot there. It made me think that someone drove her to the yard and left her there. What I don't know is, was she already dead when they brought her, or was she only killed afterwards?"

"What did you find?"

"A crystal charm for a necklace. A unicorn. She got it from a boyfriend a couple months ago. It broke and fell off in the parking lot."

"I don't suppose you left it there?"

"No," I admitted. "Otherwise I wouldn't have found out it was hers. I did get a name for the boyfriend though, and a rough description..."

"Okay, who was he?"

"His name is Win or Winter. He's a lot older than she is... was. He has all white hair."

"Yeah, we're looking for that guy. Do you have anything useful like a last name or an address?"

I considered mentioning the possibility that he could be Winston Graham but quickly thought better of it. Graham was not someone you raised unfounded allegations about to the police.

Instead, I just said, "No."

"Any chance we can get prints off that charm of yours?"

"Probably not." Too many people had handled it since I found it.

"Tainted, huh? I thought so. Well, it's a shame we didn't find it ourselves but it probably doesn't matter. All it shows is that someone took her there by car or truck which we pretty much knew. In answer to your question, the victim was dead when she got there. We don't know where they brought her from."

"They? There was more than one person?"

"Person or persons unknown, then, if you're going to be a lawyer about it. There's not a lot to go on. The M.E. puts time of death as anytime between Saturday evening and Sunday morning. We've got Bugman Fitch from the university trying to pinpoint that a little better."

"Fitch is working this?" I asked.

"He and his little friends."

Anyone who followed crime in Eola knew of Albin Fitch, the celebrated entomology professor at Eola university. He was often consulted locally and even nationally for police investigations where insects became part of the evidence. Some of his successes were spectacular enough to be mentioned in national news magazines. That the Burton County police had called him in about Rudi's death showed they were taking it very seriously.

I waited for Clark to say something more about the case but finally had to break the silence myself:

"So, is there anything else I can do?"

"Well, what else do you have for me?" Clark asked.

"Right now--nothing."

"Nothing is not much. Listen, I'm not a hard-case. If you insist on working this, I won't stop you. I'll even welcome any help you give me. I don't give a damn who nails this case so long as it gets nailed--my stats look the same no matter who clears it. But just so you know, stay out of my way. I don't want you interfering or screwing anything up. This is a police investigation and even with a PI badge you're still just a civilian. And I expect you to let me know everything you find out that might have a bearing on my case. Is that clear?"

"Sure," I said, stifling a "sir." "But I'd be in a better position to help if you let me in on more of the details."

"That's true, you would." There was a loud click on the line as Clark hung up the phone.

I put my own receiver down in its cradle and struck up a cigarette.

I was not surprised by Clark's attitude. It was about what I expected, maybe even a little better. But I was struck that he never once mentioned Rudi by name. To him, she was always "the victim" or "the deceased." She was just an object, the latest carcass on the coroner's cold steel table. In a job where violence was routine and where seeing young lives snuffed out senselessly was just something you did before lunch, Clark's detachment was probably wise. God knows, it would be hard to empathize with someone you've seen opened up like a garment bag and gutted like a perch.

But Clark's detachment came at a price; in focusing on the "deceased," he missed what was truly important--Rudi's life. Whether you believed Mrs. Sachett's glowing description of Rudi, or her principal's damning one, didn't matter. Rudi Alsmith was like the rest of us, part of a vast network of attachments and interactions that make up everyday life. She was forcibly ripped from that web. That loss was so great that nothing could be done to make up for it, and yet the need for redress felt like a crushing weight on my shoulders.

Maybe Clark was right; it's better not to dwell on such things.

I took the bottle of mezcal from my drawer and took a celebratory swig to my first murder case. I swallowed. It was thrilling and yet daunting at the same time. I owed it to myself and to Rudi not to blow it.

And to Curtiz, my client? He never mentioned anything about wanting me to find a killer. Rudi had still been alive when Curtiz called me in. The person Curtiz wanted me to find may or may not have had something to do with her death. There was no way to tell, not without Curtiz coming forward with more specifics on who that person was. So, until I heard differently, I was committed.

I took another slug from the mezcal bottle.

So many questions remained. If Rudi was killed away from the gravel yard, where did it happen? Why had she been beaten? Who had her sexual partner been? Was there any forensic evidence pointing to the killer? Clark had been silent on all these points, and I doubted the county medical examiner would be any more forthcoming. I needed to find out about the autopsy some other way.

I lifted the bottle towards my lips again but stopped. If I was going to have more, I should at least pour it into a glass. Appearances are important, even when no one is there to see.

I set the bottle back down on my desk. The agave worm slowly sank to the bottom.

What about Bugman Fitch? Insect consultants like Albin Fitch sometimes attended autopsies so they could collect their specimens right from the source. If Fitch had taken part in Rudi's post mortem, he might be more approachable than Clark or the medical examiner. In spite of all his work with the police, Fitch was still an academic, a civilian like me. He might be persuaded to give me some of the details that Clark was sitting on. At any rate, Fitch was worth a try.

I called the University of Eola's Biology Office and a gum-cracking co-ed made an appointment for me to see Professor Fitch the next afternoon at 1:00. She took my number in case she needed to cancel or make changes but she didn't anticipate any problems. She neglected to ask what I wanted to discuss with Professor Fitch and I didn't volunteer anything.

I put the bottle away, closed my window, and went outside under the greying sky. I crossed the street for an early supper at Woolworth's and tried to banter with the counter waitress, but her heart wasn't in it. When I asked what she could recommend, she suggested "Coffee." I settled for a deluxe chili dog.

The only other customers at the counter were a father with two young kids and an infant seated on his lap. The older children fussed loudly about wanting dessert and spun around on the counter stools trying to make their father pay attention to them. I sat on a stool at the other end of the counter.

While I ate, I watched the early news on a television set

mounted on the wall. The lead story centered on the latest poll numbers for Eola's embattled mayor. While his support had never been great, his numbers had been sliding lately for a variety of reasons, including his penchant for sticking his foot in his mouth.

His latest gaffe occurred two days before when he addressed a group of city teachers who were threatening to strike. I only caught snippets of the mayor's speech because of the squalls from the children, but I thought he said to the teachers, "If I had the money, I'd give it to you, honest injun..." The TV reporter noted blandly that today's newspaper editorials were all howling for the mayor's scalp over his insensitive ethnic slur. The mayoral election was only a few weeks away.

That hard-hitting news item was balanced by a fluff piece about a canine stowaway on an airliner. After a whirlwind tour of the country, the lost dog was finally reunited with his eight-year-old owner. As the camera fawned over the dog licking the boy's face, the local anchor-pair provided an unctuous accompaniment of "Ooohs" and "Ahhhhs."

I left the counter briefly and retrieved the evening paper. It wasn't much better than the television, but at least it didn't make noise. One piece quickly caught my eye. It referred to Weibrecht Gravel Yard, "recent scene of teenager's bizarre death," and how it was being used as a front company for Winston Graham's syndicate. The writer, a woman whose name I didn't recognize, spent most of the story rehashing the publicly known details about Rudi Alsmith's death and interspersing them with speculation about connections to Winston Graham. She claimed to have an unnamed official source who told her that Graham used the gravel yard to launder funds.

I left Woolworth's at 5:30 and drove back to Potters Mill to interview Sheila Lee.

CHAPTER FOURTEEN

Rush hour traffic was slow heading out of the city, and I didn't arrive back at Mrs. Kellogg's until after 6:30. I parked on the street behind a drab orange Japanese compact that had not been there that afternoon.

I guessed that the car was Sheila Lee's. Its body was shot through with rust and it was burning oil--a large soot stain radiated out from its tailpipe. The vehicle's whole rear end was covered with excited Christian-themed bumper stickers: "I found it!"; "Christians aren't perfect, just forgiven"; "† The Hours Are Long, But The Benefits Are Out of This World!" and so on. One of the slogans threw me: "If you don't know Jesus, you're in for a Rood awakening..." While the bumper stickers may not have added much to the car's appearance, at least they papered over some significant rust holes and welts.

The car's back seat was cluttered with items you normally find in a trunk: a toolbox, a bottle of wiper fluid, quart cans of oil, an oil spout in a plastic sheath, even the spare tire. A dirty towel, garbage bags, church service bulletins, and a sun-bleached paperback Bible were also strewn on the floor. A dried-out palm leaf had been twisted roughly into the shape of a cross and hung from the rear-view mirror, but actually it looked more like an Egyptian ankh.

I crossed the lawn to the steps at the side of Mrs. Kellogg's house. The sun was setting in a glorious blaze of red, orange, and pink, casting long dark shadows over the grass. There were lights on in the second story apartment and I heard rock music pounding faintly through the wall as I climbed the stairs.

I knocked loudly on the door and the music stopped.

A chain was pulled out inside and the apartment door opened.

"Yes?" Sheila Lee said, breathless from an interrupted workout. She had on a pair of dark blue sweatpants and a sleeveless white shirt. The wide open arm holes showed the edges of a grey jogging bra.

I took in her appearance quickly before answering. She was taller than I expected and more muscular. Her oval face had none of the pudginess that had marked it in the photograph. Instead it was well-formed and appealing. Her black hair was cut very short and sculpted to follow the contours of her skull. This could have given her a severe look, but it was tempered by her high round cheeks and slightly upturned nose. Her bright green eyes were fascinating. This new Sheila Lee may not have been fashion-model material, but she was certainly attractive. Given the right time and opportunity, hers would be face to linger over. Unfortunately, this was not it.

She watched me warily through the door crack, her hand held ready at the knob. Her damp shirt clung to her chest, which rose and fell quickly with her breathing. There was a sheen of sweat on her face and arms.

"Hi, Miss Lee? My name is Nash Tobin. I'm a private investigator. I have some questions to ask if you have a few minutes."

The door opened wider and I handed her my card. As she read it, I couldn't get over how much she had changed in the two years since her high school portrait. She looked so much stronger now--not just in her figure, but in her attitude as well. Her eyes had lost the swimming, squid-like quality that had been obvious in her pictures. Her gaze was hard and fiercely protective. Of all the changes I saw, this inner toughness was the most remarkable. The effort required to achieve it would have sent the most dedicated Olympic hopeful scurrying to the showers.

"What kind of questions?" She made no move to let me in.

"About a friend of yours, Rudi Alsmith."

Sheila's rose-petal lips clenched, and reluctance spread over her whole face.

"Well, I'm really busy right now and..."

"Please. It won't take long. And it is very important. I wouldn't disturb you otherwise."

She thought hard for a reason to refuse but couldn't find one. Apparently personal inconvenience wasn't enough.

"All right, I guess so," she said finally, pulling the door all the way open.

I went past her and came into a large open living area. It served as her combined living room, dining room, and kitchen.

Sheila closed the door and moved to the center of the room, leaving a wide margin between us as she passed. Her movements seemed clumsy and self-conscious. Even though she stood several feet away, her glistening body felt closer.

She glanced down and noticed how her shirt was clinging tightly to her bust. She quickly pulled the damp material away.

"Please excuse me," she said, "I just need to ... I mean, I'll be back in a minute." She made a vague gesture towards the back of the apartment and retreated into another room. She closed the door after her.

While she was gone, I glanced around her apartment. The main room ran the whole length of Mrs. Kellogg's house. At the far end, the kitchen area was equipped with a mismatched stove and refrigerator. There was a white enamel sink that had probably once been a bathroom fixture. The counters on each side of it looked homemade. There were no cupboards or cabinets, just a set of red metal utility shelves where dishes, glasses, pots, and utensils all fought for space with cereal boxes, soup cans, and other non-perishables.

Sheila Lee's dining area consisted of a simple gray card table with one matching folding chair stuck beneath it. An empty candlestick and a dry vase with wilted flowers stood at the center of the table. There was not a crumb on either the table or the small round carpet beneath it.

The living room was also sparsely furnished. A couch with threadbare blue upholstery and three folding chairs were set up against the apartment's inner wall. A low pine crate set in front of the couch served as the coffee table, and judging from the crumbs and crumpled napkins on its top, was also used as a dining table.

Across from the couch, a small television with a rabbit ears antenna stood on top of a small stand. A Singapore brand boom-box with the red power light on, sat on the floor under the T.V. stand.

Every item in Sheila Lee's apartment screamed out "cheap" and "bottom of the line." Except for one thing.

Against an inside wall, Sheila Lee had a beautiful upright piano, a Steinway, with gleaming brass pedals and a black case polished like ebony. She may have compromised on everything else in her life, but her instrument was a treasure. I had no idea how she even got it into the apartment. I glanced at the sheet music on the piano's music stand; it was an impossible-looking piece by J. S. Bach.

While I was examining her piano, Sheila Lee came back into the room wearing a bulky blue sweatshirt.

"This is a beautiful instrument," I told her.

She smiled. "Thank you. Do you play?" There was a faint glimmer of interest in her voice.

If I lied and said yes, we would have something in common and she would be more comfortable in talking to me. On the other hand, if she found out I was lying, she wouldn't tell me anything. I decided quickly I could never pull it off.

"No, I'm afraid not."

"Oh, well... Sorry, I didn't mean to leave you standing here. Please have a seat," she said gesturing to the couch. As I sat down, she took one of the drab folding chairs for herself and set it opposite me.

No sooner had she settled into her chair, than she immediately jumped up again:

"Where are my manners? I haven't offered you anything to drink. Would you like diet cola? Or I can make tea or coffee. It won't take a second."

"No thank you, I'm fine."

"Are you sure?"

"Absolutely. I had dinner just before I came."

Sheila sank back reluctantly into her chair. But she looked ready to leap up again as soon as she could come up with another pretext.

I preempted her by getting to the point.

"I don't know if you're aware of this, but Rudi Alsmith is dead."

Sheila nodded.

"I know. I read about it in the paper." She rested her hands on her legs just above her knees and squeezed them absently. Her feet, clad in flimsy tennis shoes, rocked back and forth on the floor.

“You and she were friends, is that right?"

"I guess."

"When was the last time you talked with her?"

"I'm not really sure. A long time ago. Over a year probably."

"Oh, I thought you were close."

"Not really. She was more Jim Boughton's friend than mine. Jim and I were close, of course. But Rudi and I..." She shrugged her shoulders, leaving the sentence unfinished.

Sheila's words came slowly, as if each were a weight she raised only with difficulty. My first reaction was that she was lying; she was certainly being evasive.

I shifted on the couch to take my wallet from my pocket. I removed the picture of Rudi, Jim, and Sheila that Mrs. Sachett had given me and pushed it across the crate.

"This is the three of you together in school, yes? You all look pretty close to me..."

Sheila leaned forward in her chair to look at the photograph but she did not pick it up. She sat back again quickly.

"We may have been close... for a while. But, you know, people change. Interests change. Sometimes the person you thought was your best friend in the world can turn into a stranger."

"Is that what happened with Rudi?"

"No," Sheila said, shaking her head emphatically. "That's just an example... That's how people are. It wasn't about Rudi in particular."

"But I'm asking about Rudi in particular. What was it like when you were friends? What did you do together, what did you talk about, what activities were you part of? ... That's not too hard, is it?"

For a split second, Sheila raised her head and looked into my eyes. The strength melted from her gaze. She suddenly looked like a terrified doe caught in on-rushing headlights. She took her hands off her legs and grasped the side of her chair. She quickly looked down again but said nothing.

I had touched a nerve. Her reluctance to discuss what she and Rudi did in high school made me more determined to find out what it was.

I leaned forward.

"Miss Lee, tell me about the Hill House Preservation Society..."

There was a long pause. Sheila kept her eyes directed at the floor.

"Look," she said quietly, "None of that matters anymore. It's all over and gone. I have not seen Rudi in over a year. I really don't know anything that can help you."

"Unfortunately, you are all I have to go on. If I could talk to someone else I would. But Jim and Rudi are both dead..."

"I know. But back when I was part of-- of all that, I was a completely different person. Someone I didn't even like. That person is gone now. I am all new inside, a brand new creation."

It was not clear which of us she was trying to convince.

"I know you are," I said. "I can tell. The change in your life is obvious. But you're wrong if you don't think it matters. You may have been able to save yourself..." Sheila started to protest at this, but I made a quick correction. "You allowed yourself to be saved, then. But your friend Rudi was not so lucky. She will never find what you have found. Her shot at salvation is gone forever. Someone took that away from her."

I stopped to let Sheila think on that.

For a long time she said nothing. Her response finally came in a whisper:

"Then it is too late. Nothing I can do will help her. Dredging all that up won't do any good."

"No, but you can help me. And you're the only one who can. We need to find out who did this to her. I can't do that if you won't tell me what she was involved with. It may be painful--I can see that it is--and I'm sorry. But the person who killed Rudi is still out there. If we don't stop him, he may do the same thing to somebody else. Are you really willing to let that happen?"

Sheila craned her head to look away from me towards the

kitchen, at her wall poster for the group “Found,” towards the windows, even at her piano; everywhere in short that I was not. But my question filled her apartment, echoing mutely until she could no longer ignore it.

"The hard thing to understand about Rudi," she said finally, "Is that she was so ... 'blessed' is the only word. Smart, beautiful, confident; she was a leader people liked to be with, liked doing things for. She had so many gifts—as if God had singled her out for greatness. I don't know, maybe it was too much for one person."

"You almost make her sound like a saint."

"No. Nothing like that. She was selfish, too. If someone crossed her, she got even. And she could be extremely cruel, especially when she was high. But none of that explains how things turned out."

"Then what does?" I asked.

Sheila looked at me, frowning. The answer should have been obvious.

"Sin, of course."

"Sin? What sin? What did Rudi do?"

"The specifics aren't important. All sin is the same, whatever form it takes. It is the distance we put between ourselves and God. We sin when we pull away from Him. No matter how far we go, He always remains faithful, reaching out, ready to bring us back, ready to forgive. If only we will listen..."

Sheila shook her head slowly, and went on:

"But we almost never do. Sin grows on itself; our hearts become hard with deceit and betrayal. It is like when you run down a steep hill; you may start slow but you end up going faster and faster. God calls to you from the hilltop, but by the time you hear, you're running so fast you're afraid to stop. You think maybe it's already too late and tell yourself you don't care. You block out His calls and give in to the speed and momentum, knowing you will never climb that hill again."

She took a long breath: "If you're lucky, you trip and fall. Then, Jesus Christ will carry you, broken and bruised, back up the hill. But if not, you keep running away and never get back."

By the end of her recitation, Sheila's gaze was fixed on empty space. Her words were directed as much to herself as to me. A private litany of repentance that was only spoken aloud because I was in the room.

"The things we did, Rudi and I..." Sheila closed her eyes and shook her head, "Were terrible things. But I was lucky. I crashed and burned and Jesus made me whole. Poor Rudi never stopped running..."

Sheila's lips scarcely moved and her words grew faint. Her cream-white face with its frame of black hair looked more like a ceramic mask than flesh and blood. Her green eyes were like glass. I wondered what she saw with them that I couldn't see.

I recrossed my legs and shifted my weight on the couch.

"I'm sorry," Sheila said, coming back to the present. She brushed her short bangs off the top of her forehead. "You asked a question earlier. What was it? Oh, yes, the Hill House Preservation Society.

"That was really Rudi's idea. She never believed in God, she was raised that way. But when we read the book about Hill House, she saw the first paragraph as a revelation. 'To live under conditions of absolute reality.' It meant looking at the world with nothing but your own judgement to guide you. It meant not having to rely on what your parents or teachers or anyone else said. It meant not having any pre-existing rules to follow. It meant absolute freedom.

"Rudi would talk on and on about it. She was so eloquent, we loved listening to her. And when she finally stopped, we all laughed because we could never remember half of what she said. Usually she couldn't either. Whatever it was, though, we were sure it was incredibly deep. Of course, we were stoned most of the time, so it probably made no sense after all."

Sheila stopped. When it seemed clear she had stalled, I threw in a question to get her started again.

"I don't understand. If the goal was absolute reality, then where did the drugs fit in? Wouldn't they distort your perceptions rather than clarify them?"

Sheila nodded hesitantly. "Yes, but it didn't seem like it then. We thought we could actually see more. The drugs took away our inhibitions and got rid of our conditioning. They left us free to be ourselves."

"Which meant?"

"Young and stupid mostly!" Sheila said. She tried to force her taut lips into a smile, as if glossing over some remote transgression from her past. But I could see that the memories were closer than that and they frightened her. They were waiting, full of menace and ready to surface.

"We're all young and stupid sometimes. I've done things I want to kick myself for afterwards. What was so terrible about you and Rudi?"

Sheila stiffened in her chair and her hands gripped the front corners of her seat.

"And remember," I added gently, "I'm not with the police. I'm strictly private and confidential. My only interest is to find out what happened to Rudi."

Sheila did not relax her posture any but her grip on the wooden chair seemed to loosen a bit.

"I... We..." Sheila sputtered through several false starts. "This is so hard for me!" she pleaded.

"I know it is. Take your time, you're doing fine."

"Well, there were the drugs," she began again, "And men. Many men."

The admission was coming, but only with difficulty. Her

breathing quickened and became more labored; I could hear it whistling through her nostrils. Her green eyes looked wild and unnaturally bright. Unfortunately this limited confession was neither new nor helpful.

"That's a good start," I said. "What else?"

Sheila was gripped by a sudden panic. She brought her hands to her eyes and rubbed at them pitilessly. Whatever she saw behind them must have been terrible.

"I don't want to talk about it! ... Not about that! That's all behind me!" Her fingers smeared tears down her cheeks and along her nose. She kept her elbows clamped down hard into her breasts. For all her talk about divine forgiveness, Sheila was having a hard time forgiving herself.

"That's okay, if you don't want to, you don't have to. We'll talk about something else. How about Rudi's boyfriends. Did you know she was seeing an older man, someone named Win?"

Sheila stopped abusing her eyes and nodded slowly.

"Was his last name Graham?"

"I don't think so," she said. "That doesn't sound right, anyway. But, honestly, I don't remember about him."

"All right, what can you tell me about Jim Boughton?"

Sheila actually smiled.

"Oh, Jim was a sweet boy. At first, when my mother brought me here in the middle of my junior year, he was the only one who would be my friend. We used to talk together for hours. He wanted to be an actor. He said when he got rich in Hollywood, he'd send for me to come live on his estate. He was so funny I just knew he'd make it someday. He worked so hard at making me laugh..." She sounded half-expectant that the message from Hollywood might still come any day.

While she spoke about him, Sheila's eyes grew warm and her mouth nearly smiled. Not all of her memories of Worthington High School were bad. It almost made me ashamed to press her on the unpleasant ones.

Though she never said it in so many words, it was clear from the way she talked about Jim Boughton that she had been in love with him. As much in love as a lonely seventeen-year-old could be. She still was, for that matter. Even though he'd been a year younger than her, she loved the attention he'd paid to her when no one else noticed. He remembered her birthday and brought her flowers. When Sheila's mother got in a fight with her own boyfriend, Sheila had gone to stay with Jim's family for a week. She spoke of that week as of a treasure that she would never lose or forget.

It was equally clear that Jim's feelings for her never went beyond friendship. His romantic interests lay in a different and all too predictable direction.

"... He always had a crush on Rudi," Sheila said. "Ever since they were in the seventh grade. She was always so beautiful. Jim told me how she sat on his lap once in the back of the bus on the way home from a field trip and he doted on her from then on. Even though she never even looked at him after that bus ride until a long time after, he watched her for years, seeing what she liked, how she dressed, what she read; learning how the people around her behaved. Jim told me all that! If he spent half the time studying his books that he spent studying Rudi, Jim would be in Harvard today."

During high school Jim began to insinuate himself slowly into Rudi's circle. Starting on the outskirts, he succeeded in worming his way into the central core by pretending to be indifferent to Rudi and her friends. He didn't press himself on them, rather he made them draw him into their group. And as Jim moved in, Sheila followed, ever hopeful. She joined in the frequent drug parties, the fast-forgotten sexual interludes, the petty intrigues and manipulations for prestige that characterized the group...

"Through it all, Jim was fixed on Rudi," Sheila said. "Even though he pretended not to be. The first time he slept with her, he cried when he told me about it. But the next day he hardly talked to her. It was like the biggest day of his life and he acted like it was nothing. I told Roger, who was Rudi's boyfriend then, and he didn't seem to care either. He made a joke out of it, called her Sharon Sharealike. After that, I didn't care either. I mean, I was in with the coolest group at school and that was something at least. I never thought I'd get to do that..."

I held my tongue. It was hard listening to Sheila describe her days with Rudi's friends and hearing how impressed she had been with them. I wanted to shake the girl she used to be and wake her to the truth--the kids she had looked up to were self-indulgent morons.

But Sheila herself knew that now. When the warning was needed two years ago, no one had bothered.

"This Roger, what was his last name?"

"Thornton. Roger Thornton."

"Do you know where he is now?"

"I've no idea."

"All right. So what happened to Jim?"

"Not long after she started the Hill House Preservation Society, Rudi dumped Roger and took up with Jim. Or she didn't exactly dump Roger, they didn't break up or anything. She just started seeing both of them for a time, and then she was only with Jim. It was very confusing because even after that, she'd sometimes pair off with Jim and sometimes with Roger at the Gatherings..."

Sheila winced and her voice cut off abruptly after she uttered the last word. Her hands again grasped the sides of her chair so hard that the bones of her knuckles gleamed palely through her skin. She inhaled sharply, but if she was trying to suck the word back in, it was too late.

"The Gatherings," I said. "What were they?"

Sheila shook her head adamantly.

"Were they the Hill House Society meetings?"

Again she shook her head. "I'm not going to talk about that!" she said in a loud, shrill tone. Her face and neck turned red as the blood pressure built up in her head. Her narrow chin jutted out with a petulance that would have seemed childish had it not been combined with such a distorted expression. She rocked slightly forward in her chair and her green eyes darted like a dog's in REM sleep.

I resolved to try once more, and to let it rest after that: "It's just that..."

It was one time too many.

Sheila stood up and cut me off. She grabbed her wrists and pulled her arms in tight against her stomach. There were already tears flowing down from her eyes but I don't think she noticed them. Her teeth were bared like an animal's. Drawing on all her reserves, she mustered an icy control in her voice that in no way could be confused for calm.

"You must leave now! I want you to go."

I stood up from the couch and tried to reason with her.

"I'm sorry," I said slowly, calmly. "We don't have to talk about..."

Whatever control Sheila had built up suddenly shattered.

"Get out!" she screamed. "Get out now! I'll call the police!..."

There was probably more along the same lines, but I left her and went outside. The door slammed behind me with enough force to shake the wooden stairway beneath my feet. Before I was halfway down the stairs, the crashing sounds of a Tchaikovsky piano concerto came pounding through the upstairs wall. While I thought I might have heard hysterical sobs in counterpoint, it was probably just my imagination.

I drove home through a spitting rain that was no more than I deserved. The slow pace on the road gave me plenty of time to think about my bungled effort with Sheila Lee. Applying pressure in an interview is a delicate process, requiring finesse, balance, and tact. A good interviewer must never lose track of the fine line between persistence and being pushy. One misstep, and your witness may clam up forever, never to cooperate. The line is not too hard to see actually--I generally spot it looking back over my shoulder after I've crossed it.

Sheila was my best lead so far, and I drove her to the brink of collapse. Of course, I had no way of knowing that her psyche was so fragile, but ignorance is an overused excuse. I should have read her better, paid more attention to the skittishness in her green cat's eyes, sensed the pain and fear and loathing that lay behind them. I should have recognized that her defenses could not be breached easily without collateral damage. Instead, I had blundered in recklessly, pulling at memories she barely suppressed, prodding some trauma that was scarred over but not healed.

Worst of all, I had not learned very much from her. It seemed unlikely I would get a chance to speak to her again.

* * *

I returned to my apartment. With Mara's possessions gone, the rooms seemed cold and empty. It no longer seemed like home, just where I lived.

I took a beer from the refrigerator and stretched out on the couch, sipping directly from the can. When some beer spilled out and dribbled down my chin and neck, I wiped most of it off with my sleeve. The rest would add character to my undershirt.

I had all the wild joys of bachelor living to look forward to. Hanging out at local dives, complaining about the lack of talent. Retiring my razor on weekends. Listening to talk radio for company, or if things got really bad, calling the station myself.

Throwing out broad hints around the holidays about having nowhere to go. And if no one took pity on me, I could spend Thanksgiving alone, playing electronic chess games and gnawing on a pepperoni stick.

Here it was not even nine o'clock and I was already waxing pathetic. Plenty of time for that later, I decided, let's try something useful first.

I put my beer down on the coffee table and looked in the Eola area phone book for Roger Thornton, the boyfriend Sheila mentioned.

Thornton was listed at an address not far across town. I dialed his number.

A man picked up on the twelfth ring.

"Yeah?"

The voice sounded tired and irritable. A dull rhythmic thud of rap music was loud in the background. The booming bass overpowered everything else. He probably set his equalizer ski-slope fashion.

"Mr. Thornton?"

He grunted.

"I'm a private detective. My name is Nash Tobin. Can I talk to you a few minutes?"

There was a brief pause before he responded. A note of caution crept into his voice. "Why?"

"It's about a friend of yours, Rudi Alsmith."

There was a longer pause.

"I know her," he said slowly.

"Good. I have a few simple questions. First off, how well did you know her?"

"Why?"

"Someone told me she was your girlfriend. Is that right?"

"Maybe. One of them."

"When was the last time you saw Ms. Alsmith? Was it

recent?"

"Not that it's your business, but no, it was a while back."

"What happened? You guys split up?"

"That's none of your business either."

This was not going well. I could hear from his tone that Thornton was on the verge of hanging up. If I didn't hook him soon, I'd lose him.

"You did know she's dead?"

"Of course!" he said, adding, "A shame too. Rudi was a hot number, no doubt about it. But there're plenty of others around. I won't be joining no monastery because Rudi's gone."

I believed him. But it also gave me a clue about what made Roger Thornton tick.

"How do you mean 'hot'?"

"I'm talking lava. That's how she moved, all gliding and flowing. When you're wrapped up in that, man, you know it!" Thornton was beginning to warm to the subject.

"How long did you know her?"

"From when I was a freshman. She was even younger then but already had a name for herself. When other kids were just playing doctor, Rudi already had her M.D." He laughed at his own joke.

"Where'd she come by it?"

"Who knows? Home-schooling, maybe, if you get my drift. Her mom thought maybe she learned it from dad."

"Anything to that?"

"I don't know. Rudi never said it was true. To tell the truth, I don't think her dad cared much for either of them. I think her mom was just pissed at being ignored. What made it worse was, she was getting old and Rudi was turning into a knockout."

"You and Rudi were together since junior high school?"

"Off and on," he said, and laughed again. "On and off."

His single-minded double-entendres were as fresh as a day-old condom.

"So what were you last week?" I asked. "On or off?"

Thornton went quiet. Only the pounding wump, wump, wump from his speakers was audible.

"I was right. I shouldn't have talked to you," he said.

I dropped all pretense of politeness; I was never very good at it anyway:

"... Cause if you say you were off, I know you're lying." I was lying myself—I knew no such thing.

"Rudi died. It happens to all of us. It can happen to you if you don't watch yourself."

A threat. On the first phone call. How did I get to be so lucky?

"Look. I know you saw her not long ago. Why lie about it? Why not just tell me? Unless you have something to hide. Whatever it is I'll find out eventually anyway. You may as well tell me now. Or we could do it face to face if you'd rather."

"Nuts to you, Jack," was all Thornton could manage in reply.

"Okay, what can you tell me about the 'Gatherings?'"

Thornton was silent for a moment, then:

"You're awful stupid, Mr. Tobin. But you're right about one thing. We should get together, and we will. Only we won't have much talking to do. I'll be in touch." He slammed the phone down.

For no good reason, it was my turn to laugh.

CHAPTER FIFTEEN

The next morning, I was in the kitchen getting a fork for my eggs, when a loud knock came at my front door. I dropped the fork into my bathrobe pocket and went to answer it. Through the peep-hole, I saw two men standing on the other side. The broad-shouldered man in front started pounding again and the whole door shook.

Leaving the chain in place, I opened it a crack. "Yes?"

The first man grinned and brushed pink sparkles off his tie and black sport coat. His thick glasses looked absurdly large around his narrow, skull-shaped face, giving him the appearance of a pop-eyed buzzard. His haircut was wretched and apparently self-inflicted.

"Can we have a moment of your time?" he asked in a deep but affable voice. He reached through the crack and shook my hand with a grip like a machine press. "We have so much to talk about."

"Yes, much," his friend chimed in from behind like some strange Greek chorus.

Slightly built and with a pregnant paunch, this second man wore a brown leisure suit with white stitching. Beneath the unbuttoned jacket, he had a nylon shirt with a gaudy depiction of a tropical sunset. The shirt was open at the neck and for several buttons below, exposing a gold necklace nestled in bronze chest hair. His round face was a dye-lot copper, set off by sandy blond hair and a robin's-egg-blue golf cap. He sported a broad mustache and a scruffy goatee, grown to give his weak chin definition. Unfortunately, it only drew attention to it. His eyes were small, but quick and penetrating.

"I don't think I know you gentlemen," I said. Perhaps my dues were in arrears at the Fashion Distressed Men's Club of America and these two had been sent to collect.

"Not yet," said the first man, "But that's easy to remedy. I am Cyrus Hardison. This is Tony Gerrara."

"Gerrara," his partner repeated.

"How can I help you?"

"We're here to help you, actually. May we come in?" Hardison gestured toward the chain, still smiling.

I recalled his hydraulic handshake and shook my head. "Whatever it is, we can discuss it right here."

Hardison frowned. He glanced around the open area surrounding the stairwell. He reached inside his coat and pulled out a long barrel revolver, which he pointed at me through the open door interval.

"Even this?" Hardison said.

"And this?" Gerrara said, opening his own jacket to show the butt end of a pistol protruding from a side holster.

I jumped back and tried to slam the door shut, but Hardison managed to wedge his shoe into the gap first. I strained to crush his foot with the metal door, but it was no use. The thick sole of his shoe was too sturdy.

"Stand back!" Hardison warned.

A moment later the door burst in as the security chain's hardware was ripped out of the door jamb. The door swung around and slammed into the apartment wall with a crash, leaving a deep gouge in the drywall from the door knob.

Gerrara tumbled into the middle of the room, landing face down on the floor. Hardison stumbled in right behind, losing his glasses but keeping his feet.

Hardison kicked the door shut behind him. He turned away briefly to latch the deadbolt but soon had his gun trained on me again. He showed no sign of exertion from breaking in the door. His leathery face remained cold and impassive. He walked to the center of the room and reached down to help his partner up.

Gerrara, on the other hand, was winded. He took Hardison's arm and stood up slowly, taking deep breaths. The rise and fall of his pot-belly made it look like the beach on his shirt was eroding into the sea. Although Gerrara's blue golf cap remained perched on his head, the fall had knocked it askew. He carefully adjusted it, maintaining the same moronic smile he had displayed throughout.

He would have looked almost comical if he too had not pulled out his gun and leveled it at me.

"Back up," Gerrara said.

I slowly moved backwards until I bumped into the plank bookshelves against the wall.

"What do you want?" I asked, fighting to keep my voice calm. Inside, I was shaking with anger and adrenalin. My eyes darted back and forth between the two men and all around the room, but I knew there was nothing I could do. My only hope was that my neighbors might call the police, but given their usual attitude toward cops, it seemed a long shot.

"First things first," Gerrara said. "Close up that bathrobe. You're no underwear model."

The larger goon, Hardison, was still standing behind Gerrara at the center of the room. He twisted his head from side to side, searching the floor around him. His small grey head even swiveled like a bird's.

"My glasses...?" Hardison asked.

Without looking back, Gerrara said, "They're down there. By the recliner."

"Oh, yes." Hardison leaned down and picked up his glasses from beside the chair. He put them back on his face and blinked a few times while his eyes adapted again. He reached into his jacket pocket and pulled out a pink marshmallow Peep. He pinched it gingerly to check its consistency.

Hardison moved in front of his partner, chick still in hand.

"I told you before, Mr. Tobin, we're here to help. To keep you out of trouble you may not know you're in." Hardison brought the chick to his mouth and bit it in half. A small shower of pink dust floated down to his tie.

Gerrara nodded behind him: "We're like the good Samaritans."

"Yes," Hardison agreed. "But we also need your help. We need to know who hired you to look into the death of Rudi Alsmith." He ate some more of his Peep.

"And why?" Gerrara piped in.

"Also why," Hardison agreed.

"I can't tell you that! It would violate every principle I ..."

"Principle!" Gerrara snorted derisively. "That's good! Principle..." Still chuckling, Gerrara went over and sat down on the sofa. He stuck his legs up on the coffee table and kicked over a dirty ashtray onto the floor.

"I'm sure you don't mean 'can't'," Hardison said. "Can't is too strong, too final. It leaves no room for judgement. It's true, you may not want to tell us; but there's no question you will. In the end."

Hardison took several steps towards me, finishing his marshmallow chick and licking the red sugar crystals off his thick fingers. He stopped right in front of me and looked down into my face. His eyes were dark and bloodshot beneath a heavy brow. His nose was kinked just below the point where his glasses rested. His stale breath smelled of cigarettes, coffee, and hangover halitosis. And from close up, his haircut was even worse than I thought.

I returned his stare, keeping my eyes unfocused for that steely look.

"You really should get your hair cut by a professional," I said. "Or were you going for the rat's nest look?"

Hardison smiled. His breathing continued slow and measured, giving no sign of what was to come. The gun in his right hand held steady.

Suddenly, his left fist exploded deep into my gut, knocking me back into the bookshelves. Paperback books tumbled to the floor around my feet. I clutched my stomach, convinced that some internal organs had just been scrambled. I gasped, but air seemed hard to come by.

"Bastard!" I rasped. It was a hell of a punch. I'd hate to meet the guy who broke Hardison's nose.

"Annhhhh!" From the couch, Gerrara made a noise like a game show buzzer. He was leaning back with his fingers meshed behind his head and his elbows spread out wide. His automatic pistol lay free in his lap. "You lose points for invective. Answer the question, please. Who hired you about Rudi Alsmith?"

I shook my head and wheezed, "It's against the law..."

"Not the law of self-preservation," Gerrara grinned.

Hardison took another step towards me.

I was running out of time. Another punch like the first one and I wouldn't be able to put up any fight at all. I clutched my arms more tightly against my stomach. Beneath them, I felt the fork which was still hidden in my bathrobe pocket.

I grimaced and groaned as if from renewed pain, and shifted my arms. With my right hand, I reached into my pocket and took hold of the fork, concealing the maneuver with my left arm.

"I think you broke something," I said.

"Not yet," Hardison said. "But I can if I need to." He grasped my shoulder with his left hand and bounced me against the bookshelves.

"All right!" I said. "But let me catch my breath first..." I took several deep breaths, priming my lungs with oxygen.

Hardison turned his head towards Gerrara and smiled at how easily I had been broken. His gun hand hung down at his side.

Only a fool would even have thought of trying something in my position. So I stopped thinking and just let it happen.

I yanked the fork out of my pocket and lashed out at Hardison's head. He ducked back as the blow came and I barely scratched his temple. His glasses flew across the room. I lunged away from Hardison and dove for the loose pistol in Gerrara's lap.

But Gerrara's gun was already gone.

Before I reached him, Gerrara's legs disappeared from the table and the gun was in his hand. He cracked me hard over the head with the butt of his pistol, and I crashed off the coffee table onto the floor. My elbow landed in the ashes and butts from the overturned ashtray.

Gerrara laughed: "You get an E for effort. So few even try nowadays."

"The bastard scratched me!" Hardison griped to his partner. He came over to where I lay curled up on the floor and kicked into my back with his steel-toed shoe. It tore open the scab under my bandage and caused sticky blood to flow once more down my back.

"There," Hardison said to me. "We're even. Except that you still haven't answered my question, and I'm in a worse mood than before." He kicked me again to show how bad his mood was.

"He's bleeding," Gerrara said. "Take off his robe, maybe that will loosen his tongue."

Hardison reached down and pulled my robe off, leaving me cringing on the carpet in my underwear.

"Softboy," Hardison said. "Are you going to tell me what I want to know?"

"I get it now," I said to Hardison, without looking up. "He's the brains of the operation. And you're just the mouth."

Somewhere behind me, Gerrara laughed again.

"And your operation is all mouth," Hardison said. "You just don't say the right things."

Gerrara stood up from the couch. He came around the coffee table and approached me. Holding his pistol by the barrel, he took a wide swing and clubbed the side of my head.

My vision blurred for a moment and all I could see was the fuzzy image of Gerrara's blue hat hovering in darkness like a UFO. My head was ringing and tears came to my eyes. I reached up to my left ear and felt blood there.

Above the ringing, I heard Hardison's bass voice:

"Silence is golden, but it's not an option here. You will tell us. Eventually. It's just easier now than later."

"For us too," Gerrara added. "I ruined a perfectly good shirt last night. I'd hate to lose this one as well."

I spoke towards the blue spot: "I'd guess it was ruined at the factory. Or do yours come off a Qiana boat?"

A second, harder blow struck my ear again. I pulled in my knees and curled up into a tight ball with my arms protecting my head. I was conscious only of throbbing pain--I throb therefore I am.

Their two voices seemed far away. They were addressing some other person in the room, but for the life of me, I could not understand who he was or why he didn't answer.

As my hearing refocused, I heard Gerrara's voice.

"Well, Cy, we're going to have to do him. Seems a shame, him being so entertaining and all."

I felt the cold muzzle of a gun pressed against the back of my head. It was annoying.

"You'll mess your cuff again," Hardison's voice warned.

The muzzle went away.

I raised my head. My eyes were clearing and so was my head. Gerrara had taken off his jacket and was rolling up his right shirt sleeve. His gun lay on the arm of the recliner. I recalled having the gun barrel against my head and it slowly dawned on me what it had been doing there.

"No," I said faintly.

Hardison leaned down toward me. He had his glasses on again. "No, what? No, don't shoot me, or no, I'm not going to tell you?"

"Don't..." I managed.

"This sounds promising," Hardison said. "But keep your sleeve up just in case."

I was able to stand--barely. There was blood on my left leg where I'd rested my head.

"I want water," I said.

"Tell us what we want, and we'll have champagne to celebrate," Hardison said. But he nodded at Gerrara to get the water.

Gerrara brought a glass back from the kitchen and it tasted so good and cool going down that I almost thanked him.

"Okay," I said, "I'm ready."

Hardison started the questions. "Who hired you to look into the girl's death?"

"No one. Her writing teacher hired me but it wasn't about the girl. In fact, his job stank. It was a waste of money, effort, and time. But I saw Rudi at his office once. When she died, it seemed more interesting to go after that."

Gerrara grabbed my hair and pulled my head back so I was looking up into his copper face. His mustache was stained from cigarette smoke beneath his nostrils.

"You thought it was interesting? Interesting? You still

interested, Van Gogh?" He shook my head roughly and flicked my injured ear with his finger.

I winced.

"No. Not interested. Not remotely. More like bored."

Gerrara nodded and let me go.

Hardison asked, "What else do you know about it?"

"Nothing. Except what was in the papers. I don't know anything."

A disgusted look stole across Gerrara's face. He took his golf cap off and threw it to the couch. He grabbed his pistol from the chair arm and came at me.

"I say we do him. Right here, right now. He's lying like a strung-out junkie. He knows Roger..."

"Only that he was her boyfriend," I said. "I swear, that's all I know."

Gerrara was waiting for some signal from Hardison. Hardison took another marshmallow chicken from his pocket and bit its head off. He chewed it pensively. He brought his hand to his mouth and pulled a small piece of lint from his tongue.

Gerrara and I both waited.

Finally, Hardison spoke:

"No. If he says he doesn't know anything, you only have to look at him to know he's telling the truth."

Gerrara sighed. He put the gun back in his holster and retrieved his cap from the couch. He rolled down his sleeve and put his brown leisure suit jacket back on.

"Lucky for you, you're so ignorant," he said to me. "But everyone's luck runs out sometime. Our boss knows how to handle snoops like you who poke around in matters that don't concern them. And he hates being threatened, do you get me? You are finished with that girl. Just keep your nose out of it. And you never saw us because Cy and I were never here. You certainly don't want us calling again... But you're such a smart boy, I bet you figured that out already!" He turned to Hardison. "And now breakfast I think. Those eggs smell good."

Hardison stuffed the remaining pink chick into his mouth and nodded. He took his wallet from his back pocket and pulled out a twenty dollar bill. He pinched one end of the bill and flung it at my face.

"Tha'sh fo' champay'," he said, his words muffled by marshmallow. "'Sh too uh'ly i' the day..."

Side by side, they walked to the door. Hardison brushed the sugar dust off his hands onto his pants legs. He twisted the latch and pulled the door open.

He turned and said, "Let's say goodbye..."

"...Not au revoir," Gerrara finished.

They left me alone in my living room, with a pounding head and blood-stained underwear. I sat down on the couch and held my head in my hands.

Hardison and Gerrara had done their work well. I had no desire to continue with this or any other investigation. I had no right to. I had folded at the first sign of pressure, sold out my own client. I may not have named Curtiz but I certainly told them enough that they could find him if they wanted. Lance Talbot was right; I was unfit for my profession, a failure at its most basic level. The remembrance would gnaw at me like a cancer, twisting my insides into something alien and malignant. I could not even go back to my old job at Transcontinental--I would always be Tobin the washout, the wannabe op who didn't have the mettle. I would have to find something else...

My pride had just been executed, gangland style. I felt empty and alone, and with a terrible void to fill.

I retrieved a beer from the refrigerator and a bottle of whiskey from the liquor cupboard. It was early in the day, as Hardison said, but I had no special plans. Maybe I would get a bottle of champagne later. If I ever made it out of the apartment.

I set the beer and whiskey on the coffee table and flicked on the television for noise. For now, I intended to drink like a souse at an Irish wake and the consequences be damned. I opened the can of beer and lit a cigarette to feed the cancer within.

That's when the call came.

CHAPTER SIXTEEN

Mr. Tobin, please help! Rudi's mother is out front and she's acting crazy!" The voice on the phone was an urgent croak. I recognized it instantly.

"Calm down, Mrs. Sachett. Tell me what she is doing. No, first, does she seem dangerous? To herself or to you? If she does, call the police. Don't wait. Let them take care of her."

"No. She's not dangerous. She just makes no sense. She pounds on my door and demands to see Rudi. Her eyes are wild, Mr. Tobin, I've never seen her like this. I tried to talk sense to her, get her to come in, but she won't come near me. She called me an ugly old woman, said I stole Rudi from her. And other things..." Mrs. Sachett began to cry. "She's still out there, looking for her daughter..."

"Okay, I'm coming. I'll be right there. Where is Mr. Alsmith?"

"He's not home and I don't know how to reach him. I didn't know who else to call." A loud pounding was audible in the background. "There she is again! Hurry, please," Mrs. Sachett wailed.

"It's all right. Stay calm. Keep an eye on her and don't let her hurt herself. That's the best way to help her right now. If she looks like she's turning violent, call the police. Do you understand?"

"Yes," Mrs. Sachett said. The specific instructions seemed to calm her.

"I'm leaving right now."

After I hung up, I hurriedly bandaged my back and put on a sweatshirt and jeans. I was on the road within five minutes, heading south on Easton Boulevard through Shakytown. Easton opens up into Route 63 outside the city limits, which I thought would be a faster way of getting to Avalon Estates. While I drove, I cleaned the blood off my face using a paper towel and saliva but didn't go anywhere near my ear.

I pulled into Mrs. Sachett's driveway at 9:15, only twenty minutes after her call.

Mrs. Sachett came running awkwardly from her front door as I stepped out of the car. She was out of breath by the time she reached me, her wide face mottled and red.

"She's in back…" she said, gasping for breath. "On the terrace. She's calmer now… but still not coherent."

"I'll take her home now. Thank you. You've done a good job here."

I walked around Mrs. Sachett's garage and found Rudi's mother sitting on the stone terrace, hunched over a white patio table with her head on her hands. Her black hair drifted back and forth in the intermittent breeze. She wore a green knit polo shirt, tucked primly into cream-colored slacks, and had on a pair of sky-blue canvas sneakers. She didn't seem to hear me as I came up the terrace steps behind her.

"Mrs. Alsmith?" I said. "Samantha?"

After a long pause she lifted her face like it was a heavy burden and turned towards me, drawing her right shoulder back and pushing her breasts forward for maximum impact. Her tight knit shirt strained at the pressure, and the effect was certainly impressive. It can't have been a comfortable position to hold but she made it look effortless. Ah, the fruits of finishing-school.

For a woman in her mid-forties, Mrs. Alsmith looked

amazing. Rudi's beauty was no fluke. Her mother had the same triangular face, the same high cheekbones, the same pert, upturned nose, even the same prismatic eyes, shimmering and electric--eyes you could lose yourself in. Samantha's bobbed hair was puffed up and sprayed back, except for long bangs that curled down over her forehead. She was justifiably proud of her youthful figure and liked to show it off.

But something was missing. Samantha's coral-blue eyes burned brightly enough but they were wild and desperate, with none of the ironic self-possession that had been so striking in her daughter. Instead, she had the air of a pampered pet, abandoned in the forest and forced to fend for itself. Her make-up, though expertly applied, could not cover the lines around her eyes or the fleshy slackness that was beginning to develop under her chin.

"Ye-es? You have the advantage of me." Her tone and cadence mocked those of a southern belle but her vowels fell flat. It was as if her accent were pure affectation and she wasn't sure I was worth the effort.

I extended my hand to help her up from her chair.

"Hi, I'm Nash Tobin. I'm here to take you home."

That seemed to interest her a little. A smile crept across her face like a centipede. She stood up and withdrew her hand, lightly brushing my palm with her fingers. She smoothed out any wrinkles that might have formed on her slacks by running her hands up and down her backside.

Her smile faded, though, as she noticed my old jeans and loose sweatshirt.

"Some white knight," she said.

“My armor's at the silver polisher's. Are you ready?"

"I am always ready."

Whenever Samantha Alsmith spoke, she turned her head slightly to the side and wouldn't face me directly. As she came closer and extended her elbow for me to take, I quickly discovered why. Her breath reeked of alcohol and its heavy scent permeated her skin and clothing.

"My car is right out front," I told her, leaving her arm alone.

Mrs. Alsmith cleared her throat and stayed where she was. "If I'm to be escorted, I want a proper escort."

I shrugged and took her arm. She pulled in close, clinging to me like a desperate deb on prom night. As we walked around the garage, she kept brushing her leg against mine. Her loose cotton pants glided lightly over her smooth skin. Her smile was big and phony, and her eyes swam like an animal's.

I brought her around to the driveway and opened the Impala's passenger door. She slid over to the middle of the bench seat and waited.

I waved to Mrs. Sachett as I walked around to the driver's side. She waved back from her crafts room window, cigarette in hand.

Samantha Alsmith glared through the windshield at her elderly neighbor. It was a look of hatred, but with a trace of fear mixed in as well. Something about the old woman frightened her.

As I got into the car, Mrs. Alsmith's concentration immediately shifted. She slid over beside me, flashing a grin like a kitten lapping up milk. Before I even backed down the driveway she had her paw in my lap.

I stepped on the brake hard and grabbed her wrist.

"Be careful," I said, "You don't know where it's been."

She smiled blankly, pleased at my undivided attention. She gave her head a shake and her Betty Boop curls bounced back and forth like buggy whips. She could not get over how cute she was.

I slapped her face with her own hand. Not too hard, just enough to get her attention.

She yelped, more astonished than hurt. She squirmed and

tried to pull away.

"You're no gentleman. Let me out!"

I pulled her closer to keep her under control. It was surprisingly easy. She only struggled briefly and made no serious effort to get away.

I backed onto the street and drove across to the Alsmith's driveway, two houses up. The drive curved around to an attached garage beside their large Tudor house.

Samantha was quiet until I stopped the car.

"I thought you were going to take me home."

"Your home. Not mine." I got out and went around to open the passenger door for her.

"Please," she said, staying in her seat. "Let's go somewhere else."

"Where would you rather?"

"It doesn't matter. Anywhere. Just not here!"

But as I stood there holding the door, Samantha lowered her head and a shadow fell across her face.

"Oh, never mind," she muttered, the southern accent now gone. "There isn't anywhere."

She got out of the car and trudged towards the house with slow, sullen steps.

I followed her to the first of two front entrances. Samantha opened the unlocked door and we went inside, turning left past the laundry room into a spacious kitchen. She stopped in the middle of the room and looked aimlessly around her. I went over to the breakfast area and sat down at a round glass table beside the patio door.

"I need a drink," Mrs. Alsmith announced finally. "What will you have?"

Without waiting for an answer, she stood on tiptoes and leaned against the refrigerator to reach the liquor cupboard above it. She rattled through the bottles inside.

I watched her intently, with an interest that was not even close to professional. As she reached up, her shirt came untucked from her slacks, and I could see her smooth peach skin, her fine waist, and trim figure. Her off-white pants draped closely over her firm thighs and calves and a pair of dark bikini panties showed through the light material. Watching her like this was a mistake. Now I realized how desirable she was--probably because for the first time she wasn't trying to convince me of it. Suddenly it was hard to focus on anything else.

She turned her head and caught my look.

"What do you want?" she repeated with a smile that was too coy.

"I'll have water."

"With what, though?"

"Just ice."

She shook her head and came down with a bottle of bourbon and a bottle of gin. She set them on the cooktop-and-counter peninsula that jutted out to the center of the room. She retrieved two tall glasses from another cupboard and filled each one with ice from the freezer's ice dispenser.

I looked away from her out the patio door across the large back yard. It was surrounded by a tall fence lined with small shrubs. Their yard was dotted with saplings, each one wired to a stout white post for support.

I heard the ice cracking as Mrs. Alsmith ran tap water into our glasses. When I turned back, she was adding several fingers of bourbon to her own glass. She put the bottle down and fixed her gaze on mine.

Slowly, deliberately, she undid the buttons beneath her collar and pried the edges apart into a deep V. The swell of her breasts gleamed palely in the room's diffuse light. Taut nipples raised bumps in her tight shirt. She leaned across the central counter, offering the glasses and so much more.

"Here you are."

She played her center-counter gambit like a master. I had expected something along this line, but it still took my breath away when she sprang it. Her slightest move sent my nerves spinning. Even the rhythmic rise and fall of her bosom as she breathed seemed calculated to elicit excitement. The world seemed to shrink around us two, squeezing us together and shutting out everything else.

I got up from the table and moved toward her. The air was already charged between us and that feeling of electricity increased as I got closer. Samantha's breathing quickened; her cleavage heaved and fell. She was practically panting by the time I reached her. I may not have been breathing at all. The glasses shook in Samantha's hands, and the clink of the ice sounded like chimes.

I took the drinks out of her hands. She leaned in towards me, closing her eyes and offering her lips. More than anything, I wanted to reciprocate, to lock faces with her in a feral kiss, to take her in my arms and feel her eager body beneath my hands. To give in completely to the roiling demand of the moment...

Instead, I said, "If you show any more, you'll need an exhibitor's license."

I took the glasses back to the round table. I sat down by the patio door and the fever in my brow slowly subsided. Taking a sip from the clear liquid in my glass, I tasted the cold bite of gin. No doubt Samantha thought I would be distracted and not notice.

She stood up straight behind the counter and pushed her collar back together.

"You could almost be cute," she said, "If you just shut up once in a while."

"That's what my wife says."

"You should listen to her."

Samantha picked up a pill bottle from a woven basket by the

refrigerator and brought it over to the table. She sat down opposite me, her face still annoyed. She pushed back in her chair, disinclined now even to play footsy.

"What are you doing here anyway?" she asked.

"Someone thought you needed looking after. They called me."

"I don't need anyone."

She opened the pill bottle and took three pink tablets from it. She put them into her mouth and washed them down with a long swig of her bourbon and water. She recapped the bottle and set it down on the table.

I reached across and snatched the bottle before she could stop me. It was a brown plastic container with a plain white label taped to the outside. There was no pharmacy name or prescription on the label, just the handwritten letter "V."

I held the bottle up to her and shook the tablets inside.

"What's in here?"

"None of your business." She made a grab for the pill bottle but missed it by a mile.

"Are you supposed to take it with alcohol?"

"Yes, of course."

"Where'd you get them?"

"Work, if you must know." She leaned back in her chair and ran her fingers through her hair. She let her eyelids drop.

I threw the pill bottle past her head at the wall. The top popped off and the pills scattered loudly across the floor.

Samantha's eyes shot open at the sound and she straightened up.

"Why'd you do that!? Those are from the hospital!"

"Then where's the prescription label?"

"I'm a nurse. I didn't need one." She looked in dismay at the pills on the floor. "Those are the only ones I have left!"

Samantha got down from her chair onto her hands and knees

to collect the scattered tablets. As she picked them up and replaced them in the bottle, she brushed each one off or blew on it to remove any grit or fuzz. She muttered angrily to herself but remained absolutely focused on the task at hand.

"Why don't you get more?"

"I can't!" she spat. "They put me on leave a month ago. While they do their investigation. They may not take me back."

"Why not?"

"That's none of your ..." she began, but stopped.

Her face softened and she looked up at me with wide, calculating eyes. Even her southern belle accent made a brief reprise:

"Please, can't you all at least help me with these? I am so very tired."

"No, I don't think so."

"Then you're a bastard!" she said, and her scowl at least looked sincere.

She continued to scour the floor, but the remaining pills were getting harder to find. Samantha's face turned red with frustration and her shoulders were beginning to slump.

"There must be more," she said to herself. "There has to be."

Finally she gave up and threw herself back into her chair. She placed the uncapped pill bottle at the edge of the table where I could not reach it. She closed her eyes, brought her hands to her face, and began to rock slowly back and forth. Her loud breathing whistled through her nose, eventually ratcheting up into sobs. She let out a low, piteous cry--almost a wail--but it stopped as abruptly as it began. She moved her hands and I could see that her eyes were dry; no tears had come.

"Dammit!" She pounded her fists on the glass table. The impact shook the pill bottle off the edge, and her precious tablets scattered over the floor once more.

Samantha yelped like a clubbed seal and kicked perversely at the pills by her feet. Her eyes teared over at last and a few sluggish drops dribbled down her cheeks. But her red eyes soon became dry again. It was painful to watch. Her inability to cry was far worse than if she had been a sobbing, blubbering mess.

"Is there someone I can call for you?" I asked. "Your husband, maybe?"

She wiped her face roughly with her bare arm. Her mascara smeared around her eyes and left a black cloudy smudge on her forearm.

"Don't you dare! He is the last person I want to see."

"What about friends then? Or do you have family nearby?"

She shook her head adamantly, "No one."

"No other children?"

"Only Rudi," she said. She closed her eyes and wiped the skin around them with her fingers. "Only Rudi," she repeated. "She was enough. More than enough."

"You didn't want any more?"

Mrs. Alsmith looked at me acidly.

"I didn't want her." The statement was both a confession and a challenge. She wanted to provoke a reaction in me and shook her head in disgust when she didn't get one.

"Mrs. Alsmith, can you tell me what happened to your daughter?"

"What difference does it make? It was an overdose of cocaine and PCP. Her heart and lungs couldn't take it and gave out." She shook her head. "You know, they actually told me it was quite painless. Can you believe that?"

"You don't?"

"How can I? We have terminal patients at the hospital; they're always whining, begging, or crying--sometimes even screaming. They're all scared to death of dying, and it is never painless. That's just what we tell relatives. Now I am one."

Samantha's speech was becoming slower, colder, more

dispassionate. The tablets she had taken were beginning to take effect, packing her feelings into a neat little box and stashing them all far away.

"That's all it was? An overdose?"

Mrs. Alsmith yawned: "Of course. What else?"

She showed no sign that she knew about the beating her daughter had received. Perhaps the police had spared her that.

"Do you know who your daughter was with on Saturday night?"

This question seemed to startle her a little. She tried to clear the haze from her head with a swift shake and peered at me through narrowed eyes.

"Why do you want to know?"

"I'm just asking."

"Well, I don't know. If I did, I would have told the police, wouldn't I. Could have been anyone. One of her boyfriends. That muscle-bound punk Roger Thornton maybe. Or somebody else. Could have been a complete stranger, for all I know. My daughter was never very particular. And she was often gone overnight..."

She caught my questioning look.

"Oh, yes. My husband, Dennis, tried to close his eyes to it. He usually left before she got up anyway. But I checked her room every morning. I always knew."

It sounded like she stored up each bitter occasion in her heart, forgiving nothing.

"Could your husband know who she was with?"

The caution in her voice became unmistakable:

"You'll have to ask him. I'm his wife, not his keeper. He doesn't actually confide in me."

Something in what she said, or maybe it was the way she said it, pricked at my consciousness just below the level of comprehension. Finally it broke through.

"Your husband wasn't home Saturday night either, was he?"

Samantha lowered her eyes and shook her head.

"No. He was out. All night."

She picked up her drink and quickly drained a quarter of it. She set the glass on the table with a loud and clumsy "clink." She slid down slightly in her chair.

"Where was he?"

Samantha's face was woozy, but she still managed a look of contempt.

"You want me to spell it out? Or would a picture be better? He was not here. He did not tell me where he was or who he was with. And if he did tell me anything, by God, it would have been a lie. My husband, you see, is not very particular either."

I was beginning to detect a family pattern.

"You were here alone?"

Mrs. Alsmith nodded her head twice. Slowly. Sleepily. The pills she had taken were now in full force. She closed her eyes and slid down further in her chair. If she were any more relaxed she would melt away altogether. She started humming a tuneless tune low under her breath, only stopping her song when she needed to breathe through her open mouth. Before long, she was completely gone.

I was both fascinated and repelled watching her. A few minutes earlier, she had been so seductive, almost irresistible. Her sensuality had seemed to promise everything I or anyone else could want from the world. At least for a time. Now she looked less than human, more like a drowsy lizard basking on a hot rock. Probably she was somewhere in between, like the rest of us. Samantha Alsmith began to snore.

People in a stupor always make me tired. I took what was left of our drinks and poured them out in the sink. After searching through the pantry and cupboards, I found a foil bag of coffee in the freezer. On the door of the freezer was a yellow sticky-note with "Dennis wk" and a phone number written on it. I pocketed the note and started a half-pot of coffee brewing. I stood by the sink and waited for it to finish.

The sound of Samantha's snoring blended perfectly with the churning coffee-maker. As long as she was snoring, I knew she was all right. If she stopped, I would need to watch her. I had no idea what kind of pills she took nor what she might have taken before I came. But drugs and alcohol is an unpredictable mix at best, even for an old pro like Mrs. Alsmith. Maybe the spark that had flashed between us made me feel protective. Maybe I just felt sorry for her. Whatever it was, I didn't want to let anything happen to her, not if I could help it. If nothing else, two drug-related deaths in the same family would look bad in the newspapers.

One thing was clear: the Alsmith family was a dysfunctional mess. It was as if the family infrastructure had been wiped out in an unknown cataclysm and all that was left were a few empty titles: mother, father, daughter, husband, wife. The Alsmiths' marriage appeared to be a disaster, a running battle of competing infidelities and mutual hatred. And Mrs. Alsmith fared little better as a mother. Her own promiscuous and addictive behavior could hardly have given Rudi a worse model to follow. The fact that Samantha never wanted her daughter to begin with could not have helped either. Rudi must have picked up on her mother's indifference and drawn closer to her father by default.

Maybe too close.

I recalled what Roger Thornton had said on the phone. That Mrs. Alsmith suspected Rudi and Rudi's father of having an incestuous affair. It was impossible for me to know if this were true. Perhaps Samantha's own pathologies just made her see things that way. Maybe she had shut herself outside the other two thirds of her family for so long that she could only despise what went on--or what she imagined went on--on the inside.

On the other hand, Rudi's precocious sexual behavior did fit a pattern that was consistent with sexual abuse at home. Perhaps as she got older and more experienced, Rudi even continued willingly, knowing full well what she was doing. What better way to get back at her mother for her indifference than by stealing the man from her bed? A truly explosive love-hate triangle, and all kept within the nuclear family.

As I watched the black coffee stream into the pot, my mind was struck by an even darker thought.

Rudi's father was not accounted for on Saturday night. What if he and Rudi had been together then? What if Rudi's abuser and partner that night was none other than her father? It was a sordid scenario more suited to the excesses of Greek tragedy than to a quiet American bedroom community. But that didn't mean it couldn't happen.

I looked back at Samantha who was dozing fitfully in her chair. Occasionally she whimpered in her sleep. Was that what haunted her? The suspicion that her daughter may have died in the arms of her husband? Or even by his hand? It was a dreadful image and I could see why Samantha would want to escape it by any means available.

The coffee-maker finished at last with a loud, flatulent flourish. I filled two mugs and took them over to the table. I set one in front of Mrs. Alsmith and sat down to drink the other myself. In silence I watched the steam rise out of Samantha's cup, twisting and drifting like smoke.

Before long, Samantha started to come around again. She opened her eyes slowly. It took a long time for them to focus.

"You're cute," she said when she was coherent enough to speak.

"You said that already."

"Not very tall, though..."

"And you're not very original."

"I could show you a few new things, I think."

"Stop it," I said. "You played this scene earlier. It's getting old."

"Aren't we all."

Samantha rubbed her cheeks with her hands. When she stopped, the rosy color quickly faded. She shook her head and rapidly blinked her eyes in an effort to wake up. Eventually, she noticed the coffee in front of her.

"Where'd this come from?"

"I made it."

She drank some. "It's good. Didn't we have real drinks before?"

"They're gone."

"Oh," she said, nodding.

It was nominal conversation. Shallow, vacuous, comfortable, with nothing challenging or painful about it. But it was not very productive.

"Mrs. Alsmith..." I began, unsure how to proceed.

"Call me Sam. Sam I am."

"Okay, Sam. Your husband..."

"Dennis."

"Yes, Dennis. What was... that is, how did he get along with Rudi?"

Samantha took another long sip of coffee and set her mug down.

"Why do you want to know?"

"It's my job to find out."

She shook her head vigorously.

"No, you said you were here to help me."

"That too. Don't you want me to find out what happened to your daughter?"

"I know what happened to her. I told you--she died of a drug overdose. Why do we have to keep going over these things?

Over and over?"

"Because sometimes it's not enough to know what happened. We have to know why."

Mrs. Alsmith wrestled with that for a moment and shrugged her shoulders.

"Sometimes there is no why. You just wear yourself out looking for something that's not there."

"You still haven't told me how Rudi and your husband got along?"

Samantha looked away.

"What do you expect me to say? They were close. Of course, they were close. He was her father."

"I'm not interested in 'of course.' It doesn't mean anything. I want the truth. Were they affectionate together? Did they talk a lot? Did they fight? Was there tension between them?"

Samantha squirmed in her seat.

"Well, he wanted to be close certainly. Sometimes maybe he tried too hard because he had so much to make up for. But Rudi didn't take to it. She thought he was trying to smother her. It just made her worse, even more likely to stir up trouble."

"What kind of trouble did she get in?"

"She liked to get him worked up. Even over minor things. Like the way she dressed or wore her makeup. She made herself look cheap on purpose because she knew how it bothered him. And it made him crazy when she went out without a bra on, so she started doing it all the time."

"Okay, good. What else?"

"She never told us where she was going. Or who she was with. And we couldn't trust her in anything. Sometimes she took money without asking. Or she'd have parties with her friends here while we were gone, even after we told her specifically that she couldn't. She had no sense of responsibility at all. That's why Dennis wouldn't let her go away to school. I pleaded with him to let her go, but he flat out refused. He was too afraid of what she might get into, that she would get out of control. Like she wasn't already..."

Samantha stopped, her face tight with recalled frustration. I felt a renewed twinge of sympathy for her. Caught in a loveless marriage, with a daughter she hated and who probably hated her back, Mrs. Alsmith's life was hard in spite of the material advantages she possessed. A big house, wealth, beauty; and none of it any comfort.

"Was there any other reason he didn't want to let her go?" I asked.

"What do you mean?"

It was a difficult question to phrase tactfully. In fact, it was impossible.

"I mean, was there something more to their relationship than is normal between a father and daughter?"

For a split second, Samantha Alsmith's face panicked. My question struck her viscerally and very deep. She quickly looked away and managed to fight the panic down. When she turned back, she crossed her arms over her chest.

"How can you ask that? What gives you the right to even suggest it? My daughter is dead. My only child! Don't you have even a shred of decency?"

"You only need to deny it..."

"I won't even dignify it."

"All right. I'm sorry." I paused, thinking over what she said. “Why did you go next door this morning looking for Rudi?”

Samantha was stung by the reminder and her indignation quickly deflated. She stared down at the center of the table where a reflection of moving clouds was visible in the glass. I don't know if she saw them. I'm not sure she saw anything.

Finally she looked up and her brilliant blue eyes were flooded with a bitterness that could fill the Great Lakes. At the same time, they were uncharacteristically clear and focused. And when she spoke at last, she dropped all pretense of her accent:

"How old are you, Mr. Tobin. Twenty-five, twenty-six? Wait fifteen or twenty years while your dreams slowly grind and crumble from neglect. Wait until you look back at your whole life and see nothing but a howling waste. The man I spent my life with doesn't care a damn about me, not when every year there's a fresh crop of eager MBA's and giggly interns. His desk at work sees more action in a week than our bed has in years. And I managed to screw up my job so badly that I will probably never work as a nurse again. All I had left was my beautiful child... And she hated me so hard it tore my heart out to look at her. Now she's gone too and there is no hope."

At last real tears welled up in her eyes and laid long black river tracks of mascara down her cheeks.

"Why did it all turn to shit?" she sobbed. "What did I do to deserve it? I just want to start over. Scrap it all as a misdeal and go back to the beginning. Back when I was eighteen or twenty. People noticed me then. When I came into a room, everyone looked at me and it felt warmer than fur or sunlight! I had so many suitors then, so many choices. Men did whatever I asked and gladly too. There was so much I could have done, should have done differently... Life had so much promise then. Now I have nothing. There must be more to life than that."

Her long speech left her short of air. Her face was cinched up and red. Black wisps of tear-wet hair clung to her cheeks and forehead.

"You can change that," I said, "If you want to..."

She lashed back at me:

"You really are young and stupid! How can you change your life if it's already over? When nothing is left, it's too late! It doesn't matter what I want. Wanting won't make it so. I've got thirty more years with nothing to do but look back on the mess I made of the first forty. Take a good look 'cause this is how your fairy tales end. Now if you don't mind, I want to be by myself. Why don't you run along and play with someone your own age."

I hesitated. I was less sure than ever that I should leave.

Samantha made a shooing gesture with her hands.

"Go, go. Don't worry about me. I'll be fine. I promise not to do anything self-destructive. Nothing permanent anyway. Please, just let me be."

"I don't know..."

"And I do. Frankly, you're insulting. I don't need a baby sitter. Especially one who's wet behind the ears but nowhere else. I don't want you here. Is that clear enough for you?"

I finished my coffee and stood up.

"Okay," I said. "I'll go. I'm sorry about your daughter. I hope one day you find what it is you're looking for. Whatever that may be."

She waved her hand dismissively: "And I hope you find the door okay."

* * *

Outside, a parade of cumulus clouds blundered over the sun. One after another their dusky shadows overran the Alsmiths' quiet neighborhood. The breeze that blew into my face as I walked to my car could not even raise a whisper from the few scrawny trees nearby. A cappuccino-colored leaf scuttled crab-like across the driveway; the dry rasp of its curled claws was the only sound.

I backed out of the drive and followed the subdivision's curving streets to the rural highway. I turned left and went west along the quiet road. The boundaries for the fields I passed were crude fences, just wood posts strung together with rusty wire. I drove slowly, almost on auto-pilot.

As soon as I left Mrs. Alsmith, I began to have second

thoughts. My mind pictured all kinds of dire and melodramatic consequences: she could pass out on the kitchen floor in a drunken stupor and choke to death on her own vomit. Or in her despair, she might slit her wrists in the bathtub and numbly watch her life's blood sluice out around her in an ever-reddening pool. Or perhaps she'd just finish off her bottle of pills and finish herself off in the process. The images were so graphic that I almost turned off the highway at several exits to go back to her.

But in spite of the images, I kept going. For all of her talk about life being over, Samantha Alsmith simply did not strike me as someone who would commit suicide. It would mean doing away with the only thing in the world she valued--herself. And if I did go back, what could I do for her? Her problems were all so entrenched and intractable--I was in no position to overhaul her life. Not when my own needed fixing. Samantha had wandered alone into a parched and private wilderness; she would need to find a way out on her own as well. If she said she wanted solitude, I had to take her at her word. It may have been the best thing she could ask for. Or the worst.

I turned north on Route 63 and headed back towards Eola. My mood lifted a little as the shimmering skyline came into view. My conscience continued to bother me with its grim, unwelcome peepshow, but in the heart of a city where you're surrounded by a million other lost souls, it always seems easier to ignore your conscience.

CHAPTER SEVENTEEN

As I made my way across my apartment complex parking lot, the glare of the late morning sun was almost blinding off the neighboring windshields. The city's sun-soaked buildings and pavement already radiated heat. There was no breeze to speak of, just an occasional restless stir in the air. I climbed the open stairwell to my apartment and went inside.

Nothing had changed since I left. The security chain with its wall-mount still attached hung down loose from door and swung awkwardly back and forth when I closed it. Paperback books were jumbled on the floor in front of the bookshelf that Cyrus Hardison threw me into. The same grey footprints tracked in cigarette ash led across the brown carpet. A few spots of blood were visible near where Gerrara cuffed me with his gun.

I tried to ignore it. I sat back on the couch with my feet up and lit a cigarette, my first one in hours. The nicotine sent a dizzying rush through my head but it died quickly and left only a dry cottony feeling in my mouth. I took a few sips from the can of Moosbrew beer that I'd opened earlier. The beer was warm of course, and flat, but drinkable enough as a Camel chaser. It was certainly more convenient than getting up for a fresh one. I flipped on the television to a news show.

I wanted a break. A chance to get my mind off the Alsmiths and their problems. To forget about the thugs who invaded my home and threatened to kill me.

Obscurity is generally underrated. It is a lot easier to be blissfully complacent when no one gives a damn who you are or what you do. But the signs of Hardison and Gerrara's "interest" surrounded me and complacency was no longer an option.

I had agreed to give up the Rudi Alsmith case. My visitors made it very clear what would happen if I reneged on the deal. Their threats left me no room for excuses, no way to plead misunderstanding.

Yet simply by going to help Mrs. Alsmith, I had already broken that agreement once. By itself, that might have been okay, if it were the last time, and as long as Hardison and Gerrara never found out. But I already knew I would not stop. If Rudi's father was involved in her death, then I could not just walk away and pretend to forget it. The outrage was more than I could ignore. I would just have to live with the consequences as best I could. As long as I could.

I took out the sticky-note with Dennis Alsmith's work number and dialed it on the telephone. It only rang once.

A receptionist--her voice like a talking Barbie doll--picked it up:

"Biltmore Eola, how may I help you?"

"Dennis Alsmith, please."

"I'm sorry, he's not available right now. Can I take a message?"

"It's important personal business. Are you sure you can't get him for me?"

"As I said, he is not available."

"Then can I make an appointment?"

"Certainly, sir..." There was a pause while she looked over his schedule. "How does 10:30 ncxt Thursday sound?"

"Fine," I said and gave her a name. "And could you tell me where you're located?"

"We are on the fortieth floor of the Sloane Building at ..." She gave the building's address and started to give directions. But the Sloane Building is an Eola landmark and I knew exactly where it was. I hung up the phone, cutting Barbie off mid-sentence. No need to waste her batteries.

I got up and went into the bathroom. Black knots of dried blood in my hair looked like bugs. I tried to wash and comb them out at the sink, but it was a tedious and painful process, especially around my left ear. In the end I decided it would be easier simply to shower again.

The shower was faster certainly, but no less painful. Even with a gentle spray the water jets felt like needles on my tenderized skin. I got out of the shower quickly, rebandaged my back, and put on one of my courtroom suits. There was nothing I could do to hide the purple swelling of my ear, so I didn't try. If I was going to make a good impression on Dennis Alsmith, it would have to be by means other than grooming. Think how impressed he'd be when I showed up early for our appointment... Say, by more than a week.

* * *

The Sloane Building is Eola's tallest sky-scraper, a great green finger flipped contemptuously at the sky. Built at a meander of the Eola River, the emerald glass tower is prime office space by any city's standards. From the observation deck restaurant at the top, you can enjoy unparalleled views of the city along with exorbitantly priced cuisine. And if the bill comes as too much of a shock, rest assured the windows are shatterproof for the safety of the restaurant patron and street-level pedestrians alike.

I stood waiting by the Sloane access road, while a red and white ETA bus blew by, belching blue smoke and reeking exhaust. I crossed the narrow street and approached the tower across a wide courtyard of white-pebbled paving stones. Not far from the building's entrance was a small outdoor cafe with a lot of vacant tables. I went past the cafe and pushed through the revolving door into the building's cavernous foyer.

The floor and walls--which stretched up for three stories--looked like rich green marble, the color of money. The ceiling was subtly curved to enhance the crisp echo of footsteps far below. The information and security desks at either side of the entrance to the elevator bay were dark cherry wood and probably worth more than the combined salaries of the employees who manned them. When the Sloane was built, the foyer had been designed to capture the desired image for the whole building: rich, bold, imposing, immense. But most importantly rich.

Lean times, however, had filled the foyer with chintzy souvenir kiosks, fast buck artists, and faster food carts. I plowed through the teeming sea of cheap merchandisers to the elevators and joined a handful of like-dressed people in an "even floors" cab. It was a long slow ride to the fortieth floor but faster than taking the stairs.

Biltmore Assurance and Guarantee was one of several insurance companies whose offices were on this floor. Its entrance was at the end of a long hallway. The glass walls that separated the hallway from the workspaces were all covered by heavy grey curtains with white vinyl backing.

As I went down the corridor, occasional gaps in the curtains revealed a brutal sweatshop of sharp-dressed telemarketers in cramped cubicles, armed with neckrest handsets and small computer screens. They hunched over tiny desks, heads bowed, hands quivering over their keyboards. For many of them, men and women, the narrow three foot horizon of their cubicles seemed a very tight squeeze.

I felt a twinge of sympathy for them but only for a moment. These were the same folks who brought you unwanted phone calls at dinnertime, who left empty messages on answering machines day after day, like professional burglars casing a premises. My hardboiled attitude returned quickly and in spades.

When I came through the doorway into the office, I saw that the Biltmore spaces spread back along both sides of the hall like a "U." The office was filled with the short desk cubicles, all organized into ingenious patterns of rows, squares, diagonals and zigzags. It was a maze epitomized for the modern corporate rat race. Interspersed among the cubicles were several larger modular boxes with windows on two sides and a single door that could be closed for the illusion of privacy. The walls of these offices were considerably taller than the cubicles (though well short of the ceiling) and clearly indicated "big cheese."

An elderly receptionist challenged me at the door: "Hello, sir, may I help you?" It was the same syrupy voice I'd spoken to earlier.

"Yes, I've got an appointment to see Dennis Alsmith."

The pinch-faced woman glanced quickly back at one of the managers' offices. Through its window I could see a tall balding man inside, holding a phone to his head and nodding absently. I don't think his lips moved once while I watched.

The receptionist turned back and looked down at the large calendar on her desk. She shook her head.

"That's funny," she said, frowning, "I don't have any appointments scheduled for right now..."

"Good, then I'm not interrupting. I'll go right in."

I rapped my knuckles twice on her counter with a flourish, and swaggered over to the bald man's office. The receptionist stood up and tried to call me back, but I pushed into his office before she could work up a real protest.

Dennis Alsmith spun around in his swivel chair to look at me. He still held the phone and continued making positive grunts into it. He was tall, or least appeared lanky sitting down. He wore an expensive blue suit and a hand-painted silk tie. His face was square and affable with bushy black eyebrows. The fringe of black hair around his head was grown long and pulled into a short pony tail. As he nodded to me, the reflection of the fluorescent ceiling light moved across his bald pate.

I closed the door and waited as if I belonged there.

Alsmith raised his hand and index finger to show he would just be a minute.

"Listen, I'm sorry, Lars, but I have to go... Yes, it's terrible... Awful thing... No, I don't mind your calling me at a time like this. It's just that I have work to catch up on... The last few days, you know... No, of course she can't. You can tell her from me... Uh-hunh... Uh-hunh."

Alsmith rolled his eyes and gestured at me with his hand to pull up a chair. After several more non-verbal utterances into the phone, he covered the mouthpiece with his hand and said, "Just put those folders on the floor. Sorry about the mess."

I cleared off a beige swivel chair as instructed and sat down opposite him. I looked around the office as I waited. There were several file cabinets against the back wall next to the door. Opposite them, Alsmith's paper-strewn desk was pushed into the cloth covering of the modular wall. The cursor flashed tirelessly on his computer monitor. A metal bookshelf was mounted on brackets above the desk. Alsmith's books all dealt with various spins on management strategy and human resources manipulation. The other two sides of his office-box had large glass windows with no curtains. A few curious employees momentarily raised their heads like grazing cattle and looked in at us.

Contrary to Samantha Alsmith's suspicions, her husband's office offered nothing at all in the way of privacy. The most vigorous "in-out" action this desk was likely to see would be a quick turnaround paper shuffle.

"Really..." Alsmith said to the phone. He looked at me apologetically and rolled his eyes again. "Listen, Lars, I've got a client here. Gotta go... Yes, later... Maybe... Okay, bye-bye."

He hung up the phone and let out a long breath.

"Sorry about that. A friend of mine is having marital problems."

"Lot of that going around," I said.

"Sure is. 'Stay single, young man,' that's my advice. And if it's already too late, then you know what I'm talking about." He grinned to show that he was only joking, but of course, I knew better.

"That's partly why I'm here. I've just been to see your wife."

"Oh, yes?" Dennis Alsmith was still smiling but his voice seemed a shade less friendly.

I took out a business card and gave it to him.

"I'm a private investigator. Nash Tobin."

I extended my hand towards Alsmith. He shifted my card to his left hand and returned my handshake perfunctorily.

"Dennis Alsmith," he said. "Now what business did you have with my wife?"

"It's not what you're thinking, whatever that is. She was in a pretty bad state this morning. A neighbor called me in to look after her since they didn't have your work number."

Alsmith frowned and shook his head slowly.

"She's always in some state or another. I can't go running home for all of them. What was it this time?"

"You can probably guess. The pills she keeps in the kitchen--she took a number of them. On top of a lot of alcohol."

"If that's all, I'm surprised anyone bothered to call. That's pretty standard for her."

"She was also acting very strangely, wandering around your neighborhood looking for your daughter."

"My daughter is dead." Alsmith's voice was firm, almost

stern, but it caught on the last word.

"I know. I'm sorry. I talked with your wife about it some after I took her home."

"So she's all right now?"

"I don't know about all right. She was more or less sober when I left."

"That's something at least. Still, I don't understand why you came to see me. If it's the bill, I can write you a check."

"No. It's not that. I already have a client. Taking Mrs. Alsmith home was just incidental to something else I'm working on. I really came here to talk about your daughter."

"First my wife, now my daughter? What exactly is your interest here, Mr. Tobin?"

"I'm trying to find out what happened to her. Your daughter I mean. I'm working with the police, so you don't need to worry about my interfering with them in any way."

"Are you the one who came to our house Tuesday with that glass... whatever it was?"

"Yes, that's right."

"So, who hired you? Samantha?"

It was my turn to shake my head.

"It was not your wife, but I can't say who it was. Our confidentiality rules are strict, like a lawyer's. Do you want to talk here or should we go someplace more private?"

"Here, I guess. But I wish you'd made an appointment. I came to work today to get away from all that."

"I understand and I promise to be as brief as possible. Now, first of all, I'd like to establish a few things: as I understand it, your daughter died Saturday night. Is that right?"

"Saturday night or early Sunday morning. I don't think they've narrowed it down any closer than that."

"And were you at home during that time-frame?"

Alsmith raised his head and peered at me over a jutting nose.

"What are you implying here?"

"Nothing at all. I'm just asking a question. Trying to get the facts straight."

Alsmith's lips remained tightly closed, while he thought what to say. Finally he answered:

"No, I was not home that night. I was out. Very late. But I imagine you knew that already from Sam. I don't like your trying to trap me. I don't recommend it."

"Okay, then, straight up--where were you?"

Alsmith sucked his lips in against his teeth and looked away from me out the office window. A startled female employee who had been staring in at us, quickly turned back to her desk and began typing.

"I changed my mind," Alsmith said, standing up. "I think we need to take this conversation outside."

"Fine with me."

I stood up and followed Alsmith out of his office, past the receptionist, and down the hallway to the elevators.

"There's a cafe outside. We can talk there," Alsmith said while we waited for the elevator. Then we rode in strained silence all the way down to the ground floor.

We left the foyer and took a cafe table situated far from where the wait staff congregated. The air outdoors was dry and warm, but the table's umbrella kept us shaded from the sun. There were very few other customers and no one near our table. Eventually a waiter sidled over and took our order for two coffees. Then he left.

Even after the waiter was gone, Alsmith kept silent.

I finally prompted him, "I asked you a question up there..."

"I know you did. I'm still thinking about how to answer it. Or whether I should even. I hope you don't believe I could have anything to do with what happened to my little girl? My baby? What that animal did to her!" There was a hitch in his voice like real anguish and his eyes began to mist over. He blinked slowly to keep tears from forming and wiped his eyes and brow with his display handkerchief.

The waiter returned and set two styrofoam cups down on napkins on the table. I gave him money and he went away.

"It's so awful," Alsmith said. "This guilt. Knowing I should have protected her somehow and didn't. Not just Saturday, but all along. I still don't know what I should have done, and I keep going over and over it in my head. But I don't come up with anything. The only thing I'm sure of is, I wasn't there when she needed me. And that will haunt me the rest of my life. Isn't that enough? Do I really have to go into the rest?"

"Like I said, I'm not working for your wife. I'm not interested in your private life. The only reason I need to know who you were with that night is so they can vouch for you."

"You think I need an alibi?! For my own little girl's death?!" His indignant voice was loud enough to carry across the cafe. A few of the other customers turned their heads to see where the outburst came from.

I lowered my voice and hoped Alsmith would follow suit.

"I'm not saying you need one--I'm asking if you have one. It's not the same thing. There are certain allegations I am trying to run down. I don't believe them or disbelieve them. I'm just looking for proof, one way or the other."

"What allegations?"

I took a sip of coffee from my cup.

"What allegations?" he repeated more firmly. "I deserve to know what I am suspected of."

"That's probably true. But if you are going to blurt it all out in public, I think it's a mistake to tell you. For your sake, not mine."

Alsmith gripped the edge of the metal table with his hands. The pressure of his grip created yellow crescents beneath the ends of his fingernails.

"Let me worry about me," he said. "What allegations are you talking about?"

"That maybe your relationship with Rudi was closer than the law allows."

Alsmith tightened his grip on the table, his hands visibly shaking. Blood rushed into his face, turning it a deep red, but almost as quickly, it drained out again, leaving him wan and gaunt. He looked like he was going to be sick.

"God, it's a lie!" he whispered. "A dirty despicable lie! Did Sam tell you that?" I shook my head, but Alsmith ranted on. "You're a fool to listen to her. I loved my daughter more than anything. I should have taken her away from her mother long ago. She's a damn liar and a drunk and a tramp and a ..."

"Enough!" I said. "It wasn't her. Just tell me who you were with that night. That's really all I care about."

Alsmith bit down on his lower lip. A small fly was buzzing around over his head but he either ignored it or didn't notice. At last Alsmith made his decision. He took the napkin from beneath his styrofoam cup and wrote a name and phone number on it inside the coffee-stain circle. He pushed the napkin across the table to me.

"That's her work number. She's married. I can't tell you how bad it would be if this ever got back to her husband. You've got to swear that it won't!"

"Not from me." I read the name in the circle. "Scandinavian?"

"Her husband is," Alsmith said, looking down at the table.

"I see... Lars with marital problems?"

Alsmith closed his eyes, nodded slowly.

I recalled how loyal and protective the tall Scandinavian-looking man had been when he answered the Alsmith's door on Tuesday. If that was Lars, his misplaced loyalty now seemed almost contemptible. But he was not the one who deserved blame. Dennis Alsmith had a lot on his conscience and probably would for a long time to come.

"Okay," I said. "No problem. Is there anything else you can tell me about what happened to your daughter? Do you know who she was with Saturday night?"

Alsmith's voice was low and subdued, "No, I don't have any idea. Rudi was out late Thursday with a guy named Winter. I've never seen him but Sam says he's older than we are. But I don't know about Saturday."

"Did you tell the police about who she was with Thursday?"

"Of course. I told them anything and everything that might help them find the monster who..." He stopped short, not wanting even to say the words.

A soft breeze brought the sound of bird cries across the square and the tangy scent of the river filled the air.

"It's like there's a gaping hole where my life used to be," Dennis Alsmith went on. "With Rudi gone, there's nothing left."

"Your wife said much the same thing." The warm day, the fresh breeze, and the wide open plaza made the world seem a place of infinite possibilities. As if the future was wide open and all one had to do was choose... "You should go to her," I continued. "She needs you."

Alsmith shook his head.

"No. We were a mistake. A huge twenty-three year mistake. We were young and thought she was pregnant. After we got married, it turned out she wasn't. We were lucky even to have Rudi years later." He shook his head and scowled. "A quarter century... All for what?"

"I don't know," I admitted. "Something, but I don't know what."

I looked down at my watch and realized it was past 12:30. I would have to hurry to get to my appointment with Albin Fitch at the university on time.

"I'm sorry to be so abrupt, but I have to get going. Thank you for talking to me. And I am truly sorry about your daughter." I stood up and extended my hand across the table. Alsmith shook it still sitting down.

"I think I'll stay here a bit," he said. "It may take me a while longer to get back into work mode."

I left him sitting alone at the table, staring with a glazed look at nothing at all.

CHAPTER EIGHTEEN

The University of Eola's Biology Department was housed in an eight-story concrete building just outside the college quadrangle. Long thin windows and narrow ventilation chimneys ran up its walls, making it look even taller. As I got out of the car, I realized it was situated directly across from the English Department.

That was where I had seen Rudi Alsmith in the hall while I waited outside Curtiz's office. That had been exactly a week ago, two days before she died. It was strange to think that my only direct connection to her was so mundane and fleeting, and yet I remembered it vividly: her grace and assurance, her striking beauty, her regal half-wave as she told Curtiz goodbye, her enigmatic smile to the boy and me as she passed, her hand diving into her bag for a bus pass. The actions were ordinary enough, but now they took on added significance in my memory. There's nothing like death to give everyday life meaning.

I checked my watch and hastened up the steps to the Biology building entrance. It was 1:15 and I was fifteen minutes late for my appointment.

The building's air-conditioning system was running full-blast and the temperature was downright chilly. Several stuffed birds and mammals in display cases stared at me icily. The classrooms along the main hallway that crossed in front of the entrance were all empty and dark. A wide staircase with a heavy iron balustrade wound upwards and down on my right.

A large board on the left wall listed the professors' names, office numbers, and specialties. The office for "Fitch, A.--Entomology" was in the basement so I took the staircase down.

His office was at the far end of a long corridor with cinderblock walls and a cement floor. A small notecard beside the door read "Albin Fitch Ph.D., Entomology, Forensic and Otherwise." Two sturdy locks were built into the metal door and a large magnetic sign was stuck to it: "Authorized personnel only, all others KEEP OUT!"

Authorized by my appointment, I knocked and waited. It wasn't until I knocked harder a second time that I heard shuffling footsteps on the other side and the sound of two deadbolts being opened.

The man who opened the door filled the doorway. Over six and a half feet tall, his huge body was even more remarkable than his height. You see pictures of four hundred pound wrestlers or football players on television, but it doesn't prepare you for the physical presence such men get from their size alone. This man was no athlete but he was still imposing enough. His rumpled olive drab jacket could have been used for a pup-tent and his hand-knotted bow tie must have been nearly as long as one of my regular ties just to get around his neck.

The man's head was bald as a bullet. His bland, small-featured face was pasty white and grub-like as if he spent too much time in the dark confines of the basement. His mistrustful grey eyes squinted down at me. If I'd been forced to guess the man's profession from his appearance, my first pick would be serial axe murderer--the kind fellow prisoners dub "Tiny."

He stood barring the door with his bulk, waiting for me to explain my intrusion.

"I'm here to see Albin Fitch," I said. "I have an appointment."

"First I've heard of it. And I am Albin Fitch."

"I arranged it yesterday... With the girl at the biology desk..." There was no reaction, no shift in his combative posture. "I talked to her over the phone. She assured me there would be no..."

Fitch cut me off: "The circumstances are irrelevant since, as I said, I know nothing about it. Who are you and what do you want?"

"My name is Nash Tobin. I'm a private investigator. I was hoping to ask you some questions about the autopsy on Rudi Alsmith. I understand you took part?"

Fitch's brow relaxed.

"Autopsy, eh? So you're not a student. That's fine then. I should have known from the suit. You've no idea how they pester me. Price of fame, of course." As an afterthought, he reached out a large flabby white hand which I shook. "Come in, come in. I am in the middle of lunch, but you may join me if you wish."

He moved aside and I stepped into the room, which was noticeably warmer than the hallway.

Fitch closed the door behind me and turned both deadbolts home.

"Security," he explained. "I do a lot of work with the police and have to preserve the integrity of my evidence."

I nodded and glanced around Doctor Fitch's laboratory.

The room was very large but seemed cramped and untidy. Stainless steel cabinets with black formica counters lined the walls, and matching counter islands and lab tables took up much of the floor space. Rows of fluorescent lights hung from the low ceiling, offering little clearance for Fitch's head. The floor was black vinyl tiling, except for occasional patches of revealed concrete where a tile corner had come unglued or where a tile was missing entirely.

The tables and countertops were covered with scientific glassware and other paraphernalia. There were huge jars, stoppered bottles, dry aquariums with black-painted light bulbs fixed to their sides, smaller jars with mesh covers, and display boxes full of pinned insect specimens. Fitch also had several microscopes, each one with its own assortment of scalpels, picks, tweezers, and other accoutrements. Various local ordinance and weather maps, illustrated insect books, and hand-plotted charts were strewn around the tables and sometimes under them.

But what struck me most was the incessant noise engulfing the lab, a loud buzzing that was steady in pitch and volume but which shifted subtly in its apparent direction.

It seemed to come mostly from the far end of the room where a ten-foot cage had been constructed from cheap planks and gauze cloth. Dozens of black dots appeared momentarily on the gauze wall and then disappeared again. Similar dots appeared inside the aquariums all around the room, some crawling on the walls of their glass prisons, others flying clumsily into them.

They were flies. Hundreds of them. Maybe thousands. Fitch was raising flies, and the sound of their beating wings filled the air.

I looked at the doctor, my distaste evident on my face.

"You're surprised by the noise," Fitch said in a loud voice. "Most people are. I don't even hear it anymore. When I'm someplace else that's truly quiet, it strikes my ears all wrong. As if something is missing. Come, please..."

I followed him across the room to the counter where the doctor's lunch was set out. Fitch straddled a tall metal stool and plopped his heft down on its narrow seat, like a chicken on an upright roasting stand.

I pulled another stool up to the counter and sat down.

Fitch picked up a plastic fork and plunged it into a mound of brown rice and mixed fruit on a paper plate. The fork looked puny in his large hand. He leaned forward and lifted the fork nimbly to his mouth. Before he even began chewing, he brought it back down again to reload.

"You don't mind if I eat?" he asked with his mouth still full of food. I turned away. The rice looked alive on his tongue.

"No, go ahead," I said.

Unfortunately, my averted gaze fell upon a tall open jar beside his plate. At the base of the jar was a churning layer of sand-colored maggots several inches deep. They resembled the rice so closely that I did a reluctant double-take at Fitch's plate. If any maggots got out onto his salad, he'd never be able to tell.

Noting my interest in his dinner, he pushed his plate forward.

"Actually, you're welcome to have some. My wife gives me much more than one man can possibly eat. And as you see, I've no dearth of girth..."

"That's all right. I'm not hungry." My stomach did barrel rolls at the thought.

Fitch nodded and chewed. To save time, he talked simultaneously.

"You're interested in that gravel yard girl, right? Alsmith, Rudi?"

"That's right. I talked to Detective Clark and he said the final autopsy report isn't out yet. But he mentioned that you were working on it, so I came here to see if you have any preliminary results."

"Detective Clark sent you here?"

"He asked me to help out, yes."

Misdirection is an art. The only better way to lie with the truth is to use statistics.

"I suppose it's okay, then," Fitch said. "What did you have in mind?"

"Well, for example, when did she die? And how?... And, if you know, who killed her?"

Fitch honked loudly and sprayed rice particles down his jacket and into his ample lap.

"You don't want much, do you?" he said. He stood up and brushed himself off. "Stay here. I'll see what I can do."

Fitch went over to a cabinet at the back of the room and pulled open a drawer. He carefully dialed a combination on the locked strongbox inside and withdrew a manila folder. He pushed the drawer closed and came back to his stool, clutching the folder in his hand.

"Now, without written authorization from Detective Clark, I cannot let you see or touch this," he said. "But I can describe its contents."

"That's fine."

"Let me just refresh my memory..."

He opened the folder and set it down beside his plate. He continued eating as he read. Whatever gory details the file may have contained had no effect on his appetite.

From where I sat, I could see at the top of the first page two line diagrams of a woman's body, front and back view. There was typewritten text below the diagrams, but I was too far away to read it. Someone had marked the wrists and ankles in the picture with small black X's, or perhaps the original ink had been some other color and this document was a photocopy. In the rear-view picture, a dotted line extended up across the back from the buttocks to the left side of the neck. A second, much shorter line intersected the long one at the very top, cutting obliquely across the back of the neck. There were also a number of black marks or spots drawn on the shoulders, arms, and back. The face was obliterated under a scourge of hashmarks and splotches.

The diagram wasn't all in black and white. The nose, eyes, and ears were marked with a green marker, and the short line on the back of the neck was also marked in green. The pubic and anal areas were marked in red and green.

Fitch turned the page over and glanced through the closely typed text. As he read, he grunted occasionally and referred to three pages of photographs paper-clipped to the back cover of the folder. I couldn't see much from where I sat, but they looked like Polaroid shots taken at the autopsy and then reproduced on a color copier.

From what I could see, most of the pictures showed bruises and welts all over the victim's body. Rudi's skin, already pale when she was alive, took on a faintly green hue tinged with red under the autopsy room lights. The purple-black contusions were deep and distinct.

As Fitch turned to the third page of photographs, I glimpsed something I will never forget. It caught my eye in the instant that the page flipped and was gone because it was different from the other shots. Most of the photographs were cold, clinical, greenish in cast, but this one had a warm glow, like a red chrysanthemum in the sun. Only after the photo flashed by was my brain able to draw the image together and make sense of it.

The red chrysanthemum petals were flayed flesh of what had been a human face. The lips, nose, and eyelids were razed off. Eyeballs, surprisingly intact, stared out sightless and wired. The jaw was clenched tight. Exposed teeth, cracked and streaked with blood, looked like a broken zipper. The dark pit in the center of the face where a nose had been was filled with bristling white grains of rice. A yellow-white crust had formed beneath the staring eyes, like a century's accretion of sleep dust. My mind rebelled at the thought that this grotesque mask, could be the same beautiful, intelligent girl I'd seen less than a week ago.

"It's not her," I said, giving voice to an absurd hope. "I mean, what if it's not her?"

Fitch didn't even look up from the sheets. "Oh, it's her, all right. The dental records prove it. A shame, too. They say she was a real beauty."

Of course, it was Rudi. Russell Morgan at the gravel yard had said the dead girl was really messed up by the rocks shooting off the conveyor belt. Now that I knew what he meant, I wished I didn't.

Professor Fitch sighed and closed the folder. He picked up his paper plate and scraped the few remaining food particles into the maggot jar. The scraps quickly sank into the squirming mass at the bottom. He screwed a cover onto the jar and tossed the plate and fork into a short metal waste basket beside him.

"Now then, according to the deputy coroner," Fitch began, stressing the word deputy with some disdain, "The victim died sometime on Saturday or very early Sunday morning. Of course, he originally estimated time of death as being anywhere between late Friday night and Sunday morning... But never mind. He prudently revised that estimate when he found out the girl'd been seen alive on Saturday morning.

"Using my methods, I have narrowed that time frame down considerably. As I told your detective friend yesterday, the girl died sometime at night on Saturday the 14th. With further refinements, my current results indicate a time of death between 10 p.m. Saturday and 1 a.m. Sunday."

I took out my notebook and pen.

"And how did you get those results?"

Fitch held up his hand. "Let's start with the coroner's version, shall we, while I've got it in my head. I can explain my methods afterwards... And save the best for last."

I nodded and let him continue.

"So the deputy coroner says sometime Saturday or early Sunday," he repeated. "When she was found Monday morning, her body had already reached ambient temperature and rigor mortis was completely resolved. There was advanced skin color change, but bloating had not yet begun... Are you with me?"

He paused to see if I was following him. I was. Sort of. At

least I recognized the words as English. But when I looked at my notebook page, it was as blank as my face must have been.

Fitch sighed audibly.

"You see, after death, there is a pattern of postmortem changes that takes place within a body. These changes are not like clockwork, of course; there are wide variations for when each stage occurs, but the stages themselves follow a predictable order and, broadly speaking, a predictable schedule.

"When a person dies, their heart stops beating. The blood stops flowing through the circulatory system. Body temperature starts to fall by 1 to 2 degrees Fahrenheit per hour in most cases. So it takes a while for the body temperature to fall from 98.6 to the same temperature as its surrounding environment--what is called the ambient temperature. After that, the corpse is warmed or cooled according to its local conditions like any other inanimate object. The point is, in this case, when the gravel yard girl was found, she had been dead long enough to have lost all of her animate body heat."

I nodded.

Fitch went on: "Similarly, rigor mortis takes time to become fully established. And then, contrary to popular belief, it also 'resolves' or dissipates with time, leaving the body completely flaccid."

"Okay. And you said the rigor was completely resolved when they found her," I said, a shade impatiently. "How long does that take?"

He shrugged.

"Unfortunately, it varies. More than a day usually. Around thirty hours. Longer if it's cold out."

"Okay, so if Rudi was found, say, at 7:00 Monday morning, that means she died somewhere between twenty-four and thirty hours before. Right?"

"It doesn't work that way. After rigor mortis stops,

decomposition changes are harder to gauge. That's why the coroner couldn't place time of death with any more precision than he did. The best he could do is say that death probably took place more than a day before she was found. At the same time, it was doubtful she could have died earlier than three days previously because the body had not started to bloat. Decomposition gases, you know."

The professor burped loudly and patted his chest. "Excuse me!"

The scent of his pungent rice salad wafted over in my direction. I turned my head and held my breath momentarily.

"So anywhere between 30 and 72 hours," I said. "That's a span of nearly two days. What makes you so sure she died late Saturday night?"

"I will get to that," he promised. "In good time. You also asked about how she died..."

Fitch paused for a moment. His voice became lower and his face turned more serious. The dark bags beneath his eyes looked like pits.

"The body was badly beaten. It cannot have been pleasant... There were bruises all over, but especially on the arms and back. And her left clavicle was broken." Fitch opened the autopsy folder to the photographs and, with his index finger, flicked each photo that showed the bruises. His finger continued its tattoo (flick, flick, flick, flick) as he resumed talking. "Brutal," he said, shaking his head sadly, "Just brutal. She tried to protect herself, to ward off the blows, but in the end she was overpowered.

"The coroner also found evidence of coital activity. And she had recently been sodomized as well. Whether this was consensual or forced is not clear. The beating, of course, indicates a violent rape, but the possibility remains that it is unrelated. I expect to hear very soon about the blood type of her partner. Or rather, the other involved party."

Fitch paused. "Are you writing any of this down?"

I glanced at my still blank notebook sheet. My pen hand was shaking.

"Of course," I said. "It's just, I saw her before she died. I talked with people who knew her, saw what her death has done to them. Hearing what she went through makes me want to strike back somehow. But... we can't do anything." My indignation was actually stronger than my words let on. Rudi's death had been an outrage.

"Not unless we catch him," Fitch pointed out, his grey eyes burning. This obscure specialty was not just Fitch's academic niche, it was his quest for justice. A crusade for an unlikely crusader, eccentric, single-minded, intense. Despite appearances, I decided, Professor Fitch had a nobility that was easy to miss.

When I caught up with my notes, he began again:

"The actual cause of death was cardiac and respiratory failure brought on by a massive overdose of cocaine, with some traces of PCP as well. The deputy coroner said she had just about the highest cocaine concentration in her blood that he'd ever seen. He joked that if 'Rudi Red' were on the street, dealers would have to cut it first. And there was still a lot of cocaine powder left unabsorbed in her nasal cavity. There was no possible way the dose would not have been fatal."

Fitch stopped. It took me a while to grasp what he was driving at.

"You think it was deliberate, then?" I asked.

"Certainly deliberate. Whether she took it herself willingly or was forced, we don't know."

"Forced? How?"

Fitch raised a meaty hand into the air, fingers formed into the shape of a gun, and pointed it at my head.

"You give an addict the choice: a bullet in the brain or one last unbelievable high. They'll take the dope every time. There have also been cases where an immobilized victim's mouth is taped shut and a bag of cocaine held over their nose. When he or she runs out of air, the victim can't help inhaling the fatal dose. Superficially, the death looks like an ordinary overdose. If the police don't notice the slight bruising on the face or find cocaine traces on the skin, the killer gets away with murder. But in this case, there wasn't enough face left for us to tell."

"But you say it is possible Rudi killed herself deliberately? Willingly?" Mrs. Sachett had said that somewhere deep inside, Rudi wanted to die. Somehow the thought that she could do this to herself seemed even worse than the alternative.

Fitch was pensive for a moment.

"I need to be very careful about what I say and how I say it. I learned my lesson a long time ago the hard way, testifying in court. When I say something is possible, I mean just that and no more. It doesn't mean I believe that it happened.

"It is possible she took a fatal dose as a deliberate, uncoerced act of suicide. But several factors weigh against it. She did not beat herself black and blue--someone else did that. She did not break her own shoulder. And, obviously, she never tied herself up or took herself to the gravel yard after she was dead."

"You didn't say anything about her being tied up."

"You interrupted. Before her body was taken there, it was bound into a very tight ball, knees against her chest, hands tied to her feet, and her head held down between her knees by a rope across the back of her neck. The rope marks on the body were very distinctive. Police have seen the same marks before on a couple of prostitutes who were killed for cheating their handlers, and also once on a small-statured gangster who double-crossed the wrong group of friends. Tied up like that and bundled in a bed sheet, a small body can fit easily inside a large garbage bag. They call it 'taking out the trash.'"

"And that's what happened to Rudi?"

Fitch nodded, his pale lips pressed tight together.

I scowled. To treat an eighteen-year-old girl like a bag of garbage... Like she was just another item to sort and separate from the recyclables. It seemed such a pointless indignity. But to Rudi, of course, it could not have made any difference.

A niggling thought occurred to me.

"If she was tied up in a sheet and garbage bag, how did her arm get caught on the conveyor belt?"

"Somebody untied her before they put her there. We found a knife wound across the back of her neck from when they cut the rope."

"Oh," was all I could think of to say. I had had enough. I was tired of the tawdry details of death. Tired of the way human beings treated each other. Tired of the stupid, senseless brutality that had become so common that people accepted it as natural and unavoidable. I was tired of the whole sorry spectacle of humanity. We were an experiment gone wrong and overripe for termination.

I thought of the whiskey bottle in my apartment. I wanted to crawl into my hole and drown myself in oblivion. Maybe Rudi's mother was right. Any form of escape from the howling waste was all we could hope for and more than we could expect.

The best things in life are still bad.

I stood up and extended my hand to Fitch.

"Well, professor, I think I've heard enough. Thank you for your time. It has been very enlightening."

Fitch's face suddenly became concerned.

"But you can't go yet," he said. "We haven't got to the good part!"

CHAPTER NINETEEN

"The good part?" I asked. "What could possibly be good in all this?"

"The flies, man! The flies!" Fitch said. "Come have a look."

He raised himself off his stool and lumbered over to one of the dry aquariums on a nearby table. He checked the tag, which was tied to its wire-screen cover, and removed the lid. He pulled out a foil pouch and gently brushed sand from its bottom. With a set of forceps, he carefully pried open the pouch's crimped top.

"These larvae were taken from the corpse at autopsy."

"You mean Rudi's?"

"Of course."

Once he got the pouch open, he reached in with the forceps and gingerly pulled out a small white worm. He placed it in the center of a medium-sized petri dish and handed it to me.

"Watch him," he said, closing the pouch and replacing it in the aquarium. "Don't let him get away. I've got to boil some water."

Fitch returned to the counter we had just left and began to fill a flask at the sink.

I glanced down at my charge in the glass dish. The maggot was about half the width of my pinky fingernail. It wiggled some but did not seem eager to go anywhere.

Not half as eager as I was anyway. I looked over at Fitch but saw no sign he was kidding. A new low, I thought. Reduced to baby-sitting maggots.

Fitch set the flask of water on a stand over a bunsen burner and lit the flame.

"Now, remember, you must watch that thing," he warned.

I turned back to the petri dish. The worm had moved and was already climbing up the side wall. I grabbed a long-handled cotton swab and brushed the creature back to the dish's center.

Looking closely, I could see that the maggot resembled a miniature caveman's club, thick at one end and tapering to a point at the other. As I watched, it started to make another break for it, pushing itself backwards towards the edge of the dish. It moved surprisingly quickly. Using my swab, I pushed it back again.

"Why does it move backwards?" I asked.

"It doesn't. The pointed end is the head, not the tail. He pulls himself forward with his mouth." After a pause Fitch asked, "How much do you know about forensic entomology, anyway?"

"Not much. Just that it has to do with using insects to estimate time of death."

"Mostly, yes. Strictly speaking it covers any application of entomology to legal matters. In practice, though, we spend most of our time trying to determine the time and place of death based on the insect evidence, which usually means flies. And that's what this is all about." He stood up straight and gestured all around at his buzzing laboratory. "Did you ever wonder why flies are attracted to dead things?"

I hadn't, actually.

"For food?"

"Partly, yes, but that's not the whole story. Adult flies can live on a lot of things. But a decaying carcass, human or otherwise, provides an ideal food source for their maggots. Female flies deposit their eggs on corpses so the larvae will have plenty to eat when they hatch out and start to feed."

Fitch smiled, adding, "And they are voracious creatures! Maggots can consume a pig carcass in just five days... And increase in size a thousandfold doing it. It's a marvelous thing to watch. Absolutely marvelous."

"I'm sure that it is."

"And they are so under-appreciated. They play a crucial role in breaking down complex body tissue quickly and efficiently but no one ever thinks about that. Without maggots to devour the dead, the world would sink under a mountainous layer of half-decayed putrid flesh."

Beneath the hyperbole, there was no question that Fitch had a genuine respect and fondness for the species he studied. He made them sound like an environmentalist's dream pet—feed a maggot, save the world!

I looked down at my little friend in the petri dish. Come to think of it, he was kind of cute. He wriggled smartly but stayed in place. Either he was getting tired or he was trying to lull me into a false sense of security.

"So how does it work?" I asked. "I mean, what can you learn from the insects on a body?"

"A tremendous amount," Fitch said, still waiting for the water to boil. "Most of the flies we deal with only lay their eggs on dead tissue. And since we know how long it takes the eggs and larvae to develop, a close examination of the maggots can tell us a lot about the time of death. Put simply, we can get a good idea of when the person died by determining how old the maggots are.

"Unfortunately, that's not always easy. Maggot development depends a lot on heat, so we need very detailed information on the prevailing temperatures. If we're lucky and the temperature was relatively constant, then we can estimate the maggot's age just by measuring its length... Which is what we are about to do now."

The water in Fitch's flask was beginning to boil. Air bubbled up slowly through the wide bell portion of the flask and then raced furiously through its narrow neck. Fitch turned off the gas burner and attempted to pick up the flask with his fingers.

"Frass!" he cursed, setting the flask down. "Sass'n frass!" He stuck his finger into his mouth, blew on it, and waved it through the air.

He reached up to one of the cabinets above the sink and brought down a large grey oven mitt to put on his right hand. On him, it looked like a normal-sized winter mitten. He picked up the flask with the mitt and came over to me.

"Okay, set him down on the table."

I put the petri dish down. The maggot raised its tiny head almost expectantly. Fitch tipped the flask and poured the scalding water directly on top of him. The creature lurched madly for an instant before it died, then floated to the surface.

"That gets him to his full length," Fitch explained, "So we can measure him."

Fitch took off his mitt. He scooped the boiled maggot out of the dish and put it on a microscope slide. Placing the slide under a microscope lens, he bent over the eyepiece and twisted the focus knob on the side. When he had the proper focus, he made some final adjustments by turning the eyepiece.

"Four millimeters," he said, pulling his head back. "Right on schedule. Have a look."

I moved over to the microscope and looked down into it. The magnified maggot was at the center of the view. It was creamy white and segmented. At the pointed front end, certain dark structures were barely perceptible through the smooth skin. A series of ruled marks was lined up alongside the worm's image. The maggot was exactly four of the marked lines long.

"I'm surprised," I said. "It looks so clean."

Fitch chuckled. "Yes, considering it was born and reared on excrement."

He picked up the microscope slide and brushed the maggot into a small test tube in a rack. He started collecting small bottles of chemicals and measuring tiny amounts of them into a small beaker. He sat down at his stool and continued to speak as he worked, interrupting his lecture only when his chemical measurements took more concentration than what he was saying.

"That maggot was one of the oldest taken from the victim," he said. "From the rectal area. A Musca domestica larva—a baby housefly—at approximately the 4-day growth stage. Probably a shade less. Taking into account the hours the girl's body was kept in the morgue cooler, I estimate that this maggot hatched mid Sunday morning."

Fitch became silent as he swirled the chemicals together in the beaker and poured the clear liquid into the test tube with the maggot. He stopped up the tube with a small cork. He filled out a label in a small cramped hand and pinned the string of the label to the cork top.

"Now, then," he said, turning around on his stool to face me. "Housefly eggs hatch fairly quickly on a very fresh corpse because of its retained body temperature. Based on my experiments, they take somewhere between eight and eleven hours. That means the eggs were laid late Saturday night, sometime between 10 p.m. and 1 a.m. And since they were laid quite soon after the girl died, I am fairly confident the time of death falls within that same period."

He folded his hands in his lap and smiled. His attitude was more than "fairly confident," it oozed professional certainty. It was the same self-assured posture expert witnesses are trained to use in the courtroom and I had seen it used by too many expert liars to let it pass unchallenged here.

"That sounds like circular logic to me. You assume the eggs

were laid soon after Rudi's death and then base your calculations on how long it takes the eggs to develop on a still-warm corpse. What if she actually died earlier? The body would be cooler, and it would take the eggs longer to hatch, right?" Fitch nodded. "So, even if they did hatch on Sunday morning when you say they did, how can you be so sure about when they were laid on the body?"

"Excellent question! In fact, that is what makes this case so interesting. You see, it is highly unusual for the housefly to be the first species to deposit its eggs on a body. Especially on a fresh corpse. It almost never happens.

"Other flies like the bluebottle, or greenbottle, or Phormia regina are much better adapted at finding the victim earlier and faster. They can smell a dead body from a mile away, and, believe me, it doesn't take them long to get to it once they do. Sometimes they deposit their eggs just minutes after death occurs. And they are so persistent! I've even seen them get at a body that was locked inside a car trunk." Fitch shook his head at the wonder of it.

"At this time of year," the professor continued, "We would expect Calliphora vicina, the bluebottle fly, to arrive first to lay its eggs. It tolerates low temperatures better than the others. And, in fact, we found Calliphora vicina eggs and maggots on the body as well, but they weren't as old as the Musca domestica ones. Here, I can show you..."

Fitch went over to the cabinet where he had got the autopsy report earlier. He unlocked a different drawer and pulled out what looked like a white cardboard cakebox. As he brought it back to the counter, the contents of the box clinked with jiggled glass. He set the box down and pulled open the top.

"I preserved this bluebottle maggot this morning," he said, pulling a test tube out of the box and handing it to me. A similar label to the one he had just filled out was attached to the cork stopper. "It was taken from inside the victim's ear."

Fitch had an unpleasant habit of explaining which body part each maggot came from. Between that and his table manners, I guessed he didn't get asked to many dinner parties.

I held the test tube up towards the light and examined the large maggot inside. This one was much bigger than the housefly larva and consequently more repellent. It was nearly as long as the width of my thumb and thick and clumsy-looking. Like the housefly maggot, it was a creamy white color, blunt at one end and pointed at the other. But the segments on the bluebottle larva were obvious to the naked eye. Immersed in liquid like that, it reminded me of the agave worm in a mezcal bottle. I had the unwelcome, yet distinct, tactile impression of what it would be like to bite on one--how it would compress like a grape between my teeth before bursting. It left a bad feeling in my mouth. I shook my head to dispel the image and handed the test tube back to Fitch.

"I thought you said the housefly was older," I said. "This one is much bigger."

"That's a difference in species," Fitch explained. "Calliphora vicina is a much larger fly. This maggot's development is just under three days, one day younger than the Musca domestica." Fitch placed both the bluebottle and housefly maggots in the test tube rack in the box.

"For your question, though, a more important difference between them is what attracts each species to a body. Calliphora vicina is attracted to carrion, plain and simple. Its maggots feed on the moist inner tissue of the body. That is why it lays its eggs in the orifices of the face--it gives the young easy access to the soft insides.

"The housefly on the other hand, is not interested in fresh carrion per se; it is drawn to fecal matter. Houseflies love excrement. So when the dead girl's bowels loosened, as often happens in the moments after death, it attracted a housefly to deposit its eggs in and around the rectum. After they hatched, those maggots also migrated inward, colonizing the anus and the uro-genital region."

It was not a pretty picture. Whoever coined the phrase "death with dignity" obviously did not know much about either.

"The key point here," Fitch went on, "Is that only the housefly was able to oviposit--lay its eggs--on the victim's body Saturday night. If the body had been available for a longer time, as you suggested, one of the other fly species would certainly have gotten to it and laid eggs as well. The fact that they didn't shows that the girl hadn't been dead very long when the housefly found her. And her body must have been wrapped up shortly thereafter which kept the other flies from finding her."

"So what's the bottom line?" I asked. "What does all this tell us?"

"Several things," Fitch said, counting each point on his fingers. "One, that time of death was late Saturday, between 10 p.m. and 1 a.m., as I said. That's a much narrower window than the coroner's office came up with. Two, at this time of year, Musca domestica would only be active indoors, so the victim probably died indoors. Three, although the body was left outside at the gravel yard, the housefly eggs continued to develop through the night, kept warm by the victim's ebbing body heat. However, most fly activity is greatly reduced at night, especially when the temperatures are lower. That's why the bluebottles didn't show up until the next morning."

He paused for a moment and gave me a searching look. Satisfied that I wasn't completely baffled, he continued.

"OK. So at mid morning Sunday, the housefly eggs began to hatch. The eggs from the second wave of flies, the Calliphora vicina, took longer to develop because the body temperature was lower. A few of them had hatched out by early Monday morning, but most of their eggs were still intact when the body was brought to the morgue."

I nodded slowly in acknowledgement.

"Very impressive," I said.

Fitch smiled. "Well, there was one tricky thing about the fly evidence."

He took another test tube out of the cakebox and gave it to me.

"What do you think of this little beauty? So plump, just brimming with life..." Fitch made it sound like a prize tomato.

I glanced at the label first and saw that it was another Calliphora vicina maggot, this time taken from Rudi's nasal cavity. I thought of the picture of Rudi's face from the autopsy and suddenly understood that the white grains I'd seen in her nose had been fly eggs.

I swallowed hard before looking at the white worm in the tube.

A good thing, too. The first bluebottle maggot had been repugnant enough. This one was downright loathsome. It was even longer than its sibling, but so bloated and engorged, it was almost obscene. Its fat body seemed about ready to burst from internal pressure. The urge to dump the creature to the floor and mash it beneath my shoe was very strong.

Instead, I handed it back to Fitch.

"Very nice," I said.

Professor Fitch's face fell slightly at my reaction.

"Well," he said, "The nose maggots had me stumped at first. Based on its size and development, this fellow should be over four days old. He looks even older than the Musca domestica ones." He held up the test tube to look at it.

"So what's the problem? You said the bluebottles should have got to the body first. Now it looks like they did after all..."

I knew I was missing something. Fitch would never have

overlooked something so obvious.

Fitch shook his head. "That maggot is the same age as the one we pulled from her ear. He only appears a day older. Somehow...," he paused for emphasis, shaking the test tube, "... This one has gone through massively accelerated growth. Something made it grow much larger and faster than nature intended."

"What could do that?" I asked.

Fitch waited a beat before answering triumphantly:

"Cocaine! It's like steroids for maggots!" His pasty face beamed with pleasure at the analogy. "For some strange reason, cocaine has the effect of speeding up the growth and development of maggots. This maggot, along with some others from her nose, fed on tissue that was completely saturated with the drug. And you see the result, a fat little emperor maggot."

"And I suppose it would have grown into a blow fly," I said.

"Yes, of course," Fitch said. "Calliphora vicina is a blow fly..."

He didn't get it and I didn't bother to elaborate. A joke that needs to be explained was probably not worth making in the first place.

"Yes, of course..." Fitch repeated, almost embarrassed. He put the cocaine maggot test tube back in the box and retrieved the autopsy report from the counter. He closed the box and put the folder with the report on top of it. He stood up.

"Well, I'm afraid that's all I can tell you," he said. "So if there's nothing else, I am rather busy right now..." His tone was curt, almost as abrupt as when he'd first opened the door and mistook me for a student. But, then, I had missed the awkwardness that lay hidden behind his gruff bluster. Whenever the discussion veered away from insects, or flies, or death, or some other subject Fitch felt equally comfortable with, he became brusque and defensive. Like a beached whale, the big man floundered in the shallow shoals of social nicety that most of us take for granted. He beetled his brow in an attempt to look stern, but his sad, grey eyes looked lost and forlorn underneath. He held out his hand awkwardly for me to shake.

"Thank you," I said, taking it. "I hope we meet again sometime."

"Perhaps, perhaps," Fitch said. "Now, if you'll excuse me..."

"Of course," I said. "I understand."

He followed me to the door.

"Thanks again," I said, as I stepped through. "And goodbye."

Fitch merely nodded and closed the door behind me. Walking down the hallway, I could hear the two deadbolts being shot home as Fitch locked himself away once more. Then there was only the sound of my footsteps on the cold concrete floor.

CHAPTER TWENTY

I had a bowl of soup at a university coffee shop and considered my next step. From what Fitch had told me and what I'd seen in the autopsy pictures, I doubted Rudi was killed by a stranger. The intense beating she received had been deliberate, vicious, and personal. The perpetrator knew Rudi enough to want to dominate and humiliate her completely. The power-trip of forcibly raping her was not enough. He had beaten her down until she was as limp and pliant as a dishrag--the psychic equivalent of a killing as prelude to the real thing.

Having spoken with Rudi's father, I doubted that he was the perpetrator, but I called the woman whose number he gave me to make sure. She took a lot of persuading but eventually did confirm his alibi.

Which left me in a quandary. My first thought was to try Roger Thornton again. Thornton was clearly a suspect, given his threats last night and the two hoods who tried to warn me off the case that morning. If Rudi's body had been wrapped up and dumped in the style of a local gang killing, then Thornton, Hardison, and Gerrara, were all probably part of that gang.

Which was enough to give me second thoughts, even third ones. To go against Thornton now would be a blatant affront, an open admission that I was thumbing my nose at Hardison and Gerrara’s warning. A challenge like that would not go unpunished.

On the other hand, if I ignored my best lead because I was afraid of the consequences, I might as well take the safe route and quit altogether. Why should I risk my neck for a girl who was already dead? What was it to me if Rudi's victimizers got away with murder? And even if Rudi had run afoul of Thornton's gang, that didn't prove they were the ones blackmailing Curtiz...

But I sensed there was a lot more at stake here than my neck or Curtiz's reputation. To today's ears, ideals like justice, truth, or duty may sound hopelessly abstract or quaint. As does the old notion that what we allow against others we accept against ourselves by proxy. But if we internalize those ideas— if we live them— they become visceral. They become a powerful force, more irresistible than a terrorist shrapnel bomb as it tears through a crowded marketplace, or a stormtrooper's boot heel as it crushes a baby's soft skull. Our ideals allow us to stand up in the face of evil. Without them, we are no better than animals, with no object of faith greater than ourselves.

When I finished my soup and left the small eatery, my path was clear. A little fear can sometimes be healthy, but moral cowardice never is.

* * *

The phone book address for Roger Thornton brought me to a run-down apartment complex located just across the river from Shakytown. The four-story blond-brick buildings were crammed tightly together, leaving no room for balconies. The sidewalks that passed between them were nearly choked by overgrown hedges. Even windows had been doled out sparingly, as if sheet glass were a precious commodity. The complex was crowded, dingy, and depressing. Either the owners didn't give a damn and the residents had given up trying, or it was the other way around.

Across the street to the west of the apartment complex was a derelict city park. It was mostly covered with trees but had a few open areas of unmowed grass and weeds. Abandoned by the city, the park had become a haven for the drunks, drug-dealers, addicts, hookers, and johns that no one wanted anywhere else.

This crime-infested neighborhood featured regularly in newspaper police reports. Its shabby surroundings were an object lesson that crime does not pay. At least, not very well.

It was just after 3 p.m. when I arrived. I tried the buzzer for Thornton's apartment but there was no response. I went back to my parked car and waited.

There were only a few vehicles in the parking lot and most of them were inoperable. Flat or missing tires, broken headlights, cracked windows, hoods open to the elements, all seemed to be part of the local "standard options" package. The car next to mine was a once-dapper convertible whose roof, doors, and engine had all been removed. Its leather upholstery was cracked and dry, and rust stains had formed on the pavement beneath it. The parking lot was an old-beater graveyard. Now my Impala knew where to come to die.

I continued to wait.

As the afternoon wore on, several people came and went from the entrance to Thornton's building. Most of the residents looked elderly and poor. One old woman was frankly demented. She approached the door, waving her arms in the air and arguing loudly with someone or something that wasn't there.

Eventually, the sun started to descend behind distant high-rises. Their lengthening shadows crept slowly across the bright autumn leaves in the park. Intense orange and scarlet maples, smoldering red oaks, bright yellow birches, all blazed like licks of flame in the sun's dying rays. It was a spectacle that would have given Nero something to fiddle about. But finally, the shadows stretched across to the apartment complex and snuffed out the park completely.

The apartment buildings looked grey and dreary in the

lowering dusk. The brown eaves under their roofs turned to hazy black.

It was fully dark out when I spotted a hulking figure coming out of the park across the street. The man marched forward with long strides, his hands thrust deep in his pockets. He wore a long green coat that swayed and billowed behind him with each swaggering step. As he came beneath a streetlamp, his close-cropped copper-red hair seemed to grab the light and hold it for an instant before he passed again into the gloom.

He looked like a muscle-bound punk, which matched Mrs. Alsmith's description of Thornton exactly.

I got out of the car and walked slowly towards the entrance. From the few glances I had of him, I saw at once that Thornton would be trouble. Even at rest, his boxy face was twisted into a snarl. He had a tall, powerful build with bulked-up shoulders and a thick neck. Quite young, he looked like a high school athlete who could pound holes in brick walls with his square head. Beneath his unbuttoned coat he wore faded blue-jeans and a dark shirt with a pack of cigarettes in the breast pocket. I heard the heavy clop-clop of his black lace-up boots as they pounded the cement.

When I reached the short sidewalk leading to the entrance, I turned and waited for him.

From ten yards away, he narrowed his eyes and quickly sized me up. He did not look impressed.

"What are you looking at?"

He exaggerated his snarl and increased his stride. He was coming directly at me with no intention of stepping aside.

I stood my ground, but my bravado felt as thin and misplaced as the gold foil on a French cake.

"Roger Thornton?" I said. "I'm Nash Tobin. We talked last night. You said you wanted to meet in person. Here I am..."

Thornton stopped dead only two paces away. Anger, surprise,

and annoyance all battled for supremacy on his flat red face. But what finally won out was stark fear.

"No!" he yelled.

He lunged forward and pushed me into the bush. I fell down hard on my rump. Before I could pick myself up, Thornton spun around and raced away in the direction of the park.

"Stop!" I called out, but he paid no attention.

I got up and started after him. As I ran, my suit jacket cinched around my arms so I twisted out of it and let it drop to the ground. My tie bounced from side to side until finally it bumped up over my shoulder and stayed there.

I was winded by the time I reached the street. My lungs cried out for air and my breathing whistled through my teeth.

I paused beside a bus stop shelter to let a car pass, then ran across the street and plunged after Thornton into the park.

I could hardly see anything. There were no lights along the asphalt footpath, at least none that worked. When I accidentally stepped off it, I felt the dusty crunch of dead leaves that had accumulated over the years.

Although I couldn't see Thornton, I could still hear his footsteps on the path ahead of me. It may have been wishful thinking on my part, but it sounded like he was slowing down. And no wonder. The dark path was almost invisible and its twists and turns came so quickly that I could hardly follow them at any pace faster than a trot. In fact, the best indicator I had of where I should go came from Thornton's loud footsteps marking the way ahead.

Suddenly, Thornton lost his footing. With a loud cry, he fell and let out a long string of oaths. He quickly regained his feet and started running again, but it gave me a chance to narrow the gap between us. His boot strikes definitely sounded nearer.

I picked up my own pace and almost made the same mistake Thornton did.

Around the next corner, the path opened up into a paved clearing with an old dry fountain in the middle. The empty pool was surrounded by a low circular wall, which Thornton had tripped over. I managed to veer around the fountain and kept running. The silent stone angel at the fountain's center stared after me as I went.

After the clearing, the path split in two directions. The right path led north, the other continued west. I paused briefly, listening and catching my breath. I thought I could hear Thornton's steps on the northern fork, but it was hard to tell; the sound of automobile traffic on nearby streets confused the issue.

I took the northern path, running as fast as the darkness allowed. The traffic noises quickly got louder and I lost track of Thornton's steps entirely. I guessed that I must be nearing the edge of the park.

The path I was on turned abruptly to the right. Unfortunately, I did not and fell headfirst into a thicket of bushes and trees. The spray of dead leaves and debris filled my eyes and nostrils. I jumped back up and returned to the path, wiping leaf grit off my face and sputtering to get it out of my mouth and nose. I followed the path more carefully and soon reached the park's edge.

The path let out on a small dark side street, which intersected with Easton Boulevard a long half-block away. Although there were no streetlamps, my dark-accustomed eyes could see well enough in the light spilling over from Easton.

I didn't see Thornton anywhere. If he had come out this way, he was already gone. I had lost him. I took a few panting steps towards Easton Boulevard but soon gave up. He had not been far enough ahead of me to reach the main road before I came out. Nor could he have gotten to the intersecting alley going the other way. Either he had taken the western path after the clearing or he had ducked back into the trees and I ran right by him.

Disappointed, I leaned over with my hands on my thighs to catch my breath. I spat loose phlegm into the brush beside the sidewalk. When I could finally breathe normally again, I straightened up and looked down the street.

Halfway up the block, I spotted another possibility, one that held a certain promise independent of Roger Thornton. It was a tiny bar sandwiched between the side walls of a retail store on Easton and a large warehouse that faced the back alley. The name of the place, "Murray's Tavern," was painted directly on the brick wall. Its door was propped open with a chair to let in the cool night air along with any customers lost enough to find it. It was a quiet, sleepy little place. There was no noise of any kind coming out as I approached.

Inside, Murray's was a narrow, dimly-lit dive with a long bar on the right and a bank of booths on the opposite wall. Between the bar and the booths, there were several unsteady round tables scattered over the floor. The joint was nearly empty. The only other customers were two older women in winter coats who sat hunched over their drinks in separate booths. People who choose to drink alone, choose Murray's...

A very young barmaid with a pudgy face and dark hair, stood behind the bar. She wore too-tight jeans, a sleeveless black blouse, and had a silver stud poked through the side of her nose. She was watching a miniature TV with a three inch screen. Its flickering image bathed her face and crossed arms with pale light. Her exposed skin was pimpled with gooseflesh. She looked extremely bored.

I sat down on a bar stool not far from her and craned my neck to see what she was watching--a silent movie about Napoleon.

"Evening," I said.

She glanced up. "That's what it is."

She returned her attention to her myopic epic. In closeups,

the characters were the size of grasshoppers. The battle scene which was underway looked like a raiding party on an ant farm.

"Did someone come in here a minute ago?" I asked. "A tall, husky guy about twenty years old? Buzz-cut red hair, wearing a long coat?"

"You want something to drink, or are you here to watch my TV and ask me questions?" She didn't even look up.

"I'll take a beer. What do you have on tap?"

"Moosbrew, light and dark."

"Make it light."

The barmaid reached up to a rack above her head and brought down a glass. She filled it from a tap and set it in front of me on a colorful pub mat printed with the slogan: “Have a Moosbrew! Or two!“

"That's $1.50 without the tip. And no, no one like that's been in all night. Don't I wish."

"Thanks." I put my money on the bar and took my beer to one of the tables. I drained half of the glass at a gulp. The cold liquid felt good on my parched throat. All that running had made me thirsty and burned up a lot of empty calories I would need to replenish... I took another sip and held it, letting the bubbles attack the dry mold on my tongue.

I had not really expected to find Thornton here but at least I tried. Such diligence should not go unrewarded. I signaled to the barmaid I wanted another beer. The first one was not going to last long.

I drank my beer and mulled over Thornton's reaction earlier. As soon as he had heard my voice, he ran off, terrified. It was as if he was afraid for his life. Why? I wondered.

The question was too complex for beer alone, it would take a cigarette as well. I started to reach for one but recalled that they were in my jacket pocket back at Thornton's apartment complex.

The barmaid brought a second beer and set it on the table.

"Same drill," she droned, "$1.50 not including tip."

"Fine," I said. "Do you have a cigarette machine?"

She picked up the empty glass and gestured with it to the back of the room.

"Back there by the johns. It only takes quarters though, and I charge for change."

I took the 50 cents she gave me for the second beer and jiggled it with the other coins in my pocket. Nearly enough. I gave her two more dollar bills.

"Bring me another beer," I said, "And keep the quarters coming."

She returned to the bar, filled a new glass and brought it to me. She left two more quarters on the table. She went back to the bar and stared blankly at her tiny TV.

I got up and walked down a narrow hallway, past the rest room doors to the cigarette machine against the back wall. I plunked in quarter after quarter, having to repeat some of them when the machine spat them back into the coin return. Finally, the machine accepted my money and dispensed a package of Camels. I pulled the package out of the slot and put it in my shirt pocket.

Before returning to my table I needed to make a pit stop and pushed open the door marked "Gents."

There was another patron in the bathroom already, one I hadn't seen in the bar area. He was standing in the middle of the floor, alone except for the long, gleaming straight razor he held in his right hand for company. His crazy blue eyes outshone the blade. It was Roger Thornton.

He was trapped and knew it. The fear was still emblazoned on his face, but like any great predator with its back to the wall, he turned his fear into anger. His only way out led through me and he was working himself up to do something about it. When I made no move on him, it occurred to him that I was not armed.

His fear seemed to melt away and his red face lit up in a nasty smile. He quickened his breath and tightened his hold on the razor.

He lifted the blade and came at me.

I jumped back and slammed the door on top of him. He had started a swipe at my face with the razor, but the door crushed his shoulder and halted his stroke.

Thornton lurched back and grabbed at his shoulder. We both knew he wasn't seriously hurt. I had smashed the door on him as hard as I could, and it had no more effect than slapping a bull with a two-by-four. Thornton had been stung, but it only made him more angry. He grunted and rolled his shoulder to shake off the pain. The overhead light glinted off the razor as it twirled in his hand.

I had two choices, I could try to outrun him or stay and fight it out. Neither was a good option. With my smoker's wind, Thornton would certainly catch me if I ran, and it was clear I could not survive a toe-to-toe brawl with him. My only chance was to attack first and inflict maximum pain as quickly as possible.

I rushed at Thornton, which caught him by surprise. I sprang forward, pushing through him with all my accumulated momentum. It knocked him backwards against the bathroom stall where his head smacked hard on the corner. Both boot heels slipped out beneath him on the linoleum floor, and Thornton went sliding down the wall in slow motion, his arms pinwheeling for balance. He wound up seated on the floor, stunned from the blow to his head.

It was all the time I needed. I picked myself up and moved over him. I stamped hard on his razor hand with my foot, trying to crush the bones.

Thornton yelped. He managed to pull his injured hand away, but the razor fell from its useless grip. The pain helped rouse him, however. He grabbed my belt with his strong left hand and began to pull himself up.

I kneed him in the face, driving his head against the stall with a satisfying thud. The loud crunch his nose made as it collapsed beneath my knee was even more gratifying. Blood erupted from his nose and poured down his face onto his shirt. The droplets that fell on his green coat looked like holly berries. He released my belt and started punching at my legs with his good hand.

I kneed him in the face again to make him stop. Then when he did stop, I kept kneeing him anyway just because I liked the sound. My blows rained in faster and faster, and Thornton's gruesome face sprayed blood against the grey wall with each one. Exhilarated by his weakness and exultant in contempt, I kicked him over and over, knowing he could do nothing to stop me.

Thornton tried to speak, but all that came out was a burbling, "Doh... doh, doh..."

The power I had over him surged through me, violent and absolute. I went on pounding his head against the wall, waiting for his skull to split open like a ripe cantaloupe and his brains to dump out onto the dingy floor. I wanted to go on bashing his face until the whimpering faded and died, and he along with it. I was going to kill him. I could already taste it. I felt like I was standing on the edge of a stormy sea-cliff, anxious to dive into the warm seething ocean below, but knowing if I did, I could never crawl back out. It almost didn't matter. My rage--the urge to smash and break and destroy--went far beyond temptation; it was a state of being.

I glanced at the mirror above the sink and saw a crazed, blood-spattered creature. Its inhuman face was distorted like a kabuki mask. The wildness in the eyes that stared back reminded me of Lance Talbot, Roger Thornton, Cy Hardison, his partner

Gerrara, and a host of others. But I was looking at myself.

Thornton's face was smeared with blood all the way up into his crew-cut widow's peak. His lips were swollen, his nose askew. His eyes were shut against whatever else I might do, but tears seeped out at their edges and rolled down his cheeks, clearing streaks in the gore.

I leaned over and picked up the razor from where it had fallen. I knelt down beside Thornton and crooked my left arm around his neck so my elbow could pinch off his windpipe. He still had about a hundred pounds weight advantage over me and I was not going to take any chances. I pressed the razor blade against his cheek just below his right eye.

"You know what this is?" I whispered.

Thornton nodded very slowly. The tears continued to come.

"...You know what I can do?"

He nodded again.

"Good. Now we are going to chat. Like I said last night. It could have been friendly, but you ruined that, not me. Now I want to know what happened to your girlfriend, Rudi. Where were you when she died Saturday?"

At first he said nothing, just went on panting loudly through his mouth. Every once in a while, his breathing halted so he could spit out the blood that accumulated in his mouth. His nose was going to be useless for a long time.

I slid the razor up onto his closed eyelid and pressed it firmly against the thin layer of skin.

"I'm not kidding, Rog. I know you sent those two goons after me this morning and I'd like nothing more than to hurt you bad, permanently. I'll carve my initials in your eyeball..."

"Don't... kill... me," he said. His voice was ragged and he had to pause between every word to take a breath.

"Tell me what I want."

Thornton nodded again and tried to collect himself. His

whimpering subsided and his breathing gradually slowed. He was beginning to believe he might live through this.

"My throat... loosen..."

I loosed my arm slightly around his neck.

Roger coughed and spat out a red cloud onto the floor. Finally he said, "She came over Saturday. But she left... I swear, I never killed her..."

His voice sounded too comfortable. I tightened my grip on his neck and had him panting again.

"That's not good enough," I said. "Details, Rog, I want details. You must have done something. Otherwise, why did you send your buddies after me."

"I didn't," he spat. "I wanted to deal with you myself... But Cy made me back off. He said he'd take care of you."

"Why? Why should he clean up your mess?"

Thornton started to shake his head, but the pressure of the razor on his eye convinced him to stop.

"...Don't know," he said.

It made sense that Cyrus Hardison would be the one in charge rather than a young punk like Thornton. But it still seemed strange that Hardison would involve himself in straightening out Thornton's affairs.

"Assuming you're innocent, why did you want me off the case?"

Thornton laughed, or at least made a bitter noise in his throat that I took for a laugh. He regretted it immediately. He choked and coughed up more blood that he spat to the floor.

I loosened my grip on his neck and withdrew the razor from his face. I didn't want to slice open an eyeball by accident. When his coughing stopped and he could speak again, I placed the razor blade back on his closed eye.

"Innocent or guilty," he said, his voice still a rasp, "That don't matter. All that matters is how it looks. How the cops make it look. If they knew Rudi was there that night, they'd make it plenty bad for me."

"How?"

"Look, she came for blow. That's all she was interested in, ever. I told her, fine, but she's got to work it off first. So she does... I mean, we do... Then she's ready to leave. But when I saw the coke she was taking, I got pissed off. It was way more than she put out. I lost my temper..."

"You hit her."

"A few times. She was headstrong so I had to. But after we did more coke, we made up. I did her a couple more times--around the world, you know--and she left. That's all. I swear to you!"

Roger stopped to regain his breath before he went on:

"It's nothing so bad, really. But cops and lawyers twist things, make them seem worse than they are. They'd love to pin this on me. That's why I wanted you to butt out."

Not so bad. Sure, Thornton beat her up, but it was just part of the negotiating process. Once Rudi knew what was expected of her, she performed her various duties as required and was free to go. Rudi was a bright girl, she understood these things.

"What time did she leave?"

"I don't know! I fell asleep, and when I woke up, she was gone. A long time."

"How do you know it was a long time?"

"The sheets were cold where she'd been."

"Okay, what time did you wake up?

"I think 9:30. Yeah, I'm pretty sure."

That was well before Fitch's earliest estimate for time of death, and Thornton claimed Rudi had left even earlier than that.

"If you're lying to me..." I increased the pressure of the blade on his closed eyelid.

"I'm not, I swear! I'm straight with you."

"Prove it. Tell me about the Gatherings. You and Rudi and the Hill House Preservation Society in high school."

Thornton nodded slowly, wary of the blade on his eye.

"Okay, but let my neck go," he said. "I can't breathe."

I thought for a moment and agreed. My arm was cramping up anyway.

"You better not try anything," I said, withdrawing my arm.

Thornton took several long breaths.

"That's better," he said. "Now let me open my eyes..."

I pressed the blunt end of the blade more firmly against his eyelid and pushed the elastic skin back and forth.

"Not if you want to keep them. Now, the Gatherings..." I prompted.

"All right, all right. They're supposed to be secret. Some of Rudi's friends from that group used to come, but it wasn't related. The Gatherings are basically outdoor orgies. There's some mumbo-jumbo thrown in, but the big draw is the drugs and group sex. You ask me, the rest is fluff."

"You mean they are still going on?"

"Of course! It's late in the season, but there may be one or two left. If you're interested..."

"If I am, what would I expect?"

"Middle-aged losers, mostly. Greasy, slobbery men, flabby women..." Thornton wrinkled his nose in disgust and then flinched at the pain that it caused.

"I don't go to them anymore," he went on. "I can have any woman I want. I don't need to waste time with some stinking goat out in a field. I have a waterbed, for Christ's sake!"

"What about Rudi? Did she stop going as well?"

"I don't know. If she had any sense she did. But she had a sick streak to her..." A coarse, unpleasant grin spread across Thornton's bloody face. "They were wild times, though. One girl went when she was pregnant, only she didn't know it, or at any rate didn't tell anyone. And she was high as a kite. She's doing it with this guy, and she loses it--the baby I mean. Nobody notices except the guy she's with, and he runs off leaving her crying in the middle of this bloody mess. Then this dog comes along, sniffing and licking around her. And before you can say Scooby-doo..."

I interrupted Thornton mid-sentence.

"Is there a point to this story, or is it just school-yard reminiscences?"

"No, like I told you, it wasn't school. They have these Gatherings anywhere, just so long as there aren't a lot of people around. So the girl just freaked! She went crazy with screaming, like... like..." Thornton struggled to come up with a fit analogy but failed. He finished lamely. "I dunno... She just was screaming."

Since his eyes were closed, he didn't see my reaction to his anecdote. I was tempted to smash his nose all over again, just to stop the inanity. Instead, I asked:

"And Rudi Alsmith actually went to these... orgies?"

"Yeah. She liked the old man's sermons. The guy who runs things. The 'group grope guru,' I called him. He gave what were like sermons at church, only the opposite. Pretentious garbage, if you ask me. But Rudi always stopped whatever, or whoever, she was doing to listen. Every time he talked she would get real quiet."

"This old man--what was his name?"

"Ow! Man, my eye. You're hurting my eye!"

In my excitement, I was pressing his eyelid harder than I meant. I pulled the razor away completely.

"Tell me his name!"

"Winter..." he said, "Winter Kerr is..."

But the rest was lost under a loud pounding that came from outside, and the rest room door suddenly burst open.

CHAPTER TWENTY-ONE

A lanky uniformed cop stormed into the bathroom, pounding his baton against the wooden door for attention.

"Drop it! Drop it now!" he shouted. His dark eyes burned like coals in sunken sockets, and his hair was sweat-plastered to his forehead. The rough-hewn features of his face looked unfinished, like a wood-carving that still needed to be sanded down. "Drop the knife!"

I tossed the razor under the stall door and it skittered across the floor beneath a radiator.

"Now, get up, one at a time and slow! You first." He pointed his stick at me. I rose to my feet and held up my hands.

The policeman came closer. He grabbed my left arm and twisted me around with a grip as tight as tungsten. He shoved me at the wall and I had to brace against the impact with my hands.

"That's right," he said, "Hands up where I can see them! Feet back." I stepped back and held myself off the wall with my arms above my head.

"Now you," the cop told Thornton.

I glanced back. The policeman grabbed Thornton's coat lapels and lifted him up one-handed. He brought Thornton's blood-smeared face in close to his own.

"I don't know what sick puppy games you're playing here, Roger boy, but playtime is definitely over."

He threw Thornton roughly at the wall and Roger's hand smashed into the mirror above the sink. Broken shards of silvered glass clattered down into the basin.

The policeman laughed. "Seven years bad luck. On top of everything else. For your sake I hope it's concurrent and not back-to-back."

Thornton left large red smears on the white tile wall where he put his hands. He muttered under his breath, but all I could make out was "... Officer Friendly."

The cop approached Thornton and gently bounced his nightstick against his already tender head.

"That's Friedman, Roger. Officer Friedman. I'm hurt you don't remember, but you're such a mess right now maybe I shouldn't be."

Friedman took a pair of thin latex gloves out of one of his pockets and put them on before frisking Thornton.

"You got nothing on me," Thornton said. "I'm clean. You're just wasting time..."

"I wouldn't worry about time if I were you. You got plenty coming."

The policeman finished with Thornton and moved over to me.

"And who's your friend, Roger?" he said. "From the looks of things, maybe somebody you shouldn't play with no more."

"I'm a private detective," I said. "You can check my card, if you want."

The policeman tucked his stick under his arm and frisked me quickly.

"A dick, huh? A real live one? And here I thought maybe you were a barber with that razor of yours." He took my wallet out of my back pocket and looked at my ID. "'Nash Tobin, Private Investigator.' Now that does have a certain ring to it." He tossed my wallet into the sink where it landed on broken glass. "You want to tell me what business you have here with my good friend Roger? This fine, upstanding citizen of the city, admired and respected by all?" As he named each of Thornton's supposed qualities, the policeman prodded him in the back with his nightstick. "And more important, why wasn't I invited to watch?"

"I don't know what you're talking about, officer. We were just having a friendly discussion. Until you barged in," I said.

"That's right," Thornton chimed in. "Just chatting about the weather."

The policeman glanced around at the blood that had spattered over the floor and stall door. Both Thornton's and my clothing were a grisly mess. We looked like we'd been wrestling in an abattoir. Thornton's swollen face was downright gruesome.

"Friendly discussion, huh?" Friedman said. "They told me there was a barroom disturbance here. I certainly don't need to bust up anyone's chat about the weather."

"Then can we go? No one here disturbing anyone," Thornton prompted.

The policeman sighed.

"Could be. Are you both willing to testify that any injuries sustained in this room tonight took place before I arrived?"

Thornton and I nodded.

"Okay," Friedman said to me, "you can go."

Both Roger and I started to turn away from the wall.

"Sorry, Roger. I didn't say you could move yet." He put a sheathed hand on Thornton's shoulder. "I'm afraid your case is more complicated. See, I've been hearing a lot about you lately, in all kinds of places. On the street, in the station, maybe from some balling teenager or a ripped-off junkie. They're always kind of hushed and respectful, actually downright scared most of the time, if you want to know. But from what I hear, you haven't been getting nearly enough credit for all the things you've been up to. A crying shame, of course, but then, what isn't nowadays."

Friedman shook his head at the injustice of it all.

Thornton twisted around to watch Friedman. He could tell the policeman was leading up to something but he didn't know what.

Personally, I had a pretty good idea. But it was Friedman's scene to play out and I could see that he planned to enjoy every minute.

The policeman went on, "But what I heard today at roll call, that was different. Seems you've outdone yourself, Roger. Reached a whole new level, jumped up to the big leagues. I think you'll finally get the attention you so richly deserve."

Thornton could take no more.

"What the hell are you talking about, Friendly?"

Friedman became very grave.

"Roger Thornton," he began, "It is my duty, and at the same time my very great pleasure, to arrest you on the charge of homicide. For the death of ..." Officer Friedman hesitated. "Well, I forget the girl's name, but I'm sure you know which one." The policeman took the set of handcuffs off his belt and tapped Thornton's left hand with it. "Down behind you, please."

Thornton lowered his hands slowly. He knew better than to resist. At his best, the stocky Thornton would not be much of a match for the wiry cop. But with a crushed hand and a nose he couldn't breathe through, Thornton had absolutely no chance.

"I didn't do it," Thornton said. "I already told him!" His ghastly face was desperate as the policeman crunched the cuffs on his wrists. "I swear I didn't!"

"Pay attention," the officer said, ignoring his protestations. "You have the right to remain silent..." As he recited the Miranda warnings, he prodded his prisoner across the room and opened the door.

Thornton didn't listen.

"It wasn't me," he went on, appealing to me over his shoulder. "She left that night, just like I said. You've got to believe me! I'm innocent. Help me, please!" In the stress of the moment, blood began once more to drip from his nose.

The cop laughed and pushed Roger through the doorway.

"Hey, Mr. Innocent. I asked you a question. Do you understand your rights as I explained them to you?"

The door closed behind them, blocking out Thornton's answer.

I was left alone.

* * *

I picked up my wallet from the sink and washed my face and hands. My clothes were a mess but there was nothing I could do about them. I lit a cigarette and went out into the barroom.

The beers I'd left on the table were already warm, but I took a long drink anyway. The two women customers were gone. Only the barmaid was left. She stood at the far end of the bar, pretending to watch her TV.

I took a beer and ashtray over to the bar and set them down in front of her. She moved back slowly, casually, leaning back against the counter behind her. It was so nonchalant that a casual observer might have missed the fact that it was a retreat.

I smiled.

"Hi," I said.

"Hi. You need another beer? Cause I can give you one on the house. It's slow tonight."

"You think so? I found it rather exciting."

I took another sip of my beer and looked at her. She averted her eyes, shifting her gaze to the mini-TV. But it was just to have something to look at. A bowl of stale pretzels would have sufficed.

"Did I misunderstand earlier, or did you tell me that no one like him came in all night?"

"I know, Mister, I'm sorry. But he's a regular. What do you expect? I mean, if I'd known cops were involved, I would have told you..." She sounded sincere, but then she was a bartender; it was her job to tell people what they wanted to hear.

"How old are you?" I asked.

"Twenty-three."

In a hog's monocle, I thought. She wasn't a day over twenty.

"That guy you were protecting tonight was arrested for killing a girl. She was only eighteen."

The barmaid's eyes opened very wide. The idea that one of her regulars could be a killer clearly appealed to her.

"Really? Did he do it?"

I took another sip from my beer and puffed my cigarette. She looked at me expectantly while I considered her question. This time, it was my turn to look away before answering.

"I don't know," I said.

But somewhere in my gut, I did know. In spite of myself and contrary to overwhelming antipathy, I believed Roger Thornton. Not that he was innocent, of course--far from it. But the story he told about his last drug-tryst with Rudi rang depressingly true. It was so totally banal, without even a spark of imagination or originality. Rudi had come to him and prostituted herself for cocaine. When she tried to take more than he thought she earned, Thornton first beat her, then had sex with her again. Thornton's brutish behavior in the episode came through unvarnished. But still he insisted that Rudi had been alive and had left him there.

I glanced at the barmaid's tiny TV screen close beside me, but it provided no comfort. During a commercial break in the movie, a local news update came on. The grainy color picture was claustrophobic. The sound was turned so low as to be almost inaudible. The newscasters' voices were no more than tinny vibrations.

The picture shifted from the studio news desk to a neighborhood identified as Lapins Forest earlier in the day. The camera eye focused from a distance on the front of a suburban brick rancher with tall trees in the yard. Police tape was strung around the trees, isolating the house from its neighbors. A policeman stood by the front door, smoking a cigarette, while another one combed through the front hedges for evidence. The door opened and two emergency medical technicians brought out a gurney carrying a body covered by a plastic sheet. The men were in no hurry. The camera followed their shaky progress as they wheeled the stretcher along the front walk to a waiting ambulance.

The ambulance was parked on the driveway beside a long grey Cadillac. The Caddy's metallic paint gleamed. It had greywall tires with shiny emblems on chrome hubcaps. Whoever lived there must have done pretty well for themselves.

Correction. Whoever had lived there.

While the EMTs started to put the body into the ambulance, a sharp breeze blew the corner of the sheet off the victim's head. For an instant, the cameraman zoomed in on a gaping facial wound. Then the ambulance door slammed shut.

It took me a moment to recognize what I'd just seen.

"Aha!" I said. I pounded my two fists on the bar top and swung off the stool.

The barmaid looked at me quizzically, but I left without explaining.

I limped painfully back to Thornton's complex; my knee ached from the abuse it had taken off his face. The evening temperature plummeted and by the time I got there I was shivering in my blood-soaked clothes. I picked up my jacket from the ground where I had left it, but in spite of the cold, I did not put it on. I couldn't afford to lose another suit-jacket to bloodstains.

I drove back to my office with the car's heater going full blast. When I got inside, I quickly changed clothes and threw my ruined shirt and pants into the waste basket.

I sat down at my desk to wind down, savoring some of civilization's simpler joys: a pillow behind my back, a glass of mezcal, hot water radiator heat, the soft buzz of alcohol in my bloodstream, dry clothes that don't reek of slaughter.

As warmth began to reach my extremities, I picked up the phone and had the operator connect me with the police precinct headquarters nearest to Flyte Street in Shakytown. When the desk officer answered, I asked for Officer Nance and was put on hold.

I had barely thought about the foul-mouthed policewoman since Saturday night when we met in Shakytown. Nor about the two dead muggers who'd been gunned down in the street there. To be honest, the Flyte Street shootings already seemed like ancient history. It was strange to think that--if Albin Fitch's estimate was correct--they actually took place later than Rudi Alsmith's death. Her death only seemed more recent.

The precinct desk officer got back to me finally and said that Officer Nance was not expected in until 10:00 at shift change. I said I would call back but left no message.

In the meantime, I decided to call Walter Alvarez, my friend who worked at the Eola Graphic. Walter and I had been at school together before he went to work at the paper. He was now the crime desk editor there and an associate editor in charge of investigative reporting.

I flipped my rolodex to his card and called him at home.

"Y'hello," came the familiar finicky voice, reminiscent of Truman Capote.

"Hi, Walter. It's Nash."

"Nash! How are you? Loaded?"

"Only when I'm on duty. I have a favor that requires your

criminal expertise."

"I don't do crime anymore, Nash. I got religion now. They booted me down to the religion desk."

The religion section; lowest rung on the journalist's ladder.

"Why? What'd you do?"

"The chief editor's mad about a story I ran while he was on vacation. It was a damn good story, but it involved his girl-friend's brother."

"Smart, Walter. You should have told him first."

"I did. Before he left," Walter insisted.

"And..."

"He told me not to run it. But it was such a good story, I couldn't help myself. Besides, I'm sure this religion stint is only temporary. I'll do some penance, a little-soul searching, repent the error of my ways, and all will be forgiven. It's not like I implicated his brother-in-law or anything... But enough about my problems," he said. "How about yours?"

"I'm fine," I said without enthusiasm.

"That good, huh? How's Mara?"

In the four years I'd been married, Walter had never asked about Mara once, not even out of simple politeness. He hadn't liked her even back in college and never bothered to hide it. But it was typical that he would mention her now. He had an unerring instinct for pursuing whatever his subjects least wanted to discuss. Whether it was a deceptive piece of legislation, a flawed courtroom argument, or a politician's emotional hotspot, Walter would instinctively zero in on the weak link and push at it until it snapped. It was ingrained in his character and completely unconscious. It made him a good reporter but a difficult friend.

I ignored his question.

"Listen, I need to find out about a couple of ..."

He cut me short.

"Nash, I know she's gone and I'm sorry."

After a long pause, I said, "Well, aren't you going to tell me 'Good riddance'?"

"I could, but I won't. Hopefully in time you'll see it yourself. And by then, my opinion on the subject won't matter."

"Yeah," I said, in a dead, dry monotone. "Anyway, that's not what I called for."

"Sure. What's up?"

"I need to find out about two thugs, one named Cy Hardison and the other Tony Gerrara. I had a run-in with them this morning and I'm not sure what I'm dealing with. Who do they work for and how much trouble they are likely to be? There's a couple Bass in it for you."

Walter and I frequently did favors for each other and, unless real work was involved, the token payment was a six-pack of premium beer. However, the beer was actually only an excuse to get together and drink.

There was a long pause at Walter's end.

"Nash, I don't know what you're involved in, but I doubt those two will cause you any trouble. You might as well come over now. I'll tell you the rest when you get here. Don't dawdle! You know how the bitch loves company."

"Not to mention beer," I said.

Walter laughed.

"You got that right. Sandy's just a beer-guzzling hound. See you in a few."

* * *

Not long after, we were sitting outside on Walter Alvarez's porch, drinking beer and talking shop. The night was chilly and we both had on winter coats. I looked up into the dull night sky. Walter's home was inside the city, so even though the sky was clear, only a handful of isolated stars were visible and there was nothing resembling a coherent constellation.

I had been telling Walter about my interview with Sheila Lee (without using her name) and how poorly I'd managed it. Now I understood better than ever why she had been so adamant about putting the trauma of the Gatherings behind her. And why it had been such a mistake for me to keep pushing.

"... Maybe it's my attitude. Maybe I should pick up a book on how to win friends and influence people."

"Attitude's good," Walter said.

He sat in a canvas director's chair behind a fiberglass pedestal table. He was medium height and a trifle overweight. His pudgy face and thin blond eyebrows looked blandly cherubic. Except when he smiled; his impish grin immediately dispelled any angelic illusion.

He popped off the cap to another Bass Ale.

"... At least Sandy likes you."

Hearing her name, Walter's spaniel raised her head lazily from the wooden planks of the porch and looked at each of us in turn. When she saw that she was not going to get more beer, she put her head down and yawned.

"I wonder if she can sue me. The girl I mean..." I let the thought trail off with my breath's vapor.

"Don't be so negative. Look at it this way: Count no day wasted when you've given someone a nervous breakdown."

"You mean it's a question of setting goals?"

Walter frowned. His teeth were clenched on a long black cigarette holder. He thought--incorrectly--that it made him look like Franklin Roosevelt.

"More a matter of motto, I think. Or mission statement. Apoplexy R Us, that sort of thing."

"I see." I downed more beer and wondered how many more bottles it would take before I just didn't care.

"You should make it part of your personal code. That unique set of rules all you private detectives live by."

A personal code, I thought. That's what I need. If only someone would give me one.

I pushed myself back in the green vinyl porch glider and let the springs carry me back and forth. The runner on one side was rusty, making the glider's motion uneven, like a rowboat in an ocean squall. The glider let out a loud shriek with every swing. Sandy looked up in mild protest at the noise, and I stopped myself with my feet.

"What surprised me most," I mused, "Was how different the girl was. It really seemed like she was on the road to changing her life."

Walter stretched back in his chair.

"I have two things to say to that," he said. "First, you didn't know what she was like before. You're only guessing from her high school photograph. That's hardly conclusive.

"And second, maybe you're right. If people want to change badly enough, they will. It's just that most of us--for all our complaining--never reach that point. Behavioral inertia is an awfully warm security blanket."

I lit a cigarette, underscoring his point.

"And I suppose, for her, religion is just a new security blanket," I said.

"Exactly! But don't get me wrong. Sometimes a change of linen can have a salutary effect. The main problem with religion, based on my experience of the last two weeks, is that it thrives on gullibility. On a belief in things unseen. It'd be a cinch to believe if you actually saw some poor schmoe walking on water, or saw a footpath open up through the Red Sea. Scriptures around the world are full of pseudo-depositions from people who claim to have seen one miracle or another. As if you could look up old so-and-so and ask if it were true! But without personal experience, all you have to go on is second-hand accounts written long after the fact. And I use the word 'fact' loosely. To paraphrase a lawyer I know, I wouldn't hang a dog on the basis of religious testimony."

I thought about what he said for a moment before speaking:

"Maybe it's not supposed to be easy. Maybe faith isn't something you have because of what you see, but something you hold onto in spite of what you see. Don't they call it the 'work of a lifetime'?"

Walter smirked.

"Nice work if you can get it. And don't think I'm disputing any particular creed or belief. My point is that when people are disposed to believe in things without proof, they're likely to fall for any old claptrap. Like the New Jersey puppy worship cult. Or the sect here in Eola, the Church of Divine Salivation. Its members attend every week to be spat upon by their self-proclaimed minister."

"No doubt they have great expectorations in the hereafter," I said.

"Say, that's pretty good. I'll have to use it for my column. Glad I thought of it."

Walter pulled another bottle of beer from the carton and held it out to me.

"But enough," Walter said. "You want to talk about Mara?"

"Yes to the beer," I said. "No to Mara."

Walter flicked the cap into the hedges and handed the bottle over to me. "You always could drink beer like there's no tomorro'..."

I groaned.

"Actually, I'm here to talk about Hardison and Gerrara. Remember?" I finished all but a sip of my first beer and poured the remainder into Sandy's bowl. I set the empty bottle on the window ledge beside the glider. Sandy looked over at her dish and decided there wasn't enough to get up for. She lay her head down and closed her eyes.

"To business, then," Walter said. "As I said earlier, I don't think you have anything to worry about from those two. In fact, you should probably keep a fairly tight lip about whatever run-in you had with them."

"Why?"

"Because they're both dead. They were shot earlier today. It's all over the news. I'm surprised you missed it."

"What happened?"

"Hardison was killed at a restaurant in midtown. Gerrara was killed at his home."

"In Lapins Forest?"

"That was Gerrara. The stations all ran it."

"Do they know who did it?"

"Not yet. It was definitely a coordinated hit with two separate teams. They were both killed within several minutes of each other so there'd be no chance of one of them getting a warning."

That explained why Thornton had been so frightened of me that evening. He probably thought I was part of the mop-up squads that killed Hardison and Gerrara. He must have thought he was next. I suddenly felt an unpleasant sense of vertigo as once more my investigation seemed to be spinning out of control...

"Who were they working for?" I asked.

"Hardison and Gerrara? They were both part of Angus Baird's gang. You know him?"

"Not really."

"He's relatively small time. At least for now. Officially he runs some mobile home parks on the east side of the city and in the suburbs. But he makes his real money on drugs and women. His gang is nothing like the size of Winston Graham's, say, or the Northside Legion, but he's smart, ruthless, and ambitious. Very ambitious. My police sources predict that he'll be a real problem within five years if he keeps building his organization. Of course, he lost one of his top men today with Cyrus Hardison. And his driver Gerrara was pretty high up as well."

"And the police have no idea why they were killed, or who was behind it?"

"None that I've heard. It looks like they were hit by some other gang. Theoretically, though, Angus Baird could have had them whacked himself, for whatever reason. He may actually have taken part--he's the type who likes to keep his hands dirty. At least, he has that reputation."

Walter became silent for a moment.

"Nash, I know you can't tell me what you're working on. And under the circumstances, I'm not sure I want to know. But these killings have the potential to blow up into something much bigger. Much worse."

"You mean a war?"

Walter nodded. "You should be aware of it and be careful. The cops I talked to are very worried."

"I'm always careful," I said.

"Then work on awareness."

"I'll try. And let me add, you seem to be doing a lot of work on a straight crime story for someone who is supposed to be sitting the religion desk."

Walter grinned.

"Well, I subscribe to a big-tent theology. Ultimately everything falls under religion. You know--good/evil, right/wrong, life/death. Doesn't seem like too much of a stretch to me."

"Yes, I'm sure." I glanced down at my watch. It was 10:35. "Can I use your phone?" I asked.

"Sure, go ahead."

I went inside the house and called the Shakytown police precinct again. It took a while, but Officer Nance eventually came to the phone.

"Who is this?" she asked.

"It's Nash Tobin. I'm the private detective you spoke with at the shootings on Flyte Street."

"I remember. And..."

"I have a tip for you on those killings."

"I'm not a detective. Call whoever's working the case. Someone who gives a damn."

"I called you."

Officer Nance muttered something unpleasant under her breath. The police line was probably monitored for officer courtesy.

"Okay," she said finally. "What do you have?"

"First off, you're aware of the Anthony Gerrara shooting? Out in Lapins Forest?"

"Of course."

"Well, the car in his driveway was a big grey Cadillac with greywall tires. It had chrome emblems on the hubcaps. I'm guessing they were red."

"What is this, Lifestyles of the Rich and Infamous?..." She stopped abruptly. "You mean the marks on the curb! The grey rubber smudges and the scraped red metal!"

"That's right. Gerrara's Cadillac could have left those tire marks there. Of course, it might not have been his car, but I'll bet anything it was the same model."

Nance's profanity came through more clearly this time but expressing surprise rather than annoyance.

"Okay, I might be able to do something with this," she said. "How can I reach you?"

I gave her my home and office telephone numbers.

"Okay," she said. "And thanks. I may owe you." She hung up.

Suddenly I felt very tired. I rejoined Walter briefly and

finished my second beer, but left soon after. I went back to my apartment and was asleep almost as soon as my shoes were off.

CHAPTER TWENTY-TWO

My alarm went off at 6:00. And then again at 8:15. Only the second time it was the phone.

I coaxed my eyes open to slits and peered through the blinds at a grey, drizzly morning. I sat up reluctantly and fumbled for the handset.

"Yeah," I said.

"Your bleeping phone rang thirteen times. I thought you private guys never sleep." It was Officer Nance.

"Never enough, anyway... What about you? Isn't your shift through yet?"

"Yeah, but I'm working late. Your tip on Gerrara's car checked out. It was the car on Flyte Street. The driver's side rear tire and hubcap were scratched and dented in all the right places and the color matched our scrapings perfectly. Of course, the lab'll analyze the hell out of them, but as far as I'm concerned it's a match. Looks like we got our shooter."

"Looks like somebody else got our shooter," I said.

"Yeah, I guess so." There was a long pause. "Listen, you ever hear of a PI called Wallace MacShane?"

"Why?"

"That's a yes or no question, there's no bleeping 'why...'"

"Then, no. Why do you want to know?"

"This MacShane guy requested a license check for Gerrara's car on Monday. Claimed to be a PI. Only problem is, we can't find any listing for MacShane at all, where he lives, where he works, whether he's licensed. There's nothing on him. He's a total blank."

"This is the first I've heard of him," I said, which was at least literally true.

"Yeah? OK. Well, I mainly called to thank you for the tip on Gerrara. You made me look good and I appreciate it. I won't forget it."

"I'd remind you if you did."

Officer Nance responded in her own inimitable fashion and hung up.

I replaced my phone in its cradle. I would have laid back down myself, only I doubted I could get to sleep again. Nance's call gave me too much to think about. I went to the kitchen and started some coffee. While it brewed, my thoughts came slowly, like waves of sludge washing up on a beach after an oil spill.

I had never heard the name Wallace MacShane, but I did recognize it. It was one of Lance Talbot's aliases. Which meant Talbot requested the check on Gerrara's car.

That much was easy, but it got more complicated. Because on Monday when Talbot submitted the license check, he was still following me full-time. Since I hadn't had any contact with Gerrara until yesterday morning, it raised the questions, when and how did Talbot?

A round-the-clock tail would not have left Talbot much time for anything else, so it was unlikely he ran across Gerrara on another job. Besides, to assume Talbot had an unrelated case involving Gerrara seemed unnecessarily complicated; it was the kind of loose thinking that always got William of Occam into a lather.

Saturday night was the key, I decided. That was when Gerrara and a partner—probably Hardison—had shot and killed the two muggers on Flyte Street. It seemed reasonable that

Talbot would have tailed me into Shakytown that night. While there, he might have have seen the shootings and taken down Gerrara's license number. Since he didn't inform the police about it but instead tried to find out the car's owner himself, Talbot may have intended to make some money from what he saw. This scenario sounded plausible enough and for a short time I actually believed it.

But it was ultimately flawed. The muggers were shot several blocks away from where I'd been. No matter how loosely Talbot was following me that night, he would never have laid off far enough to witness the shootings. So he must have seen something else that made him interested in Gerrara's Cadillac. But what?

With Gerrara and Hardison both dead, the only person left to ask was Talbot himself.

* * *

I drove across town through a sporadic, misty drizzle, my wipers scraping angrily across the windshield. The sky was dull pewter. I paid close attention to the cars around me and made sure I wasn't being followed.

Talbot's company address turned out to be a Victorian cottage on a corner lot. The chiffon yellow walls and bright blue porch, shutters, and trim looked like decorative icing on a gingerbread house.

The whole neighborhood had long ago turned into a commercial ghetto where houses had been gutted and renovated to serve as office space. Professional servicers of all stripes, from lawyers and plumbers to psychic advisers, had planted their signposts by the sidewalk like so many horse tethers.

Despite the spiffy paint job, Talbot's building still looked dilapidated. His roof ridge sagged at the middle and his gutter lines were visibly off horizontal. The walls were pitted and pocked, and even the thick layer of paint could not hide their defects. In fact, the bright paint made the house look worse—like an aging hooker, who, though eager to please, has stayed in the game too long.

A narrow concrete driveway looped around behind his building through a thin and patchy lawn. I crossed the street from where I parked and followed a flagstone walk to Talbot's wide wooden porch. A placard by the front door read "Axiom Security" and gave an answering service number to call if the office was closed. The door was locked. I pressed the doorbell, an ancient black buzzer affair with exposed wires, and a muffled "whir" sounded somewhere within. The long, etched-glass window in the door was covered by a roller blind so I could not see if anyone was coming.

I waited and pressed the bell again. Still nobody answered. I moved along the porch to look in at the front window but the curtains were drawn.

I stepped down from the porch and walked slowly along the driveway to the back of the house. The air felt cool and damp on my skin but at least the drizzle had stopped. The back yard was quite small. Most of it was taken up by a detached two-car garage done up in the same garish yellow and blue. I peeked in through a dirty side window and could just make out Talbot's grey Cherokee inside. The mirror on the passenger side was still broken. The other half of the garage was empty. If Talbot had a second car, it looked like he was out.

The back door to the house was set above a concrete stoop with crumbled corners. This door was also locked. A sheer white curtain in the window left gaps at the sides that I could peek through and see the kitchen inside. There were dishes stacked neatly beside the sink and pots seated on the stove. It looked like Talbot actually lived here after all. I knocked loudly on the door in case Talbot had not been able to hear the doorbell.

I didn't wait long before continuing around to the other side of the house, where a shaggy hedge ran the full length of the wall. By leaning against the bushes, I could just peer into the dark living room through either of two windows.

The furniture inside looked more functional than fancy. The chairs were unmatched and threadbare. There was an old sofa with a coffee table in front. A strip of veneer was peeling off the side of a particle-board bookshelf. The TV was off and no one was sleeping on the couch.

Still leaning forward, I glanced down through a hole in the hedge into a deep semicircular recess in the ground. The wall of the pit was made of corrugated metal and its bottom was covered with white gravel. I got down on my knees and poked my head through the stems. It was a basement window-well with a single pane of glass. The window itself was dirty and spattered with yellow paint from the house's last make-over.

I moved over to the other living room window and found a second window-well directly beneath it. Only this window's glass was broken and its frame had been left ajar.

I stood up and brushed the hedge needles off my knees. My black jeans were damp where I'd knelt on the wet ground. I looked around at the two streets running past Talbot's house. The traffic on the one-way avenue was moving too fast for anyone to pay attention to me and there was no one at all on the cross street.

I walked to the back of the house and pushed in behind the hedge. Its branches scraped my face and hands, and spiderwebs clung to my hair as I crept along the wall to the broken window. I sat down with my legs in the window-well and bent over to look inside. There wasn't much to see. Between the overcast day and the dense hedge, very little light got into the basement. All I could see were faint glimmers of broken glass on the cement floor.

As I sat there considering my options, I could feel the cold dampness of the ground leaching into my pants. I fought off the urge for a cigarette.

Now, I am a firm believer that breaking and entering should be left to professionals—no question. But when the breakage is already done, what is the harm in a little unlawful entry for the gifted amateur? Sure, if I was caught, I could be arrested, lose my investigator's license, or even be shot if I were mistaken for a burglar. But I didn't intend to be caught.

Besides, I still nursed a grudge about the way Talbot had bested me in the field. I had something to prove, not only to him but to myself. The thought of the expression on his fat face when he came back and found me waiting for him in his house was all the motive I needed.

It might also give me a chance to find out the answers to some important questions. Like why did Talbot notice Gerrara's car in Shakytown? And who hired Talbot to follow me in the first place? I might even get my stolen retainer back. In short, getting the drop on Talbot would be more rewarding than anything else I could imagine.

I leaned forward and gingerly checked the pieces of glass left in the sash. I removed any that were loose so they wouldn't fall to the floor when I went in. I pushed the window forward a few times and decided the hinges were acceptably quiet.

I turned around, facing away from the house, and knelt inside the window-well with my legs crossed and cramped. The jagged gravel bit into my knees even through my jeans. I gripped the top of the metal wall, shifting my weight as much as possible to my hands.

Blood pounded in my head. I was confident that the hedge screened me from any casual passerby or motorist, but I was still concerned that I could give myself away by sound. Just because Talbot did not answer the door and all the lights were out, did not mean conclusively that he wasn't home. In fact, I had to operate under the assumption that he was, just in case.

Keeping my moves slow and methodical, I reached back, pushed open the frame and slid my feet into the window. The gravel crunched softly as my weight settled back onto my knees. With the bottom rail of the sash resting on my calves, I regripped the top of the metal wall and slowly pushed my legs farther through the window, lowering myself with my arms. My pants made a soft whisper as they passed over the sill.

The only touchy moment came when my belt buckle scraped on the metal latch. In reality, the sound couldn't have been very loud, but to my pounding ears it was amplified to heavy metal proportions.

After my waist was through, I brought my arms down and lowered myself, holding onto the sill. For a second, I felt a sharp twinge as the swinging frame slid across the wound on my back, but I was not going to let simple poetic justice deter me and continued to squeeze inside.

When I was almost all the way in, I ducked my head in to see where I could drop to my feet without landing on any broken glass. As best I could tell, the original burglar had smashed the window very hard and the shards had scattered far into the basement. There was no glass directly beneath the window so it was an easy matter to let myself down, belly-scraping the wall. When I finally dropped to the ground, the window swung down heavily on the backs of my hands. It didn't feel good, but at least it was quiet. Once on the floor, I withdrew my arms and gently set the frame in place.

A gloomy twilight suffused the room like a grey mist, making it impossible to recognize any colors. Cardboard boxes stacked against the back wall, some flattened, some intact, looked more like an abstract collage of monochrome squares and cubes than actual objects. An old washer and dryer stood at the far wall beside a cruddy utility tub.

I stood silently, letting my eyes adjust to the gloom and straining to hear even the slightest noise from the rest of the house. At first there was nothing. Not a footstep, not a murmur, not a note of music. Then I began to think I could hear something. Was it a door closing above or just random traffic noise from the street? As I listened harder, my brain began to conjure up sounds to reward my efforts, sounds that may or may not have been there.

Suddenly the boiler kicked in beside me with a loud "ting!" and water rumbled through the radiator pipes causing crashes and bangs all over the house. It was all I could do to keep from diving headfirst into the sump hole.

When my heart slowed again and my eyes became acclimated, I made a quick survey of the basement. A long work bench was set along the front wall. There were surprisingly few wood-working tools on it however since Talbot's projects all seemed to involve electronics and optics. There were lenses and directional microphones in various stages of repair and construction on and under the bench. I noted several gadgets that looked interesting even though I couldn't guess what they were for.

Talbot had an elaborate weight machine set up in one corner of the room and he had attached a heavy boxing bag and a speed bag to the exposed wooden joists that crossed the ceiling.

Halfway across the basement, directly opposite the broken window, a wooden staircase with open risers led up to the first floor. Gripping both hand rails and trying to keep my feet at the edges of the steps, I went up as quietly as possible. My execution was nearly perfect, not even a whisper of a creak until I almost reached the top. But when I took my foot off the second-to-last step, it let out a shriek as if space-time itself were being drawn and quartered.

I stood transfixed. If anyone was home, they would surely have heard it; and there was no way I could get away through the basement window before they found me. There was no way to go but forward. I cursed my wounded ego that had got me into this mess and pushed open the door at the top of the stairs.

I stepped out into the kitchen, intent on any sound. All I heard was my own breathing and a slow, steady drip coming from the kitchen sink.

I glanced over and knew immediately I was alone in the house---perhaps my luck was beginning to change. Water dripping from the faucet had overflowed the sink and was leaking out slowly into a large puddle on the floor. Talbot must have left hours ago for the water to accumulate like that. I pushed the faucet lever down to stop the drip and moved a saucer that had been blocking the drain. The water quickly drained away in a great swirl.

Aside from the wet floor, Talbot's kitchen turned out to be as immaculate inside as it had appeared from outdoors. The counters and stove top were pristine without even a grease spot around the gas burners. The trap in the sink was so clean it could have been used as a miniature colander.

It was a small room and there were not many cabinets, which explained why Talbot had his pots stacked up on the back of the stove and dishes stored by the sink. A surprisingly formal dining table stood in a corner opposite the back door, trapping two of four dining room chairs against the walls.

I pushed through a white door at the back of the kitchen into Talbot's office. It had originally been the dining room but it had lost that function long ago. Glancing around the shadowy room, I was struck by the taste and expense that must have gone into its decor. Although Talbot's house was gradually falling apart, he kept his office a haven of class and quality. The beautiful wood desk at the room's center, the lawyer's bookshelves filled with law books against the back wall, the plush forest green carpet, the desktop computer four generations more advanced than my own, all would have worked to create an atmosphere of competence, efficiency, and security.

The formal elegance of his office coupled with Talbot's folksy personality would have made a winning impression on his clients. If I were to sit down in one of his leather armchairs for just a few minutes, I might hire him myself.

On his walls, Talbot kept autographed pictures of various celebrities and VIPs who had been satisfied clients. The practice seemed more in keeping with a trendy Italian restaurant than a private detective's office, but there was no denying the gratitude in their messages. There were also photos showing Talbot at work: here, as a bodyguard for a tough guy Hollywood actor on a local shoot; and there, as the big money bag man at a politician's breakfast. It was an impressive and enviable clientele. I peevishly wondered if Talbot had forged the autographs himself. Even if he hadn't, it was such a good idea, I considered using it for my own office.

But one thing kept me from being too impressed. His office was a shambles. Someone had turned the room upside down, apparently looking for something. File cabinets at the front wall had been overturned and the contents of several drawers were scattered all over the floor and desk. The drive bay panel on the computer case had been pried open and the hard drive removed. Even the monitor screen was smashed. I looked through the drawers and cabinets but didn't find a single computer floppy disk or backup tape. Presumably they were all taken. On the floor by his desk, Talbot's answering machine had been crushed under the searcher's heel. His telephone had been thrown across the room toward the second doorway, leading to the foyer.

A mass of papers was strewn over Talbot's desk; receipts, reports, proposals, and other documents, all related to work he'd done within the last month. Somehow he had managed to drum up several consulting jobs, lectures to corporate executives, two or three requests to locate missing persons and potential court witnesses. He even did some background and credit checks. In addition to all this, I reminded myself, someone had hired him to follow me. Unfortunately, I found no documentation relating to that job. It was an enviable work load. If I could discover Talbot's secret for landing so much business, then maybe the eight hundred dollars he took from me would end up being a worthwhile investment.

Beneath these other papers, I peeled up a number of loose sheets that were stuck to the desk. They were pages from Talbot's report documenting a city councilman's philandering. The prominent Eola politician had personally hired Talbot to do the report to see how much dirt would be available to his opponents if he chose to run for mayor (answer: a lot). But it was the tacky pink and red droplets on the sheets that drew my attention. After seeing Talbot's spotless kitchen, I couldn't believe he would be so careless about wiping up a beverage spill from his mahogany desk.

As I considered this, I glanced down at the pages on the floor. They were scattered all over and I had not been very careful about not walking on them. Where I did, I had left red footprints emblazoned with the pattern of my tennis shoe soles.

It did not take long to find the source. Although I hadn't noticed it before on the dark carpet, there was a deep stain, apparently of blood, halfway between the desk and the door to the kitchen. It was mostly dry, but my wet shoes had dampened it again. As I knelt down to examine the area more carefully, I found other stains as well. There was the main puddle where the blood had originally pooled and a series of lesser stains that led toward the other door into the front hall. Drag marks in the carpet pile confirmed the direction indicated by the bloodstains.

They pointed to a triangular cubbyhole beneath the stairs that led up from Talbot's foyer. The cubbyhole door was made of painted wood slats that matched the wall molding. The area around its black iron handle was marked with brownish red smudges. As I reached out for the little door's handle, I had the sinking feeling that my luck had not changed after all.

CHAPTER TWENTY-THREE

My own bad luck was nothing compared to the man's in the closet. His large body sat propped against the cubbyhole wall, his knees drawn up to his chest, his head angled sideways under the slanted ceiling. The sparse, stringy hair that he used to brush over his bald spot now hung down loose to his shoulder. A large round eye stared up at me, despite the fact that both his eyes were closed.

It was Lance Talbot. He wore the same drab clothes as when I'd last seen him; wrinkled beige suit, white shirt, hand-tooled leather belt, no tie. His pale, moon face had lost its patented good-ol'-boy grin. Instead, dried blood snaked down from the corners of his mouth.

Then there was that third eye... In Hindu circles it was supposed to represent wisdom and spiritual vision. But Talbot and I ran with a less enlightened crowd, and to me it looked like a bullet hole.

Talbot had been shot once in the forehead and it was enough. The skin where the bullet entered was torn and scorched and showed the phantom imprint of a gun muzzle--a textbook contact wound. Before he died, Talbot had felt the gun pressed there and knew exactly what was coming. Although I could not see an exit wound, I guessed there was one; the back of his head was not stuck to the wall by greasy kid stuff.

I reached down and carefully lifted the corner of his jacket.

He had a leather holster strapped to his belt but no gun. I removed his wallet from a back pocket and leafed through it quickly. The contents seemed no different than before. Same driver's licenses, same credit and business cards under different names, same wad of $50 bills. Wallace MacShane, the name Officer Nance had asked about, appeared on a driver's license and credit card.

My fingers lingered briefly over the cash. After all, Talbot had taken $800 from me and he certainly wasn't going to miss it. In the end, though, I left the money where it was. My position was dubious enough without stealing from a murdered man's wallet.

In fact, "dubious" scarcely covered it. I had broken into a competitor's home, left fingerprints all over his ransacked office, and even tracked footprints in the murdered man's blood. What should I do for an encore, call the police and turn myself in?

In retrospect that is exactly what I should have done—reported the body and taken the heat for being in the house. Talbot was dead long before I arrived; any investigator could see that. At worst, there might be a hard look given at revoking my private investigator's license. More likely I would get the legal equivalent of a slap on the wrist or a stern talking to. At least I wouldn't be a suspect for Lance Talbot's murder.

Not unless I did what I decided to do next.

With my handkerchief, I carefully wiped off Talbot's billfold and replaced it in his pocket. I closed the door to the cubbyhole and buffed my prints off the iron door handle.

While I had my activities fresh in mind, I went through the rest of the office, carefully removing all traces that I had been there. I picked up any papers that I may have handled or stepped on, folded them up, and stuffed them in my pockets. I cleaned the bottoms of my shoes with several sheets and pocketed those as well. I wiped down the drawer handles of the desk and file cabinets. I rubbed off the edge of the desk top, the back of the leather chair, and every other surface I thought I might have touched. I was a one-man-gang of evidence eradication.

When I was done with the office, I retraced my steps through the kitchen and basement and eliminated any possible fingerprints or other marks of my presence. I wiped the basement window and window frame completely, and did the front and back door handles. I even did a quick swipe on the front doorbell button. Fortunately, I hadn't touched much outside of the office so the rest of my clean-up did not take very long.

When I finished, I went up to the second floor, scrupulously avoiding the handrail. I was acutely aware of Talbot's body beneath the stairs, like a threshold that shouldn't be crossed.

There were three bedrooms off the upstairs hallway.

The master bedroom was decorated to strictly masculine tastes, with a dark-plaid bedspread, big-emblem nautical wallpaper, heavy blue drapes, and large, dark pieces of furniture. Judging from the books on his nightstand, Talbot liked to read men's adventure novels, the racier the better.

On the dresser, he had a framed wedding picture taken many years earlier, showing himself and a sharp-faced bride. It was the only indication that Talbot had ever been married. There were no women's clothes in any of the closets and no women's products in the bathrooms.

The second bedroom I checked had been converted into a darkroom, with several layers of thick black cloth stapled over the window and photographs tacked up on the walls. This room had also been searched with the same rigor as the office downstairs. At the center of the floor there was a large pile of smashed developing equipment, the contents of overturned desk drawers, yards of unspooled film, photographic negatives, and ripped up prints. I knelt down to pick through some of this material but quickly gave up. Whoever had been here presumably removed what they came for.

I carefully stepped around the edge of the room towards the desk under the window. The pictures on the walls turned out to be surveillance shots taken of husbands, wives, and lovers who'd been caught red-handed and red-faced in the act of cheating on their partners. Their activities were not unusual, in fact they all seemed rather banal, which made me wonder why Talbot kept the pictures in the first place. Any private detective will tell you, infidelity doesn't cut it as a spectator sport.

The photos must have been something other than a voyeur's gallery. My guess was, they were prime blackmail material. With more greed than ethics, Talbot could easily have turned a steady tax-free income from the people he'd caught on film. It would mean betraying the clients who originally hired him, but Talbot may have been too slick to let a little thing like that bother him. Seeing how he ended up, he may have been too slick for his own good.

I reached the large desk and peered into its empty drawer wells for any stray pages that might have been missed by the previous searcher, but there were none, not even any torn papers caught in the drawer runners.

A tall plastic wastebasket stood beside the desk but it was empty. There'd been a trashcan liner and crumpled cigarette packs and ashes mixed in with the other debris on the floor, so I surmised that its contents had also been searched. I picked up the wastebasket and found a small scrap of photograph an inch and a half square stuck to the bottom by some mystery grit.

The image on the scrap was very dark. As best I could make out, it showed a car in an alley at night. Part of the car's front fender was visible, as were some garbage cans next to a brick wall. Behind the car was an ambiguous blur that may have been a human being.

The only thing clear on the picture was part of the date stamp superimposed at the bottom. The scrap showed the initial digit "1" followed by part of a zero in the position that most likely indicated the month. So the picture was either taken this month, which was promising, or in October of some previous year, which was less so.

The scrap was part of an unsuccessful attempt to develop a photograph taken at night. When the print came out too dark to be of any use, Talbot had torn it up and thrown the pieces into the wastebasket. This particular piece had missed the basket and somehow become stuck to the bottom.

I didn't know if the scrap was important; the odds were certainly against it. But since it had been missed by whoever searched the room earlier, it at least had potential. I put the scrap into my wallet.

I rummaged around the darkroom for several minutes in the hope of finding something more. It would have helped a lot if I knew what I was looking for.

Finally, I moved on to the last room upstairs. Two wooden gun cabinets stood against its walls, loaded with pistols, shotguns, and semi-automatic rifles. Several wood crates containing boxes of ammunition, clips, sights, scopes, silencers, and other attachments were scattered around the bare floor. I even found a case of smoke grenades beneath an armchair. Talbot had enough weapons stashed to outfit a militia.

Whoever ransacked the other rooms apparently had no need of additional weapons, but my position was different. Talbot had taken away my only gun three days ago. After seeing what had happened to Hardison, Gerrara, and now Talbot himself, I felt it was a good time to replace it.

I smashed one of the cabinet doors and removed a Smith and Wesson .357 Magnum revolver. The barrel was longer than the one I'd lost, but overall the gun had a similar feel. I checked the cylinder and found each chamber loaded. I tucked the gun into my back pocket and pulled out the tail of my shirt to cover it.

Finished with the upstairs, I went back down to Talbot's office and took one last look around to make sure I hadn't missed anything. Using a sheet of paper, I picked up the telephone from the floor by the hallway door and plugged the wire back into the wall. I listened for the dial-tone and pressed the redial key. After a series of dialing "bloops," I heard a ringing signal at the other end.

"Riverview Mobile Home Park," a rough-sounding man began. “How may I help you?”

“This is Lance Talbot at Axiom Security," I said. "I'd like to talk with someone about--“

"The hell it is!" The man said and hung up.

I hit redial again, only this time he didn't answer.

It was time to go. I left through the kitchen door, making sure it locked behind me.

As I came around the back of the house, the twenty yards to my car felt like miles. I took a deep breath and marched down Talbot's driveway, whistling silently. The street was empty and no one was watching. Not that it mattered. I was just a guy going about my personal business with nothing to hide and nothing to fear. I was so ordinary as to be invisible. Nothing to see, folks, move along. Nothing attracts attention like furtiveness. I sauntered across the street to my car and shut Talbot's gun in my glove box. I pulled away without incident.

I drove to an outdoor shopping mall across town and bought a pair of cheap tennis shoes at the chain discount store. My old shoes would have traces of blood on them no matter how well I cleaned them. I put on the new pair in the car. My old shoes, and the crumpled papers from Talbot's office, I stashed into the store's plastic bag. Then I drove to a different mall where they had the same anchor discount store and disposed of the plastic bag in a mall dumpster. If by some miracle the bag were discovered, the clerks at the store nearest the dumpster would not be able to identify me.

Next I went to a large office plaza in another section of town where the ground-floor banks, shops and restaurants provided plenty of anonymity. Wearing a pair of leather driving gloves, I punched up the non-emergency police number on a pay phone.

When the police operator answered, I said, "There's a man dead..." and gave Talbot's address. I hung up immediately, giving her no time to ask questions. What the police don't know can't hurt me.

My civic duty done, I returned to my car and plowed through a now earnest rain to my office. Swollen clouds hung low over the city, like a bloated aerialist in a net. It was 12:30 when I pulled into the empty alley beside Alphonse Andeo's warehouse. I dashed to the entrance to keep from getting soaked.

I took the elevator up and stood dripping in the hallway as I fumbled for the key. When I pushed open the door, the mail that had been dropped through the letter slot went skidding across the floor.

I flicked on the light switch and retrieved the scattered envelopes. There were a couple bills, some offers for magazines I'd never heard of, and a red-white-and-blue express reply from the Department of Motor Vehicles. I trashed the subscription offers, tossed the bills onto my desk, and sat down to open the DMV letter.

It was the response to my license plate query for the black BMW the two men in camel had brought to Curtiz's office the previous Friday. With any luck, this would answer questions I hadn't even known to ask.

I tore open the envelope with my fingernail. According to the DMV, the sedan was a company car belonging to an Eola publishing house, the same one that handled Curtiz's most recent works. The men were Curtiz's publishers, that's all. That manuscript they had taken from Vera Marshall was probably Curtiz's current work in progress. I scowled and threw the letter down on my desk, then brushed it into the garbage can.

I don't know why I'd been so hopeful about that particular lead. Maybe it was because everything else had gone so badly lately that I figured the law of averages owed me a break. Unfortunately, breaks don't work that way and probability is a notorious welsher.

But as I sat there, a vague idea that had been rumbling around at the back of my mind finally clicked, like a rusty tumbler in an old-fashioned lock.

Curtiz, blackmail... Lance Talbot.

From what I'd seen, Talbot's name was well known among Eola celebrities, who turned to him whenever they needed the services of a private detective. Why then had Curtiz come to me, a low-rent new-comer? Talbot would have seemed a far more natural choice...

What if I was not Curtiz's first choice?

Suppose Curtiz had hired Talbot first, for whatever reason. And suppose Talbot had turned up something juicy on Curtiz, something too valuable to pass up. Lance Talbot could have been the elusive blackmailer who had so spooked Curtiz he couldn't even tell me about it... That would also explain why Talbot had been following me--he was afraid I might jeopardize his financial arrangement with Curtiz.

I warmed to the idea immediately. Obviously there was no proof, but at least one fact supported it. All of the file cabinets in Talbot's office had been pushed over, but most of the files were actually left alone. The killer or killers only emptied out the first two drawers of the first cabinet, so whatever they were looking for could be found between the letters "A" and "E." If Talbot had formerly worked for Curtiz, Curtiz's paperwork could have been among the missing files. That might even have been what they were looking for.

The notion struck me out of the blue: could Preston Curtiz be Talbot's killer? If Talbot was blackmailing him, Curtiz's motive would be strong enough. The writer was certainly obsessive about his reputation and there was no telling how far he might go to protect it. But murder? It seemed far-fetched, admittedly, but not impossible.

There were two messages on my answering machine. The first came from a British-sounding lawyer named Taggart who wanted to meet me that afternoon at his office or later in the evening at the Savan Hotel where he was giving a speech. I'd never heard of this Taggart and started to look into who he was, when the voice on the second message brought me up short.

It was Vera Marshall.

"Mr. Tobin," the recording began, "It's Friday morning, 10 o'clock. Mr. Curtiz asked me to relay to you that he is very disappointed that you have pursued an investigation completely unrelated to what he hired you for. He wanted me to tell you that he considers it, quote "a breach of faith bordering on fraud" unquote. He said you may keep the unused portion of your fee, but as of this moment, he no longer wishes to retain your services."

The voice paused and I thought I could hear a sigh on the tape. In a softer, more personal tone, Miss Marshall added something I'm sure was not relayed from Curtiz.

"I am sorry," she said.

CHAPTER TWENTY-FOUR

Fired... Just when I thought I was getting close. I sat at my desk, staring at the office walls, my gut twisted up inside.

For a week and a half I had kept busy enough to hold off my depression. By focusing on the job at hand, I managed to shut out the simultaneous train wrecks of my marriage, my profession, my life. Now the artificial support was gone, and they came crashing over me, all the more devastating for having been held in check so long.

Everything I had counted on or hoped for was suddenly snatched away. All I could do was sit there dumbly and watch the unraveling. And I alone was to blame. The fault lay in some inherent personal flaw that I could neither diagnose nor fix, so it would never get better.

This is the downside to losing yourself in work. When the job is over, you have nothing left.

No, I thought. It can't be over. I can't let it be. It was not even hope--just a grim determination. Somehow I had to change Curtiz's mind and show him I was still on the trail he'd set me. I had no other option.

I left my office and set off for Curtiz's house on Tamur Lane. The drive took twenty-five minutes; even the traffic lights were against me.

When I arrived, Ms. Marshall's VW was parked in front of

the house and I pulled in behind her car. I didn't see Curtiz's white Buick anywhere. The pavement was still slick and wet, but the air was warmer as the sun tried to break through the clouds.

I followed the cement walk to Curtiz's door and rang the bell. Vera Marshall opened it, wearing a navy blue pants suit that set off her blond hair and pale skin. She still looked like an angel.

"Oh, I thought I told--" she began, but I interrupted her.

"I need to see your boss. I have to talk with him." I shoved my foot between the door and the metal strip on the floor.

"He's not here," she said. She tried to push the door closed, but I pushed back and it was no contest. The door swung open and Vera Marshall retreated into the wide marble foyer. I entered the house and closed the door behind me.

"Then I'll wait. I won't leave without speaking to him."

Ms. Marshall stood by the staircase that led to the upper floors. She looked defiant but a little frightened at the same time. Her face and scalp were turning red. She shook her head angrily and the back and forth swish of her ponytail was like a nervous horse swatting at flies.

"You'll have to," she said. "If you don't get out now, I will call the police and you can talk to them..." She inched towards Curtiz's office on my left.

"I wouldn't if I were you."

"Watch me," she said. She ducked into the book-lined office and grabbed the phone from the desk.

I followed her in.

"Go ahead, but consider this: I know why Curtiz hired me. If you bring police in, I'll be happy to explain it to them. But I seriously doubt Curtiz would approve."

Vera Marshall's finger was poised above the phone keypad ready to hit the final "-1."

"What do you know?" she asked.

"I know enough. I know about the other investigator and

what he was up to. Now why don't you hang up? I'm not going to hurt you, if that's what you're afraid of..."

She thought about it, still holding the phone to her head. Finally, she took her finger away from the dial keys and pushed down one of the prongs in the telephone cradle. I could hear the dim dial tone even where I stood. She sank into the desk chair and hung up the receiver. She ran her hand over her face.

"I'm sorry," she said. "Sorry for everything. The whole thing was unforgivable. I know it's no consolation, but I never liked the idea from the beginning. I told him so."

"I can only talk to Curtiz," I said. "Will you get him for me?"

"I can't. He's still in L.A."

"They have phones there too. They're only a few hours behind the rest of us, so you won't be waking him up." I moved closer and leaned towards her across the desk, "Call him."

Vera began to raise some objection but changed her mind. She picked up the phone and punched in a number. Her nervous fingers misdialed the area code for Los Angeles and she had to start over.

"He's probably not even there," she said, not looking at me. "He tends to be very..." She stopped. "Yes, hello, sir. It's me."

Sir. That didn't sound too intimate. Perhaps there was hope for me yet.

"Yes..." she went on. "Yes, I gave him the message... Yes, that too... Well, the thing is, he's here now. At the office. He insists on talking to you."

I reached across the desk and took the receiver from her hand. She seemed glad to be rid of it.

"Mr. Curtiz," I said into the mouthpiece. "It's been a long time."

"What are you doing there?" he began. His tight, controlled voice sounded strained over the telephone. "I made it clear..."

"You can cut the bull. I know why you hired me."

There was a long pause at Curtiz's end--an awkward silence that spanned a continent.

"She told you, then," Curtiz said. "You must be a very persuasive young man. A shame in a way, but it doesn't change anything. If you know why I hired you, then you understand why you can no longer work for me."

I didn't even try to grasp the meaning of this paradox. I had to focus on what I knew, or what I thought I knew.

"I know all about Lance Talbot," I told him. "And what he was doing to you."

"For me, you mean." Curtiz paused. I could practically hear his thick eyebrows wrinkle. "Unless-- unless Vera didn't tell you after all... And there's no reason she should... I believe you're just trying to bluff me!" Curtiz laughed a long, loud, heartfelt laugh, the kind that normally does a soul good. "You nearly had me convinced, but you don't even know about the book, do you?"

What book?! I knew the game was lost. But like a log-roller trying to keep his balance over a freezing river, I grabbed at anything to try to stay on top.

"Of course I know about it. Talbot had it."

Curtiz guffawed once more.

"What impudence! What a shame I have to let you go. In many ways you were so perfect."

"Okay, so I don't know about any book," I admitted. "I do know about Talbot's scheme to--"

Vera Marshall shot me a puzzled look at the same time Curtiz interrupted.

"Then you know nothing! I might as well tell you now. I hired Lance Talbot to follow you. He was to report back to me on everything you did. He told me where you went, who you met, what you said, what you drank. Mr. Talbot's descriptions were invaluable, full of exactly the kind of details I needed to make my new novel come alive. A lot more detail than I ever got from you, I might add."

It slowly dawned on me what Curtiz was talking about. It was so preposterous I could hardly believe it. So demeaning, I knew it must be true.

"A novel? Based on my actions?"

As I spoke, I searched Vera Marshall's face for a sign of surprise or indignation, any hint that she was not aware of what Curtiz was up to. Instead she looked away from my gaze. She had known all along.

"Of course a novel!" Curtiz said. "My comeback project. A Kafkaesque whodunit, a noir collaboration a la Chandler and Beckett. My best book idea in years! And you were the perfect antihero, so lost and alone. The private eye hired to do an impossible job, given no background, no explanations, nothing but ambiguity. Forced to follow a meaningless case with no hope of understanding or accomplishment." Curtiz took a breath. "Don't you see? It is life itself! Everyman confronts the existential questions: 'Why am I here? What am I to do?' The symbolism is so rich, it almost borders on allegory!"

I couldn't follow all that he said, but I heard enough to know I'd been played for a sucker. I began to feel light-headed, even a little sick.

He went on "... And what answers does our investigator find? The only ones possible: There is no reason. No reason and nothing to be done. His whole sorry life makes no difference. We all wrap ourselves in such sad scraps of meaning, but they are only vanity. Vanity and ashes!"

Curtiz paused in his excited harangue. Perhaps he expected me to congratulate him on his great idea, but once again I disappointed him and said nothing.

"It will be my greatest triumph. A huge first printing, front page review in The Times, a guaranteed film deal, maybe even another Pulitzer. It will be like coming home again. I have been away too long."

"Why me?" I asked finally in a voice no louder than a Kafka cockroach. All my work, two weeks of my life, the beatings inflicted by Talbot and the two thugs, all thrown away on a fraud and a sham. All for nothing. Compared to me, a hard-shelled bug was a higher form of life.

"It didn't have to be you. Anyone would have done. I just needed a model, a not-too-bright private eye, preferably one who'd been beaten-down by life. I needed to know how such a man would react in certain circumstances, needed it for those all-important details. There were other candidates, but when Talbot found out about your wife, he suggested that you would be the best one. And he was so right. Your attitude was priceless, so young and cocky, but at the same time self-consciously tragic. Precisely the absurd mix I wanted to portray."

"And the person I was supposed to find?"

Curtiz laughed again.

"You still don't get it. There was no one! That person doesn't exist--except as a symbol of course. Instead of waiting for his Godot, my detective goes off in search of him. It makes for more action that way. Only the end result is the same."

Indignation is the surest sign of life, and I wasn't dead yet. Not quite.

"So you made me your prop, your dupe, your fool, your..."

Curtiz cut me off:

"You were a child's wind-up toy. I wound you up and set you going. I had you followed and watched to see what you would do. I don't see how you can complain of it. You were well-paid for your services. They just weren't the services you thought they were."

He was right. While I thought I was out walking mean streets for Curtiz, I was merely his street-walker.

"Well-paid?" I asked, my voice tired and hoarse. "Talbot

robbed me the first night. I came away with nothing. My wife left me. I'm broke. I had nothing left but my job and my self respect, and you've turned them both into a joke. But no, I have no right to complain."

Behind Curtiz's desk, Vera Marshall brought her hand up to her mouth and pressed the knuckles against her lips. Her eyes were watery and her nose was red.

Curtiz stopped effusing for a moment. A trace of worry crept into his voice.

"Well, I do regret that Talbot hit you that night. That was not part of the plan. But I had to ensure that you would not quit, no matter how frustrating the work became. You can see how crucial that was. As long as you had the money, you might be tempted to give it back. We had to prevent that. Now that you know the truth, of course, you'll be recompensed again for the first week. Vera has already mailed the check. You won't be out of pocket for your efforts at all, believe me."

"And what about your student Rudi Alsmith?" I asked. "Don't you care what happened to her?"

"Damn Rudi Alsmith! She is the reason you're fired. I hired you for a grand and noble task. To go after the great white whale, to hunt the questing beast alone, to plumb unfathomable depths and match wits with a witless universe… Instead, you start nosing around the tedious story of an ordinary girl whose death was sad and wasteful, but irrelevant. You took my great scheme and reduced it to kitchen table melodrama. Rudi Alsmith ruined you for me! Ever since she died, everything you've done has been a waste of your time and my money. I'm putting an end to it now. It was bad luck for both of us she died when she did. It was an unfortunate coincidence that led you astray. But that is all it was."

Curtiz had said his piece, and a mighty piece it was. Rudi was gone and nothing I could do would bring her back. That much was true. In the grand scheme of things, it didn't matter what I did. All was vanity and ashes, as Curtiz said.

But as I stood there, the phone still clasped to my ear, I felt something stir deep within, a wave of power or energy that passed through me so subtly it could easily have been dismissed or missed altogether. It centered on a pinprick of consciousness so bright, so dense, so compact, its light radiated only inward. Not darkness visible but invisible light, a hard darkness at the pit of my soul.

A voice came like a whisper from that dark place, a still, quiet voice that commanded attention; like the night wind calling over a mountain or a low vibration in black diamond. As I listened to the voice, Curtiz faded away. I didn't lose the anger I felt but it became stilled; my humiliation remained but was muted. The voice spoke to me in a language that would take a lifetime to learn, in terms I could never truly understand. A lifetime of study without comprehension; a lifetime commingling devotion and hope and fear and doubt and certainty. A lifetime of all these things and more.

A lifetime of longing to hear once more that hard darkness within--and being satisfied with silence.

"...all it was," Curtiz repeated.

The other voice was gone. I had not understood a word but had felt all that was needed.

"You can believe that if you want," I told Curtiz, "But you're wrong. You are the one who got lost, who missed what's going on around you. You thought you controlled everything, like a white-coat Poindexter with his laboratory rats. You wanted to watch me maneuver through your unstructured maze. Well, I'm through it now, and you never controlled anything! It has all gotten away from you, only you don't know it yet. When I'm gone, there will be no one to protect you from your arrogance."

Curtiz slammed down the phone and our connection ended.

I handed the phone back to his secretary and turned to leave.

Vera Marshall started to speak but I kept going. I wanted no apologies and had nothing to say to her. I walked out of Curtiz's house without a word.

Outside, I had to shield my eyes. The sun burst through a hole in clouds and blazed down magnificently upon the old earth. Before the purple clouds, an incredibly distinct rainbow arced across the sky, both ends clearly visible. A fainter secondary bow ranged outside of it, and I even glimpsed what might have been a third.

I went home.

* * *

Epiphanies don't last; intense thoughts and feelings soon lose their impact. Distractions come, petty worries and grievances invade the mind until finally the most brilliant certainty becomes only a doubtful memory.

Perhaps it's better that way. I poured myself two thumbs of whiskey into a double shot glass and set the bottle back down on my dining room table. I took a long drag on a cigarette. The acrid smell of smoldering butts rose from the metal ashtray and filled my apartment. Loud crackly jazz music poured off my stereo.

The world would be a hell of a different place if we went around all the time dazed and bewildered by deep spiritual insight. A hell of a strange place.

I had been a gullible fool, that much was clear. I had taken Curtiz's case as a challenge. As if by overcoming the difficulties it presented, I could prove myself to myself.

No, let's be honest, not even that. I had wanted to prove myself to someone else. To Mara perhaps. Or Curtiz. Maybe even to Vera Marshall. It may not have mattered so long as it was an audience, someone I could stand before with my head held high and say, "Look at what I've done..." I was no better than a trained seal with no one to rub my head or toss me raw fish.

The afternoon ground away slowly. The minutes drifted by like continents.

My glass was nearly half empty. Time for a refill.

Drinking is like any other worthwhile pursuit; you have to practice to get good at it. I was getting expert enough to recognize that the true attraction of alcohol is how it makes us regress, pushes us back to a younger state of mind. Alcohol makes us feel like we think we once were, full of moxie and purpose, ready to raise hell. The selfish, reckless, insufferable ego of youth awaits us in each bottle of Dutch courage.

I was already pretty far gone, back in my teens at least. The music was an old cassette I had taped off one of my dad's jazz LPs many years ago. As a teenager, I would sit for hours in our recliner chair with head-phones on, playing the same tape over and over. The jazz music carried me away from my stagnant life where nothing seemed important. The music would become a part of me, and I of it. At least until one of my parents rousted me from my perch, insisting that I find something useful to do.

One song in particular always put a hard lump in my throat and brought my eyes to a soft simmer. That song came over the speakers now:

There was a time
When every day was sunny
You held my heart
I was your lifetime honey
But now you've left me,
And I'm alone
There is no life
When the sun is gone

Now life is night to me
A blight to me
I lie awake and pray for dawn

The woman's voice was achingly sad, even over the tape hiss. The song became a pure distillation of loss and longing. As if a prayer of loneliness had been captured on tape, an inexorable progression of words, music, and emotion.

Despite the mournful lyrics, the woman's voice maintained a wistful, almost hidden note of grace. As if she still harbored a desperate, impossible hope that her prayer might be answered. That note of hope always got me.

Inevitably the song made me think of Mara. It was tempting to give in to that wish, to indulge in the fantasy that all could be well again. I almost gave in. To the rhythm and the meter and the rhyme.

Music gives meaning to empty time. It strings moments together from a coherent beginning through a directed middle to a necessary end. Connection and direction are what music is all about.

Too bad life's not like that. Real time can be truly empty; dead meaningless moments that can't be strung together, no matter how hard you try or what ruse you employ. Even music becomes disjointed, a chaotic jumble of notes and gibberish. Real time cannot be got around so easily.

The jazz song held no magic for me anymore. It was a plaintive address doomed to failure. The only sure promise of Love's Old Sweet Song is loss.

I am done with illusions, I decided. I will have nothing more to do with music, or rainbows, or noble pursuits. Or hope— I especially wanted no part of that. I would live with the Hill House Preservation Society under conditions of absolute reality. Now I could appreciate Jim Boughton's swan dive with firearm accompaniment as a fitting final gesture. I wondered how long I would last and didn't care much one way or the other.

I refilled my whiskey glass and brought it to my lips automatically.

Self-pity is the emptiest time of all.

At that moment, with that thought, part of me suddenly died. It was an image of myself I had carefully built up and nurtured over the years. A cherished notion about who and what I was, and what I wanted to be. In its place something new was taking shape, something still too vague and undefined to recognize. But the prospect was strangely exciting.

I took the shot glass away from my mouth in disgust and dumped its contents out in the ashtray. It sizzled briefly on some still glowing ashes. I picked up the whiskey bottle and went into the kitchen. I pulled down the other bottles from the top of the refrigerator and carried them all—wine, tequila, peach schnapps, gin, the cognac I'd bought before I knew what cognac was—to the bathroom at the end of the hallway. One by one, I emptied each bottle into the commode. When I was done, I flushed the "throne cocktail" to kingdom come. The white porcelain surface glistened in its wake.

I put down the toilet cover and sat down. Then and there, I prayed with a strength and fervor I had not mustered since I was a boy. I don't know for how long, but when I finished, I was a lot more sober, and the apartment was dark because it was dark outside.

And I knew beyond any shadow of doubt: Hope is not just a privilege, it is a duty.

CHAPTER TWENTY-FIVE

A few hours later I stood waiting at the entrance to a small reception hall in one of Eola's premier hotels, the Savan. Inside, a lawyers' group dinner was underway. As I looked out over the tables that filled the narrow room, waiters in white coats and black ties bustled expertly around their tuxedoed patrons like worker bees attending their queen. I was underdressed even for a busboy's apprentice.

At a lectern in front of the room, the evening's speaker was winding down his presentation:

"In conclusion, gentlemen--and ladies, mustn't forget the ladies--" The man leaned forward and gave a big, smarmy grin... "The rule of law is all that separates us, man in the broadest sense, from brute beasts. It is the preeminent human, and humanist, construct."

He spoke with a British accent. It was the same warm and cultured voice that had left the message on my answering machine that morning. The lawyer Campbell Taggart was medium height but looked taller because of the wild shock of silver grey hair that stood out for inches around his head like steel wool. He had a round white face with large features. Even back from where I stood, his eyes looked enormous. Bushy eyebrows arched over them like batwings.

"... But we have no room for complacency. The law of the jungle lurks just outside the light of our flickering bonfire. It stalks us, watching for its chance to swoop in and devour us all."

The speaker paused to let his complex image sink in. He needn't have bothered. Too much food and wine had left most of his listeners too drowsy and stupid to care. There were a number of half-coughs, half-throat-clearings scattered around the room during his silence. Someone somewhere started to snore.

"Then let us agree, respect for the law, and hence, for lawyers, is the very bedrock of civilized society. Indeed, without it--or us, I dare say--civilization itself could not exist. Our much vaunted humanity, Homo sapiens in toto, would revert to a species of feral primates, where the strong prey continuously upon the weak and undefended.

"Lawyers, gentlemen, you and I, prevent that from happening. We uphold the eternal beacon of law against the darkness; we feed the flames of blind justice; our hands stoke the fire that keeps chaos at bay. Let us always tend to that fire diligently; it is our charter and our most sacred trust. As lawyers, gentlemen, let us keep that legal tender ever foremost in our thoughts. I thank you."

The speaker stepped back from the lectern and bowed his head to the audience. The applause was spirited. One man stood up for a standing ovation, but was so unsteady on his feet that he quickly sat down again and contented himself with whistling raucously.

The speaker inclined his head once more and stepped down off the stage. Another man took his place at the podium to make announcements about the group's next meeting.

The featured speaker meanwhile made his way through the tables towards the back of the room, shaking hands with those he passed only when he could not avoid it. He came directly towards me at the door.

"Mr. Tobin, I take it?" He extended his hand to me.

"Yes, Mr. Taggart. Nice speech. I got your message, but not

in time to meet at your office."

"That's fine. Better this way in fact. That's why I told you I'd be here. But let's go. These things always put me off my appetite."

I followed him into the hotel lobby and waited while he picked up his coat at the check desk. It was a long black overcoat that looked as shiny and sleek as seal skin. We walked out of the hotel into the chilly night.

"This way," Taggart said, gesturing up the street. "There's a restaurant close by that I quite like. You mind?"

"Not at all." I was famished in fact. I hadn't eaten anything since lunch and all the coffee I drank before coming to meet the lawyer was churning corrosively in my stomach.

We walked up the street in silence. Taggart moved with a quick gait. He kept his gaze focused straight ahead, never once turning to the side. I glanced over at him. His age could have been anywhere between late fifties and early seventies. Bristly grey sideburns sprouted abundantly down his face all the way to his jaw. They were almost spectacular enough to draw attention away from his bulbous nose, which looked like it had been partially sculpted from a blob of putty and then abandoned unfinished. The cold night air reddened his cheeks but not with a healthy glow--it looked more like broken blood vessels. He seemed to take no notice of the cold, however, and continued along the street lost in thought.

When we stopped at a crosswalk to wait for the light, just to make conversation, I said:

"Turned chilly."

"Yes, of course," Taggart replied disinterestedly. If I'd told him "puppies taste delightful in a light Madeira sauce..." I suspect his response would have been the same.

The restaurant was indeed close to the hotel as Taggart had promised. It was actually a pub. Its painted wooden sign stuck out over the door and swayed in the cold wind. The sign was lit by spotlights from both sides. The picture showed several cows dancing happily on a hilly pasture beneath the full moon. The pub was called The Sprightly Kine.

The restaurant was much bigger inside than it looked. The door to the left of the entranceway led to a dark and crowded bar. A large dining area was on the right. It was decorated in deep red polished wood, green upholstery, tartan fabrics, and wall paintings of foggy Scottish highlands. Even at nine o'clock there were several customers in the foyer waiting for a table.

Taggart smiled familiarly to the red-haired hostess when we came in. Without waiting for an escort, he turned directly into the dining room and gestured for me to follow. As we walked through the dining room, a waiter spotted us coming. He rushed to the back of the room and opened a door for us.

It led into a private party room. Taggart and I hung up our coats and sat down at the end of a long elegant dining table. The upholstery on the chairs was real leather. The waiter followed us in, took our drink orders, and discreetly disappeared. Taggart and I had the whole room to ourselves.

"And now to business..." Taggart began. "To be quite frank, there are other private investigators I normally work with. But my client insisted on you by name. Apparently you made a big impression on him. If you impress me half as much, it could mean a lot of business coming your way."

I took out a cigarette and stuck it in my mouth.

"Mind?" I asked.

Taggart shook his head; his wiry hair continued to move even after his head stopped.

I lit my cigarette and began, "That would be great, of course. But just so we understand each other, I won't hunt snipe or chase wild geese for you. I may be young, but I'm still a professional. I am not some flunky to be deployed at the merest whim. Some clients have a hard time understanding that. If you don't, we should have no problem."

"I'm not one to waste money, sir, my own or my client's."

"Who is your client?"

"You know him," Taggart said. "Or at least he says you do. Roger Thornton. The police are holding him for suspicion of a murder and they appear quite satisfied that they have the right man. Thornton denies it of course."

"You don't believe him?"

Taggart frowned. “That's an impertinent question. And irrelevant. I'm not paid to believe or disbelieve; I'm paid to get the best possible outcome for my client. In this particular case, my professional judgement might be that a plea bargain would be a better strategy. The District Attorney's office seems to believe that they have a good case. In their words, they have 'enough physical evidence to tie Thornton to the murder and to hang him with it.' They may be right. But my client insists on his innocence, and I am forced to go along with his wishes."

"What kind of physical evidence do they have?"

"A semen sample taken from the dead girl matches Thornton's blood type. They are threatening to do a DNA test on it. Probably, they won't need to. We are willing to stipulate that Thornton had sexual relations with the girl in question on the night she died. That, at least, is no crime."

Taggart stopped. The door opened and the waiter brought in our drinks and a pitcher of water, ice, and empty glasses. The waiter filled a large shot glass with single malt Scotch whiskey and set the glass and bottle on the table beside Taggart. It smelled nothing like the whiskey I'd been drinking all afternoon. The beer I ordered tasted bitter in my mouth, so I concentrated on a glass of ice water.

After he was done pouring the drinks, the waiter asked, "The usual, sir?"

"Yes, two of your specials." The waiter nodded and went away. "I'm sure at least one of them will appeal to you," Taggart said to me.

"I'm sure you're right." I saw no reason to argue. I had made my pitch for independence and personal integrity. Now if he wanted to order my food for me, let him.

"So where were we?" he said. "That's right, sex is no crime. Unfortunately, that's not the problem. The dead girl was also beaten very badly. I've seen the pictures. The jury is going to want to convict. They will want to punish someone, and that someone will be Thornton unless we can serve up another suspect.

"Unfortunately, there are witnesses that Thornton and a girl were fighting in his apartment that night, and that the girl was yelling as if she were being hit. No one called the police about it at the time, so there is no real corroborating evidence on that count. Nonetheless, some of the bruises on the girl's body allegedly match, and I stress allegedly, the pattern on a high school ring my client wears. A detective tells me the impression is legible, even down to the year. That, of course, we will never be able to stipulate."

"It all sounds pretty damning," I said. Nothing in what Taggart said contradicted anything Thornton himself had told me before. But I had to admit that even if Thornton was actually innocent of killing Rudi Alsmith, it would take a miracle to get him off, given the circumstantial evidence.

"Yes, quite. There is also the matter of the cocaine found in Thornton's apartment. It was mixed with the same fillers as cocaine traces taken from the girl's nose at autopsy. Of course, scientific evidence is often hard to explain and frequently falls on deaf ears in the jury box. And besides, we plan to argue against the legality of the initial search warrant, so that should not be an insurmountable problem."

Taggart stopped and frowned. When his big eyebrows drooped, he looked like a weary schnauzer.

"But Thornton has a prior arrest record for both drug-dealing and battery. That is a problem. I might be able to get it suppressed as being prejudicial, but in the current hostile climate against woman-beaters, there's no guarantee that will work."

"You certainly seem to have your work cut out for you."

Taggart nodded and sighed.

"Indeed." His expression was a strange mixture of puzzlement and resignation. Thornton's case was clearly not being run the way Taggart thought it should be and he seemed perplexed about why. Behind it all was something even the high-powered lawyer did not understand.

"Is Thornton your real client here?" I asked.

"He is not paying the bills, if that's what you mean. But he is my client. And I have been instructed to do exactly what Mr. Thornton asks. Even if it means going against my judgement about what is in his best interest."

"So who is it, then? I like to know who pays my bills too."

Taggart smiled, showing grey and crooked teeth through his thick lips.

"I will pay you, Mr. Tobin. Thornton is the only client you need trouble yourself for."

The waiter came through the door carrying a tray with two large plates on it.

With a deft flick of his fingers, Taggart directed him where to put the dishes.

The waiter set a succulent orange salmon filet in front of me, delicately marinated and garnished with dill. There were also potatoes and greens on the side, but I scarcely noticed them. The fish was so tender it flaked away if I just looked at it sharply.

Taggart had fried herrings coated with oatmeal. Judging from his ooohing and ahhhing, it must have tasted better than it looked. The two of us sat without speaking for several minutes, just savoring our food. When we did talk, it was on general topics that had nothing to do with Roger Thornton or Rudi Alsmith. Such crass diversions seemed out of place during a meal as fine as this.

It wasn't until after the entrees were finished and the waiter had brought us a silver pot of coffee that we returned to the reason for our meeting.

"Assuming I start working for you," I said, "What precisely do you want me to do?"

Taggart took a sip of coffee, and paused, reluctant for the respite to end.

"Ah, yes," he said. "Thornton tells me he wants you to find out who really killed the girl. That of course is complete nonsense. All you need to do is prove that Thornton himself did not. Anything beyond that is up to the police."

"That's still pretty vague."

Taggart nodded.

"True. This is the angle I suggest you take. Thornton claims that the girl left his apartment sometime between 8 o'clock and 9:30 Saturday night. He doesn't precisely remember when it was because he passed out. No doubt the evening's festivities had something to do with that.

"If you can find corroborating evidence that the girl left his apartment alive, then the police will have to drop their case against Thornton. I doubt seriously they have been exhaustive in trying to shoot holes in their own best theory of what happened. They believe they have the perpetrator, they don't particularly want to find out that they are wrong."

"What about payment?" I asked.

"You bill my office. Your standard fee structure should be fine, plus an appreciable bonus if you provide evidence that puts Thornton in the clear. Personally, I don't care where or how you get it, provided it stands up in court. Needless to say, if you find indications that Thornton is guilty, you must back off immediately. Take up a different line of inquiry that might lead to different results. Remember, you are being hired to clear my client, not convict him."

I drank some coffee of my own.

"Okay," I agreed. “As it happens, I am available to work for you. But I do have one question. You can answer it or not, as you choose. Deep down, you believe Thornton is guilty--you as much as said so. You saw what was done to that girl, yet you go on defending him with every trick and ploy at your disposal. Just now you came very close to suborning me to manufacture evidence on his behalf, which I will not do. But my question is this: If you get guilty clients off all the time, how do you live with yourself?"

Taggart wasn't offended. In fact he smiled a crooked grin.

"I live very comfortably," he said, "And that is answer enough.”

CHAPTER TWENTY-SIX

Saturday morning I drove south across town to Roger Thornton's apartment complex. Along the way the buildings and pavements were wet, washed down by an earlier rain. Already the sky was clearing for what promised to be a pleasant, if blustery day.

The drive was invigorating. I felt alert, confident, and energized. But when I pulled in among the dingy, ash-blond buildings all crammed so tightly together, it was hard not to feel a letdown. The atmosphere of the place was shabby and soulless, utterly depressing.

I parked outside Thornton's entrance and went inside. The long, ground-floor hallway was dimly lit and stank of old disinfectant. The edges of its tan linoleum floor curled up and away from the walls. As I climbed the metal stairway to the second floor, the stairs rattled and banged like an angry ghost.

The second floor hallway was just like the first, with four apartments along each side. Thornton's was the first door on the right.

Even if I hadn't known which apartment was Thornton's, I could have made a pretty shrewd guess. There was a pretty young girl, probably no older than fourteen or fifteen, seated on the floor with her back against the wall by his door. She had her knees drawn up and her arms were locked around them. She rested her head on her arms and rocked her tiny body back and forth, whimpering.

She jerked up her head as I came off the stairs. Her face could have been pretty, but the pale skin was drawn too tight and deep circles under her eyes looked like soot. Her denim jeans were faded almost white and ripped at the knees. A cotton tank-top clung to her skeletal figure. Though I tried not to notice, her small breasts were disconcertingly pert in the cold hallway. She had sharp elfin features that made her look the perfect type for daddy's little tomboy. But there was no charm at all in her face, only a voracious, mindless hunger. Her eyes looked like they were rolling and boiling at the bottom of sulfurous pits.

When she saw I was not Thornton, she whimpered again and put her head back down on her knees. She rocked back and forth more vigorously, her curled spine acting as a spring.

"Roger's not coming back today," I told her. "It won't do any good to wait."

She looked like I'd just yanked out her appendix without anesthetics.

"Do you know where he is? I need to see him, real bad."

"The cops have him. They picked him up Thursday."

"Really?"

As if I would kid a kid about that.

"Really. He won't get out for a long time."

The girl tried to pull herself together. She put a kittenish smile on her face and struggled to her feet, pushing up against the wall. She was a tiny little thing, coming up only to my shoulder.

"What about you?" she said. "You holding?" Her voice didn't even sound young, just weary. "I can make it worthwhile. I'm very good..." She came forward, put her arm around my back and tried to twine around my legs. She moved and mewed like a cat but the stench of her breath was like a dog with bad teeth.

I pushed her away.

"Save your strength. But I have ten bucks if you can tell me about this girl."

I took out the picture of Rudi Mrs. Sachett had given me and held it out to the waif. She took it eagerly. As she looked it over, her face slowly fell again.

"Look, mister, I wish I did, but I never seen her." She started towards me again, persistent beyond her years. "But for ten bucks I could..."

"Stop. I don't even want to know." I took out my wallet and gave her the ten dollar bill. "Just take it."

She grabbed the bill and scampered down the stairs without saying a word.

When she was gone, I stood alone in the hallway for a moment with the taste of ashes heavy in my mouth and an inexplicable urge to take a shower. Finally I approached the door across from Thornton's and rapped the small metal knocker against it.

Before I even took my hand off the knocker, a rumpled old man opened the door. He had been watching the girl and me through the spy hole. His eyes were bloodshot and watery, set wide apart in a round yellow-tinged face. His expression was an uneasy mix of calculated cunning and natural stupidity.

He brought me into his untidy apartment and insisted on getting his money up front before he would answer any questions, "just like the little whore."

After he took my ten, he admitted that he had been out most of Saturday night. He had not seen or heard anything of interest to me. He claimed not to recognize Rudi from her picture, but judging from the smug smile on his grizzled face, I guessed he was lying. He was just overwhelmingly pleased with himself at the idea of getting ten bucks for nothing.

It didn't take long for me to realize the old man had nothing to offer. With a quick grab, I snatched my bill back from him. I almost felt sorry for the old guy. He was so worked up and furious, ranting and grousing and threatening to call the cops, that I let myself out.

I moved down the hallway to talk to Thornton's next door neighbor, a large disheveled black woman in a bathrobe. She quickly made it clear that she did not care for her neighbor or his activities, but just as clearly, she did not care to answer any questions about them either. She barely even glanced at Rudi's picture before shaking her head and saying she didn't recognize her.

As the morning, and eventually the day, wore on, I moved from one door to the next, then from floor to floor, questioning one resident after another about last Saturday night. Most of them remembered nothing at all related to Thornton or whichever of his girlfriends was there that night. Roger was not popular among his neighbors, although there were some who grudgingly envied the endless string of girls he had coming to his apartment. A few of the residents did recognize Rudi as one of Thornton's regulars, even if they didn't recall her being there the previous Saturday.

But one middle-aged woman on the first floor, another unsavory drunk, had seen Rudi come into the building early on Saturday evening. The woman had run into her on the way out to buy cigarettes before it got dark, so the time was probably around 6:30. Maybe a little earlier.

Residents in the apartments above and below Thornton's recalled that a shouting match broke out between Roger and whomever he was with that night. They also got the impression--independently, it seemed to me--that the argument had come to blows. They were not sure about this however, and could only base it on "a vague feeling..." They didn't even think that fighting of this sort was unusual for Thornton and his female visitors. In fact, it happened all the time. To the best of the neighbors' recollections, the argument on Saturday seemed to have died off well before 9 o'clock.

No one could recall seeing Rudi leave. No one saw Roger taking out a bundle of trash that might have concealed her body.

It was a long, tedious, unproductive day. I spent a lot of it in my car, waiting for residents who weren't home to come back. Then when they did, they generally didn't know anything.

In the end, I learned nothing that either Thornton or his lawyer had not already told me. What little I did learn confirmed certain aspects of Thornton's story, but they were the kind of details that were more likely to be used in the circumstantial case against him rather than in his favor.

It was evening when I gave up. My patience was exhausted and I was hungry.

I didn't feel like dining alone in a crowded restaurant on a Saturday night, so I went to a 24-hour donut diner. I ordered chili, coffee, and a bear-claw. Everyone else there was lonely as hell and grouchy to boot, which made me feel much better.

I finished eating after 7:30 and sat at the counter smoking a cigarette while I drank coffee.

I was missing something; I could feel it. Like an expression or an idea on the tip of my tongue, it was close by, but just out of reach. A different approach, maybe. Something obvious, I was sure.

No one I talked to had seen Rudi leave Thornton's complex. Presumably it was the same with the police, or they would not have held Thornton.

But that in itself proved nothing. If I made the assumption that she did leave, as Thornton said she did, where would that lead?

Based on the autopsy pictures I'd seen and what "Bugman" Fitch had said, Rudi had obviously been badly beaten. Her shoulder was even broken, though that injury might have been post-mortem. If Roger beat her up--and even his lawyer admitted the evidence pointed that way--then Rudi must have been in pain when she left. What would she do? Where would she go? How would she get there?

Rudi had no car, yet she managed to get around somehow. A taxi maybe. But if she had called for a cab from Thornton's apartment, the police would have found the record of it by now.

I thought back to the one and only time I had seen her, outside Curtiz's office. I tried to recall how she looked as she left. She smiled at me and the boy in the hallway but there was nothing personal in it--she was intent on something else, something she reached into her purse for...

A bus pass! And I recalled there was a bus stop right beside Thornton's apartment complex...

I went back to Thornton's and found there were actually two stops, one northbound and one southbound. The posted schedules showed that several buses stopped there, but most of them only ran during weekday morning and evening rush hours.

Only the 151 bus continued to operate at night and on weekends, stopping there at twenty minute intervals.

The next one arrived ten minutes later, screeching to the curb in front of me with a loud squeal of brakes. I climbed aboard the northbound 151 bus and bought an hour transfer. I sat on the bench directly behind the driver and briefly explained what I wanted to do. He gave his assent and pulled back onto the street.

I stood up at the front, holding one of the upright metal poles, and looked back over the passengers. There were fewer than a dozen people, racially mixed, ranging in age from some teenage boys to a pair of old women returning home with shopping bags in their laps.

I gave a shrill whistle and held my hand up.

"Excuse me, please," I announced. "I'm looking for a missing girl who may have taken this bus last week. If any of you were on this bus last Saturday night, I'd like to show you her picture to see if you recognize her."

Two passengers raised their hands, one an elderly woman and the other a teenager at the back. I moved down the aisle until I reached the woman and showed her Rudi's picture. She shook her head:

"Nope, don't recognize her."

I thanked her and moved back to the boy. He was big but had a baby face. He scrutinized her picture carefully.

"She's pretty," he said, concentrating.

"Yes," I agreed. "Did you see her on the bus last week?"

"No, sorry. I didn't see her."

One of his friends who had also been looking at the picture, nudged his young companion in the ribs.

"And you'd remember, I'll bet!"

The boy nudged him back and they started in a playful tussle. Early teens obviously. About the same age as the strung-out waif.

"Thank you," I said.

I moved up to a seat by the door and pulled the cord to signal the driver I wanted to get off at the next stop.

The stop was several blocks north of Thornton's complex beside a large glass factory. The factory lights were all off and the tall chain link fence surrounding it made it look like a concentration camp. I crossed the street and waited for the next southbound 151 bus.

I only had to wait a few minutes. I showed my transfer and asked the driver if I could question the passengers about a missing girl. He agreed.

Once again I stood up and asked if anyone had been on the same bus the previous Saturday. This time no one had.

I got off at the stop across from Thornton's complex in front of the city park. I recrossed the street and waited for the next northbound bus. The temperature had dropped since the afternoon, and in spite of my windbreaker, I was pretty cold by the time it arrived. I explained what I wanted to the third driver and went through the whole process again. Again without results.

I repeated this numerous times, switching between the north- and southbound buses, asking if anyone had seen Rudi the previous week. When I encountered the first driver again (there were only three working the 151 route that night), I showed him Rudi's picture as well.

He said she looked familiar, but he could not remember if she was riding last Saturday or not. The other drivers had the same response.

One woman on a northbound bus asked to see Rudi's picture and recognized her immediately. However, the woman had not been riding last Saturday night, so she was no use in terms of an alibi for Roger Thornton.

Despite the lack of results, I kept plugging away and bought a second transfer when the first one ran out. It was 9:25 when my persistence finally paid off.

On a southbound bus, one of the passengers remembered Rudi being on the bus the previous week. He was a young man around twenty with fine brown hair, watery blue eyes, and a weak chin. His name was Derek Osborne. He was a regular on the bus, which he took to and from oboe lessons on Saturday night. He carried his instrument case and music folder in his lap.

"Yeah, I saw her Saturday," he said. "I was glad, too, because it had been a while. Maybe a month since the last time."

"Was that long a gap unusual?"

"Not really, I guess," Osborne said. "Truth is, I've only seen her six or seven times. But she leaves a big impression. Every Saturday I hope she'll be on the bus too. I'm working up the nerve to ask her out, you see. Of course, she'll probably say no...

You say she ran away?"

"She's missing," I said.

"I hope she comes back soon." Osborne scowled, but on his soft face it looked more like a pout. "I almost talked to her Saturday, too. She was real upset when she got on. Her face was red and she'd been crying. It was the perfect opportunity and I missed it. I was even going to give her my handkerchief, but the woman who got on with her gave her a Kleenex first." Osborne shook his head. "He who hesitates is lost, I guess."

"Was it around this time she got on last week?" I asked.

"Roughly," Osborne said. "No, actually it was earlier. My lesson ran long tonight."

"Was she hurt?"

"How do you mean?"

"You said she was crying. Did she look like she was injured or in a lot of pain? Would you say that she might have had a broken bone?"

"Oh no, nothing like that. From the way she talked with that woman, I guessed it was romance problems. She just seemed upset, very upset. I would have given anything to be the one to comfort her... Catch her on the rebound maybe."

"What about the woman who got on with her? Do you know who she was?"

Derek shook his head. "She was African-American, elderly. I think she was wearing a flowery dress. I never saw her before."

"Could you tell if they knew each other well?"

"Nah, not really. I think the woman was just being kind. Offering sympathy. They didn't talk very long. Probably it was just a few comforting words."

"Did you notice where the girl got off?"

"Sure. She always gets off at the same stop, the one before mine. The first time I saw her, I started to get real hopeful... Like maybe it was fate, you know, something to tell our grandkids about."

It was too late for me to change my story about Rudi being missing. As the star witness for Thornton's alibi, Osborne would find out the truth soon enough. Who knows, maybe he would meet a young woman in the courtroom and it would "be like fate." They could hit it off right away, go out for coffee, and discover a mutual passion for woodwinds. The rest, as they say, would be history. Or at least Osborne would have his story for the grandkids: "It all started with a murder..."

I took down Derek Osborne's address and telephone numbers for both home and work. He agreed to point out Rudi's stop for me.

Our route continued south until the street ended in a T-intersection at North Shore Road. The bus turned right on North Shore, and soon after, left onto Easton Boulevard not far above the Easton Bridge.

"Okay," Derek said, "It's the first stop once we cross the river. In front of the Chinese grocer's. Not a great neighborhood actually."

The whine of the tires on the metal grill bridge was loud, even over the engine noise.

I thanked Osborne and promised to be in touch. I stood up and pulled the bus cord. My hand was shaking. Maybe it was from the coffee I'd drunk at the donut shop, but I didn't think so.

It was the thrill of recognition. Even before we were over the bridge and the bus pulled up to the curb, I knew which grocery Osborne meant--it was actually Korean. I recognized the Christian Science reading room next to it and the sleazy book and video store on the other side. I'd passed by them many times.

Roger Thornton had been telling the truth. Rudi had left his place sometime after 9:00 last Saturday. Then she rode the 151 bus south to Shakytown.

Within a few hours she was dead.

CHAPTER TWENTY-SEVEN

I stepped off the bus onto a lighted patch of dirty pavement. When the door closed behind me and the bus rumbled away, the light disappeared. Only dirt and dark remained.

The stores along the sidewalk were all closed. Judging from the soap-swirled windows and run-down storefronts, many were closed for good. The mainstay of the block, the small Korean grocery, was shut up for the night behind an impregnable steel security blanket. There was a light on in the Christian Science reading room beside it but no one was home. On the other side of the grocery, the adult book and video store was supposed to be open from noon to midnight ("for the privacy and convenience of our late-night patrons") but it too was closed.

Across the street, two vacant apartment buildings glowered at each other over a narrow courtyard. The sides of the buildings were linked together by a high brick wall, which was sprayed and scratched with gang graffiti. A wood gate led into the courtyard but it was padlocked and had "KEEP OUT" painted in large red letters on its door. The buildings were completely dark except for occasional glints of light off their broken windows.

It was a lonely, desolate spot wrapped up in uneasy silence. A flatline neighborhood with all vital signs missing. There was no music or laughter, no loud arguments, even traffic noise seemed subdued here. The few cars that did come down Easton passed through in a hurry, their drivers staring fixedly ahead. The only other movement was a cold wind that sighed in off the river, kicking up grit and pushing crumpled newspapers along the sidewalk. Here in the middle of the city was a ghost town, complete with newsprint tumbleweeds. I glanced around me and shivered. Even in a ghost town there is room for decline.

It raised the obvious question: what was Rudi Alsmith doing here on Saturday night? Saturday nights, I corrected myself; Derek Osborne recalled seeing her on the bus several times. Did she know someone who lived nearby? Maybe after the argument with her dealer/boyfriend Thornton, she sought solace here with the proprietor of a crack-flat across the street...

I found the bus stop schedule posted on a lightpole. It was basically the same as at Thornton's: at night and on weekends, only the Southbound 151 bus stopped here. So Rudi hadn't come here to change buses.

I set off down the sidewalk, peering into the garbage-strewn walkways that ran between the stores. I don't know what I was looking for. It hardly mattered anyway, since it was too dark to see much. I heard scuttling noises and squeaks or grunts from deep among the shadows, but nothing of human interest.

At the south end of the block, I crossed to the other side and started back up Easton towards the northbound bus stop. My hands searched my pockets for whatever warmth they could find, and my eyes were slits against the dusty wind. As I walked, my gait became suddenly clumsy and self-conscious.

Someone was watching me. I sensed it like a cold hand brushing my neck. I looked around but saw no one. In the courtyard behind the high wall, dry leaves rustled in the wind and tree limbs creaked like old bones. Except for my footsteps, they were the only sounds.

I quickened my pace.

I had driven through this area many times but never really

paid much attention. If I thought about it at all, it was probably no more than quiet relief that my car did not choose this particular spot to break down. It is a lot easier to feel impervious when you're barreling down the street in 2400 pounds of steel than when you're left alone to feel the blight up close and personal.

I tried to reassure myself that Easton was a major street, that nothing would happen out here in the open. But I knew better. The last time I was in Shakytown I had run across the two dead muggers on Flyte street and that was only a few blocks away. The image of that pale, young man came back to me--how he lay there helpless on the curb, his punctured lungs wheezing with each labored breath...

I was getting jumpy. I glanced back over my shoulder and stumbled on an uneven sidewalk joint. I managed to right myself without falling and hurried past the wooden gate to the northbound bus stop. Even though I had not found whatever it was I came for, I was ready to leave. More than ready.

I waited at the stop, unable to shake the feeling that someone was still watching. I could neither pin down the cause, nor dismiss it as mere nerves or imagination. When I had felt this way a week ago, it turned out that Lance Talbot actually had been surveilling me. At least I could be certain it was not him now...

A lone car rushed down Easton heading south. The bright headlamps slashed through the night and lit up the neighborhood for an instant. After it passed, the ensuing gloom seemed darker for the intrusion.

To take my mind off waiting, I glanced over the route map which was displayed in a plexiglass case. Then, I leaned forward and peered at it more closely.

As expected, the 151 bus and weekday expresses stopped here on their northern treks. But there was another route that stopped here as well--the Shakytown local, bus 214, which ran seven days a week, all day and late into the night. It followed a circular route through the neighborhoods of Shakytown. It went north on Easton for a half block to just before the river, and turned right. After traveling east for two blocks, it turned again and went south and east, following the perambulations of Flyte Street.

Flyte Street—where Preston Curtiz's mysterious condominium was located; where on Saturday night, Thornton's associates, Hardison and Gerrara had shot and killed the two muggers. Flyte Street—where one week ago, a cut-rate and sleepy private eye had been shadowed by a more expensive but sleazy one, now defunct.

I couldn't see any other reason why Rudi would get off at this stop except to transfer over to the Shakytown local. There was nothing else here. It looked like Preston Curtiz's beautiful but troubled student had been on her way to...

The sound of footsteps brought me up short. I turned and adrenalin pumped into my system.

A young man was approaching. He was twenty-something or late teens, tall and quite thin. He wore a dirty unzipped blue parka, baggy-bottomed jeans, and a dark knit skull cap. His dark brown face was an expressionless mask. He sauntered towards me slowly with his hands in his pockets. He shifted his eyes around the street but kept his gaze from meeting mine.

The tension between us built as he came closer.

What if he has a gun, or a knife? I had left Talbot's gun in the glove box of my car back in Thornton's parking lot. The closest thing I had to a weapon was the dull penknife on my keychain.

The young man came within a few feet of me and stopped on my left. He faced forward, not saying a word. I looked straight ahead, too, not wanting to do anything that might seem provocative. My face felt hot; every muscle in my body was primed to fight.

We stood there for several minutes, rigid, silent, and sullen, like opposing soldiers carefully avoiding engagement.

Finally, from down the street came the welcome sound of a loud motor. A 151 bus was approaching. The young man beside me glanced at it, but otherwise didn't move. It suddenly struck me what a fool I had been. He wasn't there to rob me, he was simply waiting for a bus. My face continued its burn, only now from a different cause.

When the bus pulled up to the curb and the door opened in front of us, I gestured for him to go ahead.

He shook his head.

"No thanks," he said. "Ain't getting on. But you weren't safe out here and I din't want nothing to happen."

He turned away and started walking back down the street.

"Thanks, then," I called after him.

He didn't turn. He waved his hand in a gesture of both acknowledgment and dismissal: "It ain't nothing," it seemed to say, "Just what people do."

I rode the bus back up to Thornton's apartment complex and picked up my car there. It was 10:30.

Although it was getting late, I was too excited to knock off for the night. I had already proven that Rudi left Thornton's apartment alive. That in itself would clear Thornton of the murder, which was more than the police had managed. But I also had a good idea now of where Rudi was heading on the night she died. I warmed up my car in Thornton's lot and drove down Easton across the river. I turned left and followed the route of the Shakytown bus down Flyte Street.

This was where so many threads of my investigation converged that I felt sure the key must be found here. Especially since it looked like Rudi Alsmith had planned to go Preston Curtiz's condominium.

I parked just up the street from Curtiz's apartment building and locked the car. There was a loud party going on nearby and its music flooded the night. The street-level stores I passed were dark, but lights were on in many of the second and third-story windows above them.

I stopped when I reached the alley beside Curtiz's building. My shadow, cast by a streetlamp behind me, stretched all the way to the metal garbage drums by the wall. The scene was perfectly familiar, of course. Nothing had changed since I saw it last. But something about it now seemed staged, like a drawing or painting...

Or a photograph. Even an incomplete one.

I opened my wallet and pulled out the poorly developed scrap from Talbot's darkroom. The picture itself was fuzzy at best and there wasn't much light to examine it by, but I didn't need details. A cursory look at the gross shapes was all it took. In addition to the image of a car fender, the photo showed three cylindrical blurs that matched three of the overflowing garbage drums perfectly. Their shapes, their positions relative to each other and to the long shadow from the building on the other side of the alley were identical.

Talbot had taken a picture of this alley on Saturday night. I turned around to gauge where he had shot the picture from and lined up the angle with my arm. As best I could judge, Talbot had been parked across the street, just ahead of the street light. It was an illegal spot--his Jeep Cherokee would have blocked the entrance to the alley on that side--but from a professional viewpoint, it was a good one. Parking had been difficult that night and I certainly would have noticed if he'd double-parked somewhere behind me. Here on the other hand, Talbot had an unobtrusive post that covered every possible route I might take when I left.

As it turned out, he was also in a good position to see my

attempts to get into Curtiz's apartment building. I could just picture Talbot watching me from his vehicle, his wide greasy face pressed up against the tinted windows. How he must have howled when I went scampering down the stairs and into the alley like a spooked rabbit.

But there was also the car in the alley to think about. Talbot must have arrived at the same time I did, yet there was no car there when I went behind Curtiz's building. It must have pulled into the alley when I was back in my car, which would have been between 12:30 and 3 a.m.

I took the scrap and examined it directly under the street lamp. There was no doubt it showed the alley by Curtiz's building. The light-colored layer of cement at the base of the brick wall was clearly delineated. Unfortunately, not much else was clear. At the edge of one tear, the slim outline of a car's dark fender and part of its headlight showed in front of the wall. Immersed in the shadows farther back was a lighter smudge that may have been a human figure. The top of the smudge had been torn away, leaving the figure decapitated at the shoulders. If it was a person and not just a trick of the light, it appeared to be a man's back, slightly hunched over. It would be impossible to identify either the car or the figure behind it based on the torn photo.

But I had more than the photo to go on. I knew that Talbot had run a license check on Anthony Gerrara's Cadillac shortly after our Shakytown excursion. As far as I could tell, during the period when Talbot was shadowing me, Gerrara's path only crossed mine the one time, that Saturday night on Flyte Street. It seemed logical, then, that the car Talbot photographed was the same one he checked the license for. The car in the alley was probably Gerrara's.

It was worth noting, too, that Talbot became interested in the Cadillac even before the shootings took place farther down the street. Something Talbot saw here prompted him to photograph Gerrara's car with night-enhanced film, something important enough that he was willing to go through the tedious trial-and-error developing process. The scrap I had was just part of an early and unsuccessful attempt. And when Talbot submitted the license check request on Monday, he had used an assumed name. Whatever Talbot had seen Gerrara do that night was worth going to a lot of trouble for.

I went over to the condo building and punched the doorbell for Curtiz's apartment. His tenants, whoever they were, had a lot of explaining to do.

An irritated man's voice crackled over the intercom:

"You're early. I'll be down in a minute." The intercom shut off before I could say a word.

I looked at my watch. Eleven-ten hardly seemed early to me.

I left the vestibule and went outside to wait in front of the building. I lit a cigarette and lounged against the wall.

After a few minutes, a large green sedan pulled up with a middle-aged man and woman inside. The man got out on the passenger side. He was large, built like a high-school football player long since gone to seed. He was dressed in expensive but loose-fitting sweat-clothes and jogging shoes. I couldn't see much of his wife but she appeared to be dressed similarly.

The man went into the foyer and pushed an apartment bell.

I could hear the response even standing outside.

"Damn it! I'm coming!" It was the same impatient voice I had heard earlier.

"Yeah, well, we're here," the man said.

The man stepped out of the foyer and started towards his car, glancing at me contemptuously as he went by. His dilated pupils made his eyes look like a cat's. I ambled away, like a vagrant afraid of being rousted for loitering. I heard the green sedan's door open and close behind me as the man got inside. His wife kept the car's motor running.

I moved back towards my own car, a new plan already formed in my mind. Instead of confronting the resident of Curtiz's condo immediately, I decided to wait and see what he was up to. If his souped-up friend was any indication, I might learn something worthwhile by following them, something that would put me in a stronger position when I finally did talk to him.

It was nearly 11:20 when a medium height man came out of the apartment building wearing a long dark coat. He had a fright-wig shock of white hair, and a pale, dissipated face that glowed like crumbling marble in moonlight. He looked like Andy Warhol on a very bad night—like a week after his death. What I could see of his unpleasant face somehow reminded me of the coke-bloated maggot in Albin Fitch's laboratory, the one I had wanted to crush under my shoe.

Although I'd never seen the man before, I recognized him instantly. This was the white-haired man who had given Rudi the unicorn charm at the Crystal Cave; her elusive older lover whom the police and I had sought so long. He was Winter Kerr, the leader of the Gatherings Roger Thornton talked about.

And he was living in Preston Curtiz's condominium.

He also matched perfectly the physical description of the older brother from Curtiz's novel, My Brother's Keeper. He moved voluptuously, with the same lazy self-indulgence that Curtiz described when he called him "a bastard son of sleaze and sloth, favoring both." At the same time, there was something reptilian in his manner, as if hidden by his slow grace was the coiled potential to strike out fast in any direction. In spite of his bleached-out skin and hair, this dangerous undercurrent gave him an undeniable, if perverse, magnetism. A girl Rudi's age could easily mistake it for more.

Suddenly I understood. This was Curtiz's brother. When I

asked Thornton about the leader of the Gatherings, he hadn't said "Winter Kerr is...", he said "Winter Curtiz." I misheard because the rest was blocked by Officer Friedman's pounding on the door.

The character of the faithless pornographer in Curtiz's novel was inspired by the author's real-life brother. And he was the man Rudi ran to after Thornton beat and brutalized her on Saturday night. Winter Curtiz may have been the last person to see her alive. He may have been worse.

Winter Curtiz moved to the waiting sedan and got into the back seat. The car started off and headed down Flyte Street.

I pulled out after them and followed at a discreet distance. My luck had been bad when I tried to follow Preston Curtiz early on--I didn't want anything to go wrong this time.

We followed Flyte Street to its end and continued east, crossing a narrow southern tributary of the river and then going past the University. Even on the major streets, there weren't many cars, so it was easy for me to keep track of the sedan. There were still enough vehicles, though, that I could shuffle my own position among them easily, making me difficult to spot.

We headed south on North-South highway, going past several successive exits for suburban towns. Most of the other cars got off at these exits, and I had to fall back even further. In the end, the green sedan--now no more than a distant blur of red dot tail lights--was the only car in sight.

As we left the city lights behind, the sky became mostly black and dull; the moon and stars covered by clouds. Once in a while, a gap in the fast-moving lower strata permitted some moonlight to creep through briefly but the stars were permanently blocked.

Finally, the sedan's brake lights lit up for a moment about a half mile ahead of me and it turned off the highway. It was instantly swallowed up by the night.

I had been concentrating so hard on the car itself that when it left the road, I had no idea where we had got to, whether we were twenty miles from the city or fifty. The empty black countryside around us provided no clues. There were no signs for a turn-off from the highway and no exit lanes on the right. For half a minute, I was afraid I would miss the exit.

Sure enough, I did. As I came down over a slight rise, I spotted the narrow access road off the highway but I was going too fast to take it. Instead I braked and pulled onto the shoulder a hundred feet past the entrance.

I shut off my headlights and peered out around me. As my eyes became accustomed, I could make out certain features of the landscape. Beyond the shoulder and berm beside the highway, a steep slope led down into a deep hollow. The access road cut across that slope to the right, descending at a much gentler angle.

The green sedan was still going down the access road. The car turned left at the bottom of the hill and went straight on for a hundred yards, trailing a low cloud of gravel dust that glowed red from its tail lights. The sedan turned left sharply and its headlights swept over a small parking area with about twenty or twenty-five cars. The driver turned off her headlights in the parking lot and the car disappeared from view.

A propitious break in the clouds gave me a glimpse of huge piles of crushed stone in the depression below. In the silver-grey moonlight, the semi-articulated mounds looked like part of a giant carcass, like the old myths about mountain ranges formed from the skeletal remains of fallen gods and heroes. Then clouds rolled in and darkness reigned once more.

We had come to the Weibrecht gravel yard, Winston Graham's cozy little money-washer in the middle of nowhere; the place where Rudi Alsmith's body had been unceremoniously dumped a week ago.

I left my car and walked over to the edge of the slope. It was steep, but it didn't look too difficult to climb down on foot. I would certainly be less noticeable than if I drove my car down the access road.

I started down the slope standing up but my feet kept getting tangled in the weedy ground cover. I nearly tripped several times and quickly switched to a crab position. By the time I reached the bottom, the palms of my hands smarted from some stinging plant, but I was fine otherwise.

My eyes were now fully adjusted to the dark and I could see surprisingly well. Ahead of me, the boundary of the gravel yard was marked by a thin row of cypress trees. Beyond the trees a string of hopper cars sat idle on a shunt of railway track. They looked like they hadn't moved since the days of the steam locomotive.

As I approached, I couldn't see much beyond the railcars except for the tops of the gravel mounds. But in the still of the night, I could hear plenty.

It started out faint and low, so I thought it was my imagination or the wind. But as I got closer, the sounds became unmistakable. Low grunts and yelps seemed to permeate the yard; muffled moans mingled with the sound of crunching gravel.

When I reached the railway tracks, I was startled by a sudden thump that shook the wall of the nearest hopper. A woman inside the railcar unleashed a low droning wail. Her partner's wild huffing and panting, like a hungry boar sniffing out truffle, was also clearly audible. All this heavy respirating was punctuated by more loud thumps, as one or the other of them pounded their fist against the wall. I moved on quietly, careful not to disturb their concealed assignation. I needn't have bothered. The couple inside was far too preoccupied to take any notice of me.

I moved along the tracks and crossed them where the string

of railcars ended. An enormous mound of gravel stood directly in front of me. As I moved around its base, the insistent sounds of love-making grew louder and more raucous, hovering like a wet fog over the whole yard. When I finally got around the large mound, I could see why.

A narrow hollow was formed between the large piles of stone like an artificial valley nestled discreetly between mountains. But what went on in that hidden valley, concealed from prying eyes, was anything but discreet.

CHAPTER TWENTY-EIGHT

The area between the gravel mounds was full of naked flesh. Stark naked, buck naked, all kinds of naked. Dozens of men and women lay scattered on blankets across the hard ground in pairs, trios, and larger clusters. They climbed and clung to one another like nuptial swarms of ants, twitching, gasping, bobbing, thrusting. Some preferred a rougher, dustier trade; they skipped the blankets entirely and did their squirm-and-heave on the bare gravel.

I watched from twenty yards away through a gap between the large gravel pile and a yellow power shovel parked beside it.

The people fit no particular age or race demographic. They came in all shapes and sizes, a mix of young, old, short, tall, thin, fat, light, dark. They were ordinary people with ordinary lives and problems. Some of them probably left kids at home with baby sitters to come here.

But they all shared an extraordinary passion which they pursued with witless abandon. Their frenetic adventures ran the gamut of every lewd act imaginable and included a few that imagination might have shied at. It was as if the gravel yard had been declared an inhibition-free zone, where every impulse was given free rein and nothing was forbidden. There was no position too awkward, no contortion too painful, that someone wouldn't entertain it.

Certain accommodations had to be made of course. One

elderly pair, unable to keep up with their younger brethren, slunk off to a corner of the lot where they engaged in making a rickety beast with two sore backs. Love in the geriatric ward, two hearts murmur as one.

Only love had nothing to do with it.

These were men and women in moral free-fall, drugged-out and completely depraved. Their teeming antics reminded me of the maggot mass at the bottom of Albin Fitch's scrap jar. With every gesture fumbled, each embrace self-serving, and each profession dishonest, they looked more like lecherous zombies than human beings. The whole scene was pure Hieronymus Bosch--a great, grim dumb-show acted out by eager participants in their own abomination.

Yet beneath the group's unbridled hedonism was a gnawing frustration. In spite of their passion and stamina--which in some cases were remarkable--the members were too jaded to enjoy even the most extreme consummations. When someone finished with one partner or group, he or she brusquely moved on to someone else, to start up some new desperate frolic, panting after a truly peak experience that was always out of reach. They had created a world of instant and total gratification--and found it wanting.

This was one of the Gatherings that Roger Thornton had spoken of, and that Sheila Lee had been so reluctant to discuss. Even Thornton had seemed queasy over what went on here and he was not the sensitive type. Now I understood. The brave new world they had created was repellent. Even Thornton could not help recognizing it.

Still I watched, fascinated in spite of myself. It was the thrill of curiosity that comes from wondering, how far can they go? They had obviously shed the kid-glove niceties most of us grow up with. What core constraints, if any, were left? Or is the human capacity for selfish debasement truly unlimited?

I could only shake my head. Dogs behave better, I thought. At least they have a master to look up to. We are not so much a lost generation as a lost cause.

In time, the group's ardor waned. The people who had migrated to other parts of the gravel yard started to return to the central group. As they moved across the crowded lot, they stepped carefully so as not to disturb the remaining trysts. They picked up unoccupied blankets from the ground and wrapped themselves in them against the cold.

No one had spotted me yet, but I definitely needed a better hiding place. I crept out from behind the gravel mound and climbed into the cab of the Caterpillar wheel loader next to it. Crouched inside, I spied out the window as the debauched festivities petered out below.

Those who were done talked quietly amongst themselves around the central area. Some put on blankets, others sat together in very close groups, hoping body heat would warm them. No one made any effort to get dressed. As they waited, they passed around cigarettes and metal pipes that lit up their faces when they drew on them.

A few serious die-hards refused to stop and redoubled their sexual efforts, fiercely pounding and scratching each other in a futile attempt to make their last hurrahs something to cheer about.

Eventually even they subsided and the crowd was spent--satiated but not satisfied. As if on cue, the group began to congregate in front of the tallest gravel pile on the lot. They seemed to be evenly divided between practicalists, who stood with blankets around their shoulders, and purists, who did not. One woman from the unblanketed-school continued to stroke herself absently. She did not seem to derive any pleasure from it but seemed to be acting out of habit.

A man in a long dark coat came out from behind the mound

and started to climb the front of it. The gravel cascaded down around his feet and he made slow progress. The others fixed their eyes on the man and watched as he worked his way up. When he had ascended 3 or 4 feet above the crowd, he turned to face them. Even in the dark, I recognized the white stringy hair that swirled around his face. It was Winter Curtiz.

In his elevated position, he raised his arms above his head for silence and began to speak. I opened the wheel loader's window a crack. In a deeply resonant, yet slow, tired voice, he delivered a sermon from hell:

"... she was one of our own, who is no more. Her body—that incomparable body!—was found here, as cold as the stones heaped 'round us. The Phlegethon fire that burned within her has been extinguished.

"While she was with us, we shared in her fire, gained passion from her youth, relished her cool intelligence and biting wit. We will miss all of these. But her future is our greater loss. For Rudi truly had no limits, no heights were beyond her. What levels of pleasure and pain might have been ours had she lived to grow and mature? For us, all of that now belongs to the realm of regret. The cliche is true: Rudi blossomed for too short a time, like a flower too early for spring. We must content ourselves with having known her while we could."

Winter paused and regarded his audience. His words had touched them. Several in the crowd were weeping openly, while others brought their hands to their eyes to wipe away more reticent tears.

Winter continued:

"Do not deceive yourselves in thinking Rudi will live on in our memories. Memory is a pale, selfish mirror that reflects only what we have lost, what her death has taken from us. If we remember her at all, it is only for our own sakes, not hers.

"No trace of our young friend remains. She is dead, she is

gone, she is finished! And so shall we all be. Our light of experience winks on one morning and dies the same night. The length of our days may vary, but the night's darkness lays claim to us all. Nothing is gained at our arrival and nothing is changed by our passing.

"My friends, in your hearts you know the truth: we have only our selves, here-and-now. Each one of us is the center of our universe. What can exist beyond its boundaries? Nothing. No one.

"Look around you. Deep down, can you care for another person a hundredth of what you feel for yourself? Would a million other lives make up for your own extinction? Never!

"In a world of nonentities only you matter. The long slow creep of history was but prologue to your presence and when you exit the stage, the show folds, the set is struck, and the theater shuts down forever. There is nothing shameful in feeling this way. All of human nature is based on the 'sanctity of me.' It is a nature that has served us well and enabled us to conquer the world.

"But we mustn't be misled; there is no truth to our self-importance. It too is an illusion, an empty instinct that evolved out of our primitive compulsion to survive. At heart, it is the same automatic response that made our animal ancestors cower and hide when large carnivores went by. The very ground of our identity and existence is a lie—the lie that it matters whether we live or die. The vile lie that our lives have meaning."

Winter stopped. His silence stretched beyond a dramatic pause into an uncomfortable one. I was beginning to think he had finished, when he resumed:

"Meaning is our enemy! Meaning is the tyrant who enslaves us. Meaning is the cloying, choking trap that keeps us from our true selves. The grotesque idea of a watchful, vengeful, judgmental God who measures human lives against a scale is only false meaning personified! Believe me, my friends, if ever there were such a god, he would long ago have died of boredom.

"We must escape the tyranny of meaning, be done once and for all with illusion and fear. Only then will we have the freedom to be who we are, what we are, while we are. The freedom to take what we want, what we can, even knowing we will lose it all in the end.

"My friends," he went on, "your lives are your own. You are free to make of them what you can. But you will never make them more than they are. Life is impermanence, loss, and betrayal. It is an unsought affliction with suffocating symptoms and no cure. Strive to mitigate it with all your strength and all your cunning. You will fail, of course, for no one can succeed. But at least in so doing, your calling will be honest."

Winter raised his arms once more, this time in benediction. The voices of the congregation joined with his, chanting in rapt unison:

"They babble of light who are surrounded by darkness. Embrace the darkness! For though we see nothing, we see it clearly."

As they spoke the word "clearly," a shift of air-masses miles away and thousands of feet up punched a hole in the clouds. A focused shaft of moonlight shot through the breach down to earth. The crowd in the gravel yard turned en masse to witness the phenomenon as the bright beam of light fell full upon the yellow power shovel behind them, exposing the face of an outsider within.

The cold glow that suddenly surrounded me made my predicament seem unreal, like an anxiety dream. It was as if I had stumbled onto the stage of a play and been trapped by a spotlight in a performance I had no part of. The hostile audience gawped at me with blank faces, too confused to move.

For a moment, their leader fixed his gaze upon me and our

eyes locked. We stood at the same level, he and I, with a good view of each other. A malignant smile came over his face, and I knew I was looking into the eyes of a killer. I just didn't know how.

He shouted roughly to those below him and pointed at me. His gesture, at least, was unnecessary since everyone could see exactly where I was.

I didn't wait to find out what they would do. I opened the door and jumped down from the cab into a knee-jarring squat. I took off across the yard, running from the congregants as fast as I could. I needed to get around the string of railcars in a hurry or I stood no chance of evading them. A stampede of crunching footsteps followed after me.

I ran towards the place where the cars ended on the railway tracks. Just before I reached them, a man wearing a dark windbreaker and baseball cap jumped out from behind the last hopper car and took me down with a diving tackle. We rolled heavily across the ground; the loose stones dug painfully into our skin.

I snarled and picked up a handful of gravel during the roll. I pulled back my fist of stones and smashed it into the man's face. I could feel a crunch under my knuckles as his teeth broke. He screamed in pain and clasped his hand to his mouth, blood seeping out between his fingers.

I jumped to my feet. The others were much closer now, an enraged naked mob in swift pursuit, shouting deprecations.

A small rock sailed out of the darkness and hit the back of my head. Some of my pursuers had stopped running and were pelting me with stones while the rest continued to give chase. I ducked around the railcars and sprinted towards the hill and the highway fifty yards away.

The stones kept flying even after I went over the tracks but they no longer came close to hitting me. The people who were throwing them couldn't see over the railcars and were just throwing blind. Loud metal "thunks" and "tings" came after me as their missiles went astray and hit the hoppers and rails. As I passed through the ring of cypress trees at the edge of the gravel yard and started across the remaining flat ground to the hill, the remaining runners shouted back angrily at the stone-throwers to stop. They were only hitting their own people and I was out of range.

Their voices came from well behind me. They must have lost a lot of ground. I glanced back and saw that many of them had already given up and were heading back. A few were actually sitting down, massaging their bare, bloodied feet, which had been cut cruelly on the sharp gravel. Even those who still made a show of chasing after me, ran with such slow, painful steps that they could never catch up.

But three or four men had not slowed down at all. Like the man who jumped me at the railway shunt, they were fully dressed, wearing shoes and jackets. Probably, they did not take part in the Gathering at all and only acted as lookouts. If so, they had failed miserably by letting me slip past them on the way in. Their failure made them all the more determined not to let me escape.

I reached the slope leading up to the highway a few seconds before my closest pursuer. I flung myself onto the hill and clambered up as fast as I could, grabbing hold of anything that would give me purchase. The sting of the thorny weeds was nothing to what I would feel if I didn't reach my car and get out of there.

When I was halfway up the slope, a man's voice shouted down at me from the top, "Who's there?"

At first, I was elated. Here was someone who could help me. I was on the verge of crying out to him, when paranoia set in. What if he was another lookout from the Gathering?

Two of those men were already scrambling up the hill behind me. I could hear their exertions to either side. My own wind was almost gone. I tried to pick up my pace but found that I could not even maintain it. I had no choice but to take my chances with whoever was at the top of the hill.

"Here..." I croaked. "Help!"

A bright searchlight flashed down the hill and came to rest on me as I climbed. A second later, blue lights started swirling atop the police cruiser, giving me a place to climb to.

As soon as the police lights went on, my pursuers abandoned their chase. I heard them scurry and slide down the weedy hillside. At the bottom, they scattered and fled into the dark.

"What's happening there?" the policeman said. His searchlight left my face and started sweeping across the hillside. "You there, stop!"

I continued my breathless climb, too tired even to croak out a response.

When I had almost reached the top, the voice came again, more calm now, reassuring.

"You're okay," it promised. "Whoever they were, they're gone. You can take it easy."

In another moment I saw the policeman silhouetted against the bright light. He reached out a hand for me to take and pulled me up.

"Am I glad to see you," I said, panting.

Not that I could see him. My eyes were still blinded by his spotlight and blue flashers.

"Looks like," he said. "What's going on down there?"

I held up my hand to stay his question until I could catch my breath.

"Sure. No rush."

He leaned against his car, with his arms hanging loose at his sides. His gut stuck out over his belt.

Finally I recovered enough to answer.

"It was an orgy," I said. "A God-damned orgy."

"With naked people and everything?" He reached over and trained his spotlight down on the lot but there was nothing to see. The central area where everyone had been was blocked by the large mounds. "You kidding me? At a gravel yard?"

I started to shake my head, then nodded.

The policeman directed his light farther back, dimly capturing the parking lot.

"Some folks leaving in an awful hurry," he noted. "They didn't even turn on their lights. Looks like whatever it was, I missed it."

We watched as the string of cars headed away from us along a dirt road into the wooded countryside. Within two minutes they had all disappeared.

"You okay now?" the policeman asked. He was medium height, and portly. He was older than I was, but his smooth baby-face made it impossible to tell by how much.

"Yeah, fine," I said. "Like I said, you saved my life."

"It's my job. I stopped to check out this car by the highway. Is it yours?" He gestured back at my Impala five feet behind the cruiser.

"Yes."

"Mind if I look at your registration?"

"No, of course not."

I walked back towards my car on the passenger side. The policeman followed.

"So what were you doing down there?" he asked.

It was a tough question to answer. The truth would have been easy enough, but complicated, and I didn't feel up to it. I was simply too drained. I just wanted to go home and to bed.

"I noticed something going on and stopped. I guess I'm just nosy." I shrugged.

"Uh-hunh." He looked from the road to the gravel yard and back again, evaluating the angles from which I may or may not have seen something. When he finally arrived at a judgment, he seemed less convinced than ever.

I opened the door to my Impala and leaned inside. I opened the glove compartment and removed my car's registration card. The cop was standing right behind me, watching over my shoulder.

As I turned to hand it to him, the policeman gave a peremptory order:

"Okay, Mr. Tobin, stand back from the car!"

The tone in his voice surprised me. So did the fact that he knew my name before he took my card. His face was not at all friendly now; it was stern and wary.

"Now turn around and put your hands behind your back."

"You've got to be kidding..."

"Do it now!"

I turned around and did as he asked. I felt the cold clasp of handcuffs as he closed them around my wrists.

"What is this about?" I asked. "There's some kind of mistake. I haven't done anything."

"That's you and your lawyer's problem, not mine." The officer craned his neck to peer into the still-open glove compartment.

"That looks like a gun there," he said. "I hope it's registered."

It probably was. Only not to me. It was Lance Talbot's. That was definitely too complicated to explain.

"Listen carefully," the policeman went on, "I am placing you under arrest. I will read you a list of your rights. When I am done, I will ask you if you understand the rights I read to you. Do you understand?"

"Of course, but it's ridiculous..."

"Mr. Tobin, just listen. 'You have the right to remain silent. If you give up the right to remain silent, anything you say can and will be used against you in a court of law. You have the right to speak with an attorney and to have the attorney present during questioning. If you so desire and cannot afford one, an attorney will be appointed for you without charge before the questioning begins.' Do you understand these rights, and do you wish to waive your right to be silent?"

"I understand my rights," I said, "What I don't understand is what I'm being arrested for. Those men back there were chasing me, not vice versa! Why are you doing this?"

The policeman sounded genuinely surprised.

"There's a warrant out," he said. "And an APB on your car. 'Suspect may be A and D. Wanted on suspicion of murder.'"

CHAPTER TWENTY-NINE

"Tell me why you did it, damn you! Then we can get some sleep."

Detective Otto Ryan's loud frustration filled the interrogation room. He'd been badgering me constantly since 4 a.m. without result and now his voice sounded thick and tired. After two hours on the receiving end, I was sick and tired of it myself.

We sat in a small yellow room that was crowded with just our chairs and the narrow wood table between us. No one else was present. There was a mirrored pane of glass across from me with an observation booth behind it, so maybe someone was watching from there. The room had no windows. The only light came from a long fluorescent bulb that hummed incessantly over our heads.

When he first came in, Ryan had been wearing a blue sports coat, but that was now draped over the back of his chair. His once-upon-a-time white shirt was open at the collar and a red knit tie hung down from it in a lazy loop.

The detective leaned forward, sticking his face right up into mine. His complexion was pockmarked and greasy, fretted with tiny veins around his nose. His jawline, chin, and neck were covered with salt-and-pepper stubble. He was so close that I could have plucked luxuriant nosehairs from his nostrils with my teeth.

In a shoe-box room with no ventilation, it was far too close. I pushed my chair back away from him and the table. It didn't help. The stale smell of sweat and cigarette smoke was ingrained in the walls.

The room's close quarters were supposed to be intimidating. So were the clumsy red smears on the wall behind me. I could see them reflected in the mirror in gaudy contrast to the yellow paint. They were probably ketchup marks, placed there deliberately to make suspects uneasy with subliminal hints of blood and violence. If a cleaning crew ever ventured to wipe them off, I was sure the stains would quickly reappear. It was a cynical touch that showed how much contempt the cops had for the criminals they interrogated here. I frowned. I refused to be cowed by kitchen condiments.

"I told you before," I told Ryan again, "I didn't kill anyone."

His round, unpleasant face flushed an unhealthy red. It did that whenever I gave an answer he didn't like, which was most of the time. He ran his hands through the disappearing halo of grey hair that ringed his head and left strands of it sticking out in all directions. He didn't bother to smooth them back down.

"Dammit!" he said, slamming his fist down hard on the table. The yellow legal pad, which he'd brought to take notes, jumped at the impact and knocked his blue felt tip pen to the floor. "I know you killed Lance Talbot," Ryan said angrily. "The commissioner knows it, even the mayor knows!"

"Then one of you should have let me know."

Ryan clenched his teeth and growled. He was so sure of my guilt and the strength of his case that he had never even considered the possibility that I would not confess. Especially when I waived the option of having my lawyer present. This was a big case for Ryan--both the mayor and the commissioner were interested--and here I was, gumming up the works by refusing to admit the obvious.

For my part, I was so tired that the whole process seemed unreal. It was as if I were standing outside myself, watching from a great distance away, with only a vague interest in the outcome of events. It had been that way all through the booking procedure and during my brief period in the lock-up. I had protested dutifully at each stage, but no one listened or seemed to care that they had the wrong man. Eventually I got tired of complaining and just played along. I got the feeling that a lot of what was happening was beyond the control of even those who should have been able to change things. They couldn't, and consequently nothing I said made any difference.

Ryan brought himself slowly back under control. He picked up the notepad from the table and looked over it carefully. I don't know what he hoped to glean from his sparse notes. Mostly he had used it to make doodles of stick figure men with X's for eyes who were killed in any number of gruesome ways; hangings, shootings, even lightning strikes. Call me paranoid, I know some of you will, but I couldn't help but take the drawings personally.

Ryan sighed. He reached down to floor and retrieved his pen.

"Okay," he said, "Let's try this statement again... You admit that Talbot was following you?"

"You've got his microcassettes that prove it."

"That's right, we do. Now why was he doing that?"

I shook my head.

"I can't answer that now. I have to talk with my client first," I said. Since Talbot and I had both been working for Curtiz, I could not explain why Talbot was shadowing me without also exposing my own client.

"Oh, no. That won't wash," Ryan said. "This is murder and the rules are different. I'm asking you, not your client. You can refuse to answer, sure, but only on the basis of your constitutional right to avoid self-incrimination. Of course, if you do refuse, you'll make yourself look guilty as hell."

In other words, by invoking the Fifth Amendment, I would defeat the purpose of having it.

Ryan waited, but I remained silent.

Finally, he said, "Okay, we'll let that pass for now. What time did you go to Talbot's house on Wednesday--"

“Thursday,” I corrected.

"Whatever. What time?"

"About ten. Maybe 10:30."

"What were you doing there?"

"What difference does it make what I was doing there on Thursday morning if Talbot was killed on Wednesday? I've got plenty of people who can back me up on where I was Wednesday."

"I'm asking the questions," Ryan said. "What were you doing there?" Ryan's take on bulldog tenacity was to repeat his questions endlessly until his beleaguered suspect finally broke down and changed his story. It was an effective technique; I wanted to change mine just for variety.

"If you must know, I was searching for the next incarnation of the Panchen lama. The portents all pointed at Talbot."

The detective closed his eyes and puffed out his cheeks. When he expelled the air, he looked at me and scowled.

"You know, they don't pay me enough to listen to your crap. Nowhere near. Now why were you really there?"

"On Thursday…" I began.

But Ryan cut me off. He ignored my answer and provided one of his own.

"What about this then? Talbot had something you wanted. Maybe something he blackmailed you with, since that seems to have been a sidelight of his. You wouldn't pay, or couldn't, so you went to his house to confront him. When he wasn't there, you broke in."

"I didn't br--" I began, but Ryan interjected loudly:

"Don't even think it! We found Talbot's gun in your car! We found your prints on the broken glass outside his basement window! Did you forget you were fingerprinted when you got your PI license? We have your prints along with every other lowlife's."

"I didn't break in," I repeated. "The window was broken when I found it. It looked suspicious so I went in to investigate. Looking back, I probably shouldn't have."

"Which? Break in or kill him?"

"You have only to prove it."

"We'll prove it all right. We basically have all the proof we need. After the ballistics test comes back on the gun you took, we probably won't even need your statement. You have a very narrow window when I actually give a damn what you say. But it's closing fast. And when it does, you'll just be meat for the fryer."

I yawned. It was the same argument he had tried several times already under different guises and it still didn't impress me.

When he saw I wasn't responding to intimidation, Ryan turned and took a package of cigarettes from the inner pocket of his jacket. He shook a few up from the pack and offered me one. I took it and Ryan took one as well. He lit both of our cigarettes with an old-fashioned gold lighter. He smoked a heavy menthol brand that was like cool syrup on my throat.

"That's better," he said, blowing blue jets of smoke out his nose. "Isn't that better? Of course. Now look, I know how you feel. Your wife left you. I bet I know what that's like. If I was ever married, I'd feel the same way. It's a raw deal and you're angry--so angry, you could just kill someone. It's understandable, believe me. I see it all the time. Lance Talbot did something that set you off. You lost all control of your actions. You went to his house in a blind rage and killed him. Juries can understand that!"

he said.

I shook my head in disgust.

"I'm not an idiot. No court would buy that cheesy blind rage ploy and you know it. I broke into the basement of Talbot's house, lay in wait for him, and then killed him when he came home... And all this time, I'm supposed to be too crazed to control my own actions? It's ludicrous!"

"Then you admit you broke in and killed him!" Ryan said triumphantly.

"Of course not. I'm just playing along with your hypothetical. I told you: I didn't go to Talbot's house until Thursday morning. That's the day after the fact. There's no way you can prove any different because that's what happened."

"You're lying," Ryan said. He stood up and started marching back and forth across the small room, like a bald gorilla prowling an office cubicle. "Talbot came back Wednesday evening and you were waiting for him in his office. You had already smashed his computer and started to go through his file cabinets. What were you looking for? Just tell me that."

"I didn't do it."

"What did you want? Information of some kind, a record of something? Whatever it was you didn't find it. Talbot came in and found you there. You forced him to kneel on the floor and questioned him with a gun to his head. You were the tough guy. You called the shots." Ryan came forward, formed his fingers into the shape of a pistol and pressed the "barrel" roughly against my forehead.

"You threatened him," Ryan went on rapidly, increasing the pressure of his finger on my head. "But he wouldn't come across. Or maybe he did, but you just liked making him cringe, you liked playing God. Did you make him beg for his life? Is that what you wanted? What?!"

I shook his finger off my forehead.

"Nothing," I said. "You're loopy."

Ryan thrust his hands down on the table and leaned at me again, putting his face just inches from mine. His loud voice drummed into my ears.

"He did what you told him at first, but then something went wrong. Talbot stopped playing along. He showed that he didn't care what you did, that he was a better man, a tougher man. Some gesture that proved, even with a gun staring him in the face, he was above you. What was it? Why did you pull the trigger?"

Ryan was practically shouting now, and his words were punctuated with flecks of saliva that flew off his lips. He seemed out of control, but his eyes remained alert, watching me for any tell-tale sign of recognition.

"He spat on you, didn't he?" he went on. "You had the gun on him, and he still spat right in your face! Only not just spit, there was blood too. He bit off the tip of his own tongue just so he could mark you with his blood! He sprayed it all over you, your face, your hair, your clothes. All stained indelibly. He showed you what he was made of." Ryan shook his head. "A man who could bite off his own tongue... Jesus! Do you have any idea what that would take?"

"Teeth?"

Ryan slammed his fists on the table again and the concussion echoed through the room.

"I'll remember that. When we find his blood on your clothes and present them as evidence, I'll be happy to tell your little joke to the judge and jury. I'm sure they'll appreciate it."

"They'll laugh you out of court long before you deliver any of my punchlines," I said. "You have no proof I killed him. You can't and you won't because I didn't. He was dead when I got there. Check with the people I told you about. They'll tell you where I was Wednesday."

"You told me a lot of hooey," Ryan said. "We'll check with those people all right, but if there is one hour, even one minute of your day unaccounted for, your ass is mine. In fact, it is already. You might as well confess. You've practically admitted you broke into his house. We can revoke your license for that alone."

"But you won't if I confess to a murder? Come on, detective!"

"You can't tell me you're not mixed up in this. Your name showed up in connection with some shootings down in Shakytown as well. Seems wherever you go people wind up dead."

"You're a homicide dick--I'm sure you know how it feels."

Ryan stood back from the table and turned to look into the mirrored panel. Resignation flashed across his tired face. He'd been trying to shake my story for hours, and now he was the one getting rattled. Bringing me in so early in the investigation was a mistake. It left him clutching at straws when, with a little more time, he could have known the answers he needed without asking.

But in spite of all his bluster, I could see he was beginning to believe me. That was what frightened him. When they found my fingerprints on the glass shards outside Talbot's window and put out the APB for me, I was already a likely suspect. Then when the police found Talbot's gun in my glove compartment, they were confident, even arrogant, that they had nabbed their killer.

Only now Ryan had doubts. In spite of the evidence, my story was unshakable because it was the truth. I'd given him an extensive list of people who could corroborate my whereabouts on Wednesday. At least for most of it. And the phone company could verify the calls I made in the morning from my office. Nevertheless, I had to remind myself that no alibi is airtight and that if Ryan really wanted to force a case against me, he could do it.

Ryan clenched his fist and pressed the side of it against the mirrored window. He pulled his hand down the glass, leaving a long greasy streak. He came back to his chair and sat down, his shoulders hunched.

"All right," he said. "For the sake of argument, let's assume for just a moment that you are telling the truth. That you didn't kill Talbot. That you only went to his house Thursday morning. Then you gotta help me here. The shit's coming down on my head like an avalanche. All the way down from the mayor's office. Hizzoner is on the commissioner, the commissioner's on the captain, and the captain is all over me.

"Is it my fault crime in the city is out of hand? That's all the papers and the news shows talk about. The public can't take it, and the mayor's reelection campaign can't take it either. Talbot's murder is the last straw. The press smells blood--the mayor's--and they're going play this killing up for all it's worth.

"The mayor wants to show we are putting an end to it. He could get a lot of mileage out of it if we solved a high profile killing like Talbot's. Especially this close to election day. I don't really need to add that I could get a lot of mileage out of it too. If you know anything that will help me, I'm begging you to tell."

Ryan's fears were well-founded. If I was telling the truth, then the most important case of his career was crumbling to dust while the mayor and commissioner looked on. Ryan was as much a victim of the circumstantial evidence as I was. Maybe more so. We both had careers on the line, but he had a lot more time invested in his.

The politics also explained why I'd been picked up so fast. As word got passed up the chain that there was a prime suspect in the Talbot murder, the orders came back down even faster that I should be picked up immediately. With the election just weeks away, the mayor and his appointed cronies were hoping to turn

Talbot's killing from a liability to an advantage.

"Just look how fast our crack police force tracked down this heinous killer. That's exactly the sort of performance I expect and demand from our city's law enforcement bodies, because that is what you, the voters, expect and demand from me, etc..." I could practically hear the scratch and clack of the mayor's speech writers hard at work.

The only problem was they had arrested the wrong man, and Detective Ryan was starting to realize it. The consequences for his job were likely to be severe and permanent.

"I sympathize," I said, meaning it, "But I don't know anything that--"

But I stopped. Because I did know. Something Ryan said earlier came back to me in a flash. It was his crack about using my bloodstained clothes as evidence. Suddenly I knew exactly who killed Lance Talbot. And the implications were more grave than Ryan could imagine.

"Listen," I said, "I may be able to help after all. But I have to do it my own way. You'll have to let me out first or I can't make it work. In fact, if you don't, I guarantee things are going to get worse--a lot worse--and Hizzoner can kiss his swank office goodbye."

The detective looked at me.

"Are you nuts?"

"No, and you don't have much choice. If you let me go, I can solve your case and at the same time help put a lid on the city's crime problem. At least until the election. I'm not talking about any vigilante stuff either. Your boy gets re-elected and you get detective of the year. I get to keep my license and have the Talbot mess expunged from my record. That's a pretty good deal for all of us."

"Maybe, if I believed it, but I don't. How are you going to do all that?"

I shook my head.

"I can promise you one thing. If you don't let me try, in the next few weeks crime in Eola won't just be a problem, it will be an explosion. And all of us--you, me, the mayor--will all go down the tubes together. And the only thing worse than the ride will be the company."

Ryan leaned forward and set his elbows on the table. He cocked his head to the side and his eyes searched the air.

"I don't know... It sounds like a lot of horse--"

"Look, you've got nothing to lose. Sure, you could keep me here a few more days, but you're going to have to let me go eventually. We both know I'm not your killer. I can only help you if you let me out now. Otherwise, it will be too late and the whole thing will blow up in your face. It's your call."

Ryan was quiet for a moment as he considered the options.

"It's intriguing," he said finally. "I'll give you that. And I can raise it with the right people. But first, we have to understand each other. If you screw up, I'm history in the PD. Bringing you in now was stupid. It doesn't matter that I had no choice. It's my investigation—my neck. If the Talbot case stays bungled and the mayor goes down, then Hizzoner won't be the only one looking for a job. I'll lose everything I've worked for during the last 19 years, and I'm too old, too tired, and too cranky to start over. If you don't deliver, I will make it a personal crusade to have your license taken away at a minimum; and more if I can make it stick. You got that?"

I did.

"You better hope you can carry this off," Ryan added. Then the detective stood up and left the room.

Since there was no clock and my watch had been taken away, I had no idea how long it took before he came back. When he finally did, all the arrangements had been made. I was to be released on my own recognizance, pending a future court date still to be determined. Ryan set it up so I was free to go wherever I liked, provided that I didn't leave the state before the hearing.

I collected the things that had been confiscated from me earlier and signed all the forms the police set before me. I probably should have called in a lawyer to look them over first, but the only one I could think of was Taggart and I didn't think it would look good if the cops saw I shared a lawyer with Roger Thornton. Besides, that would have taken hours and I was in a hurry to get home. I had been up for nearly 24 hours and wanted nothing so much as sleep.

* * *

It was a bright Sunday morning when I finally walked out of the police station. It was a prime fall day, still cool, but promising to warm up as the day progressed. I found my car in the lot where they had brought it, and apart from the pressure the sun put on my tired eyes, had an easy drive home. Which was good because I was not up for complications.

When I got there, the parking spaces near the stairway to my apartment were all full. I drove past, noting a car and driver I'd never seen before parked directly across from my entrance. I pulled into another spot and watched the driver through my side window.

He was sitting in a dark green BMW that glistened with a show-room shine that was missing from the rest of our cars. His luxury sedan was backed into its spot, giving the driver a clear uninterrupted view of my open stairwell.

The driver looked more appropriate for the neighborhood than he did for the car. He had a long thin acne-scarred face and a small nose that barely kept his sunglasses in place. His short hair was sandy blond, the color of cement. He wore a ratty white T-shirt with a picture on the front. The man looked as out of place in the sweet leather interior as a cockroach at a presidential dinner.

He sat patiently smoking a hand-rolled cigarette and never took his eyes off my entranceway.

My shoulders tightened and a sharp pain shot through my stiff neck. I turned away. I was much too tired to deal with someone staking out my apartment. I could barely think straight. I didn't even want to know who he was working for. I had rubbed so many people the wrong way lately, it was more surprising there wasn't a whole string of people lined up outside my place.

If he was waiting for me, I decided, let him wait.

I restarted my car and followed the horseshoe-shaped parking lot around the back of the complex, coming out at the second entrance.

I drove to a nearby convenience store and called Walter Alvarez from the pay phone there. He answered after several rings.

"Hello," he said uncertainly.

"Walter, it's Nash. I need a favor."

"Sure, Nash, shoot."

"There's a guy waiting outside my apartment, and I can't go home right now. But the police kept me up all last night and I am ready to drop. I need someplace to stay. Can I come over and crash at your place for a couple hours?"

"It's fine with me, but it's a little awkward. I'm not really at home, I'm over at Demeter's. I'm expecting some news from the editor, so I'm having my calls forwarded here. If you want, you can come here and pick up the keys..."

I wanted. Walter gave me instructions on how to get to his girlfriend's house and we hung up. It took another twenty minutes for me to get to her place, and then another fifteen to get to Walter's after that.

I let myself in and let Sandy out into the fenced-in back yard.

I lay down on the couch briefly with every intention of getting up in a few minutes to let Sandy back in. Instead, I fell asleep on the couch, and all the scratching and howling in the world would not have been enough to wake me.

CHAPTER THIRTY

My nap lasted only two hours. Then, my mind started grinding relentlessly over what I needed to do, playing out the same unpleasant scene over and over, consigning me to a restless doze. Eventually I gave up on sleep and just got up.

I opened the back door off Walter's kitchen and found Sandy sleeping on the stoop in the late-morning sun. The day was warm and fine and clear. At least Sandy hadn't suffered any from my neglect. I prodded her with my foot. She stood up lazily, shook herself with a jangle of collar tags, and sauntered into the kitchen. She stretched out on her rug in the corner and went to sleep again. I started a pot of coffee and watched her. Whatever dreams she had looked a whole lot better than mine. How many karma points does it take before you can come back and live life as a dog?

While the coffee brewed, I retrieved the duffle bag of clothes from my trunk. I took a fast shower and dressed quickly. It felt good to be in a change of underwear, newer pants, and a fresh if wrinkled shirt. I made do with the same jacket I had worn on Friday but had to borrow a tie from Walter's closet.

I gulped down several cups of coffee and had a bowl of cereal at the kitchen table. While I ate, I looked up the address for the Riverview Mobile Home Park, the last place Lance Talbot had called from his office. According to the yellow pages, it was located just east of the city--in exactly the area where Hardison and Gerrara's boss, Angus Baird, was said to own several trailer parks. I took the torn scrap of photograph from my wallet and slipped it into the phone book to mark the page. If anything happened to me, I hoped that Walter would understand to pursue it. And if he didn't, well... I shrugged. I would not be around to care.

* * *

The Riverview Mobile Home Park sounded much grander than it turned out to be. For one thing, there was no river, only a dirty creek that ran along one edge. The thirty or so weathered trailers were situated in a crescent around the base of a steep hill. They rested on cement blocks with tall grass sprouting up where the wheels should be. A high fence at the bottom of the hill kept anyone in the crowded trailer area from encroaching on the grassy slope.

A long cement stairway with a black iron railing led up to a tall Victorian house at the hill's crest. The house had a large porch and a high turret in front; it seemed to watch broodingly over the small community below. A driveway wound up and around the hill to the house but it was barred with a wrought-iron gate.

I left my car in the gravel parking lot and made my way across a small open area towards the cement steps. A few of the residents were outside; some were busy washing the walls of their trailers, others sat out in canvas chairs just shooting the breeze and enjoying the day. None of them took any particular notice of me. A handful of chickens scratched for grubs in the patchy grass and clucked reproachfully as I passed. When I came too close, they fluttered away to the center of the yard, where a bright red wheel-barrow glistened in the morning sun and signified nothing.

Not everyone ignored me, however. The man at the bottom of the stairway seemed to take a very keen interest in my approach. He wore a whiskey logo T-shirt and blue jeans, had crew-cut blond hair and a face the color of boiled lobster. His sun-damaged face and bad teeth made him look a lot older than he probably was. As I came closer he shot a bolt of brown spit into a coffee can beside his faded chair. He shifted his shotgun on his knees to make sure I noticed it.

"You there. What can I do for ye?" His voice was high and nasal.

"I need to see your boss," I said. "Mr. Baird."

"You got an appoin'ment?"

I shook my head.

"Make one. Then mebbe you can see him."

"I think he'll see me anyway. It's about his boys Hardison and Gerrara. I know who killed them."

"You do? Well, we'll just see if he'll talk to ye."

The man set his shotgun down on the ground beside him. He took a small walkie-talkie off a clip on his belt and spoke into it briefly. After a pause, he nodded and turned his attention to me.

"They want to know, who ye are?"

"Nash Tobin. I'm a private detective"

The man repeated this into the walkie-talkie and listened again to the response.

"Yeah, okay. They say go on up."

The man stood up from his chair, took a key from his jeans pocket and unlocked the gate to the stairway. He pushed the gate open and I went through. As I started up the steps, I could hear him close and lock the gate behind me.

It was a long climb, and by the time I reached the top, the muscles in my legs burned.

A man was waiting for me on the porch. Even from a distance, I could see he was big--body-builder big. His shoulders were massive and his arms were so choked with muscle that they couldn't hang straight. His torso tapered into an impossibly narrow waist, and then his over-developed legs expanded out again beneath him. He had a perfect hour-glass figure, though I would never have said so within earshot. He looked like he'd spent a lot of time in the prison weight room to become the biggest con on the block. He wore khaki shorts and a tight-fitting turtleneck shirt because he liked to see his body flex. If I were a crime boss buying muscle, he'd be high on my list so long as I wasn't paying by the pound.

I reached the porch, climbed the steps, and waited for the man to tell me what I should do next.

"Stop," he said after a moment's thought, even though I already had.

He came up to me, loomed over me, in fact. He stooped and patted me down all over looking for a concealed weapon. When he was satisfied that I didn't have one, he said, "Ok. Come on."

He walked to the front door with a wide-legged stance and very little knee-bend. He knocked and someone inside opened it. My muscle-bound greeter stepped aside to let me go in first and then followed close behind.

I stepped into an opulent entrance hall that would have done justice to any civil war costume drama. The walls were burnished wood and hung with a variety of large oil paintings. A grand staircase with a sweeping banister led up to a second story hallway that also served as a balcony over the foyer. An elaborate crystal chandelier hung from the cathedral ceiling, but it was not switched on. Instead, the room was incidentally lit by desk and floor lamps whose light was swallowed up by the rich red paneling.

Another large man met me inside, this one wore a sports jacket and tie. He was nearly as big as his partner but the look on his face was a lot more sharp. His grey eyes sparkled with suspicion.

"What can we do for you, Mr. Tobin?" the new goon said. He walked back to a wooden desk by the stairway and sat down behind it. He looked like a docent about to charge me for admission.

"Like I told the guy down the hill, I want to talk with your boss. I know who killed Hardison and Gerrara."

The seated man frowned.

"What makes you think we don't? If that's all you've got, you're wasting our time."

"There's more," I said. "Plenty..."

Now the man smiled. "That's easy to say, dick. But unless you tell me what it is, I'll have Hank here kick your ass down the stairs outside. He'll be happy to oblige."

Hank, who was standing by the door with his bulging arms folded, chimed in, "You bet."

"Okay, I also know why they were killed. And I know about the other private detective," I said. This, of course, was the key point. If I was on the wrong track about Talbot's death, Baird's men would recognize me for an impostor and kick me out for the long bumpy goodbye down the hill. For an uneasy moment, I watched for the seated goon's response.

His square face slackened and his eyes went dead. His expression instantly became impenetrable.

I smiled inwardly. If he needed to cover his reaction, then there was no question--I was on the right track.

"Fine," he said. "That'll do. Hank, take him to the library. I'll get the boss."

Hank moved into a dark hallway on the left and I followed. He opened the door at the end of the hall and gestured for me to go inside.

When I did, the door closed behind me and I was alone in a large round room at the base of the turret. Built-in bookshelves lined most of the curved walls and stretched almost all the way up to the high ceiling. The top shelves were only accessible by wheeled library ladders attached to a rail in front of the shelves. A wide bay window with a view down the hill brought in enough light to keep the room from feeling oppressive.

An oil portrait of a red-haired man in a kilt-tuxedo hung on the back wall in a space that was specifically designed for it. In the picture, the man rested his arm against the mantle of a stone fireplace, while a pair of rough-and-tumble terriers gamboled at his feet. The man's piercing green eyes stared out of the canvas with steely control. Here was a man not to be crossed under any circumstances.

Walter had said Angus Baird had a reputation for liking to keep his hands dirty. Looking at his portrait, I could well believe it.

The books on Baird's shelves were all beautiful cloth- and leather-bound volumes, many of them masterpieces of the book-maker's art. It was a collection any true bibliophile might have killed for. But it didn't take long to realize Baird's library was strictly for show. His books were shelved randomly with no thought given to how they might be retrieved or read. Many were placed upside down. Probably the only attention they got would be a weekly dusting by the servants. The best of humanity's thoughts and aspirations from 5,000 years was collected on those shelves and ignored, like crops left to rot in an abundant field, just so the room could "make a statement."

"You're admiring my collection, then. Good."

The voice from the doorway startled me.

Baird strode across the room to the mahogany desk in front of the window and sat down. The painting on the wall had perfectly captured his chiseled good-looks, the unruly mop of red hair tinged with gold. But his eyes were even more arresting in person than in the picture. They were the color of jade but cold and remorseless as an arctic sea. In his mid- to late thirties, Baird had an air of absolute confidence that went far beyond arrogance.

His long hands stroked the supple leather of his desk chair.

"Sit down. Can I pour you a scotch, or would you prefer something else?" He spoke with a trace Scottish accent.

I was so tired that I didn't feel much like drinking but I didn't want to seem ungracious either.

"Sure. Scotch is fine."

Baird reached down to one of his desk drawers and pulled out a bottle of single-malt Scotch whiskey and a small glass. The whiskey brand had too many consonants and not enough vowels in its name, but after sitting in an oak cask for 25 years, it was entitled to a few eccentricities. Baird poured some into the glass and handed it across to me. He leaned down and put the bottle back into its drawer.

"Aren't you having one?" I asked.

"At this time of morning? Certainly not! I did not get where I am by indulging myself. What you do, of course, is your own business. Now what are you doing here? And don't waste my time. You told my men you know something about who killed Cy and Tony."

"Right," I said. "Only I lied. You probably know more about the triggermen than I do. I know who gave the order and why. But I doubt that's news to you either."

"Probably not. So why are you here?"

I took a long breath.

"I'm a private detective," I said. "My firm is small, but I do a lot of contract work with the bigger agencies. Your lawyer Taggart or Roger Thornton may have mentioned me..."

"I never heard of you. And that still doesn't explain your being here."

"I worked with one company in particular, Axiom Security,

run by Lance Talbot. I'm sure you've heard of him. I understand you terminated him recently."

Baird leaned back and his eyes narrowed.

"That's the American way. If someone doesn't give good service, they get fired."

"Fired, yes. Well, Lance Talbot was like a partner to me, even a mentor. He taught me a lot about the ins and outs of the business, and how you should always, always take advantage of a profitable opportunity, whenever it arises."

"What has this to do with me?" Baird asked.

"The important thing is, he showed me how to cultivate a new type of client, someone who is willing to pay to retain my services--and to keep on paying--even when they don't have a specific job in mind."

"They're daft, then. Why would they pay for something they don't need?"

"Surprisingly, no one ever complains. At least not to me. I guess they like the security of knowing I will always keep their interests at heart. Now, Talbot--he was an expert at figuring out how much that kind of peace of mind was worth to our clients."

Baird's mouth tightened. The burr in his voice became an angry rasp.

"I don't recognize this Talbot of yours. But if he chose you for a partner, I'm guessing he's missing something up here," Baird said, tapping the center of his forehead. The comment sounded innocuous enough, until I realized he meant it quite literally.

"Talbot knew you," I went on. "In fact, he had a particular interest in you."

"Did he tell you what that interest was?"

"Not in so many words, but he didn't need to. One time, though, he did tell me, 'To hell with grammar! Certain cases require double negatives...' And that's where I came in."

The expression on Baird's V-shaped face was turning ugly. I was playing word games with a dangerous snake and from the looks of it, he didn't find me at all charming.

"Double negatives. I see," Baird said, slowly. He reached down and took out the bottle of scotch again and poured himself a drink in a larger glass. "I guess I will have one after all. I believe you have a proposal to make, and business is best discussed over drinks. But I tell you up front, my answer is no. Partnerships of this kind don't last--they turn sour very quickly. Maybe your friend found that out."

"You haven't heard my terms," I said. "Talbot was greedy. I'm a reasonable man."

"You disproved that by coming here. But I can at least hear you out. If it's the last thing you do."

"Before we go into my terms, let's talk about what you want. And I'll be blunt: I see you as a second-rater with ambitions to move up. And the only way you can become top dog in the junkyard, is to take out the current top dog. Am I right?"

Baird set his drink down on the green blotter pad. He placed his elbows on the desk top, leaned forward, and tented his hands in front of him.

"There is nothing second-rate about me. Nothing!"

"But we know who currently holds first place."

Baird nodded: "Winston Graham."

I took a deep breath. I had considered this scenario from every possible angle and believed it held up. But in every chain of reasoning, there is always the danger of missing links.

"Winston Graham, exactly. And as part of an effort to get rid of Graham, your men Hardison and Gerrara dumped that girl's body at his gravel yard. You wanted to draw attention to his connections there and tie him in with the murder."

Baird raised his eyebrow, nodding coldly, almost imperceptibly. Until the last word.

"We never killed that girl," he said, pronouncing the last word like squirrel. "She was dead when we got there. All we did was move the body for a little public harassment, like you said. And it worked better than I hoped. That picture of her hanging from the conveyor belt was beautiful! I was going to place an anti-Graham story in one of the newspapers, but after that photo, all the papers started going after him on their own. It even went national. Now Graham is bleeding black ink and weakening by the day, all because of one picture."

"And he retaliated by killing your guys. For leaving her there."

"Yes. Tony was never good at keeping his mouth shut. Word got to Graham about it and he went after them... Now, he will pay for that. I'll make him pay."

Baird leaned back in his chair, picked up his highball glass and took a small sip. He left the whiskey on his tongue for a moment before swallowing. "Did you ever wrestle, Mr. Tobin?"

"Back in high school."

"Good. Then maybe you'll understand when I say it's not primarily a question of strength or toughness. You need those of course, but many people have them and still never amount to anything. What makes a wrestler great is his balance. Sometimes you grapple with an opponent, using all your strength to dislodge him, but he simply can't be moved. He stays perfectly stable. Then, suddenly, you feel a shift in his center of gravity; it can be so slight that he may not even recognize it. But you feel it, feel it in your bones that he has gone from strong to weak, from untouchable to vulnerable. That's where Graham is now. He looks strong as ever, but there's been a shift and he's ready to fall. It cost me two men already, and it may take more. But in the end, I'll be left standing and Graham will be history."

"What if you're wrong? What if you miscalculated or are just seeing what you want to see?"

"I'm not wrong. Look at the way he hit Cy and Tony. He had them both done at the same time, which was smart enough, but he used three guys on each one. That's overkill, two should have been fine. And he did Tony at home where his family was. That's against the rules. It shows me that Graham is scared and he's trying to keep me from knowing it. It could turn very ugly--like no one's seen here since the thirties. But I am willing to use every man at my disposal plus more that I can buy. If I need to, I'll throw every cent I own into destroying Graham." Baird's green eyes gleamed too brightly as he looked across the desk at me. "It's my time to take him out."

I swallowed hard.

"No," I said quietly.

"What?!"

"...At least not yet. That's what I came for."

Baird picked up a heavy brass-letter opener and shook it at me.

"No one tells me 'no'!" he said. "Least of all a dumb rent-a-cop. I can arrange it so you never walk out of here..."

"Maybe, but that's not good for you. Remember, I have the picture from Shakytown. Now that Talbot's dead, that gives me even more leverage than he had."

Baird growled viciously and hurled his letter-opener past me at the wall of books. Its point struck deep into the spine of a large antique volume and dug a nick out of its leather before falling to the floor. Baird glowered at me and rose from his chair.

"You must be the one who called from his office. You should have paid more attention to what happened there."

"I did," I said. "Very close attention. That is why I thought out my terms so carefully. I wouldn't have come if I didn't think we could both live with them. It will actually be in your interest to agree. You lose nothing by listening."

Baird leaned forward, resting his hands on his desk.

"Then tell me. Before I get annoyed enough to kill you myself."

"You only need to lay off Graham until after the November elections. Then I'll give you everything Talbot gave me and our business will be concluded. That's the difference between Talbot's demands and mine. You knew he would never stop trying to bleed you. But after November, you will never hear from me again. I promise."

Baird slowly lowered himself back into his chair.

"Your promise doesn't mean anything."

"It does to me. And for you, it will be less trouble to trust me than to kill me. It's only for two weeks."

"If I do what you say, Graham will think I'm backing down, that I'm weak."

"Probably. But that will just make him overconfident. As you said, he's already taking a beating in the press. Things are going to get worse for him, not better."

"He killed two of my guys. I can't let that go."

"Your group hurt Graham, and he retaliated. But he overreached with those killings. Now the cops are involved. Let them take care of it, at least for now. The police want Graham as badly as you do. When they go after him, they'll be doing your work for you, like the servants of the public they claim to be."

I didn't add that as long as Winston Graham thought he had won in the latest skirmish with Baird, he would not feel the need to make any more trouble for a while. Graham would have established his supremacy, and the city would stay relatively quiet.

"I see," Baird said, nodding slowly. "I may think about it. What else?"

"The police also need someone to go down for Talbot's death. Hardison and Gerrara are ideal since they actually killed him. Plus, there's no way they can be turned against you. Do you have an alibi for Wednesday?"

"If I need it."

"I doubt you will. The cops should be happy enough to pin it on those two and leave it at that. All they want is to wrap up Talbot's murder fast and neat. They probably won't go out of their way looking for loose ends. But because Talbot called your office, you may need to get a story set up that either Hardison or Gerrara took his call. Just to keep those two front and center."

"We can do that. But what about motive?"

"With solid physical evidence against Hardison and Gerrara, the police will probably not worry much about motive, or whether they were acting on their own. Frankly, there were a lot of people who wanted Talbot dead, too many for the police to sort them all out. You aren't the only person he tried to blackmail."

"But I am the last. Bear that in mind."

"I do, believe me. No other outsider knows anything about you and Talbot. As long as I stay healthy, it won't come out. If you do as I suggest, you can sit back and watch as everything comes together and gets handed to you on a silver platter. The police take care of Graham, and you get off scot-free for Talbot's death. It's a real-life example of good things coming to him who waits. All you have to do is hold back for two weeks. After election day, our deal is over and you can play it however you want."

Baird thought for a moment.

"What do you get out of this?"

"The cops let me keep my investigator's license and my freedom. In my line of work, I have to make deals with some pretty unsavory characters."

"And that's all?"

I hesitated. "There is one more thing."

Baird's face grew suspicious again:

"And that is..."

"The dead girl. You say you and your men had nothing to do with her death?"

"On a stack of bibles, I swear it."

I didn't ponder what such an oath would mean to a criminal kingpin.

"Then I want the person who's responsible to be caught. He needs to be held accountable," I said. "I'm sure you can convince him not to implicate you in moving the body..."

Baird smiled. "I could if I needed to. But he never even saw me. Or Tony. He never left the apartment. The only one he knew was Cy. And Cy's not talking."

"Then you have no objections?"

"Not if you keep your end of the bargain. If after the elections are over, I never have to worry about you again."

I nodded.

"You better be playing straight with me," he said. "You know what happens if you don't."

I did. I'd seen the consequences in Talbot's little cubbyhole.

"Is it a deal then?" I asked.

Baird extended his hand across the desk and gripped mine in a granite clasp.

"It is," he said. "And a pleasure doing business with you."

CHAPTER THIRTY-ONE

It was quiet back in my office. The nervous energy that had carried me through my meeting with Baird was exhausted. I felt half dead and probably looked a little worse. More coffee didn't help, it only made me jittery.

I called police headquarters and asked for Detective Ryan. Remarkably, he was still on-duty despite having worked a schedule much like mine.

"Yeah, who is this?" Ryan sounded like I felt.

"You don't recognize me? I'm hurt."

"No, wait. Your voice does sound familiar. It's like..." Ryan paused. "Oh, yes--it's the sound an asshole makes."

"Believe it or not, I didn't call for the banter."

"What a shame. I sat around all night waiting to show it off. Why are you calling then? Something go wrong? Need to renegotiate?"

"No, it's all arranged. Things should stay quiet through the election. No escalation anyway. I'm actually calling to give you an anonymous tip on the Talbot murder. You have something to write this down or do you think you can remember?"

"I may have to look up 'anonymous,' but I think I can handle the rest."

"All right. Check the bullet that killed Talbot against any guns you can find belonging to Anthony Gerrara or Cyrus Hardison, the two hoods who were shot on Thursday. You might get lucky."

"Okay, I'll do that."

There was a long pause where neither of us said anything.

"You know, if you actually deliver on this, I'm going to owe you big time," Ryan said. Or maybe he didn't say anything remotely like that and it was simply understood between us.

"I'll keep you posted," I said, and hung up.

For the time being at least, I was squared with Eola's finest.

My next order of business was to find the man who killed Rudi Alsmith. And now I knew exactly where to look.

* * *

I drove down to Curtiz's condominium building and rang the doorbell in the foyer. It was time to make the confrontation. I didn't know yet what I would say, but like most things, I figured I'd play it by ear. When there was no response to the bell, I pushed the button again. And again.

Still nothing.

I stared blankly at the doorbell panel, not knowing what to do next. The thought of staking out the apartment again made me wince. The last time, while I was sitting slack-jawed and snoring just a block away, Rudi Alsmith's life had been snuffed out forever right upstairs. The killer had called on Cy Hardison to come remove the body. Hardison, Gerrara, and Baird must have driven right by me as I slept.

I could have helped her, I thought. If only I'd known.

I mashed my thumb against the condo's bell-button and left it there. Still no answer. I was either being ignored or no one was home.

I went over to an outdoor payphone across the street and got Vera Marshall's home phone number from directory assistance. She answered on the second ring.

"Hello?"

"Miss Marshall. It's Nash Tobin calling."

"Oh, I didn't expect to hear from you. Vera, please. I'm glad you called."

That was a pleasant surprise. Her voice had the same lilting quality I'd taken to so easily when she came to my office.

"Okay, Vera. Sorry to bother you at home but it's business that won't wait."

"No problem. What can I do for you?"

"I need the phone number for Curtiz's brother, Winter. The one in Shakytown. I can't find a listing."

"What do you want that for?"

I hesitated before answering.

"He may be--only may be--involved with the death of that teenage girl, Rudi Alsmith. But it is urgent that I talk with him before the police do."

"I thought Mr. Curtiz let you go."

“If I talk with his brother, I may be able to keep Curtiz out of the picture for the police. If I don’t…” I left her to imagine the potential fallout for her boss.

Vera was silent while she weighed what she should do. Finally she said, “You only need to speak with him?"

"That's all."

She thought some more.

"Well, I guess it will be all right. But I don't have that number here. I'll have to get it from the office."

"Okay, I'll meet you there. I hope I'm not ruining your Sunday..."

"Nothing to ruin. I'll be there in fifteen minutes."

"Great. Thanks very much. Fifteen minutes, then."

It actually took me more than twenty to get to Curtiz's house, and Vera Marshall's red VW was already parked in front.

As I stepped onto the sidewalk leading to the entrance, Curtiz's door opened. Vera emerged from the small shadowy portico, wearing crisp blue-jeans and a green T-shirt with elbow length sleeves. Two loose strands of hair had escaped from her blond ponytail and they drifted lazily in the afternoon breeze. She pushed them back and smiled. Nothing flashy or broad or with a great show of teeth. Nothing enticing or intense, just the subdued, private, everyday smile you sometimes see on a stranger's face when they are lost in thought. Still, coming from her, its subtle radiance left me breathless because it was meant for me.

She raised her right hand, holding a small piece of paper.

"I'm still not sure I should give you this," she said.

"I know. But it's better me than the police."

"Maybe I should call Mr. Curtiz in California first..."

It seemed a reasonable suggestion but it would spoil everything.

"I already know what his answer would be. He'll never agree unless you explain why I need to talk to his brother. And that's not a good idea because the less he knows about what Winter may have done, the better it will be for him."

Vera looked at me, still hesitating.

"Forgiveness is easier than permission, I guess. You want to call from here?" She moved back towards the door.

I followed her into the sheltered porch alcove and took the note from her hand. Our fingers touched in the exchange and our faces were scant inches apart. My eyes looked deep into hers, searching.

She returned my look unabashed. Close as we were, we drew closer still, our bodies like two stormfronts converging on a frenzied squall.

Suddenly, she lunged at my face like a lamprey, her kiss ferocious and demanding. I pulled her tight against me and our hearts surged at one another. The flux continued to build as her body melded with my embrace. We locked together in that enclosed doorway, the center of a storm, the center of nature. And for the brief time we kissed, the whole of creation seemed to smile on our union.

Finally, Vera pulled back and caught her breath.

"You want to come inside and make that call?" she repeated. She took my hand, pulling me gently towards the house.

I squeezed her hand...

And let it go.

"I'd never get around to making the call. And I have to."

She picked up my hand again and kissed it.

"Then whatever it is, I hope it is over soon."

She dropped my hand and went inside. For a moment, I stood alone on the front steps, my heart pounding and my head in a daze. Finally I turned away and went back to my car.

I returned to my office and dialed the number Vera had given me. It was answered promptly, as I expected. No one would have access to this phone number who was not supposed to.

"Hello." It was the same hoarse and haggard voice from the gravel yard.

"Mr. Curtiz?"

"This is he," he said suspiciously. I must not have sounded like someone who was supposed to have this number.

"It's Nash Tobin."

There was a pause.

"I don't know you. Goodbye..."

I interrupted before he hung up.

"Actually, you do, Mr. Curtiz. And I believe you know why I'm calling. I know all about Rudi Alsmith's last night there. I'd like to talk with you about it."

"I don't know what you're talking about. You're mistaking me for someone else."

"I don't think so. I know exactly who I'm talking to and I'm quite sure you know what I'm talking about. It's time we met.

One last time. Tonight at 5:30. You know the place."

"I have no idea where you mean," he said. "Leave me alone or I will seek help from the authorities."

"Do that. It will save me the trouble of calling them myself. If I don't see you at 5:30, that's exactly what I'll do."

I hung up before he could protest further.

I swiveled round in my chair and looked out into the bright fall sky. One kiss and the world suddenly seemed a remarkable place. I tried to focus on what had happened to Rudi on the night she died, but it seemed too remote. My thoughts kept returning to Vera instead. It's amazing what suckers we mortals be.

And we wouldn't want it any other way.

I allowed myself one shot of whiskey and called Walter at home. His girlfriend Demeter answered; Walter's calls were still being forwarded to her place. She put Walter on, and I thanked him for letting me use his house that morning. In exchange for his hospitality I had one more favor to ask.

CHAPTER THIRTY-TWO

Sunday evenings are slow at My Cat Jeoffry's and the club was much quieter than during my last visit. Only one waiter was on duty and he doubled as host. One glance at my suit and tie, and he led me without comment into the dining room.

"Can I have that booth back there?" I asked, pointing. "I'm expecting another person."

"Certainly, sir." He took me to the booth and left two menus on the table.

"May I get you a drink while you wait?"

"I'll start with coffee," I said.

"Very good, sir." He spun around on his heel went to fetch it. It was a good sign.

After a few moments, he brought my coffee and went away again. I sat alone in my booth, perusing the menu and nursing my $3 java. I would have ordered it with cream but that might have come with a surcharge. I smoked a cigarette or two while I waited.

Mr. Curtiz came in at 5:30 sharp; punctuality was important to him, I recalled. The host brought him in from the hallway and the pair halted until Curtiz spotted me across the dining room. He was dressed casually, with a simple tie wrapped around his neck and no jacket. He nodded dismissively to the host and came over to sit down.

His square jaw was unshaven, maybe for two or three days. His deeply tanned face looked puffier and slacker than the last time I'd seen him. He had been burning the candle at both ends for over a week now and was paying the price for it. Dark pouches surrounded his cold brown eyes. Those eyes had previously radiated confidence and control, but now they were edgy and hostile.

It was Preston Curtiz, of course. He had left the white wig and pale powder makeup at home. I was again meeting my famous client, the world-class novelist, who also happened to be either a borderline schizophrenic or a simple sociopath.

He stuck one of his expensive party-colored cigarettes into his mouth and lit it, drawing deeply.

"So, what have you to say for yourself?" he said, the cigarette bobbing on his lips like a blue baton.

"Welcome to California," I said. "How do you like the weather?"

"The weather's fine, but I could do without the locals."

I laughed. I could afford to.

"How did you know?" Curtiz asked finally.

"That you weren't actually gone? I thought it might be you last night at the gravel yard. I didn't know how the phone trick worked until this morning. When your secretary called you in Los Angeles, it never occurred to me you could be somewhere else. Until later. But it was a simple enough matter to have the phone company forward your calls back to the condo in Shakytown. Simple but effective."

The waiter came over to us, uncertainly. Something about the way Curtiz and I looked together made him uncomfortable.

"Can I bring you anything? A drink? An appetizer? Are you ready to ..."

Curtiz shot him a look of utter contempt and scowled, "Just go away."

The waiter did.

"But I still don't understand why," I went on, ignoring the interruption. "Why the pretense of making phony trips to California? Why bother with the charade of a brother who doesn't exist?"

"You don't understand because you're a nobody, a null. You don't know the pressure that comes with being important and having to maintain a public image. Bourgeois respectability comes hard—too hard. I manage for a while, sometimes months at a time, but I always slip..."

"So you duck out from the pressures and scrutiny of home by pretending to go to California. In reality, you're off on a coke jag in Shakytown, impersonating a brother who can take the heat for your actions. You get to indulge in all the wild excess you want and still keep your reputation intact."

Curtiz's eyes fairly blazed.

"Wild doesn't even come close! It is absolute freedom, complete abandon! You have no idea what being truly free makes one capable of."

"I got a feel for it last night at the gravel yard."

Curtiz flinched. "I'm not talking about the common herd--they can be led to anything. I mean the leaders, the elite, those of us who recognize the world for what it is. We see the impertinence of your puny sense of right and wrong."

"What happened to Rudi Alsmith was wrong."

Curtiz took the cigarette from his mouth and tapped ashes into the metal ashtray on the table.

"You'll excuse me if I don't know what you mean."

"Then let me explain: Rudi came to you last Saturday night, to 'your little California retreat.' She was crying. She'd been beat up. As I see it, she came because she saw you as something better than what went on in the rest of her life. To her, you were special, someone she could count on. She must have known you as both Preston and Winter--you couldn't have hidden that from her—but still she accepted you. You may have been the only man she truly loved."

Curtiz pouted his lips. "Rudi Alsmith was a student of mine. That was all."

"To you maybe, but I saw the way she looked at you in your office. I read a poem she wrote for you. Rudi surrendered herself to you completely, heaven knows why. Maybe it was because she was eighteen and naive in spite of everything. Whatever her reasons, she did love you. And thought you loved her."

Curtiz was quiet for a moment.

"She may have been my best student, it's true. Not her writing of course, but the one I was most proud of. I will certainly miss her, but only as a mentor misses his protegee."

A thin smile played across Curtiz's face. He blew smoke down over the tabletop, like a gauntlet being tossed. The challenge was in his eyes, too, daring me to read it. His expression was tired, amused, and malevolent, all at the same time.

It only took me a second.

"Jim Boughton!" I said suddenly.

"What?!" Curtiz was shocked. My guess clearly rattled him.

I didn't give him a chance to regroup.

"Rudi was your protegee. The way she manipulated people, toyed with them, played on their desires, like you do! Like last night at the gravel yard, like what you tried to do to me. Rudi twisted the lives of those around her, the teacher she seduced, the schoolmate she drove to kill himself. But she did it all for you. Jim Boughton's suicide was a love offering to you! You must have been so proud!"

By the time I finished, Curtiz had regained his confidence. His smile was gleeful and completely depraved.

"I deny it, of course. Categorically."

"That changes nothing. You are responsible for that boy's death as surely you are for Rudi's."

Curtiz laughed.

"Now you're being ridiculous."

"Then try this amusing anecdote. Rudi came to your apartment somewhere between 10:15 and 10:45. You saw her bruises, knew she had just been with another man. Maybe you were jealous and angry. Maybe you got into an argument over something else. Whatever it was, you began to beat her yourself. You grabbed her roughly by the shoulder and somehow broke it. Maybe she started crying out. You couldn't let the cops come by and find out who you were, so you tried to shut her up. Only it went too far and you killed her. You shut her up once and for all."

"You're crazy. You can't prove any of it."

I shook my head.

"You still don't get it. How could I prove anything? I can't turn in my client. What kind of future would I have if I went around proving my own clients' guilt? How could I make a living if that got out?"

"Ah, but you don't work for me. I fired you."

"No, but I did. I'm still bound by that confidentiality."

"Then why do you care what happened Saturday night? There's nothing you can do."

"I want to know. For myself. Too many lives get cut short for no reason. I want to know why Rudi Alsmith had to die."

Curtiz shrugged. "What difference does it make?"

"Why did you kill her?"

"I didn't. She did it to herself."

"Then you maneuvered it somehow... She never broke her own shoulder."

"No," Curtiz said. "That must have come after. When— he dropped her off the balcony."

I breathed a sigh of relief. An admission. At last.

"So she was at your apartment Saturday night?"

"Since you can't do anything with the information, yes, she was. But none of it happened as you suggest."

"How was it then?"

"She came over a little before eleven. She'd been crying and looked like hell. We did some of the coke she brought, and went into the bedroom. Despite her bruises, I can tell you she was feeling no pain. But after a while, she started to get cloying and demanding. Even paranoid. She insisted that I tell her I loved her."

"And..."

"So I did. They're just words, after all, and they seemed to calm her. But at about midnight, some maniac started pushing on the doorbell downstairs. The chimes were going off in the apartment over and over, loud enough to drive one crazy. They set Rudi off again. She thought they were some kind of a church bell.

"She got out of bed and ran to the door to let the person in. She kept chanting, 'It tolls for me, it tolls for me, it tolls for me!"

I raised the cup of coffee to my lips and took a long drink. It had been around midnight when I was ringing the condo's doorbell to find out who lived there.

"What happened next?" I asked.

"I couldn't let anyone in, not with her the way she was. I had to stop her somehow. I grabbed her arm and pulled her back into the bedroom. The whole time, she kept saying, 'No, you must let me answer it! It tolls for me, it tolls for me, it tolls for me!' She fought me, but I got her back in anyway.

"All that contact with her made me excited again. I put her on the bed and brought out more cocaine. To get her mind on other things."

"What happened then?"

"It was odd," Curtiz said. "She looked at me, and for a moment her eyes seemed to clear. She smiled, but not in a pleasant way. Then she grabbed the bag of coke and tried to inhale its full contents. She even licked the residual dust out so that nothing was left."

"What did you do?"

"Well, I was a little worried about her. The bag wasn't full, but I knew it was more than she should take. But then she pulled me down on top of her. Suddenly, she was insatiable, more insistent than I'd ever seen her. I couldn't stop either one of us.

"Eventually she did start to slow down. At first it looked like she would be fine. But she wasn't. Her system slowed down so much, she shut down completely. Her eyes closed and her breathing stopped. She lay there on the bed as still as a statue. When I couldn't feel any heartbeat or respiration at all, I started to panic. I pulled her off the bed and put her under a cold shower to revive her. That seemed to work at first, but then she went under again. I took her out to the living room to help her walk it off, but..." Curtiz shook his head. "Her bowels just let loose. When that happened, I knew it was too late."

"So you had a dead body and a mess on your living room floor. What did you do then?"

"What else could I do? I called someone I know who can handle a situation like that. I told him I needed his help right away."

"Who was this person."

"A contact. I'm not going to say more."

"So what time did this contact arrive?"

"About twenty minutes later. He came up to the apartment and tied the body up so it would not draw attention when we got rid of it. He wrapped her in a bed sheet and put the bundle into a plastic garbage bag. That part took only fifteen minutes. He asked what other stuff she had brought with her. I showed him her clothes and her purse, her keys, etcetera, and he put them all into a paper sack and twisted the end shut. Then he carried her body out through the kitchen to the balcony.

"He had two other men waiting outside in the back lot. He dropped the body down to them. In the darkness, one of the men dropped her. I heard something crack when she hit the ground, even from the kitchen. Then the men picked her up and carried her away to the alley. That was the last I saw of her."

I nodded: "Then what?"

"Then Cy--" Curtiz began, but quickly stopped himself. "Then, see, the guy told me what I needed to do to clean the apartment. After that, he left. He took the paper sack with him and went to meet his men down below."

Curtiz pulled out another cigarette and looked at it for moment without lighting up.

"Cleaning up wasn't so bad really. They're all hardwood floors so it was fairly easy. The shit was the worst because there were some flies buzzing around it. But I took care of that and everything else. I wiped off all the door handles, fixtures, counters, tables, chairs, ... anything that she might have touched. I washed the sheets and pillow cases and burned the lint from the dryer in case there were any of Rudi's hairs that might be left. It took me most of the night. I didn't get to sleep until about six that morning."

I could picture it only too well. Curtiz would have been machine-like in his efficiency, painstakingly going over his apartment to remove all evidence of the young girl who only hours before had been a warm, breathing human being. She had loved him, and he spent the night blotting out every trace of her existence.

Something about it got to me. I think it was the part where Curtiz said Rudi's smile had turned unpleasant and her eyes became clear. Rudi Alsmith knew exactly what she was doing when she took her final overdose.

"You killed her," I said again. "As surely as if you put a gun to her head and pulled the trigger."

"I just told you what happened. She killed herself. It had nothing to do with me."

"It had everything to do with you! She came to you, beaten, abused, made to feel she was worth nothing. She came because she loved you, looking for some sign that she was worthwhile. All it would have taken was some gesture of affection, something to show you valued who she was.

"Instead you treated her like a coke whore. You tried to shut her up with drugs and used her body as if it were a blow up doll. You may not have coerced her in any way, but you are still to blame for her death. It wasn't just suicide—you drove her to an act of total self obliteration. She wasted herself once and for all on a binge of drugs and sex with the one person in the world she wanted more from. Only you had nothing more to give."

"It wasn't my fault!" he said, showing perhaps a chink in his emotional armor. "If it hadn't been me, it would have been someone else. It could have been anyone!"

"But it was you. That's what matters. Legally, your guilt may be minor. Probably a good lawyer could get you off, it being your first recorded offense and all. But what you did was a scandal. You were in a position to protect her, but instead you provoked her self-destruction. The law may not recognize it, but you are still guilty. Guilty as sin."

"Sin," Curtiz sneered. "There's no such thing. And why would I need a lawyer? As you said, you can't reveal a word of this. Even if you were willing to face the consequences, there's no proof for any of it. Nothing can link me to her. No one but you thinks I was anywhere but California when she died, and you can't touch me. There's no scandal if I don't admit to it, and that I will never do."

He paused before continuing:

"I've actually enjoyed our little tete-a-tete. They say confession is good for the soul. I don't know anything about that. But seeing your impotence—knowing how she died but not being able to do anything about it—that is ample reward for me."

There was a creak on the wooden bench from Curtiz's side. The man on the seat behind him stood up and came around to our table. He was medium height, rather pudgy, and held a cigarette holder tightly in his teeth like Franklin Delano Roosevelt.

"I thought I recognized your voices," the man said. "Nash, it's nice to see you again. And you, Mr. Curtiz, I've long been an admirer. I guess I should have warned you that your discussion was clearly audible from where I sat. I apologize for not mentioning it sooner. Nonetheless, I'm sure we'll be in touch soon, Mr. Curtiz. At a minimum, I'll be asking you for a comment. If you'd like to schedule an interview, here's my card." Walter Alvarez pushed his card across the table to Curtiz. "Give me a call—our lawyers can do lunch. Bye gents."

Alvarez left, clutching a large notebook in his hand.

Curtiz looked at the card, "Walter Alvarez, Reporter Eola Graphic,"and blanched. His faced turned as white as a sheet or a ghost. Winter-white.

He looked across the table at me, mouth open but speechless.

I shook out a Camel and lit it.

"Don't look at me," I said, blowing smoke. "Like I said, when I work for you, my lips are sealed. I'll go to jail on contempt charges before I say anything against you. But as for what you say aloud in a public restaurant..." I shook my head. "I don't know. My professional advice is, you should be a lot more careful."

I stood up and pulled my wallet from my back pocket. I took

out a twenty dollar bill and threw it on the table.

"Here, this one's on me."

I left Curtiz sitting there.

EPILOGUE

It was two months later. Vera Marshall and I walked mitten-in-glove along Old Hanover's Main Street. It was a cold, crisp December night, with snow falling steadily all around us. The layer of fine snow on the sidewalk compressed like down beneath our unhurried footfalls. The old-fashioned light-posts we passed were decorated with pine ropes and wide gold ribbons.

Last-minute Christmas shoppers rushed by in stark contrast to the slowly swirling snow. They thronged the sidewalks, bustling along with heavy shopping bags, dashing in and out of the stone shops that were open late for just such an occasion. The scene was like a paste-up job for the ultimate Christmas card.

I turned to look at Vera's face, struck by her beauty as always, and the chameleon shimmer in her eyes. Her cheeks were red in the frosty air, and occasional snowflakes settled on her nose or caught in the blond bangs that peeked out under her knit cap. She smiled back and pulled in closer. Our parkas made a familiar rustle as we trudged up the hill.

Alphonse Andeo and Judith Sachett followed behind us. I had introduced them over a month ago and knew from Alphonse that they had seen each other several times since then. Although not "a couple," they certainly made a comical pair. He was toothpick thin and pasty-white. She was as wide as two of him, and applied makeup to her face with the same verve and abandon that marked her paintings. Nonetheless, they enjoyed each other's company whenever they went out, and—Alphonse assured me with a wink—even more so when they stayed in...

Our destination was a small club on Main Street where they brewed their own beer and played different types of jazz. As we opened the door to go inside, a lively salsa number escaped into the wintery night.

Most of the club space was crowded with tables, but several couples were dancing in a cleared-out area at the center of the room. Our party was brought to a square table in the front window where we could watch either the dancers or the snow coming down outside.

"Tonight's celebration is on me," I said as we sat down. "Money is no object!" I leaned across the table towards Vera and added in a mock whisper, "You brought money, I hope?"

"Of course, dahling. I know you too well," she said.

The waiter came and took our drink orders. Vera and I ordered the house beer, Mrs. Sachett took a red wine, and Alphonse had a martini. The drinks soon arrived, and Vera held up her tall glass.

"The first toast of the evening," she said, "To my former boss, for his exceptionally wise decision not to tangle with Nash in the courtroom."

"I'll drink to that," I said.

"Hear, hear." Alphonse said and three of us clinked glasses.

For many weeks, Curtiz had been threatening to sue me for "breach of faith." But late that afternoon his lawyer notified mine that the writer had finally abandoned the idea. Curtiz was afraid that a new lawsuit would just resurrect the bad publicity that was only now starting to die down around him. My lawyer was not surprised by this decision: he believed Curtiz's case would have been hard to win, especially if we insisted on making it a jury trial. It was especially hazy since I was no longer working for him at the time of our second meeting in My Cat Jeoffry's. But to me, Curtiz's decision to drop the suit came as a great relief and was definitely worth celebrating. It also meant I could now talk more freely about the Rudi Alsmith case, which was why Vera suggested we invite our older friends to join us. My reticence during the past months had been particularly hard on Mrs. Sachett.

The old woman refused to join us in our toast and kept her wine glass firmly on the table.

"I can't drink to him," she said. "Not after what he did. I can't believe he got away with probation and community service."

"He also lost his job at the university," I pointed out. "And the mandatory drug treatment will be confinement of a sort."

"It's not enough. Not nearly."

I happened to agree with her.

Curtiz's trial had concluded two weeks earlier. As expected, the whole affair began as a highly publicized circus. It was a chance for celebrity-starved Eola to put itself on the national media map. Curtiz gave interviews to all the network morning shows, swearing his innocence and promising to fight the charges all the way to the Supreme Court. But when the trial actually began, his lawyers immediately sensed that Curtiz's self-serving testimony and condescending attitude was quickly turning the jurors against him. Within days, his lawyers convinced him to get his fate out of the hands of his "so-called peers" and to cut a deal. Given the lack of physical evidence against him, the prosecutors were happy to oblige. Curtiz pled guilty to the charges of failing to report a death, improper disposal of a dead body, and possession of a controlled substance.

For the reduced charges, Curtiz was sentenced to a year's probation and required to undergo drug rehabilitation and continuous drug testing. He was also required to perform community service by putting his talents to work for the anti-drug programs in our area. I heard from Walter Alvarez that Curtiz had already penned a searing script for a 30-second TV spot that had the state health authorities very excited.

And even if Curtiz's sentence was light on punishment, there was no question about his suffering. The reporting in the Eola Graphic and other newspapers about Curtiz's illicit activities was extensive and damning. It changed forever the way the world looked at Preston Curtiz the writer. No longer would he be "Eola's preeminent literary figure." From now on, he would be known as "that crazy Eola writer who had a teenage girl OD in his bedroom." For some, perpetual notoriety might seem easy to live with, but not for Curtiz. His permanently tarnished reputation was going to be a lifetime sentence both cruel and unusual.

"I still don't get what happened to that other detective," Alphonse said, spearing the olive in his glass with a toothpick.

I paused for a moment before answering. This was the part I still had to be most careful about.

"He was killed by the two thugs who helped Curtiz get rid of Rudi," I said. "When they arrived at Curtiz's Shakytown apartment, Talbot saw one of them go inside and the other back their car into the alley. Something about the way they acted made him suspicious enough to start taking pictures."

Actually three men had arrived in Gerrara's car that night. After Cyrus Hardison had gone inside, Talbot could see easily that the driver was the third man's flunky. That's why he directed the blackmail scheme against Angus Baird rather than the Cadillac's registered owner, Gerrara. Although I never knew for sure, I gathered that one of Talbot's pictures had been clear enough to identify Baird.

"After 15 or 20 minutes, the driver went behind the building and picked up a heavy garbage bag, which he put into the Cadillac's trunk. Then the first man came out, and the two drove away.

"Talbot probably realized there was a body in that garbage bag. He certainly knew something fishy was going on. On Monday, he ran the Cadillac's license number through the Department of Motor Vehicles. When he got the results, he tried to put the squeeze on the car's driver, Anthony Gerrara.

"But Talbot made a serious miscalculation. He was used to having his blackmail victims simply pay up with little or no resistance. This time his intended victim was a gangster who was not afraid to strike back. Gerrara and his partner Cyrus Hardison went to Talbot's house and killed him. They removed all the evidence Talbot had against them and left."

I took a long drink from my beer.

"At the inquest, the police were able to identify Gerrara's gun as the weapon that killed Talbot. They also had physical evidence that conclusively placed both Hardison and Gerrara at the scene of the murder. In short, they had an airtight case."

Minute traces of Talbot's blood were eventually found on Hardison's glasses and on the gold chain Gerrara wore around his neck. At the very end, when Talbot knew he was going to die, he bit off the tip of his tongue and spat on his killers to mark them with his blood. Gerrara must have destroyed the shirt he ruined by shooting Talbot at such close range—the one Hardison mentioned at my apartment—because it was never found.

"Obviously the police didn't need me as a suspect anymore, so they dropped all charges. They were even kind enough to let me keep my license. In the end, everyone was happy."

Detective Ryan, the commissioner, even the mayor, who won reelection by a narrow margin. And I certainly had nothing to complain about either.

I was surprised, however, that the authorities never seemed

to tumble to the fact that Talbot had called the number for Angus Baird's Riverside Mobile Home Park. I had warned Baird he would need a plausible cover story to explain it if they did, but it never even came up in the proceedings. It was hard to believe the police had missed it. Perhaps Baird had resources of his own within the PD and managed to have it suppressed...

"Of course, Hardison and Gerrara also miscalculated. When they took Rudi's body from Curtiz's apartment, they deliberately dumped it at a gravel yard owned by the head of a rival crime gang. He retaliated by having them killed as well. Hardison and Gerrara's actions nearly sparked a gang war."

Only Baird's restraint after his men were killed kept it in check. On election day, I sent him the fuzzy scrap of Talbot's photograph, along with a note explaining that this was all I really ever had on him. Frankly, I was worried about how he would react. But several days later, an expensive bottle of scotch—the same brand Baird had in his library—appeared outside my apartment door without any note or explanation.

After the election, there were a few minor skirmishes between Baird's group and Graham's, but they didn't last very long. Winston Graham suddenly decided he wanted to retire (in one piece and unincarcerated) and promptly moved to Florida. I could only guess that Baird came to some agreement with Graham's successors, or that he took over from Graham himself as the leader of a combined group.

"I don't care about any of that," Mrs. Sachett said impatiently. "What matters to me, is that bastard killed Rudi and the police let him go."

"Technically-speaking, or at least legally, Curtiz didn't kill her. The police couldn't do anything else. There was so little evidence against him, and the bulk of what they had was circumstantial."

"No!" Mrs. Sachett interrupted. "Don't tell me about 'legally-this' and 'technically-that.' He killed her! I just want to know how he could do it."

Vera turned and took one of her hands. "Are you sure? Most of it was in the papers already and none of it was pleasant."

"No, you don't understand. I read those horrid stories; I forced myself through them. But all they had were details. They never explained 'How?' How could he drive Rudi to throw away her life when it was so full of promise? When she could have had such a bright future?"

Mrs. Sachett turned to me and our table turned quiet while I tried to come up with an answer. Time passed. Gradually I realized I didn't have one.

It was Vera who spoke up finally:

"I think he made her feel, once and for all, there is no such thing as hope."

Mrs. Sachett looked at Vera and nodded sadly.

"Yes," she said. "I think that's probably right. Thank you." She took a paper napkin and daubed at the tears in her eyes. It was a gesture of goodbye to her lost young friend.

After a long moment of silence, Alphonse Andeo cleared his throat and stood up from his chair. He reached out a hand towards Mrs. Sachett and swayed from side to side on his feet in synch with the Glenn Miller tune on the sound system.

"Come on, Judy. Let's cut a rug. I lost my virginity to this song... More'n once!"

"You old fool," Mrs. Sachett said. She smiled and went out with him to the dance floor.

Vera and I stayed at our table. I signaled to the waiter to come over and I ordered a shot of vodka for both of us. When he brought them, I held out my shot glass and clinked it against hers.

"Stoli and beer--I'm glad you're here."

"Here's looking at you, kid," she said.

We each took a sip of the frozen vodka. It burned my throat going down, but the alcohol's warmth soon began to filter through to the rest of my body. Vera and I looked at each other and the intensity of our mutual gaze was like a force of nature quietly unleashed in that noisy room.

It was a feeling not unlike the flush of love. Not unlike it at all.

THE END

About the Author

Ray Turner has been writing for most of his life— but there was usually a proverbial day job to contend with. Now retired (after 40 years in government service), he is thrilled to be able to pursue writing full-time. He is a distant relative of Edgar Allan Poe (according to family lore, anyway), so it is not surprising that his favorite genres are mystery and horror. A Hard Darkness is Ray's first novel. He and his wife Lenore are transplanted Midwesterners currently living in Maryland.

Made in the USA
Columbia, SC
06 January 2025

add9c787-a808-428a-9777-6ed56063f97dR01